ASP OF ASCENSION
A Nefertari Hughes Mystery

Receive a signed book-
plate with proof of

purchase.

Details:

http://fierceinkbooks.com/
collectors-edition-content/

www.fierceinkbooks.com

ASP OF ASCENSION
A Nefertari Hughes Mystery

BR MYERS

FIERCE INK BOOKS

CANADA | est. 2012

Asp of Ascension: A Nefertari Hughes Mystery
Copyright © 2015 by BR Myers
All rights reserved

Published by Fierce Ink Books Co-Op Ltd.
www.fierceinkbooks.com

First edition, 2015

Library and Archives Canada Cataloguing in Publication information is available upon request.

ISBN: 978-1-927746-62-2
Also available in electronic formats.

Edited by Penelope Jackson
Cover by Emma Dolan

The text type was set in Century Schoolbook.

To my big brother, Brad for making me watch Star Trek *on Saturday mornings instead of* The Smurfs. *I see the wisdom of your ways now.*

Chapter One

Terry had three rules for surviving high school:

1. Don't attract attention.
2. Don't get involved.
3. Don't make trouble.

She squirmed in the front row, trying to shrink into her hoodie, wishing it were big enough to hide in.

"Brett Furlong," Ms. Bernard said. Her eyes never left the paper held in front of her pointed nose. A grunt from the back of the class was the only response.

Terry didn't need to glance behind to know it was one of the three varsity jackets in the very back. They'd sauntered in after the bell rang smelling of spicy body spray. She knew the type: cocky, stupid and impulsive. A bad combination.

Her finger traced a crude sentence that had been etched into the desk's surface, probably with the tip of a protractor.

Crystal Peters is a whore.

Someone had used a pen to mark in the lines, as if gouging the letters permanently into the surface wasn't enough. Terry slid her textbook across the desk, covering the sentence. A heavy sensation from inside pulled down her shoulders. After moving to three different high schools in six months, she discovered the safest course of action was to stay under the radar — and knowing who to avoid was essential. Everyone could be categorized … except for herself. There was no identity brand for Terry. She didn't belong in this stuffy classroom. She didn't belong in this gray northern city. She didn't belong anywhere.

The history teacher continued to drone out the attendance. "Tanya Godfrey." The paper in front of Ms. Bernard's face wavered with each name. A girl nodded from under a dark knit cap that had been pulled down low. Her fingernails were painted with black skulls. *Emo*, Terry thought automatically.

A few more names were called. Terry picked out another jock, a nerdy guy wearing a *Clone Wars* T-shirt, and a few princesses clothed in skinny jeans and knee-high riding boots.

Terry had begged her dad to let her do online courses this time, but he was adamant she try to live like a normal teen. It was ironic, actually; being on archaeological digs with her parents all over the world, cramped inside caves and tombs, was way safer than any high school. But Terry couldn't complain. Her dad had too much to deal with. Pretending she didn't hate school and forcing a smile or two at supper was the least she could do for him after everything they'd been through.

"Allison Harris," Ms. Bernard read next.

One of the princesses with enough blond hair to make Rapunzel envious gave the teacher a perfect smile. "Present," she said, sounding like she meant the kind wrapped with a bow. Terry noticed the other girls' reactions. She changed her mind. Allison wasn't a princess, she was the queen — even more dangerous than a group of jocks.

The door at the front of the class burst open. A girl rushed in with an armload of loose papers clutched to her chest. She landed in the seat next to Terry, breathless and red-faced. Terry smelled strawberry bubblegum.

"Sorry, Ms. Bernard." The girl handed over a mauled note.

"Glad you could join us, Maude," Ms. Bernard said.

Terry snuck a sideways glance. The stack of papers were some kind of advertising flyer. The girl was wearing a pink T-shirt that said, "Maude-Cloth Rules." Terry watched as she opened her backpack, then pulled out three glitter pens and a pink Hello Kitty binder. She neatly placed everything on her desk, keeping the pens in line.

Terry's recycled navy blue binder was peeling at the edges. Her pen was from the hotel she and her dad had stayed at last week while they looked for an apartment. She squirmed in her chair again. Her knee brace dug into her thigh, but she ignored it. Tangible pain helped her ignore the real heartache inside.

"Nefertari Hughes?"

The room became dead silent.

A vice gripped around Terry's stomach, threatening to squeeze its contents up her esophagus. "T-Terry," she stammered. "You can call me Terry." *Damn it.* She should have been paying closer attention.

A tiny voice chirped up. "Nefertari?" Allison pressed her lips together and rolled her eyes, poorly disguising the insult. Terry hated how Allison elongated her name, exaggerating all four syllables. And how her voice went high at the end like a question. *Nef-er-tar-i?*

Terry slouched further into her chair. Ms. Bernard stared at her, apparently waiting for an explanation. "Um … my parents," Terry began. She didn't want to give the long version. When she was born in a tent in the middle of a sandstorm, her mother took one look at her scrunched-up purple face and named her after the first and most beloved wife of Ramesses The Great, a name that means, 'the most beautiful.'

A lump rippled up Terry's throat. She swallowed it back down, tasting bile. "That is, I mean, my dad is an Egyptologist."

Ms. Bernard studied the sheet of names again, then her face cracked into a smile. "Is your father Gunther Hughes?"

Terry's cheeks grew warm. She was failing rule number two miserably. "Yup," she said, wishing Ms. Bernard would just get on with attendance.

"*The* Gunther Hughes!" She said 'the' as if Terry's dad was a rock star or something.

Terry wanted to pull her hood up over her head and disappear. She nodded back to the now beaming Ms. Bernard.

"The big discovery was in all the archaeological magazines!" Ms. Bernard forgot about the sheet of paper, now pressed against her chest as she began to pepper Terry with questions. "Is he here because of the upcoming exhibit?"

Terry didn't even have a chance to speak before Ms. Bernard answered herself. "Yes, of course, it must be." She tapped her lower lip with her pen. "Would he be willing to be a guest speaker in the class? I wonder what his views are on the proliferation of artifacts for display versus natural preservation?"

The snorts and giggles from the class buzzed around Terry's ears like annoying wasps.

"It's frustrating that most people are only interested in curses and the gold." Ms. Bernard glanced at the ceiling. The edges of her mouth drew down. "What about the simple thrill of finding something from a lost civilization?" she asked to no one in particular. The ceiling stayed quiet.

Terry touched her right knee. It had been throbbing all morning. She grimaced to the side and caught Maude staring at her. She smiled at Terry and gave her a little wave, even though only an aisle separated them.

Terry blinked. Maude's neon lip gloss matched the pink stripe in her hair. Slowly, Maude's smile faltered and she looked away as the tips of her ears glowed. An unexpected twinge of guilt hit Terry. She started clicking the hotel pen.

Ms. Bernard continued with her modern archaeology monologue, despite the growing mumbles of boredom from her students. "This is a much-needed boost for Devonshire," she continued. "It's been fifty years since the museum has had this much attention." Ms. Bernard's voice faltered. Her features sharpened as she turned toward the windows. The dull gray sky of late February did nothing to improve the sudden melancholy of the room.

Terry was unsettled by her expression, and the entire class had grown quiet. The eerie silence lasted longer than a natural gap. Ms. Bernard came out of her daze and snapped back to attention. "Well," she said, regaining her composure, "welcome to the class, Nefertari." She cleared her throat and continued taking attendance. Her face was noticeably flushed.

Terry didn't care what Ms. Bernard thought about curses. All she knew was that before her parents' infamous discovery, she'd been part of a happy family, traveling the world, and learning by experience — not from dated textbooks and falling-apart binders.

Cursed or not though, Terry knew she'd never walk properly, or see her mom alive again.

Chapter Two

Terry can hardly breathe. The darkness presses down on her from all around...

"This is it." Her mother's voice is high, quivering with excitement. Her breaths come in short gasps. "The fourth chamber—"

A roar of air pushes Terry off her feet. The sound of crunching rock and raining debris fills the air. Terry's leg bursts open. There's a flash of light. Then the pain makes her pass out.

"—one of the most famous figures in Egyptian history," Ms. Bernard's nasal pitch pierced through Terry's memory. "You'll be pairing up for this project."

Terry winced under her long bangs as the entire class grouped themselves into teams. She closed her eyes and let out a puff of air. Deep snickering echoed from the back of the class. *The jocks must be looking at porn on their phones*, she thought disgustedly. High schools were all the same.

There was a nudge at the leg of Terry's desk. Maude gave her careful smile. They were the only ones left who hadn't paired up yet. Terry glanced at the neon flyers Maude had carried into class.

Maudern Style — A touch of grace for every face!

Maude ran a hand over the fancy font. "My mom and my grandma own a beauty salon." She beamed. Then she stuck out her hand. "I'm Maude Sanchez, by the way." Then she added, with a hint of nobility, "The third."

"The third? As in roman numerals?"

"More like as in white trash." Terry recognized the perfectly biting annunciation. She turned to see Allison smirk while pretending to write in her book.

Maude lowered her voice and leaned closer to Terry. "I come from a long line of strong, independent women," she said.

"Okay," Terry said slowly.

Maude stayed quiet, lining up her glitter pens. Terry felt stupid sitting there while everyone else paired up. She finally motioned over to Maude.

Maude scooted her desk closer. "I'm so glad we're partners!" she gushed. "You must know everything about ancient Egypt." She grabbed one of her pens and started making a chart. "Is it okay if we concentrate on Cleopatra's jewelry? I'm really into fashion." Maude opened her textbook and methodically smoothed out her folder, turning to a fresh page. Terry didn't even bother opening her own textbook. Nothing in there could tell her anything she didn't already know.

"Isn't it romantic?" Maude sighed, entranced with a particular image of Mark Antony. "Being buried with your true love?"

"Not particularly." Skulls flashed in Terry's mind. She blinked a few times trying to get rid of the image. A burst of laughter exploded from the back of the class as a basketball bounced down the aisle and rolled to a stop near the teacher's desk.

"Zachary Breton!" Ms. Bernard's nostrils flared. "This is *not* the basketball court!" She pointed to the empty desk on the other side of Terry. "Join Nefertari's group."

"It's Terry." She winced.

Ms. Bernard stared at the back of the classroom. "Coach Carmichael will be hearing from me." She paused to take a breath into those massive nostrils, and then added with low snarl, "Again."

There was an exaggerated huff, followed by chair legs scraping on the floor. Ms. Bernard tapped her foot. Terry instinctively ducked her chin down as the jock eased into the desk beside her. Long legs in jeans stretched out straight, creating a mile of denim.

Terry snuck a sideways glance. Zachary's fingers started to tap out a beat on his lone blank sheet of paper. He had clean fingernails. She detected a faint scent that reminded her of laundry detergent. *A clean-cut jock.* He also had no pen or textbook. *Talk about a walking cliché.*

Ms. Bernard began to drone on again, her nasal voice having a hypnotic effect. Terry pictured her in a crowded marketplace in Cairo, trying to charm snakes for tourists. The edge of her mouth curled up in a smile. Movement to her left made her look over. Zachary was staring at her. She dropped her gaze, the smile vanishing instantly.

"A paper on Cleopatra's life is due next week and worth half your term mark," Ms. Bernard announced. She ended by staring at Terry's newly formed trio. Something in her eager expression made Terry press her back into the chair, putting more distance between them. Maude began flipping through her book, talking excitedly about gold earrings. Terry remained tense until Ms. Bernard looked away from them.

"And that would make a cool poster." Maude pointed to an image of a bust of Cleopatra.

Zachary leaned over, his knee brushing against Terry's. She froze, wondering if he could feel the brace through her cargo pants; the bulky knee hinge always poked out the side when she sat. He was all legs and arms, like a gangly octopus, and the tiny desk couldn't contain him. Heat rose up and colored Terry's cheeks. She pulled her textbook closer and opened it to a random page, at least pretending to be working. The sentence etched into the desk was uncovered now.

Crystal Peters is a whore.

Zachary's attention shifted to her desk, and the heat in Terry's cheeks doubled.

Maude stopped talking. Without hesitating, she reached into her pencil case, then leaned in front of Terry and put a star sticker over the word 'whore.' She smoothed it out with her pink fingernail. "Better," she said.

For the next half hour Maude was secretary, planner, idea girl and basically the only one doing any work on the Cleopatra project. Terry lightly interjected a few facts every few minutes when it was obvious Maude needed clarifying.

"Her mummy must be buried with so much jewelry!" Maude's eyes danced.

"Her tomb has never been found," Terry said, and her deadpan tone made Maude look up from the book. Then Terry added, "Or her mummy."

Maude's glitter pen hovered in midair. Terry guessed she was hoping for some hint to a treasure hunt. Zachary stayed quiet, bent over his paper, totally immersed in doodling. Terry imagined 3-D cubes covering the page, or whatever juvenile designs clean-cut jocks drew to kill time while their partners completed all the school projects. She hadn't realized she was staring until he caught her eye.

The bell rang, making Terry jump. She snapped her book shut, hating how frayed her nerves were. Everyone began stuffing their backpacks and making their way to the door. Zachary unfurled himself from the desk and stretched to his full height. He snatched his doodling off the desk before Terry could get a better look and tucked it inside his purple and gold varsity jacket.

When she stood up, the school crest on his jacket was directly at her eye level. She wished he would step out of her way so she wouldn't have to hobble around him.

"Um," she said, still looking at his chest, "your coat of arms is in my face."

"Look up then," he said. She could hear the tease of a smile behind the suggestion.

Terry's eyes followed all the way up to his tousled light brown hair. She was surprised he didn't gel the tips: most clean-cut jocks did that kind of thing. "You're tall," she said.

He grinned down at her, and this time the smile took hold and was real — Terry had seen enough fake ones full of pity to last a lifetime. "That's fascinating," he said. "Do all daughters of Egyptologists have such an eye for detail?"

"No … I mean yes." Terry was too surprised he'd been paying attention to Ms. Bernard talk about her dad that she couldn't think of a proper comeback.

"Relax, I'm only kidding." He tipped his head slightly. "I'm Zach, by the way."

"So I heard during roll call, plus I can read," she said, looking pointedly at the embroidered name on his sleeve with 'Captain' underneath. Terry had the urge to prove his height — and his perfectly tousled hair, for that matter — were of little consequence to her.

"Hey!" a voice called out. Terry turned to see one of the other jocks whip a basketball directly at her face.

"Whoa." Zach's hands were lightning fast. He clutched the ball in time before it hit Terry and tucked it under his arm in an effortless and completely natural maneuver. The grace was unexpected for someone so lanky.

Terry's ears burned — she hadn't even tried to duck; her knee would never allow her to move fast enough. He looked at her questioningly. "I'm fine," she murmured.

"Murphy," Zach said to the other dark-haired jock with the brush cut, "your passes suck." He left Terry and joined his teammate, ushering him out the door and into the hallway, now full of students. Terry pushed down the familiar bubble of hate and desperate self-pity. She put her attention on packing up her own stuff, but she couldn't find her hotel pen. She frowned down at her beat-up binder. There was a tiny unicorn sticker in the top corner now. Terry was about to say something to Maude, but she had already disappeared into the hallway.

After taking three wrong turns, Terry finally found the cafeteria. The open space was buzzing with five hundred different conversations. Terry limped past the lineup for hot food, the smell of Tuna Surprise assaulting her nose. She craved spicy falafels and figs soaked in honey.

She ignored the half-filled tables and perched on the low sill of the windows that lined one wall. The rain was turning all the snow-lined paths to slush. She watched as kids ran between buildings with books and jackets over their heads as makeshift umbrellas. Her dad had warned her the East Coast winters could be unpredictable and long. Tomorrow it would probably be snowing again.

Terry unwrapped the sandwich her dad had made that morning. She couldn't explain how American food had no taste for her or how everything had been dulled since the accident, even her interest in eating. But the dark circles under his eyes this morning had been enough for her to take the pathetic lunch without complaining.

She forced down a few bites of what looked like cheese and mayo. Her mom had always toasted the sandwiches so that they were crispy on the outside and chewy on the inside. Terry suddenly felt a wave of tears threaten to spill. The lump of food in her stomach matched the lump in her throat. She grabbed her backpack and made a beeline for the washroom. With her head down, she pushed through the swinging door.

There was an echo of the door slamming against the tiled wall. Terry stood in place, her hand slowly dropping to her side. Maude's back was pressed up against one of the sinks, and two of the princesses from history class stood on either side. Allison was in front of them all. She leaned to one side, letting her hip jut out.

"Oh," Terry said. There was only silence, then she added, "Sorry."

Allison's smile slid into place, but her blue eyes bore a cold, hard stare. Terry mumbled a few words and stepped backward. For a few desperate seconds Maude held her gaze, then she looked down. The door handle nudged Terry's side. She took one last look at Allison's expression and escaped back into the crowded hallway.

Goosebumps peppered Terry's arms. She limped haphazardly, then dropped her backpack on the floor by her locker, not caring when the books spilled out. She closed her eyes and pressed her forehead against cool steel.

1. Don't attract attention.

2. Don't get involved.

3. Don't make trouble.

She repeated this in her head, and her pulse started to calm. Terry let out a slow breath and opened her eyes. Staring up at her from the floor was her blue binder, the new unicorn sticker in all its sparkly glory demanding to be noticed. *Damn.*

She had to go back for Maude.

"Fire!" Terry shouted as she pushed open the washroom door again. "Get out..." her voice faltered. Nothing she had ever seen with her parents on their archaeological digs had prepared her for what she saw.

Chapter Three

Terry's jaw dropped. She wanted to turn around and run, but her body ignored every signal her brain was firing down her nerve endings. She stared at three backs, two in varsity jackets, side by side in front of the urinals. Zach's ruffled light brown hair was unmistakable. In her rush to stop whatever Allison was doing to Maude, she'd gone through the wrong swinging door.

Zach's teammate gave Terry a look of amusement, as if her sudden appearance was a pleasant surprise. Murphy hollered out a greeting worthy of a hero's welcome. "Hey, babe." He grinned over his shoulder. "Sorry about earlier. Zach's right, my passes do suck." He turned back to the urinal, and then flushed.

There was a cascade effect immediately following his announcement. The other two guys did a double take, then almost jumped out of their sneakers. Zippers were quickly tugged up.

"Whoa, Jesus!" Zach tucked in the front of his shirt.

Terry finally blinked, breaking the spell. "I ... um." She pointed with her thumb behind her. "I thought this was ... like, the girls' room."

Murphy gave her a salacious grin. "This is the *men's* room." He laughed at his own joke. "But I'm cool with co-ed."

Zach gave him a look that made his smirk disappear, then said, "I don't think Nefertari is stupid enough to do anything co-ed with you."

At the sound of her name, the third boy, now at the sink wash-

ing his hands, caught Terry's eye in the mirror. His dark bangs
touched the top of his tortoise shell glasses. His wrinkled Oxford
shirt was open at the top, but his tie was a perfect knot, resting
just below the second button. Terry guessed he was trying hard to
look disheveled, but in a stylish way. Sloppy and formal at the
same time.

The door opened behind Terry. "What the—?" She whirled
around and pushed past the confused guy.

The hallway was jammed with bodies rushing to last-minute
activities before the afternoon bell. She took small steps trying to
disguise her limp, but her knee throbbed more than usual. Terry
suspected the crappy weather. *I'm like some old lady in the nursing
home, able to predict the next storm by how much my bones ache.*

"Nefertari!" a voice came from behind.

Terry cringed and kept walking, but her stride was quickly
outmatched, and soon the boy with the fancy glasses was walking
beside her. "Nefertari, right? I'm sorry," he started, "but I didn't
get a chance to introduce myself back there."

"It's okay," she said, looking straight ahead, trying not to
blush. "You were busy."

He slowed down his pace, staying in step with her. "I'm Fraser," he said, holding out his hand. Terry shoved her hands in her
pockets.

He bent his head closer and dropped his voice. "I did wash my
hands," he said. There was a knowing pause before he added,
"Remember?"

Terry relaxed her pace; it was easier to hide her limp when
she walked slow. "Right," she said, giving his hand a quick shake.
"Nice to meet you, Fraser," she said. "And you can call me Terry.
Actually, I'd prefer it."

He stood a little taller and made a grand sweep of the hallway
with his arm. "Welcome to Roosevelt High."

She couldn't tell if he was being sarcastic or not. Still, he
seemed genuine, and he made her smile — something that didn't

happen very often these days.

"Thanks," she told him. "You're the first one to say that."

"Really?" He looked like he didn't believe her. Terry only shrugged. The school secretary was nice, but hearing it from someone her own age was better. "It's a sad commentary on the school's hospitality if you're required to crash the washroom looking for friends."

An image of Maude held captive Terry a sudden jolt. She needed to get back to the girls' bathroom.

Fraser started whistling. Terry glanced back down the hallway, hoping Maude would emerge unscathed. She wasn't sure what to do next. Fraser seemed content to join her for a stroll. Was he actually going her way? With her dark hair hanging down over her eyes, some bits sticking out in the back, plus her baggy cargo pants, Terry was sure she wasn't putting out the 'hot new chick' vibe. She was more like the shadow that stayed in the corner.

"Since you're new, you might want to join some clubs and stuff," he suggested. "You know, to meet other students who share your interests."

Terry stayed quiet. She doubted anyone in this school *shared her interests.* "Ah," he said. "The universal 'piss off' sign. I know it well."

"No," she said. "You're really nice—"

"No worries," he said. "My ego is still intact." Then he grinned at her.

Terry tugged at the neck of her hoodie. "I'm not the club kind of girl, I guess."

"What about the school paper?"

"Uh ... probably not."

She stopped by her locker and started to work the combination, thinking Fraser would leave, which would give her the chance to go back to the bathroom. He gave her a quizzical stare.

Terry's leaned on her good leg. "What?" she asked.

"I don't know many girls named Nefertari. In fact, the only

15

one I can think of is the daughter of a world-renowned Egyptologist who has just been hired to oversee a secret project for the city's museum."

"Oh," she said. "That's why you're so interested." She left off the 'in me' part. "Word gets around fast, even in a school this big."

Fraser's eyes crinkled at the edges. "I'm a curious guy. I'm also one of those kids who works for the school newspaper — I'm the editor, actually."

Terry turned back to her locker and started to shuffle papers around, peeking under textbooks, trying to find her hotel pen. "Well, my dad and I don't talk about his work much," she lied. "There's probably nothing I can tell you."

He didn't take the hint. "It's not so much the secrecy of the project, but *why* it's coming here. I mean, why not the Museum of Natural History in New York, or the Smithsonian in Washington, D.C.? Devonshire's too small. It doesn't make sense."

Terry shrugged, silently wishing Fraser would disappear.

He continued. "I mean, the museum doesn't exactly have the best track record with priceless artifacts. There's a story about something being stolen once."

That got Terry's attention. The image of Ms. Bernard's expression in class came back to her, and a shiver ran down her spine. "In history class, the teacher mentioned the museum got attention for something that happened a long time ago. She looked ... scared ..." Terry purposely let the sentence fall away, testing to see if he'd fill in the rest.

"Oh yeah?" He rubbed a hand over his chin. "I happen to know someone who can get us access to the museum's history. It would be easy for me to find out." A slow grin curled at the edge of his mouth. "If you promise to give me an exclusive for the paper."

A few kids across the hall nudged each other, motioning toward her and Fraser. "But I don't know anything about the upcoming exhibit," she said.

He pushed up his glasses. "I bet you can come up with something. At least consider it," he said. "The newspaper office is desperate for new faces."

Terry chewed her lower lip. He wasn't leaving until he got her to agree. "All right," she said. "If I find out anything, you'll be the first to know."

He winked and started walking backward. "This is the start of something big, Neffie," he teased. "I can feel it."

Neffie?

As he strutted toward the stairs, people in the hallway stared — including Terry. She tried to ignore the sense of dread. She'd never so blatantly ignored the rules before. Now here she was, signed up to be Fraser's research buddy, promising to give him information on the one thing she had no desire to ever discuss again. All to find out what had scared the crap out of her history teacher.

Terry's phone vibrated. It was a text from her dad.

Running late. Meet me at the museum on your way home. Pizza? Chinese?

She didn't bother to reply. It wasn't much of a choice. They'd had takeout every night since they moved. Terry's dad wasn't much of a cook, and she could only make toast.

Terry slammed her locker. She wanted to scream. She wanted to find someone to blame for ruining her life. But that was impossible — she couldn't fight a curse.

She picked up her backpack, then limped down the hallway, staying close to the walls, avoiding the fast lane of laughing boisterous people in the middle. No one noticed her. She could count on one hand the people who'd been nice to her that morning.

Then her heart dropped.

Terry rushed as fast her brace would allow. This time she made sure to go in the girls' washroom. It was empty except for a crumpled pink piece of paper in the corner. Terry crouched down and smoothed out a flyer.

Maudern Style — A touch of grace for every face!

Chapter Four

The cold late February rain came down in sheets, and Terry's Converse high tops were soaked through. Sidewalks were lined with slush from all the melted snow. She'd lost the feeling in her toes on the walk from the bus stop. Still, she stayed in the frigid weather, staring at the pink awning across the street.

The neon flyer, now soggy with the letters blurring together, confirmed she had the right address. *Maudern Style* was, indeed, a beauty salon. Terry crossed the street, hobbling between speeding cabs. The last one barely missed her. A horn blared as the car hit a puddle, spraying the bottom of her cargo pants. The fabric now clung to her leg, outlining her brace.

She approached the large front window, making sure to keep her hood up. Light from inside cast a warm glow onto the cold, wet sidewalk. A slim woman with a long dark waves was cutting another woman's hair. She paused and turned, talking to someone out of Terry's field of vision. Then both the hairdresser and the client laughed.

Terry craned her neck to see more of the shop, careful to stay hidden under her hoodie. Maude was sitting at the reception desk studying a large book. Terry recognized the profile of Cleopatra on the front.

Maude would pause every few pages, then write something on

a sticky note and paste it in the book. Movement from the back of the shop caught Terry's eye as a gray-haired woman in an apron came out and hugged Maude from behind. She planted a kiss on her cheek and placed a cupcake with fluffy icing beside the Cleopatra book.

Terry tried to swallow the unexpected lump of jealousy that had begun to grow. She wasn't prepared for this snippet of domestic bliss. Her guilt for not coming to Maude's defense in the bathroom slowly dissipated.

Her pocket buzzed with another text.

Are you on your way?

Terry put her head down and walked into the wind, both hating and relishing the stinging rain. She had money for a cab, but she was miserable and wanted to arrive at the museum in a mess, just to let her dad know how hard this was for her.

She turned the corner and saw the familiar castle-like facade and stone steps that led to the massive oak doors of the front entrance. Devonshire's crowning achievement had been reclaiming a crumbling hundred-year-old cathedral and turning it into a museum. Keeping the original masonry intact, the architects added a glass stairwell at the front, connecting all five levels and installing a massive domed skylight.

Her knee protested the last few steps. She pushed through the massive doors and was hit by an aroma of floor polish and old books.

A family of Velociraptor skeletons stood center stage in the rotunda to greet visitors. She crossed the lobby, noting how there was only one ticket wicket open. Ms. Bernard was right about one thing: The museum was in desperate need of some publicity. Presently, half the building was closed due to poor attendance. Less money coming in meant fewer staff, and fewer staff meant decreased access.

Her dad was supposed to change all that, though, plus the big secret exhibit — the secret Fraser had been nettling her about.

Terry knew what was coming, but it was pretty small. She wasn't sure if it would be enough to save the museum. Of course, she didn't care much anyway. The sooner her dad set up the exhibit, the sooner they could leave.

Terry's shuffle echoed through the nearly empty reception area. Five floors encircled the rotunda, leaving a large open area in the middle of the museum all the way to the domed skylight in the roof. The design enabled natural light to pour into the middle of the building, keeping the main lobby well lit.

It made Terry unsteady to look all the way up; she was suddenly reminded of Zach's towering height. Lightheaded, Terry stepped into the elevator and hit the second floor button where her dad's office was located, down the hallway past the mastodon exhibit.

Terry mentally prepared a speech to protest going back to school and why being homeschooled was more beneficial for her education. Phrases like 'outdated textbooks' and 'crowded classrooms' would have to be used. She could even come with him to work every day. The museum was the perfect quiet place to do online courses.

Terry readied herself in the hallway, then pushed into his office. A wide set of shoulders in a smart suit faced her father's desk, blocking him from her view. The man's blond hair was slightly gray at the edges.

"Gunther," the man prodded, his hands held out to the side, "I promised the city a big unveiling by the beginning of April. That gives you two months."

"Five weeks, actually," Terry's dad replied with restrained anger. Her stomach did a little flip. Her dad was hardly ever angry.

"I'm sure your team will do a splendid job," the man chirped. He put his hands in his pockets and rolled back on his heels. Then he added, "I don't have to remind you how much money my people are providing for this to go forward." His voice grew serious. "The museum is counting on you — the *city* is counting on you."

Terry's dad said, "I'm fully aware of the expectations—" He stopped when he saw her. His face instantly relaxed, and he motioned for her to come in. "Alex," he said to the man, "this is my daughter, Terry. She started at Roosevelt High today."

Terry wasn't prepared for the handsome face that turned to her. He smiled and shook her hand, his palm warm and pudgy.

"Roosevelt High." Alex's blond eyebrows lifted. "My daughter goes there. It's a fine institution. Harvard takes some of its brightest graduates."

Terry's dad was wearing the sweater he'd worn the day before. One of the cuffs had begun to unravel. "So," he asked her, "how was your first day?"

Terry flicked her gaze to Alex, dressed like a rich stockbroker, then back to her dad and his holey sweater. "It was great," she said. "Everyone was really … nice." She forced a smile. Her upper lip stuck to her teeth.

Alex beamed back, pleased by her answer. "I'll be touch, Gunther," he said, then strode out of the office. Terry's shoulders didn't relax until his footsteps faded down the hallway.

"I had no idea the curator was such a hard-ass," she said.

"Language," her dad scolded. "And that wasn't the curator, that was the mayor."

"Oh," she said.

"You'll meet the curator later," he said, dipping his head low, rummaging through a desk drawer. "She's at a conference in San Diego."

"She?"

"Mm-hmm," he said, still keeping his head under the desk. "Sarah Mathers. An old grad school friend of mine. She's the reason we're here, remember?"

"The offer you couldn't refuse," Terry said. "Right, of course. But you never mentioned anyone's name, you just said the museum was giving you a once-in-a-lifetime opportunity."

"True," he replied.

"Ease up with all the specifics, Dad."

"Uh-huh," he replied distractedly.

Terry plopped into a cheap vinyl chair. There were boxes piled in the corner, and an empty coffee mug and several granola bar wrappers littered the desk. There was only one photo framed on the desk. Terry remembered that day in Giza perfectly. The sun was low in the sky, her mom's curly dark hair loose around her shoulders. She and Terry were wearing the bright scarves around their necks. Her dad was in the middle with his arms around both of them, smiling. It was the last family picture ever taken of them. Her friend Awad had taken it.

Terry's dad finally sat up. His cheeks were pinkish. It was like looking into a mirror; same unruly dark hair, same dark eyes — same dark circles *under* the eyes.

Her previous anger melted away. "How was your day?"

He ran a hand through his hair. The piece in the back stuck up in protest, just like hers did. "I'm slowly getting used to the desk thing, I guess. It's okay, though; your mom was more of an adventurer than me." His eyes became glassy. He blinked a few times.

Terry's own eyes threatened to fill. She picked at the loose piping on the chair. "Everything here is old," she mumbled.

He dad let out a tired laugh. "Come on," he urged, tugging at the shoulder of her hoodie. "I'm going to take you someplace that feels like home."

Chapter Five

They took the elevator to the fifth floor and walked along the hallway. Terry peeked over the railing at the empty rotunda down below.
"Pizza all right for tonight?" her dad prompted.

Terry imagined them sitting opposite each other at the square
white table in their stark dining room. They had moved into their
fully furnished apartment three days ago. Her dad said it was only temporary. Everything was clean, but there was a lingering
smell of stale cigarette smoke and a weird stain on the bathroom
ceiling. With its IKEA tables and thin-cushioned chairs, the flat
had more of a college dorm atmosphere than a family dwelling. It
was bland and worn out — exactly the way Terry felt.

"They've already started updating this area," he said, using a
key to open a large glass door.

The room was only illuminated with dim lighting, but it called
out to Terry. She was almost able to smell the myrrh. *I'm home,*
she thought. She gave her dad a weak smile.

They slowly walked around the Egypt room, pausing at the
older exhibits and seeing where the new and updated displays
would be showcased. In the center of the room, a roped-off area
was bare. Terry frowned at her dad. "How will you fill this entire
area with the coins?" she asked.

"The coins?" He was absentmindedly picking at the loose

thread on his sleeve. "Oh, right. They're coming too."

"What do you mean, 'too'?" Terry said. "I thought the coins Mom found with Cleopatra's profile engraved on them were the big secret." She stared at her dad, but he remained quiet. "Isn't that why we're here?" Her voice cracked. "That's what this Sarah person is so excited about … right?"

He took a long breath in through his nose, then dropped his head. After her mom's death, Terry had been in the hospital for weeks, followed by rehab for months, learning to walk again. Her dad hadn't mentioned much about the coins, and if he'd talked about any other discovery, she had been too emotionally numb to understand or even care. Once she was well enough, her dad had insisted they needed to lead a safer life. They'd moved back to America, and he'd started working freelance in various museums, moving them three times in the last six months.

"Dad?" she prompted.

"The coins are a small part of the new exhibit," he admitted. "It's much bigger than anyone suspects." He stopped and studied her for a moment.

When he didn't elaborate, she huffed and crossed her arms in front of her chest. "I think I'm ready to hear, Dad!"

"Only a select group of people know about this." He gave her a steady gaze. "But I think you're old enough to appreciate the con-sequences." Terry swallowed and tried to erase the image of Fra-ser from her mind. "There's a sarcophagus," he said. "It was found in the fourth chamber … after." He cleared his throat. "The Egyp-tian delegates were reluctant to send it overseas." He offered no further explanation.

A sarcophagus in the fourth chamber. A rush of blood pounded in Terry's temples. "Why here?" she asked. "Why not New York or Washington, D.C.?" Fraser had made her suspicious. "What's here that those cities don't have?"

"Me, for starters, with an offer he couldn't refuse." A woman stood in the doorway, leaning on one hip. She wore a tight gray suit and red stilettos that matched her lipstick.

"Sarah?" His mouth dropped open.

The woman smiled and walked over to him, her heels tapping on the tiles. "Gunther," she said, enveloping him in a hug. "It's been too long."

Terry's dad stepped back and ran a hand through his hair, patting down the stubborn piece a few times. "It's good to see you … you look great. The museum looks great too."

Sarah tossed a wave of brown hair over her shoulder. "Not too bad for an old church. I especially love the narrow passageways the clergy secretly used — although the stone steps are a killer on my shoes." She laughed at her own joke, then her expression became somber. "The past few years interest has been diving. The museum is so empty, it's more like a mausoleum. But you're going to change all that, Gunther."

Terry cleared her throat. "Dad?"

Sarah's blue eyes softened. She looked Terry up and down. "Look at you! You're practically a grown woman." She drew Terry into a quick hug. Her grip was tight. "I haven't seen you since you were a baby."

"Oh," Terry said, taking a shaking step back. "You're the old school friend."

Terry's dad let out a laugh, then tried to cover it with a cough. "And the curator."

Sarah pouted at Terry's dad and put a hand on her hip. "And her godmother, thank you very much." She turned to Terry. "Your dad and I were undergrads, both taking art history. We even talked about opening an art gallery. Do you remember, Gunther?" She quirked an eyebrow. "That is until I introduced you to my roommate. You dropped art history and switched to archaeology, charmed by the notion of traveling all over the world with her."

"Your mom," he said softly to Terry.

"Talk about love at first sight!" Sarah said. She pointed her finger at Terry like a gun and winked at her. "You owe your existence to me, kiddo."

"Um ... thanks." Terry glanced at her dad. She'd never heard of someone named Sarah before today.

Sarah squeezed Mr. Hughes' elbow and lowered her voice. "I'm so sorry I didn't make the funeral. Naomi was special. She went too soon."

All of the air left the room. Terry tried to take a deep breath, but her chest was being squeezed.

"Thank you." Mr. Hughes grimaced. The lines on his face were a map of grief.

Terry still wasn't use to the sudden stabs of loneliness. Daily living was a guise, a list of activities to accomplish to make them feel normal. But it only took a simple reminder, sometimes even one word, to bring all the sadness washing over Terry and her dad.

After a few beats of stifling silence, he said, "I thought you were in San Diego."

"I got word *she's* coming tomorrow," Sarah said. There was a greedy glint in her eye.

"There's another expert involved," he explained to Terry. "Working with her is the offer I couldn't refuse."

Terry narrowed her eyes. "I thought you were the expert."

Sarah ignored her remark. "I've never met her. Dr. Mullaca's more research than hands-on. In fact, she's known for her knowledge of reptiles, but her reputation as an Egyptologist precedes her."

A look passed between Sarah and Terry's dad. He turned to Terry. "We hope she can decipher the hieroglyphs and open the case — literally." He smiled at his own pun.

Terry was taken aback by how much the smile made his eyes brighten and soften the lines on his forehead. She'd forgotten how handsome he was. "I don't understand," she said. "They've had it for a year and it's still closed?" Nothing happened fast in the preservation lab. There was meticulous cleaning, cataloguing, picture taking, the documentation was extreme, but still, a whole year was a long time to work on something with zero results, even for archaeologists.

Sarah led her over to a prominent display encircled by a red velvet rope. There was a mannequin made to look like Cleopatra wearing a white dress fashioned from the Hellanistic era. Over her straight black bangs sat a cobra headdress and, on the right upper arm, a golden asp. Terry rolled her eyes at the cheap glitter paint on the jewelry. Anything worth value was under or behind glass. This mannequin display was purely for ambiance. And judging by the layers of dust and dulled texture, it had probably been here since the museum opened.

"You don't need to know the particulars," Sarah said. "But yes, it's coming here for the purpose of being opened safely, Dr. Mullaca insisted upon it. I promise it will be unforgettable."

"And perfect for a big unveiling?" Terry guessed, choosing to use the mayor's phrase.

Sarah winked. "You've met Mayor Harris, I take it."

"Harris?" Terry's heart sped up. He'd mentioned a daughter. *What are the odds Allison's father is the mayor?*

"Terry's uncannily perceptive," her dad said.

Sarah arched her pencil-perfect eyebrow. "An essential talent for all young women," she said.

The flattery was improving Terry's mood. It made her more assertive than usual. She forgot all about Allison. "What's so important about this coffin that no one has been able to open it?" she asked. She imagined priceless artifacts and gold that were usually wrapped within the layers of the mummy's bandages. "What do they think is inside?"

Sarah shook his head. "Not what, but *who*." Her eyes traveled up to the mannequin's face.

Terry stared up at the charcoal-lined eyes, and the hair on the back of her neck stood up. "Cleopatra," she whispered.

Chapter Six

The library in Roosevelt High had a modern, open concept with numerous study pods composed of low, round tables and soft, cushy chairs. The librarians had visual access to the whole area except in between the rows of high bookcases, which Terry soon discovered was where everyone who was assigned study hall went to make out.

She'd been looking for a book on Roman history when she stumbled upon the first couple. The girl was wearing a studded leather jacket and pressing her boyfriend up against the shelves. Her painted nails with black skulls pushed at the back of his head, bringing his mouth closer to hers. Terry was unprepared for this display and her toe caught on the carpet, knocking her into the bookshelf. Her face grew hot when the couple finally broke apart and looked her way.

It was Tanya Godfrey, the emo girl from her history class. "Sorry," Terry stammered. "I'm just leaving." Her gaze flitted everywhere except Tanya's heavily lined eyes. "Um, carry on." There was a snicker at her back as she limped away. By the time she reached the end of the bookcase, she guessed the making out had started again.

Last year, just before the accident, when Terry was fifteen, her parents had taken her to a dig in Giza. One of their colleagues had had a son who was seventeen. Awad had olive skin, thick black hair and arms and legs that looked too long.

They had spent that summer staying cool by exploring the tombs. Awad had retold the stories of the pharaohs she already knew by heart, but the tone of his voice brought shivers over her sunburnt skin. In the evening they would lay outside the tent, eating the last of the Domiati cheese and figs, talking for hours. She had been in love but too shy to tell him.

On the night before she and her parents were scheduled to leave, he had taken her on a hike to watch the sunset. While the sky had been changing from orange to pink and then indigo, he'd kissed her. She'd kissed him back slowly, learning how to move her mouth with his. And they'd not stopped kissing until the sky was dark and speckled with stars.

She never saw Awad again, but they kept in touch online a bit. She'd heard from him after the accident, but too full of remorse, she hadn't replied. Still, Terry's stomach still swooped whenever the sunset hit that perfect moment of three colors all at once.

She slouched under the weight of her new life. The burden seemed greater this morning. Terry had hardly slept the night before. The home-cooked meal Sarah had offered them turned out to be mac and cheese and pre-packaged salad with the little bags of dried cranberries and wonton strips. Her dining room table was piled with magazines and newspapers. Terry had eaten off her lap in front of the television while Sarah and her dad had emptied a bottle of wine, reminiscing about grad school days. Sarah did most of the talking. Very rarely did Naomi's name come up.

When they finally went back to the apartment, Terry had asked her dad about Sarah. "How come I have a godmother I never heard of before?"

He winced. "It's kind of complicated."

"Was she really roommates with Mom?"

"Yes."

"And she really introduced you two?"

"Yes." He winced again. "Your mom always felt a bit guilty about what happened with Sarah." Then the phone rang, interrupting him. It was someone from the museum; one of the construction workers had an issue in the Egypt room. Terry fell asleep before he finished the call.

She had woken in the middle of the night, unable to get comfortable, and ended up taking an extra anti-inflammatory for her knee. She was still full of aches by the morning. She wanted to ask her dad about Sarah again, but by the time she got up he had already left for the museum.

Now, wandering the library, Terry absentmindedly rubbed her back as she turned the corner of the next bookcase. One of Allison's princesses and Murphy, the brush cut with the bad aim, had taken over the middle of the aisle. Terry didn't bother to say anything. She only turned away, careful not to trip again.

"Hey," Murphy called out. "Wanna meet up in the bathroom again?" This earned him a swat from his partner.

Terry gave up on the book hunt and made her way over to the little table that Maude and Zach had claimed. She gingerly sat down, careful of her right knee. Maude didn't even look up from her notes, but he took notice, his eyes lingering on her legs.

Terry guessed he was probably wondering when he could ask if she was born that way, or if it was an accident. Most people took around one week. Terry usually lied and said she'd always had the limp.

"Any luck?" Maude asked. Her pink glitter pen flew across the page. The Cleopatra book sat open, and loads more sticky notes had been added since yesterday afternoon. There was a slight twinge of guilt inside Terry — Maude must have put a ton of time into this.

Terry started to play with the zipper on her hoodie. "Nothing on Caesar," she lied. She didn't want to explain how she kept interrupting couples.

Maude frowned back, like she knew Terry wasn't telling the truth. For one horrific moment Terry thought she was going to call her out for bailing on her in the bathroom, or even say she saw her lurking outside her mom's beauty salon yesterday. But Maude didn't press further.

Earlier, when they had first met up in class, there had been an awkward pause between the two of them. Terry had planned on apologizing about leaving her in the bathroom with Allison, but when she'd seen Maude all decked out in pink and looking like she didn't have a care in the world, she'd convinced herself nothing bad had happened.

Zach leaned in his chair, balancing it on the back legs — no small accomplishment considering the size of the furniture. His black crew neck sweater had the sleeves rolled up to the elbows, showing off his toned forearms. Terry took the chair next to him. She could smell the spicy body wash he must have used in the shower this morning.

He didn't bring any reference books or even the class history text. It enforced Terry's earlier suspicion that he was used to the benefits of popularity. Instead of pens or paper, he had a basketball. He kept twirling it until the librarian warned him. Zach put the ball under the table, then started to tap a steady beat on the side of the chair — his fingers were never still.

"Maybe a Rubik's Cube will help with that nervous twitch," Terry said. She'd been waiting all study period to come up with a clever line. Terry could handle this high school. She'd become an expert at deciphering personalities. Zach liked playing the hero, and she wasn't in the mood for rescuing. She hated looking like a victim.

"By 'nervous twitch' do you mean my awesome ability to balance this chair and practice my piano concerto at the same time?" he said.

Maude's noise crinkled as she laughed.

He grinned at Terry.

"Hey, Zach!" A pair of cheerleaders flounced by in matching purple and gold uniforms. "Good luck in the big game," they sang in unison, all smiles and hips swaying. He'd been getting 'good lucks' and winks for the whole study period.

"Thanks," Zach said, barely glancing their way. He was still staring at Terry, but the grin had changed to an expression of intrusive curiosity. She suddenly wished her sloppy sweatpants would turn into designer jeans. She fought the urge to hide behind one of Maude's books. In contrast, Zach seemed to grow taller in his chair, completely comfortable in his skin.

"Trying to get work done here," Maude complained in a loud whisper as the two girls lingered by their table.

"Bitch," one of the cheerleaders shot back under her breath.

Terry supposed they wished they were doing a project with Zach. They probably would already have him in one of the aisles with their arms wrapped around him, pressing up against his chest, breathing in his shampoo as he kissed their neck.

"Earth to Terry." Maude snapped her fingers.

"Sorry, what?" Terry shook her head, then tucked a stray piece of hair behind her ear — her neck felt hot.

"Do you want one?" Maude was holding out an opened roll of Love Hearts.

The soggy breakfast burrito Terry'd heated in the microwave had been tasteless despite the exorbitant amount of fat and salt. Its partner had been rolled up in a leftover bread bag and shoved in her backpack for lunch. The last thing Terry's stomach needed was sugar. "Um … no thanks," she said.

Zach dropped his chair down on all fours and took the top candy.

"You have to read it first," Maude told him.

"Are you serious?" He gave her an odd, almost panicked look.

"I'm always serious about candy." Then she took another Love Heart and read, "You belong to me … in bed with no clothes on." Maude snort laughed at her joke, and it was so genuinely goofy Terry couldn't help but smile.

Zach pressed his lips together, pretending to consider this important information. He brought the heart close to his face and squinted at the phrase. "You are hot." He paused and raised his eyebrows at Maude.

"In bed with no clothes on," she finished for him. He popped the candy in his mouth, and all three laughed together. The librarian sent a pointed shush their way.

Chapter Seven

A few more Love Hearts were shared between Maude and Zach. Terry's mouth began to water, but it felt stupid to ask for one now.

"Okay," Maude started, "Ms. Bernard said this was worth half our grade this semester. She gives extra marks for originality, so I was thinking we could do a mock-up article, like you see in a fashion magazine."

She held up one of several magazines she'd brought with her as an example. "But we could make it from ancient Egyptian times, you know? It would be beauty tips from Cleopatra." Maude finished by holding open the Cleopatra book to a famous painting of Egypt's last pharaoh.

"Like with a cover and everything?" Zach said. His expression was sincere as he waited for Maude's answer. Terry wasn't sure if he was asking or adding to her idea. He didn't sound convinced, but he acted curious. Terry studied him from behind her long bangs. In class the other day, he'd doodled the whole time. What made the project more interesting today?

"Exactly," Maude said.

Zach reached across the table for another candy. "That'd be cool," he said. With Zach's approval, Maude's other ideas began to gush. Terry stared at the bust of Cleopatra. She imagined the mysterious coffin making its way across the Atlantic guarded by Egyptian officials at this very moment. What *if* it really was Cleopatra?

Her mother's lifetime of work had accumulated into solving one mystery: to find Cleopatra's final resting place. Except in the end, the quest had claimed her life instead and left Terry scarred, inside and out. She'd never forget her mother's excited whispers, suddenly cut off by the crushing roar and flash of light. The memory became too big for Terry and her chest grew tight, like an expanding balloon threatening to burst.

Maude's voice hit a high note, breaking through Terry's haze. "She invented milk baths!"

Terry snapped back to the present. All at once the magazines and beauty tips seemed surreal and ridiculous, insulting even. "You want this report to be about makeup?" Terry's voice sounded harsher than she intended.

Maude's expression crumbled, but she leaned back in her chair and crossed her arms, inviting Terry to plead her case.

Terry looked down, realizing she had to at least back up her outburst of a challenge. She played with a frayed thread on her sweatpants. "Cleopatra was more than a charming woman. She was a shrewd politician and a genius at warfare." Terry wrapped the thread around her finger a few times and pulled tight, then she released it and started over again. "When her father died, he left the welfare of Egypt to Cleopatra and her younger brother, but the brother forced her out, keeping all the power for himself."

Maude's arms were crossed, still unconvinced. Terry let out a breath. She wasn't used to being the expert. "A year later Cleopatra had formed an army of mercenaries, but she still wasn't ready to overthrow her brother. When she found out Caesar was visiting Alexandria, she had herself rolled up inside a carpet and smuggled into the inner sanctum of his palace." Terry paused and swallowed. "She seduced him that night."

Zach and Maude had grown quiet. "He not only became her

lover," Terry explained, "but a powerful ally as well. He helped her build an even stronger army, and they easily defeated her rivals, giving her back the throne, making Cleopatra the sole ruler of Egypt."

"What about Mark Antony?" Maude sounded deflated.

"He came later," Terry said, a little embarrassed she'd snapped at Maude.

"I don't get it," Zach said. He leaned forward and planted his elbows on his knees. "Why would she have to smuggle herself in? If she was so hot, why didn't Caesar jump on the chance to make out with her?"

A few more cheerleaders sashayed by with effortless grace, but Zach kept staring at Terry, waiting for her explanation. She met his gaze and didn't falter. "Maybe because she wanted to be seen as a clever warrior," she said, "and not just a woman asking for help." They held each other's stare a beat longer than felt comfortable.

"Neffie!" Fraser sauntered over from the information desk, oblivious to the reproachful stare from the librarian. "I got something for you." He patted his worn leather satchel resting on his hip. He was wearing one of those T-shirts that had a tuxedo printed on the front — except the bow-tie was a mustache. "My friend came through big time."

Terry tried to shrink into her chair. She wasn't quite ready to spill about the sarcophagus. "You're faster at getting information than I am," she lied.

"It's pretty juicy too," he said.

Zach pushed himself out of the chair and motioned to the far end of the room. "I'll go check out some stuff."

"Don't get so technical on us, sport," Fraser said to his retreating back, but Zach didn't even bother to turn around.

Maude purposely slipped out of her pink shrug. Today her T-shirt read *Maudern Woman*. Terry wasn't sure if she should admire or pity her.

"Here, Fraser." Maude held up the half-empty tube of Love Hearts. He took one and popped it in his mouth. "What's it say?" The tips of her ears were the same color as her shrug.

"Huh?" Fraser crunched down on the candy.

Maude's ears threatened to spontaneously combust. "Nothing." She waved it off with a fake laugh.

Fraser glanced at his watch then turned back to Terry. "Can you meet me during lunch break?"

"But I don't have anything for you," she said.

He lifted a shoulder. "Then today will be all about you," he said. "You can find me in the newspaper office, one floor directly above our heads." With barely a glance at Maude he breezed away, headed toward the long row of bookshelves.

Wordlessly, Maude bent her head and began to shove her magazines and all the reference material she'd brought into her backpack. She sniffed then mumbled a quick goodbye to Terry.

Terry fought the urge to follow her, unsure how to make Maude feel better. But maybe nothing was wrong. Terry had been raised among grad students and historians; she was clueless about kids her own age.

She nudged her own backpack with her toe. She only had the class textbook and another free pen — this one was from the dry cleaner on the first floor of her apartment building. She clicked the pen a few times, wondering what Fraser had found out about the museum.

She grabbed her backpack and chose one of the aisles she thought he'd gone down. Instead, she found Zach. He stood at the far end, head tilted to the side, squinting at the titles. He looked lost. He straightened again, then reached up and touched the edge of his left eyebrow. The movement made Terry hold her breath. It was refined — elegant, even. He repeated this mannerism a few times, then chose a book and started to pull it off the shelf.

"Hey," Terry said. "Find any good stuff?" She used his lingo, but it sounded wrong, like she was making fun of him. To redeem herself, she quickly added, "I mean, I didn't have much luck earlier." She walked closer, concentrating on each step. She stopped a few feet from him. The top of her head barely reached his shoulders.

"I'm not surprised," he said. "I bet you know more about Cleopatra than Ms. Bernard. What could a book tell you that you don't already know?"

"Just because my dad—"

Zach held up a hand, interrupting her. "Hey, take some credit," he said. "My dad sells used cars, and I have no idea what a twelve-month lease with an informational APR means." He smiled when Terry laughed. "See? It's totally different. You're more than book smart. I've learned more from listening to you in a few days than a whole year with Bernard."

"Thanks." Terry put a hand on the bookshelf to steady her balance. The floor felt suspiciously tippy with Zach so close.

The tips of his fingers slipped into the front pockets of his jeans. "You make it interesting," he said. Zach took a step closer. "You should be the teacher. I'd pass for sure."

The warm bubble that had been slowly growing in Terry' chest suddenly deflated. "You see me as the teacher?" Her tone was flat. *I wish he didn't see me at all, then*, she thought.

"Not exactly." His heel tapped against the toe of his other sneaker. The topic had exhausted itself, and they were left standing like bored statues in the aisle, staring at each other, unable to leave.

Zach nodded to one of the books on the shelf and pulled it out halfway. "Anyway," he finally said. "Since Maude is definitely the creative one of the group, I thought something on Egyptology would help her come up with a few more ideas."

Terry only shrugged, still bruised by the teacher comment.

The familiar golden boy grin vanished. Zach slouched closer and lowered his voice. "This is more than some lame class project," he said. "If I don't pass history, old pointy-faced Ms. Bernard is going to make sure I get kicked off the team. If I get kicked off the team, we don't make it to State Championships. If we don't make it to the final, I don't have a chance at a scholarship to college."

The transformation was startling. Gone was the effortless confidence he usually exuded. Zach's Adam's apple rose and fell and the color was high in his cheeks. But he didn't look away. He kept his gaze drilled into Terry, almost daring her to reply.

Terry opened and closed her mouth a few times. It was unnerving to have him get so close and intense. "Oh ... I just ... um," she stammered, but no other words came out.

His blush deepened. "Never mind," he said. "You don't get it. I doubt you'll have to fight your way into a college." The lunch bell rang, making both of them jump. "Thank god," he murmured, brushing past her.

Terry stayed in place, using the bookshelves to help her stand. Her knees were shaking. She shut her eyes tightly and whispered, "Don't attract attention. Don't get involved. And don't make trouble."

Terry opened her eyes and pushed away from the shelf. The book Zach had been looking at was still sticking out. She frowned at the title. *Ecology.*

Chapter Eight

Terry sat at the empty table furthest from the hot lunch line. Today the offering was some kind of beef and cheese combination. Pools of grease dotted the mounds of hamburger meat.

Instead, she got a large chocolate milk from one of the vending machines along the wall. Terry placed her history textbook on the table with her pen. If she looked busy doing homework, no one would notice her pathetic lunch.

She peeled back the top of the milk carton, but only one corner opened. Terry used the pen to gauge a hole through the seal. She ended up having to pry the whole thing back. Now the spout was a huge, yawning opening. She calculated the trip to the counter for a straw and decided it wouldn't be worth the pain or the stares at her limp.

She took a sip of chocolate milk. A tiny dribble trickled down her chin, and she dabbed her face with the back of her sleeve.

"Classy." Allison stood beside the table holding a tray with a salad smothered in bacon bits and creamy dressing. She was wearing a miniskirt with knee-high socks that perfectly matched the blue and green argyle print of her vest. The princess who'd been making out with Murphy in the library flanked her.

"It was an accident," Terry said, not sure why she felt the need to explain herself. Allison had a way of putting her on the defensive. Terry smoothed out the side of her hair, feeling it stick out under protest. She wished she'd at least put a few clips in today.

Allison started. "I heard you were making friends in the guys' washroom yesterday."

Terry couldn't tell if she was anxious to spread gossip or truly angry. "That was an accident too," she said.

"Rumors get started quickly here," Allison said. She was smiling, but the threat was obvious. "You'll be known as the school slut if you're not more careful about who you hang out with." The princess threw a glare in Terry's direction, giving a silent 'hear, hear' to Allison's declaration.

"Roger that," Terry said under her breath, giving the empty table an obvious sweep of her eyes. Allison turned red. She nodded to her princess. Without hesitating, the girl thrust her hand forward, tipping the chocolate milk, sending a wave over the table and down onto Terry's lap.

"Whoa!" Terry jumped up. Her knee screamed at the quick movement. She came down hard on the bench.

Allison's eyes gleamed. "Oops, I guess that was an accident too."

Terry's lap was darkened and soggy. She looked around at the other tables. People had seen what Allison just did. Some were still staring, but no one said anything. No one offered to help.

"I can't wait to see your soggy ass limp down the hallway. Everyone will think you started your period," Allison said.

"It'll make a great picture for the yearbook," the princess added. She held up an iPhone. "I'll be waiting."

Allison and her princess then strutted to their table, already filled with beautiful girls in stylish clothes and guys in varsity jackets. Terry was starting to despise the colors purple and gold. A few of their heads turned toward Terry. This was followed by a burst of laughter.

Terry sat in a daze, afraid to move. The liquid seeped between her legs, soaking her backside as well. There were napkins at the

# BR Myers

lunch counter, but there was no way she could limp up there with a wet lap and butt. Another wave of snickers came from Allison's table.

Terry went into survival mode. She took the textbook and propped it up in front of the chocolate puddle, hiding the mess. Now all she had to do was sit there and wait for everyone to leave or at least until she dried enough to escape school and head back to the apartment.

She repeated her school rules in her mind. It always calmed her down.

A familiar, easy gait caught her attention. Zach's tray was heaped with the mystery beef and cheese concoction. Terry kept her eyes glued to the textbook, hyper aware of him entering her peripheral vision. He paused by her table.

Terry was at war. She wanted him to stop. The way he'd stormed away from her in the library felt unfinished and undeserved. But she also wanted him to keep going, since her lap was a sodden mess.

The table full of jocks and their girlfriends turned their heads, one by one. The chocolate milk had soaked all the way through Terry's sweatpants to her skin.

"Zach?" one of the guys asked anxiously. They waved him over, as if luring him back to safety.

His feet finally became unglued from the floor. He joined the others without glancing back. Terry pretended to look for something in her backpack, wishing she could crawl inside and die. Her fingers felt the cold breakfast burrito. She pulled it out and let it plop onto the table. The sight of that rubbery cold thing made her eyes burn with tears. She blinked hard. Her phone buzzed, and Terry's hands, covered in half-dried milk, made sticky fingerprints all over the screen. There was a text from her dad.

Apartment building has black mold. Decontaminating until next week. Booking hotel. Come straight to museum after school.

Terry pressed her lips tight and tried to shut out Allison's stu-

42

pid squealing and giggling about the next basketball game. Then someone was beside her, bringing the scent of cotton candy. There was a flash of pink nail polish, then a travel-size package of wet wipes was gently placed beside the burrito.

Terry didn't need to see the face that went with the kindness. "Thanks," she said. Her voice warbled. She took a few wipes and began to discreetly clean her hands.

"It pays to be prepared," Maude answered, allowing several beats of silence. "Tie your hoodie around your waist until your pants dry." Terry gave her a questioning look. Maude shrugged, unfazed. "Allison isn't exactly original."

"Thanks," Terry repeated. She sucked in a quick breath, held it, then said, "I'm sorry about yesterday ... the bathroom thing, I mean. I went back for you, but I ended up ambushing the guys' washroom by mistake."

Maude made a face. "Seriously? That's kind of gross and yet hilarious at the same time."

Terry dropped her voice. "Still, I shouldn't have left you."

"It's not like you think. I pretended to be scared." She motioned toward Zach's table. "I'm only nervous she'll figure out I'm faking and escalate her game."

"Her game?"

Maude started unpacking her lunch. She talked from the corner of her mouth. "Allison isn't the usual Queen Bee. She's a viper, a power freak. She's on practically every school committee, and it's no secret she'd gunning for the big prize next year — president of the student council."

Terry's mouth dropped open. "You can't be serious."

"Half of the school is afraid of her, and the other half is jealous." Maude groaned. "God, senior year is going to be hellish. I wish she only cared about being pretty, then we could all vote for her as prom queen and move on. But she's more interested in being a tyrant. Guess who'll win 'most likely to become the next Mussolini'?"

"Why would anyone want her as school president?"

Maude snorted. "Having Zach on her arm gives the illusion she's human. She's almost guaranteed a win next September. Zach's going to be some star college athlete who's obligated to keep showing up for stupid high school dances as her date."

A sudden weight lodged itself inside Terry's chest. "*He's* dating *her?*"

"They've only been together for a few months." Maude looked around, and then leaned in closer. "He wasn't even on her radar until he became a star on the basketball court. Now she has her claws in him. If he ever broke up with her..." Maude shivered.

Terry dared a glance at the jock's table. Zach was already halfway through his massive lunch, with Allison planted next to him. The sports hero and the Queen Bee: Terry should have guessed as much. She tried to shrug off the wave of gloom that had settled around her.

Maude's voice lightened like she was trying to make a joke. "I was considering getting a bodyguard for the library to protect us while we worked on the Cleopatra project. Allison has a jealous streak."

"No kidding." Terry assessed the damage by lifting one of her thighs. There was a sucking sound from all the spilled mess. Maude handed her a pile of napkins. Terry sopped up the milk around her, trying to accomplish the impossible task of cleaning up while trying to be invisible.

Maude's lunch was a sandwich of thick bread, bursting with fresh slices of tomato, bean sprouts and humus. There was also a small bag of potato chips, a bottle of fizzy lemonade and a curiously shaped container. Maude flipped off the lid. It was a cupcake with fluffy icing. Terry glanced at her burrito, lying lifeless and unimpressive as a day-old banana peel.

"Sorry," Maude said.

Terry's face burned with shame. It wasn't like her dad didn't have money; he just wasn't domestic. "My dad isn't exactly Julia

Child," Terry explained.

Maude opened her bag of chips. "I'm talking about the beauty project idea for history class." She gave Terry a sober face. "I can't help it, everything reminds me of makeup." She crunched a few chips. "You're right. We should showcase how strong Cleopatra was. My mom says strong women don't get enough recognition in the world."

Terry smelled the chips, and it made her mouth water. "Actually, now that I think about it, your idea's really original and we should go with it."

A smile spread over Maude's face. "Yeah?"

"Yeah."

Maude pushed the open bag of chips between them. "No thanks," Terry said, the blush creeping up her neck. "That's okay."

"Your lunch got ruined by that freak," Maude said, putting half her sandwich on a napkin and passing it to Terry. "I hate seeing Allison get her way."

Terry took a small bite of the sandwich, her taste buds startled by the tangy garlic and lemon flavors. She swallowed it whole and took a larger bite, licking the tomato juice off her bottom lip. When she was done, her stomach was full and content. Terry didn't mind the dampness on her clothes, and even her knee stopped hurting.

Maude nibbled at her crust while flipping through a fashion magazine. From the first day, Terry had everyone neatly placed in a category, except for Maude — she remained a mystery.

"Why are you being so nice to me?" Terry finally asked.

"I'm just a super nice person," Maude answered, still looking at the magazine. She took the cupcake out of its container. She gave Terry a guilty smile. "And I was hoping I could tag along when you go see Fraser."

Terry had forgotten all about Fraser and his promise of 'juicy information.' What had he found out about the museum? And why hadn't he just given her the information in the library?

Maude's neck became blotchy. She started to talk with her hands. "I've been trying to get him to let me do a column for the paper for months."

Terry picked up on the way Maude's voice quivered. "Oh … really?" She pictured Fraser's mustache bow-tie T-shirt.

Maude peeled the paper wrapper away from the cupcake perfectly. Her ears glowed again. "You two seem close," she said. "I thought you could put in a good word for me."

"No more close than me and Ms. Bernard," Terry teased. Her gaze went between Maude and the cupcake.

Maude sensed victory. She offered the whole treat to Terry. "Deal?" she nudged.

Terry took the cupcake. "No problem. Of course, if you really wanted to make an impression, we could always sneak you into the newspaper office rolled up in a carpet."

Chapter Nine

The newspaper office was more like a long closet. Terry guessed it might have once belonged to the janitor. Three desks lined one side of the wall, and the middle one had the only computer. Plastic organizers were stacked on top of the other with papers sticking out. Every visible surface was covered. There was a chaotic feel to the office, but it also had some semblance of being organized.

Terry realized this room was exactly like Fraser, messy but in a purposeful way. He grinned when she and Maude appeared at the half open door. He wheeled back in his chair, abruptly hitting the opposite wall. Terry tried to hide her laugh.

"Welcome," he said, ushering them in. "Would you like a tour? These are the desks." Fraser waved his hand like a game show model.

"Lovely," Maude said.

"And these are the wheelie chairs." He gave it another push to demonstrate. "And that's my co-editor." He motioned with his head to the girl sitting at the far end of the room. She had a pair of Beats over her ears, the volume high enough for them to hear the lyrics. She leaned over a spread of papers with a highlighter in one hand and a red pen in the other. Terry recognized the black skull nail polish.

"Say hello, Tanya," Fraser said loud enough to be heard over her music.

"Hey." She nodded at Terry and Maude briefly, then went back to reading.

Terry's eyes zeroed in on Fraser's leather satchel hanging over the back of a chair. He followed her gaze. "Ah, right." His voice became dramatic. "Insatiable lust for knowledge has brought you two fine ladies here. And I was hoping it was my suave charm."

Maude glanced around the room, everywhere but at Fraser. "As if," she snorted. Her pretend sarcasm was poorly disguised. She riffled inside her backpack and produced a pink sheet of paper. She thrust it at Fraser. "Here's that piece I was telling you about?" Her voice ended high and uncertain.

Fraser took the paper. His brows knitted together. "Top ten reasons unicorns are better than zombies." He looked up at her. "Seriously?" Maude nodded encouragingly. Tanya's head inclined toward them, her music softer now. Fraser's lips moved as he scanned the rest of the sheet. Maude held her breath. "Hmm," he said, placing the paper on the desk behind him. "Maybe."

Maude's expression blanked for a second. "Well, zombies are hot right now," she defended. "And who wouldn't want to see a badass unicorn fight?" She got a smile out of Fraser that time.

Terry inwardly cheered for Maude. Then a small gap of silence followed. Maude swallowed loudly and started to stammer something about needing candy.

"Sorry?" he said, frowning at her.

"How about that information you promised?" Terry interrupted. "You said it was juicy," she reminded him.

"So I did." Fraser made a great show of pulling out the documents. Maude was unwrapping a Tootsie Pop, hanging on his every word — or at least how his mouth was moving, Terry guessed.

He handed Terry photocopies of what looked like old newspaper articles. "My brother works for the *Devonshire Daily*, so he has access to the newspaper archives," Fraser explained.

"Doesn't anyone have access to the archives at the library?"

Terry asked.

Fraser folded his arms. "Yeah, sure. See how that works for you. Do you have any idea how long it would take you to collect the stuff I found? You'd be there until next month. With my brother's account I was able to go through the database for stories pertaining to the museum since it opened. And, ta-da!" He pointed to the headline, now in Terry's hands.

"Missing museum showcase piece has local police stumped," Terry read.

Maude made an excited noise around the sucker as she read over Terry's shoulder. "Only two weeks after a mysterious foiled burglary attempt at the Museum of Natural History, officials are scrambling for clues to the whereabouts of a priceless Egyptian artifact. The gold piece, known as The Sacred Asp of Cleopatra, was the museum's main draw and was set to tour major cities across America before its return to Egypt."

Maude paused and gave Terry a peculiar look that bordered on apprehension. "That's a weird coincidence." She turned to Fraser and explained. "Ms. Bernard has our class doing a project about Cleopatra's life."

A sting of panic took root at the base of Terry's spine. She shook off the shiver, ready to dissect the issue the way her mother used to tackle her work, by looking for evidence. "But this doesn't explain why she looked so freaked out in class the other day," she said. "Why would a robbery make her so frightened?"

Maude pointed at the article with her sucker. "Look at the picture. Is that the asp? I was imagining a statue or something."

Terry said, "It's like a bracelet, but worn higher. The piece wraps around the upper arm like a snake wraps itself around a tree. One end resembles the head. The eyes are usually a gem of some kind."

"Gross," Maude said. "I hate snakes." She continued to read. "The Devonshire police are at a loss as to how the piece disappeared into thin air. The priceless artifact was under constant guard. This bizarre incident, coupled with the recent missing person case, has fueled rumors of The Sacred Asp's legendary curse."

"Curse," Tanya chuckled from across the room, clearly eavesdropping.

Maude ignored her and scanned the article further. "Egyptian delegates refused to comment. This latest blunder by the museum is another headache for the mayor. Coupled with pockets of vigilantism on the rise, voters are demanding his resignation and crying out for new leadership."

Terry became quiet, remembering the scene in her dad's office with Mayor Harris. She looked at the date on the top and her eyes grew wide. "This is fifty years old," she said.

"You can have those copies," Fraser offered.

"Thanks," she said distractedly. "Say, is Allison's dad the mayor?"

"Didn't you know?" Maude replied. "That's why she's so power -hungry. The apple doesn't fall far from the tree."

"Christ!" Fraser said. "Can you imagine the headlines if she follows his footsteps?"

His warning almost sounding like anticipation. "I hope I'm working for the *Devonshire Daily* when she takes office."

"Oh, yeah?" Tanya said. "From what I've seen, Allison has no choice. During the science fair, he showed up for the award ceremony, and when Allison got second place he pulled her aside and yelled at her for like fifteen minutes."

"He yelled at her?" Terry asked skeptically. "In front of everyone?"

"You couldn't really hear too much," Tanya replied. "They were away from the crowd. He wasn't yelling the whole time, but I was … you know, close by, eavesdropping, and he said some pretty twisted stuff about always being the best."

The room was quiet for a moment, then Maude said. "Still, you always have a choice about how you're going to treat other people."

Tanya shrugged. "Whatever. He's a total jerk if you ask me."

Maude chomped down on her sucker, cracking it in half. Terry sensed she wanted a change in topic. She held up the article. "Was the asp ever found?" she asked Fraser.

"Doesn't say."

Terry leaned against the desk, her knee threatening to lock up. "Why would Ms. Bernard be so upset about a fifty-year-old robbery?" Something was itching at the back of her mind, just out of reach.

"She's a freak for old stuff." Tanya leaned back in her chair. The Beats rested around her neck. "She once did this weird mummy thing. It looked like an alien autopsy."

Fraser laughed. "She demonstrated how the brain was pulled out the nose," he explained to Terry.

"In class?" Terry was horrified.

Tanya yawned. "She made a model with gelatin molds and a straw."

"It was gross," Maude said. "It looked so real." She threw the rest of her sucker in the garbage can under a desk.

Terry read the article again, paying closer attention. Something stood out for her this time. When she was finished, she caught Fraser watching her, waiting for the inevitable question. "What about the missing person case?" she asked.

Fraser smiled and reached into his satchel again. Then he handed her another copy. "Her name was June Macallum. She disappeared two weeks before the asp went missing. The last place she was seen was the museum." He pushed up his glasses. "She was only sixteen."

Maude gulped behind Terry. "Was *she* ever found?" she asked. The room grew quiet.

Fraser merely lifted a shoulder. "The foster mother was brought in for questioning, and there was a night security guard who was under suspicion for some time." He buckled up his satchel. "But I couldn't find anything else in the database."

Terry read in a hushed tone. "With no evidence to support the contrary, officials are reluctant to give a comment. However, several museum staff who wish to remain anonymous lay claim to unfounded gossip and believe that The Sacred Asp was indeed cursed and has ruined the lives of all those who came in contact with it."

"Curse," Tanya huffed. "People were stupid back then. There's no such thing."

Terry's knee began to throb.

Chapter Ten

Terry's pants were practically dry by the time she stepped off the bus. It was a sunny afternoon, but the winter wind was raw, and it chilled her face. Devonshire had plenty of tree-lined streets, but the bare winter branches looked like claws to her. She tugged at the drawstring of her hoodie, tightening it around her neck.

Her phone buzzed. It was another text from Maude, the third in the last half hour. The first two had been about the Cleopatra beauty project, and this last one was about the upcoming basketball game.

Super. My house. Pre-game. CUPCAKES!!

Terry slipped her phone away without replying. There was too much to think about. She was still convinced her rules were essential to getting through this bout of high school, but she was secretly charmed at Maude's invitation. She hadn't had a friend close to her own age since Awad, and that felt like a hundred years ago.

Truthfully, a basketball semifinal was the last thing she wanted to take in, but Fraser had given Maude an assignment to cover the game, and if she did well he'd consider publishing her 'Zombie Versus Unicorn' piece. When he had made the offer, Maude had lit up like Christmas.

She'd then ensnared Terry into accompanying her. "You'll get to see Zach play," she added. "He may not be much for Egyptology, but he makes the whole school scream in unison."

"And that's important?" Terry had asked, her mind far away, picturing him in the library, frowning at the titles.

"Sure," Maude had affirmed. "I'm not cheerleader material, but it does sort of make you feel a little proud of the school." Terry finally agreed, and they'd parted ways.

She was only a few blocks from the museum now, and Terry's mind was full of Zach. It happened without her realizing, starting with the ease with which he'd grabbed the ball before it hit her, then the image in the library; the subtle tilt of his head, the way his fingers touched the edge of his eyebrow several times when he was concentrating.

He'd left her so briskly after that. But during lunch he had stopped by her table. Had he wanted to talk to her? Maybe apologize? What would he have done if his teammates hadn't been there to call him away? Did he know his girlfriend was a bit psycho? And what had he been doodling that first day? He'd become a frustrating enigma.

Terry nodded to the museum staff at the front counter as she shuffled by on her way to the elevator. A sticky note on the door of her dad's office told her he was on the fifth floor.

The Egypt room was full of activity. Construction workers were setting up lights, drilling holes in the floor or constructing platforms. The air was thick with dust. All of the permanent exhibits were covered in plastic. Terry looked up at the antique Cleopatra mannequin protected by several layers of cellophane sheets. It was creepy. She rubbed her arms, trying to calm down the sudden goose bumps.

Her dad was at the far end of the room, talking with someone in a hard hat. When he saw Terry, he waved her over. She self-consciously picked her way around the various extension cords zigzagging across the floor. Tripping in front of all these people would be the perfect end to her humiliating day.

She waited as her dad went over instructions about one of the exhibits. To her right, standing up against the wall and covered by more plastic, was a closed mummy case, the unnaturally bright gold and black paint chipped and peeling away. Terry peered closer. Like the Cleopatra model, this looked original to the museum and was only for show; the eyes on the face mask were hollowed out. Terry reached up and poked a finger toward one of the empty eye sockets.

"Terry!" her dad shouted over the noise of drills and hammers. "You got my message about the apartment?" he asked.

Yup, right after the school psycho decided to pour lunch on me, Terry thought. Instead she replied, "Yeah." That one word seemed to take all of her energy.

He ran a hand through his hair and yawned. "We'll pick up a few things to get us through the week," he said. Terry could hear the exhaustion in his voice. "I'm not worried about food, we'll eat at the hotel." He paused. "But we'll need socks and ... stuff."

Terry looked down at her stained pants and worn hoodie. A shopping trip was desperately needed, but these days she couldn't care less. She and her mom had loved to spend hours in the crowded markets trying on brightly colored scarves and long, dangling earrings. Every place, no matter how remote or small, had Terry and her mom bartering with enthusiastic merchants.

"But I've got some exciting news to make up for the sudden move," her dad said. "It arrived today." There was a hint of a smile on his face. When Terry didn't respond he added, "The coffin." He motioned around the room. "That's why the frantic action. The new exhibit should be up within a few weeks."

Terry's eyes grew wide. "I thought you said they couldn't open it!"

"Opened or not," he explained, "the museum will have it on display by the end of April. The mayor insists on it."

"Can he do that?" Terry asked. She knew this museum had its own agenda for staying open, and boasting the premiere of a controversial find was apparently its priority. A dull ache began to pound behind her eyes. "What about the expert?" she asked. "I thought that's why the coffin was coming here? I thought that's why you brought *us* here." She concentrated on keeping her voice level, but it cracked at the end.

"Terry." Her dad said her name slowly, trying to be soothing.

She stared at the floor, fighting the tears. She didn't want her dad to see her cry. Terry turned quickly, her footfalls landing unevenly as she made her way to the entrance. She didn't know where to hide. The apartment was off-limits, and she had no idea what hotel her dad had booked. Terry felt hollow no matter where she went, she had no home. The tools stopped, and all the workers grew silent.

"What?" she said to a group of staff near the entrance. Her voice sounded dopey with exhaustion. "Haven't you ever seen a cripple before?" She limped toward the doorway, blinking back a gush of unwanted tears, then stopped dead in her tracks. A woman in a wheelchair blocked the entrance, staring darkly at Terry.

Her dad's voice came up behind her. "This is Dr. Mullaca," he said. "She's here to unlock the sarcophagus." The woman had olive skin and sharp features, her white hair pulled back in a severe bun. "Dr. Mullaca, this is my daughter, Terry," he said, finishing the introduction.

"I know who Nefertari is," she said. Her eyes trailed down Terry's side and stopped at her knee. "So," Dr. Mullaca said, with a hint of an accent, "you're the girl who survived."

Chapter Eleven

Terry and her dad followed Dr. Mullaca's wheelchair down the long corridor of the museum's basement. The air was cool and dry. Doors lined either side of the hallway, and Terry read labels like 'Paleontology' and 'Biodiversity' and 'Invertebrate Zoology.'

She pinched her dad's elbow and motioned to Dr. Mullaca, but he waved off her silent query about the elderly expert. Terry eyed the back of Dr. Mullaca's head, studying the white bun, a prickly trail of unease creeping down her spine. She looked at her dad again, but he was more interested in the doorway at the end of the hallway.

The plain door had a keypad over the lock. There was no indication that beyond it lay one of the greatest mysteries of ancient Egypt. Dr. Mullaca punched in a code. Her dad's expression changed from contained excitement to confused disappointment; obviously he didn't have the combination yet.

"Gunther," she said, her Egyptian-style accent curling her words. "I'm not in the habit of letting unqualified people access to my work, but I think this is something Nefertari should see for herself."

There was a thick-sounding click, then Dr. Mullaca turned the knob and pushed open the heavy door.

Terry's dad put a hand on her elbow to hold her back, allowing

Dr. Mullaca to wheel in first. Terry hadn't realized how anxious she was to see the coffin in person. Her heart began to ache. This was what her mother had died for.

The white room was brightly lit. Several shelves with numerous drawers lined the wall. A long counter ran the length of the room. Everything was neat and organized. *It's the exact opposite of Fraser's newspaper office.* The thought of Fraser and their agreement made her gut twist. She was about to lay eyes on something only a few people in the whole world had seen.

A low table dominated the room, burdened with a mummy case. The intricate hieroglyphics called out to Terry. She stepped forward, but a severe warning from behind made her freeze. Two men in black suits appeared at the doorway and quickly approached her.

Dr. Mullaca said something in Arabic. She spoke so fast and with such a thick accent that Terry could barely understand it. The men eased back and stood with their hands clasped behind them. There was an awkward silence for a few beats.

Mr. Hughes was the first to speak. "The Egyptian delegates take guarding this particular artifact seriously." He smiled at them, but the men only stared back, sizing up both him and Terry.

Dr. Mullaca gave him a look and said, "Gunther, they're the bodyguards."

"Should be easy, since the body is over two thousand years old." He laughed at his own joke and Terry loved him for it. She added her own laughter, forced as it was in the presence of all these peculiar strangers.

"There is more than one body they protect, Mr. Hughes," a male voice said. Terry recognized the accent, but the tone was more dignified than Dr. Mullaca's. The bodyguards separated and a tall sheik in a white robe and headdress walked between them.

He stopped in front of Terry and her father. "I am here to represent my country in this international venture." He waved a hand toward the men in black suits, still rigid and straight-faced. "And they are here to protect me."

"This is Prince Kamal," Dr. Mullaca explained. "He's the delegate that accompanied the coffin from Egypt."

Terry was suddenly aware of her frumpy appearance, beggarly compared to the prince's impeccably clean robe and expensive gold watch. Terry wasn't sure if she should bow or curtsey. She peeked at her dad. The prince, Terry saw with relief, shook her dad's hand and gave him what might have been a warm smile.

"I am pleased this matter is being given such special attention, Mr. Hughes," Prince Kamal said. "My country is indebted to you and your team of specialists."

Terry's posture straightened with the prince's kind words. She took a longer inspection of his dark olive skin and cleanly shaven face — he even smelled rich. She was pretty sure his cologne didn't come from Hollister. He was older than her, she guessed, but not by much. She reasoned the sophisticated manners and designer jewelry made him appear older.

"Then perhaps we should let the specialist work," Dr. Mullaca snapped. She wheeled over to the low table with such ease, Terry wondered how long she'd been in that chair.

Dr. Mullaca put on a pair of white cotton gloves and picked up a magnifying glass. She began pointing out several symbols along the side of the coffin. "I've been examining this particular inscription all morning."

Terry, her father and Prince Kamal stood behind Dr. Mullaca. "There are three similar versions of the story on each side of the case, and the top," she explained. "Each line has clues as to how to open the case correctly, and each shows what will happen when the proper technique is ignored."

"You mean if it's forced open?" Terry's dad asked.

Dr. Mullaca pointed to a tiny painting. "This image is indicative of an elaborate trap within the case itself."

Terry squinted at the picture. She was familiar with hieroglyphics, but she was completely stumped as to how Dr. Mullaca was so certain. "What kind of trap?" she asked. She looked to her father, but his expression was clouded.

"There's no harm to the person who opens the case," Dr. Mullaca replied matter-of-factly.

Prince Kamal's jaw tightened. "Then what is the real concern?" he asked.

She turned to the prince. "If we try to force this case open right now, a chain reaction will be set off, spilling acid throughout the entire case, essentially flooding everything inside. And given enough time, the mummy would be compromised as well. The result would be disastrous."

"But how much damage can be done to a few jars of organs and spices?" Terry asked. "If there's a team assembled as soon as you open the case—"

"Extremely unwise and reckless," Dr. Mullaca interrupted. "I'm shocked your parents didn't teach you better."

Terry's face burned like she'd been slapped. "They would have used papyrus," Prince Kamal kindly explained to her. "Any documents would be destroyed immediately."

"That's highly irregular," Terry's dad said. "Are you suggesting this case may contain transcripts about Cleopatra?"

"Perhaps," Dr. Mullaca said. "Plus anything that would lead to the whereabouts of her original tomb. If this is indeed Cleopatra, then where is Mark Antony?"

"It would be a find of unequalled treasures," Prince Kamal declared majestically.

Terry whispered, "Of Egypt's most celebrated doomed lovers."

She couldn't help but think how cruel it was that her mother had died for this discovery. This last project of her mother's — this chance to solve a thousands-of-years-old mystery — was the only connection Terry had left to her. She turned to Dr. Mullaca. "You said the hieroglyphs show how to open the case correctly?"

Dr. Mullaca only nodded.

Terry's gaze fell on the coffin. Had this really been what her mother had been racing toward that day?

The room began to spin. Her mother's voice surfaced from a deep memory. *"This is it … the fourth chamber—"* Then as always, her sentence is cut short by an earsplitting roar and flash of light.

Terry glared back at the woman who was stealing all her mother's hard work. She tried to swallow her anger, but the lump was too painful this time. Dr. Mullaca owed her more than a nod.

Terry's voice filled the small room. "If you know how to open it, then why are we all standing here? What are you waiting for?" Her dad sucked in his breath, but he made no motion to stop Terry. "My mother is the only reason we're all here. Why are you keeping secrets from my father and me?"

Dr. Mullaca pressed her lips together. She gave Prince Kamal a glance, then craned her neck and stared pointedly at the two bodyguards lurking in the periphery. Prince Kamal made a swift hand signal and the two men bowed and left the room, closing the door behind them.

Terry pictured them standing guard just outside the door. Of course, she reasoned, feeling like an idiot, a project this secretive wouldn't be shared with the prince's bodyguards.

Prince Kamal turned to Terry. "My deepest condolences, Miss Hughes. I understand your family has given much for the sake of preserving my country's past."

Terry was grateful for his genuine tone. "Thank you," she managed to say, her words much less barbed than earlier. The heat of an embarrassed blush made her cheeks glow.

He turned to Dr. Mullaca. "You may speak freely now," Prince Kamal announced. "Tell us what you've learned."

Chapter Twelve

"I need a key," Dr. Mullaca said. Her white-gloved hand hovered over the chest of the coffin. She pointed to three identical grooves imprinted into the chest, directly below the face mask. "See these markings?" she said. "This is the keyhole. A special trigger is needed to activate the latch — a key of a particular shape. Only by pressing into each groove at the same time can the case be opened safely."

Terry stated what she thought was the obvious. "Can't you make something that will fit?"

Dr. Mullaca gave her an exasperated look and let out a long sigh. "The latest technology will not do, Nefertari. I've seen the digital scans. The contents are far too valuable to play with."

Prince Kamal's eyebrows raised in silent surprise at Terry's true name. She ignored his stare.

Dr. Mullaca tilted up her chin as she grew taller in her chair. "There's only one shape that can fit into the grooves perfectly." She looked at her audience, but they remained silent. "A spiral," she answered. Then she motioned to another section of the case, one with an image that made Terry's pulse quicken. Dr. Mullaca paid particular attention to her. Her voice took on an eerie quality as she asked Terry, "Do you know how Cleopatra died?"

Terry peeled her eyes away from the image of the cobra. "She had a poisonous snake smuggled into her prison tower," she answered. Terry could hear the tremor in her own voice. It sent a shiver all the way down to her feet. She remembered her parents taking her to a gallery in London, showing her the famous painting of Cleopatra holding the snake to her breast. It had given her nightmares for weeks.

"Yes." Dr. Mullaca's eyes widened. "Can you imagine holding a snake inches from your heart, with its fangs dripping with venom, knowing the painful death you were about to suffer?"

Terry was repelled by the woman's strong gaze. Who was Dr. Mullaca to ask about suffering?

"Cleopatra wasn't afraid to die," Dr. Mullaca began. "She wasn't going to let Octavian have power over her. She was going to die like a queen."

Terry shuddered. She wanted to leave this cold, sterile room and get as far away from Dr. Mullaca as possible, but the temptation of new information about her mother's last project kept her feet firmly on the floor.

Dr. Mullaca's controlled tone took on a nervous edge. "Do you know the symbol for Egyptian royalty?" she asked.

"The asp," Terry answered automatically. The words sounded like an echo from the past. She imagined colored glass tumbling around a kaleidoscope, and how one slight turn changed everything. A whole new picture appeared in Terry's mind. "A spiral," she said.

The excitement at making the connection overshadowed Terry's earlier desire to leave the examination room. "That's why you're here, isn't it?" Terry said to Dr. Mullaca. "Instead of New York or Washington." She imagined Fraser's reaction if she ever hinted at this kind of scoop. "You're looking for The Sacred Asp. That's the key, isn't it?"

Dr. Mullaca peeled off her white cotton glove, looking satisfied.

Terry's face was glowing with an unexpected rush of heat, then slowly her smile melted away. "But it's been missing for fifty years," she said. "It was stolen."

"Let's not jump to conclusions," Terry's dad said. "I've known about this theory since Sarah first contacted me, and I confess I find it hard to believe that anyone with your credentials, Dr. Mullaca, would travel across the ocean on some kind of Indiana Jones quest."

Prince Kamal spoke up, the emotion thick in his voice. "The Sacred Asp was a priceless artifact on loan from my country to this very museum. If there is a chance it could be found, I would not hesitate to give my support."

Terry's dad touched his lower lip with his finger. "This is an ambitious interpretation of the hieroglyphics, Dr. Mullaca," he said. "It sounds like you're hoping the asp is a convenient coincidence."

"I don't believe in coincidences," she replied.

Great, the expert is crazy. Terry was starving and had no idea where she was going to sleep tonight. She rubbed one of her temples.

Dr. Mullaca narrowed her gaze at Terry again. "How did you know about a burglary that happened fifty years ago, Nefertari?" Then she added, "An event your father didn't think was important enough to share with you."

Terry went through the timeline of bizarre events that led her to Fraser's newspaper office. She hugged her elbows. "Just something my history teacher said," she answered.

Dr. Mullaca wasted no time. "Do you think it was fate or coincidence that brought you to that class on that certain day when that certain teacher mentioned the museum?" Before Terry could answer, she continued. "And do you think it's fate or coincidence that the artifact your mother died finding can only be opened by this missing asp?"

Terry's dad interjected angrily. "That's out of line."

She ignored his red face and continued to grill Terry. "Fate or coincidence, Nefertari?"

"It's Terry," she said, her voice quivering. "And I don't believe in fate or miracles or wishes or happy endings." She took a quick breath and steadied herself. "So I guess I'll go with coincidence."

"Wrong!" Dr. Mullaca didn't even blink. "There's no such thing as coincidence."

Chapter Thirteen

Terry's dad frowned at her armload of clothes. "Are you sure you've got everything?" he asked, his tone uncertain.

"Yeah." She shuffled as the lineup for the cashier inched forward. Pop music played in the background. At least enough to last a few days until they were allowed into their apartment again.

"Really?" he probed. "Because there's a lot over there." He motioned to the ladies' section. "Like sweaters and skirts?" His voice rose at the end like an uneasy suggestion.

Terry silently groaned inside. *A skirt? Is he serious?* With her clunky knee brace and limp, nothing flowed on her when she walked. Secretly, she had taken off the hateful brace in the dressing room earlier and pulled on a pair of skinny jeans. She had looked normal, even kind of sexy, but all she could do was stand — walking was impossible without her brace. It always felt like her knee would pop out of the socket. The jeans were added to the discarded pile, and she chose the usual baggy pants instead.

"I got everything I need, Dad," she mumbled. Terry stared at the deep red and orange sweaters — colors that reminded her of desert sunsets — but she was anxious to leave Old Navy. She hated shopping now. At least the store had everything both of them needed to last the week. They took a few more steps ahead as an extra clerk opened a new register.

Each movement took all of Terry's energy. An hour of shopping with her dad on an empty stomach with Dr. Mullaca's words echoing through her head was enough to make her want to go to bed and pull the covers over her head and forget the world.

No such thing as coincidence, Nefertari.

Terry's hopes of leaving Devonshire and its cold, wet sidewalks anytime soon were crushed. Her dad was now saddled with a crazy expert who would keep him hostage at the museum, looking for an artifact that was stolen fifty years ago. And Terry would have to keep going to Roosevelt High. Her dad had made that clear on cab ride to the store. "We can't leave," he'd told her when Terry insisted Dr. Mullaca was nuts. "That would mean breaking my contract with the museum." He had to stay until the exhibit was up and running.

Finally, it was their turn at the counter. She unloaded her choices: black cargo pants, navy sweats, two black T-shirts and a fleece zip-up hoodie. *God, I'm turning into a thirteen-year-old boy.*

"A hot shower and room service will be a nice way to end the day," he said encouragingly. "Right?"

The promise of food and smoke-free accommodations was comforting, but Terry was too exhausted to show any gratitude.

Her dad chatted with the saleswoman as she scanned and then folded his beige chinos and bundle of plaid shirts. Terry looked away when the clerk sorted through the boxers he'd picked out. Her dad took out his credit card and absentmindedly tapped it on the counter.

"Is it snowing yet?" the clerk asked, now reaching for Terry's pile. "The weather's supposed to turn cold again."

"No," he answered.

The clerk meticulously folded the sports bras and underwear Terry had picked out. She fidgeted on the spot, wishing she had her own credit card. No girl should have to buy underwear with her dad.

A bevy of giggles sounded through the constant music beat.

Terry glanced over and her stomach dropped. Allison and two of her princesses were in line.

Terry concentrated on the music, trying to block out their voices. She watched the clerk's hands, willing her to work faster. Allison was wearing a red Canada Goose coat. She plopped down her choices in front of the cashier: a pile of skinny jeans, patterned camisoles and cashmere sweaters spilled over the counter. It was a cruel contrast to Terry's wardrobe.

"Nefertari," a familiar voice giggled. *Nef-er-tar-i?* It wasn't a greeting, but part of a whispered sentence, laced with cruelty. Terry stared straight ahead, her heartbeat in her throat.

"I told Daddy I was going to buy new clothes to donate to the poor," Allison said loudly. "I mean, even though it's this cheap crap, it's better than something that's already been worn by a stranger."

Terry grabbed the huge plastic bags from the clerk as her dad swiped his credit card. She held them in front of her, conscious of the faded chocolate milk stain. She could feel Allison's eyes bore into her back.

"Terry?" Her dad's voice sounded far away.

She stared at the space between her sneakers. There was a hole in her spirit, and it was growing every day. Soon she'd be so hollow, the wind would pick her up, rip apart her limbs and scatter her all over the world.

"Terry!" The urgency in her dad's voice made her look up. His expression was hard to read, angry but embarrassed at the same time. He reached for the bags.

"I can carry them myself," she said, pulling away. *I'm so pathetic, he believes I can't even hold a bag of crappy clothes.*

"No," he sighed, taking them anyway. "The credit card has been declined."

The clerk's face was blotchy and panicked. The cashier waiting on Allison and her friends paused for a moment, then began to scan their massive mountain of fashion for charity; clothes that looked fun to wear, that would make a guy stop in the cafeteria and sit down at your table instead of pretending you didn't exist.

"I *told* the principal our school needs a free breakfast program," Allison whispered loud enough for everyone in line to hear. "I understand why people want to hide the embarrassment of being poor, but everyone has the right to healthy food ... especially milk."

The heat started in Terry's toes, then slowly rose all the way to her face. Her dad mumbled something about the bank. He took out three twenty-dollar bills. Terry picked out what was essential; the underwear, sweatpants and a few shirts. Leaving her dad to deal with the clerk, she made her way outside the store, trying to blink back the tears in the cold night air.

Clad in bomber jackets and high black boots, the princesses followed behind Allison's long red coat as she strutted up to Terry. "Too bad you can't afford all those boys' clothes," Allison said with a dramatic pout. "I was really looking forward to the hot sweatpants ensemble you'd picked out." She leaned in and sniffed. "You stink like sour milk!" Allison stayed close, challenging her to make the next move.

Terry swallowed dryly. Only five feet away, on the other side of the glass doors, people were picking out sweater sets to match new jeans. *Why does no one see this?*

"You look scared, slut," Allison goaded. "Are you?"

Maude's advice about acting scared echoed back. Terry had no other plan. She dropped her gaze to the cement sidewalk, feigning defeat.

"That's smart. You should be scared of me," Allison said, the smirk coloring her words.

Terry stepped around the trio and went back into the store. She was surprised Allison had let her go so easily. Maybe she got off on knowing that she scared people, like Maude had said. Or maybe, she worried, Allison was planning something worse for the next time.

Her dad held their much smaller bag of new clothes. He'd

managed to make the salesclerk laugh. Terry forgot how charming he could be with the opposite sex.

"Sorry," he said to Terry heavily. "I'll call the bank tomorrow.
There's obviously a mistake. Your mom and I made sure we had
enough insurance that the family would always be okay." Then he
tried to lighten his tone. "It was lucky I happened to have enough
cash on me to get us a few things."

They paused outside the store. Mr. Hughes pulled up the collar of his coat, then checked his watch. "I don't have enough for a
cab. We have to take the bus to the hotel."

"Oh." Terry did the math. The bus stop was another ten
minutes through the bitter night, and her knee was already
screaming.

"Or I could call Sarah to give us a lift?" he suggested.

Terry's shoulders drooped. The talkative curator always exhausted Terry, but tonight she'd take any form of rescue. "Sure."

After her dad made the call, they slowly walked to the corner
where Sarah would pick them up. He put an arm around her
shoulders and squeezed. They walked in silence for a block.

"So really, how come I've never heard of Sarah before?"

"It's kind of complicated."

"You already told me that."

Terry's dad let out a sigh. "When your mom and I decided to
get married, we eloped halfway around the world at an archaeological site we were scheduled to work. When Sarah found out,
she was quite upset — apparently she'd been expecting to be your
mom's maid of honor."

"Seriously?" Terry asked exhausted. "That's the reason? That's
so lame."

He nodded. "Well, it was important to Sarah. When we
brought you back to America, you were six months old. Your mom
thought it would be a nice gesture to make her your godmother,
you know, to make up for not being at the wedding."

"But you don't keep in touch, right?"

"No. That was the last time I saw her. She had her own life to live. After grad school it's natural for friends to drift apart. Everyone was happy in the end." His last sentence hung in the cool air. A melancholy silence settled over them.

Gradually, Terry leaned into her dad, and he effortlessly took her weight.

"Some day, huh?" he said softly. "But we've survived worse than an eccentric archaeologist, haven't we?" He lifted his chin and took a deep breath of crisp night air.

"Don't forget the prince," Terry added, her mood lightening as well. His optimism always shone through.

He chuckled. "Don't get any ideas, he seems quite the ladies' man."

"You're kidding, right?"

"Dr. Mullaca took me aside," he said, "warning me about the young royal Casanova and not to leave my impressionable daughter with him." He looked down at Terry and laughed at her shocked expression.

"He's so not my type, Dad," she said. "The guy is way too refined for me." She didn't bother to add that she would be the last person Prince Kamal would find attractive.

"Good to hear," he replied with a smile. He was definitely in a better mood. "Promise me you won't date anyone until you're married," he joked.

Terry smiled, but stayed quiet. She thought about the skinny jeans, abandoned in the change room. Snow flurries began. There was a beep, and a red sports car zoomed by them. The driver looked very much like Allison. And if there was any doubt, the license plate added to Terry's suspicions — 2GOOD4U.

Terry supposed it was only a coincidence. She also supposed the horn was meant for another car, not a signal to Terry. *It was only a coincidence*, she tried to tell herself. But the sudden chill had nothing to do with the weather. Dr. Mullaca's voice wafted from memory, like a warning: *There are no such things as coincidences, Nefertari.*

Chapter Fourteen

"This is so cool." Maude's voice came from the behind the massive library book standing upright on the table in front of her face. "The mascara tube Cleopatra used is almost the exact same as you'd buy at Sephora today."

Terry covered her yawn. "Mm-hmm," she said. There was some kind of convention at the hotel last night, and her room happened to be beside the hospitality suite. The paper-thin walls vibrated all night with loud laughter and music. Her eyelids felt like sandpaper every time she blinked. They had only spent two nights at the hotel, but it felt like a hundred years.

"It was made of stone," Maude continued in an animated voice, "but the wand and the bristles are identical to modern brands." Several heads turned in her direction. Her exuberance earned their study table a warning from the closest librarian.

Zach looked up from the notepad balanced on the arm of the chair, his pen stopped in mid stroke. His fitted plaid shirt had the first two buttons undone, and there was a hint of chest hair. On anyone else it would just be a shirt, but on Zach it looked fashionably aloof. It wasn't so much his looks, but his confidence. Terry was certain he'd never had someone spill chocolate milk on his lap.

He sat across from her with one foot resting on his knee and his varsity jacket slung over the back of his chair. He ignored the librarian and leaned forward, taking a candy from Maude's opened tube of Love Hearts. She also had several Tootsie Pops ready for backup.

Terry watched him from the corner of her eye. He squinted at the candy, then lightly tapped the edge of his left eyebrow with his pen a few times. Then he smiled. "Let's kiss," he read.

"In bed with no clothes on," Maude whispered automatically. He laughed with her as he popped the candy into his mouth.

Terry smiled. Hanging out in the library, snacking on candy with Maude, and having Zach's attention every time she spoke of Cleopatra was refreshing enjoyable — even if he only saw her as a teacher. For the past few days she and her dad had been eating every meal at the hotel restaurant or at Sarah's cluttered apartment. The food was usually pre-packaged or takeout. Sarah joked about having a large wine fridge instead of a place for vegetables — her teeth were purple by the end of most meals. What Terry wouldn't give for a simple kitchen with a warm oven of home-made food.

"Like, she invented mascara!" Maude was reaching some kind of red zone of excitement. Terry caught Zach grinning at her. The stare held until Terry was positive her warm blush would give her away.

She took the pen she'd nabbed from the hotel room that morning and wrote 'mascara' on a list she'd started. Their fake beauty article was shaping up nicely. Terry had to admit it was an interesting slant on Cleopatra, plus it helped fight all the creepy feelings Dr. Mullaca evoked every time Terry set foot in the museum.

Her dad hadn't mentioned much about the coffin since that first meeting, but Sarah had let it slip that Dr. Mullaca's constant talk of ancient curses was responsible for some of the construction staff working in the Egypt room to quit. Plus, the fact she was a snake expert fed into paranoid rumors she was keeping a pet cobra in the basement. "She even has a snake tattoo on her arm," Sarah had said over the rim of her wine glass. "I saw it when she was putting on her lab coat."

"Terry!" Maude's voice pleaded.

She looked up to find both Maude and Zach staring at her. "Sorry, what?"

"Did you get that last one?" Maude asked, pointing to the list. "The milk and honey facial mask?" Terry shook her head and yawned again. Maude's expression softened. "What was it last night?" she asked. "Elementary school choir or fighting newly-weds?"

"Convention," Terry moaned. "Plumbers, I think."

Maude nodded toward the pile of candy on the table. "You need sugar," she advised, as if it were prescription.

Terry reached for a Tootsie Pop and took great interest in peeling off the wrapper. She could feel Zach's curious stare, but she offered no further explanation. She'd already told them enough lies. According to Terry, her apartment was being painted — ever since Allison's poverty remark, Terry had become uncharacteristically sensitive about her living arrangements.

And since her dad was so deathly allergic to the fumes (another lie), they had to wait at least a week before they moved back. Hence the stay at the horrible hotel. There was no way she was mentioning the black mold. She put the sucker in her mouth and hoped the sugar would wake her up.

In truth, money wasn't an issue. Luxury held no interest for them. Terry and her dad were suffering from grief, not poverty. They were poor on joy, and that loneliness seeped through their pores, covering them in a gray fog. Terry found herself making excuses to avoid talking about her mother. She'd never met anyone who was important enough to share her mom's memory with.

"Do you think we should do a pamphlet instead?" Maude asked, smoothing out her pink streak of hair.

Zach answered first. "No," he said, "stick with the article idea. A pamphlet will be too small."

Maude frowned back at him. "That's more work, though."

Terry guessed she was wondering why a super jock was so interested in this project. Even though he hadn't said it was a secret, Terry kept his situation with the basketball scholarship to herself. This project could be the difference between him landing a good college or not going at all.

"I think Zach's right," Terry said. "An article will be more impressive. Also, we'll get more information down. More information means a higher mark from Ms. Bernard, right?"

Zach gave her a grateful nod. They both looked at Maude, waiting for her verdict as she twirled her hair, mulling over her decision. Terry added they could even add blocks of advertisements, showcasing what ancient market vendors would have been selling at the time of Cleopatra's reign. Maude's eyes grew wide. She straightened up and tucked her hair behind her ear.

"Oh, Neffie," Fraser sang from behind. He leaned over the back of her chair, practically resting his chin on her shoulder. "A reliable source told me that Egyptian royalty is staying in Devonshire. I'm guessing a world class Egyptologist and his daughter would probably have a better chance at meeting this delegation than the editor of the local high school paper."

Terry started to add a few words to her list, pretending to be busy. "I guess I might have met a prince or something," she mumbled.

"Holy crap!" Maude's mouth gaped open at her. "Are you serious?"

Fraser came around the chair and faced her. Today he wore jeans, a white dress shirt and a tweed vest. He stood there in his black high tops looking formal and yet casually unconcerned at the same time.

"You know," he started, "I would consider that news." He gave her a long, persuasive stare. "Something that would make a reporter ask questions."

Terry only shrugged, keeping her eyes on the paper. It was like he already knew everything and was testing her. "I guess we don't find the same things interesting," she answered.

Maude held up her hands. "Wait, you said a prince. Like a real, 'I have a castle and rule a kingdom' kind of prince?"

"See?" Fraser said, waving a hand at Maude. "People are already talking about it, so you might as well tell me the rest."

"There isn't anything else," Terry said, squirming in the chair.

Fraser read her body language. "So you don't know anything about several museum staff who quit recently?"

"If you know everything, why are you asking me?" She underlined a few words on her paper for emphasis, hoping he'd suppose she was deep in studies and clueless about her father's secret project.

Fraser laughed. "I suppose you don't find the museum staff gossip interesting either?" he asked.

"Nope."

"Rumors?"

"Nope."

"And I guess that goes for curses too?"

Terry grimaced. His tenacity was irritating, compounding her exhaustion and aching knee. "No," she snapped. "But Dr. Mullaca would love to talk about it for hours. You should go interview her."

"Dr. Mullaca?" Fraser helped himself to a *Love Heart*. Maude didn't even bother asking him to read it this time. "Fascinating name. Sounds like a bean dip."

Terry snorted. "She looks like one of the mummies. I wish someone would put *her* in a coffin."

Fraser's eyes lit up. "Coffin? Is that the secret project your dad is working on?"

Chapter Fifteen

The air stuck in Terry's throat. How could she have let that slip? Her dad would never forgive her. His career would be ruined by her stupid mistake. Instead of a hotel, they'd be staying at a homeless shelter.

"Um..." she started. She glanced around for a distraction or some kind of quick escape. Cleopatra stared back at her from the cover of Maude's book.

"What's inside?" Fraser prodded. "Or do they even know yet?"

"Hey." Zach stood up so quickly, his notebook fell to the floor, face down. He glared at Fraser. "She already said she doesn't know. She's tired, all right? Leave her alone."

Terry looked back and forth between the two guys. She'd never been in this kind of scenario. It gave her a secret thrill to have someone stand up for her — literally.

"A bunch of plumbers kept her up all night," Maude added as a form of explanation.

Fraser pushed up his tortoiseshell glasses. "Now that's an interesting headline." He motioned his chin to Zach and said, "Big game tonight, huh, sport?"

"Something like that, yeah." Zach stood his ground, hands loose by his sides. Terry could see his chest rise and fall under his plaid shirt.

Maude cleared her throat. "I'll have that piece for you first thing tomorrow morning." Fraser frowned down at her. "The one you asked me to do about the game tonight," she hinted.

It took a few more beats, then his eyebrows lifted. "Sure, awesome." He smiled at her. "Saves me the trouble of having to go." He looked at Zach. "Tanya wants to do an interview with you for the school paper. Something about how you're saving Roosevelt High from certain disgrace or death or something. Interested?"

"That's an extreme description of basketball," Zach said. He grabbed his notebook off the floor and tucked it under his arm. "But sure. I'll talk to her."

"Cool," Fraser said. "I'll warn you, though, she likes to go for the unexpected twist. You don't have any dark secrets, do you?" His voice was flat, completely serious. Maude rolled her eyes at his back.

Zach said, "Just one." A grin pulled at the corner of his mouth as he looked at Terry. "Not many people notice this, but I've been told I'm tall."

A flurry of butterflies danced inside Terry.

With a smash the library doors flew open. In a sea of purple and gold, Roosevelt High's official school spirit committee spilled into the area, singing the school song.

With her long blonde hair tied back with a purple ribbon, Allison led the pep squad around the room, holding a clipboard and singing instructions into a megaphone. Cheerleaders followed, pom-poms shaking wildly. The fox mascot jumped onto tables, whipping the students into a dancing frenzy. The librarians let it carry on, knowing it would be over soon. Resistance was futile.

The parade stopped in front of Terry's table. The mascot leaned over and grabbed her arms, his huge fox head moving in quickly. "No, I can't. Please..." she pleaded with the eyes behind the mask.

"Are you crazy?" Allison sang above the crowd. She was wearing designer skinny jeans—not 'cheap crap' from Old Navy. She

77

took Zach's jacket off the back of his chair and slipped it on. "It's bad luck. You have to dance with Foxy or we'll lose tonight. Dance! Dance! Dance!"

The cheer caught on like fire.

Terry braced herself as the mascot dug his paws into her armpits and pulled her to her feet. He spun her around haphazardly. Her foot caught and twisted her bad knee. Terry cried out. The students circled around them, a few filming the scene with their phones. Terry stumbled to the side, one hand flailing for support. Foxy started to mimic her awkward dance.

Laughter joined the cheers, and soon the humiliating chant took over the library.

"Dance! Dance! Dance!"

There was a blur of purple and gold all around Terry. Through the bodies she saw Zach make his way to Allison. He whispered in her ear. She smiled widely, then kissed him on the cheek. He led the pep squad to the doors. Allison started another round of the school song, eager to take over another part of Roosevelt High.

Terry panted as Foxy dumped her in the nearest chair, running to join the others. Maude and Fraser pushed through the dispersing crowd but stopped short when they saw Terry. "I'm fine," she lied, holding up a hand to block them from coming any closer. She couldn't stand the pitying looks on their faces.

She left everything and headed for her locker. Her brace clinked dangerously, threatening to break. Each step made her wince, but Terry took it grimly as payback for abandoning Maude in the bathroom the first day. She reached into her pocket for the bottle of anti-inflammatory medication. After fumbling open the cap, she dry-swallowed two pills.

"Shit," she whimpered, spinning her locker combination through a blur of tears. A freshman dressed in purple and gold ran down the hall, drumming up excitement for tonight's game.

Terry rested her head in the crook of her arm. She closed her eyes and took some deep breaths. When it was quiet again, she sniffed and looked inside her locker. A piece of paper was folded over with a pen clipped to one end to keep it closed. Terry recognized the pen as the one she'd lost in history class on the very first day of school.

She unfolded the paper. It was a sketch of Cleopatra, or at least a beautiful woman made to look like her. She couldn't believe someone had drawn this portrait with that lousy pen. The hair was straight and dark, with severe bangs. The traditional headdress was unmistakable. But it was the eyes that mostly impressed Terry. Her fingers lightly ran over the dark lines of ink, outlining the eyes, done in the ancient Egyptian style.

She continued to stare at that face, its familiarity slowly dawning on Terry. Those high cheekbones and knowing half smile. She was unable to look away. Her throbbing knee was now forgotten. It was a face she hadn't seen in over a year — her mother's.

Chapter Sixteen

"It's kind of small," Maude said. She paused outside her bedroom door. Terry could hear the uncertainty in her voice.

After the library episode, Terry had gone to the tiny newspaper office, hoping Tanya might have been there to let her seek refuge, but it was locked. Maude had found her sitting in the hallway, hiding behind a textbook. She gently reminded her of the supper invitation at her house before the basketball game. The only mention of the library was a mumbled "Sorry" on Maude's part. Terry had shrugged, unsure what Maude would have to be sorry about.

The cloud of awkwardness had followed them from school, lurked under the bus seats and swirled around Terry's ankles as she limped up the stairs to the apartment over Maudern Style.

Now they stood at the end of a tiny hallway lined with pictures of Maude at various ages. Terry could name every milestone from the photographs: first steps, first bike, first day of school. In one particular shot an elementary-aged Maude held a huge trophy.

"Nerd alert," Maude laughed. "It was for a cryptoquote contest. I'm kind of good at codes and stuff." She played with the bottom of her pink T-shirt. "It's useless, of course, but the trophy was cool."

Terry was fascinated. She watched Maude's grandmother age from one frame to the next. The tiny woman's smile and sense of style remained consistent even as her hair started to gray.

"Grandma calls us Charlie's Angels." She blushed and her voice grew timid again. "It's always been just me, Mom and Grandma."

Terry nodded. They shared weak smiles. It had been that kind of day.

"Okay." Maude took a deep breath and opened the door. Terry had a vague reminiscence of Dr. Mullaca unveiling the sarcophagus. "It's not much," she said, carefully watching Terry's reaction, "but it's home."

Terry's eyes grew wide, trying to take in all the details. To the left of the door was a vanity covered in bowls of sparkly eye shadow and tiny bottles of nail polish. A poster of Willy Wonka dominated one wall. Pink feather boas stretched over the curtain rod, and an old dressmaker's mannequin stood in the corner, sporting layers of necklaces with several hats towered upon its neck.

"Wow," Terry said. She felt like she'd been dropped into one of those *I Spy* picture books.

Maude let out a nervous giggle then plopped on her twin bed. It was arranged at an angle from the corner, covered in a pink satin duvet and adorned with numerous pillows.

Terry heard a sickening clank. She gripped her knee, biting the inside of her cheek.

Maude clambered to her side. "Did you break something?"

"Yeah." Terry grimaced. "My brace."

"Should I call 911?"

"No." Terry lowered herself to the floor and sat against the bed. She stayed still until the throbbing subsided. She carefully felt through her sweatpants. The outer joint had separated. "I think the screw popped out."

Maude's face relaxed at Terry's matter-of-fact tone. "Does that happen often?" she asked.

"Only when a massive fox throws me around the room." Terry's fingers worked over the material of her pants, trying to assess the damage. She was careful not to expose any skin.

"Oh." Maude's voice went small again. "Sorry."

"Why? It's not your fault."

"Yeah, it is."

Terry's hands stilled. "Are you telling me it was your idea for the mascot to pick me out of the crowd?"

"No, but I know who did." Maude became interested in picking at the pink shag carpet. "I should have stopped her. But ever since you came Allison's been…" She paused, then let it spill out. "She's been leaving me alone."

Terry narrowed her gaze. "You told me you pretended to be scared."

"I totally lied," Maude confessed. "I was so embarrassed to admit that crazy freak gets to me. She knows exactly what to say to make you cry. Her words get under your skin and fester like an infection." Maude stared at the floor. "At night, when it's quiet, is the hardest time to ignore her."

Terry stayed quiet. She understood what it was like to cry in the dark.

"She calls me white trash because my mom got pregnant, dropped out of high school and never married." Maude blinked hard a few times. "No big deal except my grandma had my mom the same way. And Allison has the whole school believing I'll do the same thing."

A delicious waft of meatballs curled under the door, making Terry's mouth water. She gave Maude a critical stare. "You have an awesome family. Your grandma is like Martha Stewart, and your mom is gorgeous and runs her own business. I don't understand why it bothers you what Allison thinks."

"Being a single mom isn't scandalous, but Allison branded me as a loser back then and it stuck. After awhile no one remembers why they hate you, only that you're a social outcast."

"Are you really a social outcast?" Terry asked.

Maude shook her head. "You have no idea what it's like. You're the first friend from school who's come to my house in two years." She took a pillow off the bed and hugged it to her chest. "Guys look at me differently too. It's not fair, but they do. That's the power Allison has; if she says something, everyone thinks it's true."

Terry wasn't sure what to say. Maude always seemed bubbly and confident most of the time, but maybe she was confusing energy with happiness. The little room grew darker. Maude blotted a tear on her sleeve, then turned on a few of her lamps around the room. The area glowing in pinks and soft yellows.

Maude rubbed her face and let out a small laugh. "Where were we? You have a broken screw or something, right?"

"Yeah." Careful not to move her leg, Terry shook the bottom of her pant leg, hoping the screw would fall out.

"It might be on the floor." Maude got on her knees and combed her fingers through the thick carpet. "How tiny is it?"

Terry held up her thumb and finger a half-inch apart. "I'll need it if I'm to help cheer on the team tonight. Maybe they'll put me on the top of the pyramid," she added dryly.

"Maybe this is a sign, you know? Like maybe we should stay home and not bother to go tonight."

"I don't believe in signs," Terry said vehemently. "Or coincidences. Besides, what about your piece for Fraser?"

Maude moved to another part of the floor, fingers still searching. "We both know he's only humoring me because he likes you."

That caught Terry by surprise. "The only thing about me that he's interested in is my connections to the museum and Cleopatra's coffin." She froze. Two slips in one afternoon? She'd never been so careless. What was happening to her?

"You said no one has ever found the location." Maude pointed a finger at Terry's pale face, her voice becoming excited. "The very first day, that's exactly what you said! Is it true? Is Cleopatra in the museum ... like, for real? *The* Cleopatra?"

"Uh ... I don't know."

Maude raced to her vanity and grabbed a handful of makeup. "She invented mascara! If anyone deserves to know, it's me!"

"What? Why?" Terry suddenly laughed.

"Duh, we're both beauty experts."

Terry returned her attention to the broken brace. Things were falling apart in her life, literally. She'd been surviving by keeping people distant — that way she never had to explain her accident and about losing her mom. She only shared her grief with her dad. It seemed too private for anyone else to understand. Too precious. But the weight of keeping all that sorrow had been building. There were cracks in her carefully constructed shell. Things were starting to spill out ... secrets she'd been trusted with.

Maude sensed the topic had been changed. She put her makeup back. "If you can't find the screw," she asked carefully, "what are you going to do?"

"I can't walk without it."

"Grandma is pretty good with fixing stuff. I bet she has something in her little tool kit. Maybe if you let her look at it—"

Terry clamped two hands around the ankle of her sweatpants. "I can do it myself. All I need is the screw." She continued to feel for the missing piece. Maude didn't say anything, but Terry could feel her stare. "The scars are pretty gross. I only let the doctors look at me."

Maude finally asked, "How did it happen?"

"I was born this way." Even though Terry had said that same lie fifty times over the last six months, this time it felt wrong.

There was more silence, then Maude said, "Remember when you walked in on me and Allison in the girls' bathroom?"

Terry nodded, a blanket of remorse wrapping around her. She should have recognized that Maude's fear was real. "What did she do to you?"

"She made one of her princesses give me a facial," Maude said, an edge to her voice. "With the toilet."

"I left you. I'm so sorry."

Maude sat down beside her. "I'm guilty of the same thing."

Terry looked at her useless limb. She was tired of feeling beaten down. Tired of life flipping her the finger. Tired of everything that reminded her of what she had lost and would never be, but most of all she was tired of being alone. *Screw the rules.* Maybe it was time to reconsider her code. She didn't get involved, she kept her head down and she didn't make trouble. But this also meant she never made any friends. Maybe it was time to stop lying. She turned to Maude. "Over a year ago my mom discovered what she thought was Cleopatra's tomb."

Maude's mouth fell open.

"The morning we set out for the dig was still and perfect," Terry continued. "Everything she had worked so hard for had come down to this day. She and her crew had finally broken through one of the barriers. They were certain a fourth chamber existed — Cleopatra's final resting place."

Terry closed her eyes; the darkness of the memory practically suffocated her. "I wasn't supposed to be there, but I managed to talk Mom into letting me go. Little by little, I inched my way past the various grad students and local archaeology assistants, until I was right behind her. When she discovered me there, she took my hand and told me that it was only fitting we should find Cleopatra together."

Terry's throat squeezed tight. The only noise in the room was Maude's breathing. "Something propelled us forward, urging us on deeper into the tunnel. Soon it was only the two of us. It was right ahead, only a few feet ... and then the world exploded."

Terry could never forget the blinding flash of white. "The top of the cave collapsed as my mom and I were passing under. She was crushed and died instantly." Terry motioned to her useless limb. "And I was pulled out, mangled but still alive."

Maude put her manicured hand over Terry's. "I'm sorry."

"Thanks." Terry reached for her backpack and pulled out the sketch of her mother. She gently unfolded the paper and handed it to Maude. "This is her."

"Wow," Maude breathed. "I didn't know you could draw. You look just like her!"

"You think that's me?" Terry's brow knitted together. "Someone left this in my locker. Look." She pointed to the three capital letters done in bold in the bottom right hand corner. "It says ICU. Who in the school has those initials? And why would they leave a picture of Cleopatra in my locker?"

Maude squinted at the paper, then her face relaxed and she smiled. "In bed with no clothes on."

"Excuse me?"

"It's like the Love Hearts; ICU means I see you." Maude looked triumphant. "It's not a threat, it's kind of a coded message. Trust me, I'm always right about this kind of thing." She tapped her lower lip with a pink fingernail. "When did you find this?"

"Right after my hot dance number in the library." Terry took the sheet away from Maude. "I wonder if I've gone viral on YouTube yet." Her fingers grazed over the three initials. "ICU," she repeated. "I wish no one could see me."

Maude grinned mischievously. "That's too bad, because it looks like you've got an admirer."

Terry kept her suspicions to herself. She stared at the picture of the beautiful woman. Could that *really* be how he saw her? It was impossible. It made no sense. *He's dating someone else — someone who walks perfectly and has style.* Still, the day she lost that hotel pen, Zach was sitting right beside her in history class. Had he whispered something to Allison in the library to persuade her to leave and put an end to the humiliation?

Maude grew quiet as well. They both stared at the Willy Wonka poster with Gene Wilder promising a world of pure imagination. "What are we going to do?" Maude finally asked.

"About Allison or my leg?"

"Both, I guess."

"It's simple," Terry said. "We need a hero."

"No, we need Cleopatra."

"You're right. She wouldn't put up with Allison's crap."

"And she wouldn't be afraid to go to a stupid basketball game," Maude answered. "Or write a stupid newspaper piece for a stupid guy who happens to be hot."

"Maybe we need another sign to tell us what to do," Terry's teased. "Clearly we're not in control of our own destiny." Her pocket buzzed. She read her dad's latest text and frowned.

Dr. Mullaca and I staying late. See you back at the hotel. There's extra cash in the top drawer of the dresser if you want to have supper early.

Terry texted him back a quick note about her visit to Maudern Style and how she'd be going to the game with Maude.

He responded immediately. *Have fun. Text me when you get to school. Make sure to take cab back to hotel after game. Don't take bus on your own. Let me know when you get back to hotel safely.*

"Do you have to go?" Maude asked cautiously.

"Nope." Terry smiled. "I reminded him I made plans with my friend."

Two perfect dimples appeared on Maude's face. "I'll see if Grandma can fix your brace," she said. "We need to get you off the floor." She pushed herself up, but then squealed in pain. A small pink indent was on her palm. She held up Terry's missing screw. They locked eyes. "It's a sign," Maude declared.

Chapter Seventeen

"More potatoes?" Maude's grandmother motioned to the flowered serving dish; only a few scoops were left. "Or maybe more casserole?"

Terry had already had two helpings of the macaroni and cheese with caramelized onions and bacon. "No, thank you," she sighed.

"Barbecued meatball?" Maude's grandmother waved her hand over the table like a game show model. Several strands of colorful beads clinked and swung as she stood up to put more food on Terry's plate. Maude's mother, also named Maude, was still working in the beauty salon downstairs and wouldn't be eating until later.

"Grandma!" Maude said. "She's not a duck, we're not making pâté."

"You girls don't eat enough," she replied. "You spend all your money on coffee with sprinkles and chocolate syrup. It's ridiculous. If you want sprinkles you should have a piece of cake. But what do I know? I'm only an old lady with a nice figure."

Terry gave her a critical look. "How can you be such an amazing cook and stay so slim?"

"Pole dancing class on weekends," she teased. She left the two girls at the table and poured herself a cup of coffee in a mug that read 'World's Greatest Grandmaude.' "At least save room for dessert," she advised.

Terry's eyes grew wide at the angel food cake on the counter, a
bowl of whipped cream and fresh fruit off to the side. It was an
embarrassment of generosity. Terry pictured her dad all alone
with the withered Dr. Mullaca, down in the basement of the museum. He probably ate a dried-up granola bar from the vending
machine for supper.

"I wish I could," Terry said. "But I think I might explode all
over your pretty kitchen."

Maude's grandmother patted Terry's shoulder. The gesture
was so natural. She was just one of those people who did everything out of love.

Earlier she had helped with Terry's brace, showing up at
Maude's bedroom door with her little toolbox. Maude had stayed
on the other side of the room while Terry carefully rolled up her
pant leg, accepting various tiny screwdrivers from Maude's grandmother as if the two of them were performing surgery. The white-
haired woman kept her eyes averted, turned slightly away to give
Terry the privacy she wanted. She lightly whistled as Terry tightened the brace.

When Terry rolled her pant leg back down. Maude's grandmother said, "They say that under every scar is a battle that was
won." She gave her a thoughtful smile. "I bet you're a real fighter,
kiddo."

Terry liked her right away.

Now at the table, threatening to burst, Terry watched
Maude's grandmother cut into the white spongy cake. She hated
to be rude by refusing any more food. "Just a small piece," she
said weakly.

Terry's phone buzzed in her back pocket. Maude's grandmother turned around, looking worried. "It's just my dad," Terry said.
"He's working late tonight."

Enjoy the bball game with yer bestie. Hunch about the key ;)
Wish me luck!!

Her dad *never* used exclamation marks. She looked up and saw Maude watching her. Terry could tell she was dying to ask about the coffin.

Maude's grandmother cleared her throat, breaking the silence.

"Terry's dad works at the museum," Maude told her.

"Is this about that school project?" she asked over the rim of her mug.

"Terry is an expert on Cleopatra," Maude beamed. "I totally lucked out getting her as a partner."

Terry's cheeks grew warm. With a stomach full of homemade food and a fixed knee brace, she knew she could say the very same thing.

"I loved that movie," Maude's grandmother said dreamily. "Elizabeth Taylor as Cleopatra and Richard Burton as Mark Antony set the screen on fire."

Maude helped herself to an extra dollop of whipped cream. "Did they do the carpet scene?" she asked. "You know, when Cleopatra snuck into his tent?"

Her grandmother gave her a confused look.

"Um ... that was with Caesar," Terry corrected.

"Oh, yeah." Maude took a mouthful of cake. "So, why was Mark Antony so special?"

"Richard Burton was incredibly sexy," Maude's grandmother said. "I think it was the confidence."

Maude raised her eyebrows. Terry helped herself to some cut-up fruit. "Cleopatra gave Caesar a son and moved with him to Rome," she said. "After Caesar was assassinated, she fled with their son back to Egypt, since they were no longer under his protection, plus there were rumors she had helped one of his enemies. At the time, Mark Antony was the commander of the Roman army, so he summoned her for an explanation."

Maude's grandmother played with her beads. "I loved that scene. He was expecting an apology, but she seduced him instead. And when they finally kissed." She paused and let out a low sigh.

"Well, it was enough to curl your toes." She took a long sip of coffee and then set her stare on Maude. "That's what you need, Maudie. Someone to curl your toes."

Maude took her empty dessert plate to the sink. "I'll keep my toes inside my shoes for now, thanks." She tried to keep the tone light, but Terry could hear the tired embarrassment. She was sure Maude kept the bullying to herself.

The trip back to Roosevelt High on the bus with Maude was more enjoyable than most of Terry's solo trips. The parking lot was crammed. They stood in line outside the gym, listening to the crowd getting pumped up.

They managed to score a tiny spot on the end of the bleachers that was just big enough for both of them. The gym was a sea of purple and gold, gaining energy, making the room vibrate. "Good thing our butts are small," Maude said, digging out a notepad and pen.

"Not if I keep eating at your house," Terry joked. She was gratefully stuffed, but she worried her dad was still hours away from finishing his work at the museum. She pictured him rubbing his eyes, straining under the fluorescent lights. She read his last text again.

Enjoy the bball game with yer bestie. Hunch about the key ;)
Wish me luck!!

Since when did he do winky faces?

She started to call him — he never ignored a phone call. A scream from the crowd made her jump.

"Geez, scare much?" Maude teased. Music throbbed from the speakers as Roosevelt High's basketball team poured into the gym. Terry decided to tuck her phone away. Maude began scribbling like mad. The only game Terry knew was backgammon. She took cues from the crowd, Maude's interjections, and of course the scoreboard. But even without all of those things, Terry saw that Zach was the best player. He seemed impervious to the chanting, only listening to the coach and his teammates. He used his full height to outreach the other players and wasn't afraid to fight for the ball. On the bench, he'd pat teammates on the back and talk intensely to them. Sweat dripped down his face, but he stayed focused, never looking away from the action of the game.

Terry was struck by how opposite they were. He was in the spotlight, but it didn't scare him. He thrived on the attention. The ease with which he skillfully dodged his opponents and his picture-perfect layups were a stark contrast to the boy Terry found squinting at the library shelves. She tried to follow the other players, but her eyes kept seeking Zach.

He never looked up at her once.

By the fourth quarter, the score was too close for either side to be comfortable. The gym had become a living mass of bodies and screams. Terry envisioned the Colosseum, wondering when the lion would be released. A few security guards took stations, anticipating a meltdown in the final minutes of play. Terry knew if Roosevelt High won tonight they were headed to the State Championships in a few weeks, and with it went Zach's hopes for a scholarship.

Terry scanned the crowd, wondering if Ms. Bernard was here. Did she really have the authority to prevent him from playing? She shuddered, imaging the crowd's reaction if that ever happened. Zach raced up the court, but he was fouled halfway and slammed to the floor. Yells of protest spiked the air. Maude turned the page and continued to write feverishly, pink loops filling the lines.

Zach stood at the foul line. He bounced the ball twice, then stared at the hoop. The yelps and jeers halted. Terry held her breath. Zach squinted, but only for a moment. Terry imagined him reaching up to touch the edge of his eyebrow.

The ball was airborne. It bounced off the rim. The gym came alive again as rumbles rippled through the bleachers. One clean-shaven man in a polo shirt a few rows ahead stood up and yelled, "Follow through. Straighten your arm!" The woman sitting beside him clutched the purse in her lap.

The crowd fell silent again. Zach zoned in on the hoop, and this time he sank the shot. Roosevelt High fell into a last ten-second countdown — they were down by one point. The opponent fumbled the rebound. Zach dove for the ball and passed to a team-mate. They both ran up the court. Zach caught the final pass. With only two seconds left he made the last shot from the three-point line.

Terry jumped to her feet with everyone else. Her knee didn't even hurt; she only felt the electricity of the crowd.

The bleachers emptied into the gym floor but Terry stayed in place, practically hugging Maude so she wouldn't be swept down the stairs. Allison separated from the mob of gold and purple and made her way to Zach. The other team disappeared into the lock-er room. The crowd thinned, already planning post-game parties. Allison pushed her way through and wrapped her arms around Zach's neck. Her heels brought her closer to his height.

She turned and smiled as one of the cheerleaders aimed her phone at them, taking pictures. Terry wanted to look away, but the voyeuristic curiosity was stronger than the painful bruise to her pride. She watched until Allison unlatched herself and joined her friends, the exuberance of the victory adding volume to their voices as they left the gym. The man in the polo shirt made his way to Zach, still encircled by his team. Terry recognized him as the man who had yelled earlier. He pulled Zach from the huddle and gave him a quick slap on the back. The woman with the purse followed with a more genuine hug.

The man took Zach back to the foul line, talking the whole time. Terry squirmed on the spot as he took practice shots while the man continued to lecture.

Maude was saying something, but her words weren't reaching Terry's ears. She caught a glimpse of Allison's blonde ponytail as she left the gym with the last of the cheerleaders. Finally, the coach came over and got the man's attention. Zach stood by himself. He turned and looked straight at Terry.

ICU

Terry dared herself to hold his gaze. He raised his eyebrows in surprise as if to say, "You came."

She casually lifted a shoulder in reply — it was the only part of her she could feel at the moment. Everything else had turned to mush. The corner of his mouth curled into a smile, then it grew.

Terry smiled back, broken knee brace and jealous girlfriend completely forgotten. Maude gasped and gripped Terry's arm.

Two policemen were walking toward them. Hurrying alongside with an anxious countenance was Sarah. Her French twist and makeup were perfect, but her coat hung off her shoulders as if she hadn't had time to put it on properly. She looked at Terry. "I'm so sorry, honey," she said. "It's your father. There's been an accident at the museum."

Chapter Eighteen

Terry's shoes squeaked on the freshly polished floor, and she wrinkled her nose at the waft of disinfectant. Sarah was beside her saying something softly, but Terry couldn't make sense of anything.

The ride in the police cruiser to the hospital had given her few clues as to what had happened. Sarah told her that she was the one who found him unconscious in the Egypt room with his cell phone by his side. Earlier, he'd told her about Terry's plans to attend the basketball game, so when the ambulance left, she headed straight to Roosevelt High with the police.

Terry shuffled like a zombie with Sarah next to her. The two uniformed officers kept a steady pace ahead of them. *He has to be all right.* Maybe he had a weak spell because he forgot to eat.

At the end of the corridor a group of people were huddled off to the side, several dressed in white lab coats. A man in a suit nudged his similarly dressed partner and motioned to Terry. She recognized them as Prince Kamal's bodyguards.

Why would there be such a fuss over a fainting spell? Sarah squeezed Terry's hand. "Don't worry," she whispered. "I won't leave you."

One of the white lab coats extended a hand to Terry. "I'm Dr. Jacquard," she said. "I'm taking care of your father." She had a loose ponytail and dark circles under her eyes. Despite the small smile she gave Terry, her tone was careful.

"What happened? Can I see him?" Terry asked. "Is he in any pain? Is he going to be okay?"

"There was some kind of episode at work," Dr. Jacquard began. "His co-worker found him unconscious but still breathing." She talked with her hands, palms upward. "We've run a number of tests, and although there is no cardiac failure or any indication he's had a stroke, his condition remains unchanged."

"Unchanged?" Terry asked. Her voice sounded small and far away.

"Follow me." Dr. Jacquard led Terry through a heavy swinging door and into the intensive care unit. Several nurses moved efficiently and quietly around the curtained sections. Terry ignored their sympathetic glances and numbly followed Dr. Jacquard. She stopped at the foot of her dad's hospital bed.

Gunther Hughes lay unmoving with an oxygen mask over his face. Numerous tubes and wires flowed from him to machines built into the walls, their gentle beeps a cruel insult to Terry's racing pulse.

Sarah put a hand to her mouth, stifling a sob. She quickly turned and disappeared around the curtain. Her heels faded back to the hallway.

"As you can see," Dr. Jacquard said in a soft tone, "we're giving him fluids intravenously. and oxygen, but he's breathing on his own and his heart rate is normal."

Terry's vision blurred as her eyes filled with tears. *This can't be happening. He's all I have left.*

"We think there was perhaps some kind of neurotoxin he may have come in contact with," Dr. Jacquard explained. "I understand your father was restoring some antiquities for the museum."

"This was no accident," a raspy voice said from behind. Dr. Mullaca wheeled herself closer. "It was the curse." The nurses at the front station exchanged looks. Dr. Jacquard let out a tired sigh.

"Find any toxins in his bloodwork?" Dr. Mullaca demanded, clearly insulted by the physician's reaction.

"Those results won't be ready for a few weeks. Of course, not all toxins show up in bloodwork," Dr. Jacquard said, deliberately enunciating each word.

Terry ignored the women and moved to her dad's side. Her fingers slid under his hand. His palm was cool.

"—not safe," Dr. Mullaca continued in the background. "If you ignore the curse, you ignore the cure."

Dr. Jacquard whispered harshly. "I'll have to ask you to leave."

Terry squeezed her dad's hand, but there was no response. It was like he was in a deep sleep. She gripped his hand harder this time. "Dad?" Her voice cracked. "It's Terry, you have to wake up." The walls started to swirl. Terry's knees unhinged, and she dropped to the floor.

"Umph!" a voice exclaimed beside her ear. Two hands were under Terry's arms, lifting her up, helping her stand. A strong arm wrapped around her waist. "Are you all right, Miss Hughes?"

A pair of black eyebrows were arched in concern, waiting for her response. Terry blinked a few times; a white headdress and robe came into view. "Prince Kamal?" she said. She managed to regain her footing.

He stepped away respectfully. "I'm sorry we have to meet under such troublesome circumstances, but when my people alerted me to what occurred at the museum this evening, I rushed here as quickly as possible." He motioned toward Dr. Jacquard. "I am personally making sure your father has the best medical care possible."

"Thank you," Terry said, her eyes lingering on her father's unmoving figure.

Dr. Mullaca dug her fingers into Terry's upper arm and pulled her down with surprising strength. "You're his only hope, Nefertari," she wheezed, her nose only inches from Terry's. "Only you can save him."

"What?" Terry winced.

Prince Kamal cleared his throat and motioned to the hallway.

"Perhaps we should continue this outside," he suggested.

Dr. Mullaca spun abruptly and wheeled her way toward to door.

Terry stared at her dad, trying to ignore the whispers of the nurses. She had a sinking feeling they weren't telling her everything. She gave him a kiss on the forehead, then limped out to the hallway.

Dr. Mullaca and the police had left, but Prince Kamal and his bodyguards were still there. Sarah leaned against the wall, a Kleenex pressed against her face.

"Terry?" Maude rushed up the hallway with her mother. "Mom wanted to make sure you were okay ... I mean..." Her voice cracked. She put an arm around Terry to finish the sentence.

Ms. Sanchez pulled back the hood of her long black coat. Terry recognized Maude's fine, straight nose and large dark eyes. Her chandelier earrings tinkled softly as she pulled a small package of tissues from her black shoulder bag and handed them to Terry. "Maude called as soon as you left with the police. We'll do anything to help."

"Thanks," Terry sniffed. She looked expectantly at the specialist.

Dr. Jacquard repeated her diagnosis to the group and that the best thing was to keep performing tests and monitoring his status. "There are many documented cases when the patient woke up several days later with no ill effects or lasting medical conditions," she said.

The hallway was quiet. "You can stay with us," Maude's mother offered. "You shouldn't be alone."

Prince Kamal spoke up. "Actually, Ms. Sanchez, I'm proposing that Nefertari be my guest at the hotel," he calmly explained. "Since Mr. Hughes was working on something that directly affects my government, I feel I should offer hospitality that ensures the safety and well-being of his daughter."

"That's very nice of you to offer," Ms. Sanchez said, "but I don't believe you have any legal authority over where Terry stays." Her gentle yet firm tone was soothing. Terry inched closer to Maude's mother.

"Does this mean Terry has to go to foster care?" Maude sounded panicked.

"Of course not." Sarah pushed herself off the wall. "I'm her godmother, so if she's going anywhere, it's with me." She smiled weakly, lipstick stuck on her front tooth. "We're good pals, aren't we, Terry? We'll get through this. It's good luck I'm here to take care of you."

Prince Kamal bowed slightly, considering Sarah's speech. He turned to Terry. "I have security guards patrolling my floor of the Plaza twenty-four hours a day. You would have your own suite, of course. Every requirement and service will be provided for you."

Maude's eyes widened, "Did you say 'Plaza'? As in *the* Plaza?"

Prince Kamal smiled. "Yes, that Plaza."

Maude continued, her voice growing higher. "As in *the* Plaza that One Direction stayed at three months ago?"

"My family owns the hotel," he admitted. "I have the entire top floor to myself."

"Holy shit!"

Maude's mother cleared her throat and gave her daughter a pointed look.

Terry remained quiet, staring into space.

Sarah stiffened her posture. "Well, Terry, you've got three places to stay, but I'm sure your father would want you in the safest one. And since I'm working full-time at the museum, I think what the prince is offering is the best solution … for now."

Terry couldn't feel the floor under her feet. She'd gone numb. Fancy Plaza or cluttered apartment with Sarah crying and winking at her. It made no difference. She wished she could take a blanket and sleep on the hospital floor so she wouldn't have to leave her dad.

Ms. Sanchez gave Terry a thoughtful look. "It's been an incredibly exhausting day, but you need to get settled." She put an arm around her shoulders. Terry smelled flowers. "Maude and I will go with you to gather your things, and then we'll meet the prince at the Plaza. If you want to stay there we'll help you get settled. If not you're more than welcome to come home with us." She glanced inquiringly at Sarah. "If that's all right?"

"Whatever Terry needs," she said, dabbing her nose with the Kleenex. "I'll be staying with Gunther a little longer."

Terry's throat was raw. "Okay," she said.

The prince pressed a hand to his chest and slightly bowed. "As you wish."

The trip to the hotel was unmemorable. Terry's things were quickly packed and stuffed into a duffel bag. She even took her dad's belongings, plus the extra cash he'd left in the top drawer. There was enough for a week of taxis.

"You won't be returning anyway, since your apartment will be finished being painted by the time your father has recovered," Ms. Sanchez reasoned with a gentle smile. Terry appreciated the hopeful comment.

An official-looking man in a dark suit met them in the luxurious lobby of the Plaza and personally escorted them to the top floor. Through her zombie haze Terry only noticed the details when she caught bits of Maude's gushing commentary. The fountain in the lobby was inlaid with Swarovski crystals, and ornate chandeliers dripped from the ceilings. More than once Ms. Sanchez shot Maude a warning glance.

As promised, Prince Kamal had private security guards for the top floor. Ms. Sanchez seemed impressed by that detail. Maude waited at the threshold as Terry was shown her room.

"The prince suggested this suite for you," the man in the suit explained. "It has the nicest view of the park."

Terry blinked at the room and finally came out of her fog. Fine leather furniture created an intimate seating arrangement in front of a large, flat-screen television. A vase of fresh flowers on a circular table dominated the space off the main entrance. Long diaphanous curtains framed floor to ceiling windows.

Maude spoke for both of them when she said, "Holy flippin'

gorgeousness!"

"I shall leave you to unpack," the man said, quietly exiting the room.

Maude let out a slow whistle. She walked around the plush furniture and stared at the night skyline of Devonshire. "How much would this cost a night?" she asked.

Terry went through a pair of French doors and found the bedroom. A massive king-sized bed was decorated with a duvet so fluffy it looked like lemon meringue pie. Terry placed the duffel bag on the floor and noticed how out of place it looked in the beautiful setting.

"There's a kitchen too!" Maude's voice bellowed out excitedly from the other room. "With a cappuccino machine!"

"This is lovely," Ms. Sanchez said to Terry, "and I know you'll be perfectly safe here, but you can still come with us for tonight."

Terry sunk down on the corner of the bed, the duvet slowly deflating around her. Waves of heavy exhaustion came on strong. "Thank you," she managed to mumble. "But I'm so tired. All I want is to close my eyes."

It took a few more minutes to convince Ms. Sanchez that she would be fine. Terry leaned against the door frame, watching as Maude and her mother made their way to the elevator. She looked down the hallway, wondering which door was Prince Kamal's.

She went back to the bedroom and then through to the bathroom. Terry was confused by all the spouts and knobs in the shower until she discovered it was a steam shower as well. Carefully, she slipped off the brace, grateful the shower had a bench built in. After washing her hair, she turned on the steam and let all the tension slowly ebb from her muscles. Her knee even stopped throbbing.

She strapped the brace back on, then slipped on the plush bathrobe from the back of the door and hobbled into bed. Her breathing slowed down, and she felt herself begin to drift off to sleep.

Her eyes flew open. Terry's heart was hammering against her

ribs. Then she heard the hotel phone on the bedside table ring. Realizing that was what woke her, she rolled out from under the duvet and blindly groped for the phone.

"You're in danger, Nefertari!"

Terry almost dropped the receiver. "Dr. Mullaca?"

"I needed to contact you. We couldn't speak freely at the hospital ... not while Prince Kamal was there."

Terry tried to blink through the mental haze. She squinted at the alarm clock; it was half past midnight. "Prince Kamal is taking care of me and my father right now. He's paying for the hospital, and he has a security guard stationed outside my—"

"Bedroom door?" Dr. Mullaca finished candidly. Terry could hear a slight disgust in her voice. "The prince has no interest in keeping your father alive. He's only trying to trick you into trusting him."

"The price has no interest in me."

Dr. Mullaca made an exasperated noise then said, "He's interested in the same thing you desperately need, the thing that will save your father."

Terry let out a breath through clenched teeth. There were still red marks encircling her right upper arm from where Dr. Mullaca had grabbed her. "You're not making sense," she said. "Even the hospital doesn't know what's wrong with him."

"Do you want your father to die?"

"Of course not!" Terry was close to tears.

"I warned him." Dr. Mullaca's voice became eerily calm. "Your father tried something foolish today, and now he's paying the price. The curse can only be lifted once the coffin is safely opened."

Terry's patience grew thin. "What am I supposed to do?" she demanded.

The line was dead quiet except for Dr. Mullaca's steady breathing. Finally she said, "That should be obvious, girl. You have to find that missing asp."

Chapter Nineteen

Terry squinted at the computer screen and read, "The police have no leads and are at a loss as to how the piece disappeared into thin air. This bizarre incident coupled with the recent missing person case has fueled rumors of The Sacred Asp's legendary curse." She leaned back in the plastic library chair and rubbed her red eyes.

Maude snapped her bubbled gum. "Seriously?" She sounded agitated. "What the heck's the point of having the Internet if all it spits back is stuff that was in the paper fifty years ago?"

Terry yawned behind her hand. After Dr. Mullaca's frantic call about the asp, she spent most of her first night in the Plaza going over every newspaper article Fraser had given her about the burglary at the museum. Finally, at four in the morning, she fell asleep on the plush rug in the sitting area, surrounded by photocopies.

"Maybe Fraser's holding out on us," Maude suggested. "I still have to give him the article on the game last night." She offered a hopeful smile. "I mean, he's a reporter ... sort of. I bet he can think of another angle we haven't tried."

Terry leaned forward and put her head in her hands. "I have no idea what I'm doing," she said helplessly. "My dad is in some kind of coma, and a crazy old bat wants me to solve a fifty-year-old burglary to cure him."

Maude put a hand on her shoulder. "He's going to be okay. Maybe that crazy old bat is just trying to distract you, like take your mind off worrying about your dad?"

"Plus, she thinks Prince Kamal is some kind of dangerous stud. It's ridiculous to think he'd be interested in me."

"I bet she's jealous he's not putting her up at the Plaza."

Terry grunted.

"Why don't we call the hospital?" Maude suggested. "Your dad could have improved overnight."

Terry kept her head down. "Prince Kamal called the ICU this morning. He texted me that Dad's condition hasn't changed, but he said Dr. Jacquard took that as a good sign since he isn't getting any worse."

"See? That's good news." Maude gave her a few pats on the back. Her voice took on a dreamy quality. "I liked Prince Kamal as soon as I saw him." She leaned across Terry and typed in a few words. Within seconds several celebrity tabloid sites appeared. Maude began clicking on images. She let out a frustrated sigh. Most of the pictures had been shot through a telephoto lens, and in every shot Prince Kamal wore his head scarf, robe and sunglasses.

Maude scrunched up her nose. "These pictures must be a few years old. He's totally gotten rid of that fat gut. He must have gotten a trainer." Terry gave her a sideways look. "What?" Maude said. "He's matured nicely into a hot dude, that's all I'm saying. Besides," she began to count on her fingers, "he's making sure your dad is getting excellent care at the hospital, and you're his private guest at the swankiest place in the city, which includes gourmet meals from room service *and* a limo ride to school."

"We picked you up on the way too," Terry interjected.

Maude smirked and gave Terry's ponytail a playful tug. "All he needs is to take you shopping, and it's just like *Pretty Woman*."

"What's that?"

"A movie about a prostitute who becomes this rich guy's private escort. They end up falling in love." Maude's voice trailed off. "It sounds bad when I describe it like that, but it's really romantic. Don't freak. I'm hardly suggesting that you and Prince Kamal are going to—"

"Please. He's totally not my type."

Maude nudged her shoulder. "Oh really? What is your type, then, Nefertari? A Roman soldier?" she teased. "Someone with their own army?"

"No," Terry said softly, remembering how Zach's smile gave her butterflies. "I need someone who will make my toes curl." Movement at the front of the library got her attention. "Why is Zach here?" Terry clumsily got to her feet. She hated how he made her flustered.

Maude looked confused. "I asked him to meet us here to work on the project. It's due in three days."

"Awesome. I'll get us a book ... or something." Terry left Maude at the computer station and made her way to the back of the library, choosing the row of shelves farthest away — she needed to concentrate on finding the Asp, not replay the staring contest she and Zach had had last night.

Terry leaned on the bookshelf and checked her phone. Since Prince Kamal's message this morning, there hadn't been any other calls or texts, not even from Sarah. Her finger hovered over the phone number to the museum. Dr. Mullaca had said her dad was trying something foolish. Then Sarah found him unconscious on the fifth floor.

Terry closed her eyes and pictured the Egypt room. If he was working on the coffin, why was he found on the fifth floor? Maybe whatever the neurotoxin Dr. Jacquard mentioned was in the Egypt room and had nothing to do with the secret case in the basement? Terry's mind grew sharp, imagining every detail of that room.

The last time she'd been there, the workmen had been preparing for the new display. She remembered how creepy Cleopatra appeared under the protective sheets of plastic with the blank stare behind the charcoal-lined eyes. The garishly decorated headdress and asp had layers of gold paint to hide years of fading. That's how Terry knew all the jewelry was fake; nothing of any value would be so tastelessly adorned.

But maybe they had painted some of the displays to freshen them? The mummy case with the carved-out eyes had an elaborate design. What if the workmen had mixed paint improperly? What if the room had been closed off and not properly ventilated?

Terry let out a long breath. There was something tugging at the back of her memory. It was like trying to remember a dream that she'd woken from too soon. She closed her eyes more tightly, willing the idea to come to the surface.

Fingers closed around her elbow. Terry jumped and her eyes flew open.

"You okay?" Zach stood beside her. His disheveled light brown hair framed his face, which was lined with concern. Terry suspected he'd spent time in front of the mirror to get that messy look.

She shook her head as the floor took an unexpected swoop. "I'm—" Terry halted as the next words got stuck. "I'm looking for a book."

Zach rested his arm on the shelf beside her. He was in his usual jeans, but the light blue Henley shirt was new. The fabric looked soft. "I came looking for you. I just saw Maude," he said. "She told me your dad is in the hospital."

"He um … collapsed at work." Her words felt like they were being spoken by someone else. "They think he might have come in contact with a toxin or something." Terry left out Dr. Mullaca's theory — it was too embarrassing to share.

A crinkle appeared between his eyebrows. "I'm sorry," he said. "Can I do anything to help?"

The kindness in his voice was a salve to her frayed nerves.

"The doctor says he'll probably be fine in a few days." She wished she believed them, but Dr. Mullaca's phone call had wedged a pinpoint of doubt, ready to spread like a crack in the ice. Terry had to keep her paranoia in check or else she'd lose her mind.

"That's good," he said. "But what about you? It's just you and your dad, right? Or do you have other family?"

"No." Terry dropped her gaze this time. She bit the inside of her cheek to keep her voice steady. "It's just me and Dad. And I'm staying at the Plaza."

"The Plaza!" Zach's flabbergasted expression was immediate and comical. A modicum of humor lighted Terry's spirit, and she smiled as she explained about the prince's offer.

"I'm glad your dad will be okay," he finally said. "I was worried when I saw the police come to the gym last night. You looked scared." He shifted his weight. "I would have called, but I didn't have your number." He looked at Terry expectantly.

She made no movement. Her back was glued to the bookcase. A rush of heat made her clothes feel heavy and too bulky. She pictured the matching camisole and sweater from Old Navy and silently cursed her boyish wardrobe.

He tilted his head and asked, "So, can I have your number?" He reached into his back pocket and held out his phone for her.

Terry resisted the urge to dry her sweaty palms on her cargo pants. She took the phone, praying it wouldn't slip from her grasp. *He means because of the Cleopatra project.* Why else would he want her number?

After a long pause he prompted, "If that's okay."

Terry tried not to shake under his gaze. She cursed the fact that her ponytail was probably showing off her red ears. She put in her number then handed his phone back.

Without anything to occupy them, her hands hung limply at her sides, flimsy and awkward. The casualness was forced. Terry crossed her arms in front of her chest, but that motion seemed too gangly as well. She concentrated on staying still.

Zach looked down the aisle and then back to Terry. She sensed he'd run out of words too but seemed reluctant to go. He ran a hand through his hair, the tips still wet from his shower.

Terry thought about her steam shower at the Plaza and considered telling him about it. Would a guy find that interesting, or would he give a strange look and then walk away? She decided on a safer topic instead. "So," she began, "you really can play basketball. You weren't kidding when you said the team needed you to make it to the State Championships."

He smiled, then reached up and grazed the edge of his eyebrow with his finger. Terry's grinned at the familiar gesture. "You should do that before every free throw," she suggested. "I bet you'd never miss."

He looked surprised, but in a pleasant way. "Think so? I've tried everything else." Then he shrugged. "Or rather, my dad has."

Terry remembered the well-groomed man who made Zach practice right after the game while the rest of the team was celebrating. "I guess he just wants you to do your best," she offered.

"He knows it's my only way into college." His voice was unwavering, but Terry could hear the catch at the end. "Why do you think I'm taking a history class meant for juniors? I'm taking the bare minimum to graduate."

"At least you get to leave the school," she said. She wasn't sure how else to respond. Her ears continued to burn as the seconds of silence grew between them. Zach stayed quiet as well, studying the floor. Then slowly, he raised his gaze, trailing up her legs, past her chest, then finally stopping at her eyes.

A pool of warmth spread from Terry's stomach all the way to the tips of her fingers. The pull toward him was undeniable. She wondered how soft his Henley shirt would feel against her cheek.

"I didn't think you'd come to the game," he simply said.

Terry's cheeks glowed with a hot blush. "I went with Maude," she started. "She had an article to do for Fraser."

Zach practically flinched, but kept his stance. "You guys hang out a lot, huh?"

"Maude or Fraser?" she asked with a mischievous lilt. Terry had no idea where this ability to flirt was coming from.

There was another pause. He pressed his lips together, looking pained. "I'm sorry for what Allison did the other day with the mascot."

Terry's warm glow vanished. A cool, prickling sensation took its place. "Yeah," she said, hugging her elbows, "everyone's sorry but her.

His expression crumbled slightly. "I wanted to help you."

Terry rolled her eyes. "I'd say you're the one who needs help," she said dryly. "She's your girlfriend."

"Appearances can be deceiving."

"You looked like the perfect couple after the game last night."

"She got her photo op — that's her priority."

The bookcase dug into Terry's back, but she stayed still. Neither one of them made a sound. Soon their breathing matched. A blanket of heat unfurled up from her toes, covering her in a body length blush sweat.

She couldn't fight the hope that Zach had drawn that picture of her, that he saw her as someone strong and beautiful and not a cripple that needed saving. She knew what she was thinking was dangerous, but her imagination wouldn't stop. She tried to clear her head by concentrating on his Adam's apple. It was the only part of him she could stare at without blushing.

He slouched down to her height. "Terry?" His voice sounded wounded. "Look at me," he softly urged. "I'm not like them." He moved closer — much closer than a friend or history partner would stand. Terry couldn't tell if the heat wave was coming from him or her own racing pulse.

A couple stumbled into the aisle with their arms entwined. Terry recognized Tanya and her boyfriend. "Oops," Tanya smirked, mid-kiss. "Looks like this one's already taken, babe."

Zach stepped back, but it was too late. Tanya's boyfriend had already seen them. The stupid grin on his face melted into a mask of disbelief. "Holy shit! What the hell are you doing, Zach?"

Tanya snorted, then pulled him away. His head snapped around, still trying to look back before they crossed to the next aisle.

Terry pushed by Zach, ignoring his pleas. "I'm sorry," he said. She didn't turn around. She didn't even care that he was watching her limp away. All she could think about was getting as far away as possible. Fear was taking root.

When she passed the next bookcase, Tanya's boyfriend voiced Terry's very thoughts. "Allison is going to kill that chick for sure."

Chapter Twenty

"If you can all get settled." Ms. Bernard's voice went up an octave, fighting to be heard over the various conversations. "I have a special announcement."

Terry followed Maude to their usual desks at the front, eyes focused on Maude's *Hunger Games*–style braid. Allison and her princesses were already in their seats, heads bowed together.

Terry slumped into her chair, purposely being evasive. Earlier, she'd met up with Maude outside the newspaper office. In Fraser's absence Tanya had taken the article about the basketball game. She'd smirked at Terry and asked if she'd found anything useful in the self-help section of the library. Maude had given Terry a quizzical look, which she mirrored, hoping that her burning blush wouldn't give her away.

Sitting in the front row of history class, Terry dared to glance over her shoulder, but Zach's usual chair was empty. Instead she made contact with Allison's hard stare. There was an eerie sense of anticipation behind her icy baby blues. Terry whipped around, silently praying to the front wall of the classroom.

Maude went through their Cleopatra notes. "And then the last column can be about henna," she said, flipping through a few pages. "I'll do up the copy tonight and print it off at the office supply store in the morning." Then she added, "The glossy finish will be the perfect touch."

"It'll be awesome," Terry said, grateful for the distraction. She couldn't help but feel proud of their little project. Ms. Bernard would definitely give them top marks, she reasoned. Then Zach would only have to worry about making those free throws at the final.

The thought of him sent Terry's pulse racing. She pulled out her ponytail, letting the hair cover her ears. Since the library episode that morning she hadn't seen him, something she wasn't able to decide was good or bad.

Ms. Bernard raised her voice even higher. "I have a special surprise. As you know, the museum is planning an extravagant night for its latest showcase exhibit." She beamed around the class, hoping for a response, but only a few yawns replied.

She tried again. "Everyone else will have to wait for the grand unveiling, but we…" She paused and did another scan of the blank faces. "…*we* get to see it in advance."

Terry's mind reeled. Had Dr. Mullaca decided to put the coffin on exhibit without even trying to open it? What about her dad and finding the asp?

"And this wouldn't be happening if it weren't for a very special student." Ms. Bernard stood in front of Terry's desk. There was a long spell of silence. Apparently, Ms. Bernard was hoping to build the anticipation with a dramatic pause. Ms. Bernard looked at Terry and a flash of sympathy crossed over her bony features, then the pointy-nosed history teacher averted her gaze to Allison.

Allison smiled, showing all her teeth. Terry was reminded of a jackal. "It was no trouble," she said. "My father is eager to show off the museum's new exhibit."

Terry had seen enough of that smile to last a lifetime. She wished she'd thought of faking being sick to get out of school and instead had gone to the museum to talk with Dr. Mullaca. Maybe it wasn't too late. She considered raising her hand for permission to go to the bathroom and get out of class.

The door at the front of the class opened, and in walked Zach. He handed a pass to Ms. Bernard.

"Take your seat, Mr. Breton," Ms. Bernard ordered impatiently. "This isn't basketball practice. You're not captain here."

The distraction of Zach's appearance made Terry rethink her plan of escape. She moved to the side as he started in the direction to his usual spot at the back. She stared down at her desk. The sticker Maude had placed last week was still there, declaring Crystal Peters was a star.

Zach cleared his throat, then slick as snake slid into the empty desk beside Terry. There was a muffled comment from the back of the room. Terry concentrated on keeping her breathing steady. The side of her body closest to Zach was popping with electricity, and she imagined their tiny molecules bouncing and mixing in the air between them. All of her senses were focused on him: the smell of his spearmint gum, the beat of his fingers on the desk, how the sleeves of his Henley shirt were pushed up to his elbows, showing off his toned forearms.

Ms. Bernard instructed the class to work on their Cleopatra projects.

"How's this for a title," Maude began from Terry's unaffected side. "'Beauty Secrets That Rule.'" She grinned. "Get it? She's a queen."

Zach's leg pressed up against Terry's knee. She went rigid. He reached across Terry and took the rough copy of the article.

"What is it?" Maude asked him defensively. "You've got a lemon face on."

Zach squinted at the paper. Terry watched as his finger grazed the edge of his eyebrow.

"It's just words," he finally said.

"Thanks, Einstein," Maude replied. "It's an article."

"I mean it needs artwork." He handed her back the copy. "Clip art or something."

Maude pursed her lips, considering this.

Terry barely inched her face toward him. "Too bad we don't know any artists."

He looked indifferent, not even a hint of blush. Terry could have easily mentioned how gray the sky looked today, and he would have given her the same bland expression.

"Oh, wait!" Maude said, her eyes bright. "How about we name some of the products? Like a lipstick can be 'Night Life on the Nile' and one of the perfumes can be called, 'Anything for Antony.'" Maude pouted at the silent response. "You know, as in Mark Antony."

"The guy she rolled up in the rug for?" Zach asked.

"No," Terry corrected. "That was Caesar."

"*Et tu, Brute?*" he teased.

The Shakespeare reference caught Terry off guard. Zach had pretty much admitted he did terribly in school. She was curious but could barely keep eye contact, let alone study his face to see if he was sincere. Her armpits were sticky, and bouncing ping-pong balls had taken over her stomach. She was a hormonal wreck, yet he was the picture of cool — and had obviously been toying with her in the library.

Terry cleared her throat, determined to conquer her nerves. "After Caesar was assassinated, Cleopatra and her son fled Rome. But Mark Antony wasn't going to let her get away."

"Was he already in love with her?" Maude asked, wide-eyed.

"He was the commander of the Roman army, and he demanded to question her about Caesar." Terry paused and imagined her mother's voice, retelling the story with a passion built from decades of study — no one had loved the story of Cleopatra more.

Terry sat a little straighter. "But Cleopatra was nobody's possession to be handed over. She arrived at his camp on a golden barge dressed like Venus." She turned to Zach and managed to hold his gaze. "You know, the goddess of love."

"The direct approach," he said. "I like it." There was a quality to his voice that made Terry blush.

Maude wiggled closer. "So they…" She made hand gestures to finish her thought.

"Yes," Terry said, trying not to laugh at Maude's obvious discomfort. "They became lovers. After she gave birth to twins, he made her his queen. Their love for each other was only matched by their limitless aspiration for territory. You could say they were the original power couple."

"Markopatra," Maude said, nodding thoughtfully.

Terry glanced at Maude's lipstick names. A hollowness deflated her spirit. "It was later that they were both defeated by Octavian. Cleopatra's fleet surrendered, while Mark Antony's army was conquered on land. Popular legend says Cleopatra spread rumors that she had been killed. Overcome with grief, Mark Antony stabbed himself. When he realized she was still alive, his followers carried him to her with little time to spare — he died in her arms. Unwilling to become Octavian's prisoner, Cleopatra had a poisonous asp smuggled into her tower."

All three are quiet for a moment, then Maude said, "No happy ending for anyone." Terry remained in a fog, thinking of Cleopatra's last hours. Two asps — one real with poisonous fangs, and one golden and coiled — kept penetrating her thoughts.

When class was over she grabbed her backpack and followed Maude. Once in the hallway, she pulled out her phone and turned it on. The battery was almost dead. She was going call to Dr. Mullaca at the museum about the upcoming unveiling, but there was already a message waiting for her.

Chapter Twenty-One

Terry stood in the middle of the hallway, staring at the message. "He wants to take me out to dinner tonight," she read out loud.

Maude unwrapped a sucker and popped it in her mouth. "Who?" Her question sounded garbled around the candy.

"Prince Kamal."

Maude craned her neck to read the text for herself. "What are you going to tell him?"

"I don't know." It seemed like a kind gesture, but Dr. Mullaca's warning had planted a seed of doubt. In the back of Terry's mind a small voice advised caution. She moaned. "I wish everything wasn't so complicated."

"What's the big deal? He's a twenty-two-year-old millionaire who happens to be royalty. Seems pretty simple to me."

Terry gave her a sideways glance. "How do you know his age?"

"I looked it up when I was scanning his pictures online." Maude's sucker made her cheek bulge out on one side. "He'll look cute in his robe and head scarf at McDonald's."

"I doubt we'd go to McDonald's. Besides," she said, noting the time on the message, "it was sent a few hours ago. He's probably changed his mind by now." Her phone suddenly went black. Terry let out a tired sigh and returned it to her backpack.

"Maybe he'll take you shopping first," Maude said mischievously. Then she proceeded to sing the song "Pretty Woman."

"Oh please," Terry moaned.

Maude continued to serenade Terry, using the lollipop as a microphone.

"Thank you! I get it!" Terry tried to sound angry, but Maude's horribly off-key voice was making the whole scenario ridiculously comic. It felt good to laugh.

When their giggles petered off, Maude gave Terry an earnest look. "Okay, seriously, though, what the heck is up with you and Zach? You took off when we were in the library, and then in class you kept leaning away from him like he had head lice." She patted her braid protectively, then leaned forward, dropping her tone. "*Does* he have head lice? I hear the cleaner the hair the more likely you'll get lice."

Terry limped a few more steps before answering. The crowds in the hallway were especially thick this afternoon. Maude played with her sucker, patiently waiting. "Um, we kind of …" Terry was unsure how to explain what exactly had happened between them in the aisle of the library. "Well," she started again, "we were talking and he sort of…"

"Stop with all your big words and fancy description," Maude interrupted. "What did he do, confess he's a vampire? Fart? What?"

"What."

"Huh?"

"He didn't fart," Terry blurted out. She was a little disenchanted that Maude hadn't even considered that Zach may have kissed her. A few heads turned in their direction. Terry dropped her voice. "He got close."

Maude crunched her sucker, chewing on the bits loudly. "He got close?"

"Yes." Terry found she was embarrassed to admit such a simple gesture had made her knees turn to water — even the one inside the brace.

"That's it?"

Terry hiked her backpack up her shoulder. "Forget about it.

Obviously it's no big deal."

"Then why are you freaking out?"

"I'm not freaking out!"

Maude was about to protest when she looked down the hall and her face lit up.

"Neffie." Fraser's bright orange polo shirt was buttoned to the top and paired with a navy wool blazer. It was a stark contrast, but Fraser totally pulled it off.

All of his attention was on Terry. "Tanya told me I missed you earlier," he said. "Next time let me know you've got something to drop off, otherwise I'll think you're playing hard to get."

Terry was all too aware of Maude's dysphoric expression. The white stick of her sucker pointed out straight from between her lips, then slowly sloped downward as if it too were dejected. "Actually," Terry corrected, "the basketball piece is from Maude."

Fraser glanced at Maude, then a smooth grin took over his face. "Right, the chick with the candy issue who loves unicorns."

Maude pulled out her fake smile.

"But," Fraser began again to Terry, "you'll be glad I caught up with you, because I have these." He held out a new pile of photocopies. When Terry reached for them, he pulled back teasingly. "That's if you're still interested?"

Maude made a disgruntled noise and tried to disguise it with a cough.

"I'm still interested," Terry said, taking the papers, "in the missing asp."

Fraser tapped the top paper. "There's a bit more about museum security that night and the guard they brought in for questioning."

Terry's eyes scanned the articles. She became hopeful for the first time that day. Somewhere in these pages was the answer to the missing asp — and her dad's cure.

Fraser stood taller. "You owe me, Neffie," he said.

"And my article?" Maude asked, playing with the end of her braid, the other hand clutched her sucker.

"You got another one of those?" he asked, pointing at the sweet.

Maude looked incredulous. "Are you kidding? I'm a freakin' candy store." She rummaged in her backpack, then held out a chocolate-flavored one, beaming up at him.

"Cool," he said, unwrapping the sucker. Then he turned on the spot and started down the hallway.

"Guys suck," Maude whispered.

"That was almost rude," Terry said. "I'm impressed. Next time try saying it to his face."

"Why is it so hard? Why can't a guy be nice and sweet? Why can't a guy smile at you, and say 'Your pink hair smells nice?'"

"Fraser's only interested in getting the inside scoop about the museum's exhibit," Terry said, hoping to soften Maude's mood. Then she shrugged tiredly. She was the last person who should be giving advice on guys.

"Where's my Mark Antony?" Maude pouted.

Terry couldn't tell if she was joking or not. "You're looking for someone who doesn't exist," she said. "The knight on the white horse is only in fairy tales."

They started down the hallway, both consumed with their own forlorn thoughts. When they turned the corner and headed down the main hallway, Maude found her voice again. "Do you want to come for supper?" she offered. "We can use the living room floor to spread out all the articles."

Terry smiled at the thought of being surrounded by the smell of Maude's grandmother's cooking. There would be no confusing guys, no crazy Egyptologists and no probing royalty. They squeezed through a circle of freshmen with books open in their hands, having an impromptu study session.

"Hey, slut!" a voice pierced through the crowded hallway from behind. A wave of nausea washed over Terry. She and Maude slowly turned around.

Allison and two of her princesses strutted toward them. Kids moved to the edge of the hallway, parting like the Red Sea did for Moses. It became quiet. "So you do know your name," Allison said, that cool smile perfectly in place. "That's all the proof I need."

"Proof of what?" Maude said, her sucker dropping to the floor.

"We heard you were making out with Zach in the library," one of the princesses said.

Maude stepped in front of Terry and said, "What Zach and I do is none of your business!"

Allison rolled her eyes. "Jesus, not you." She pointed to Terry. "The cripple is the one who's been trying to get into my boyfriend's pants."

"That's a lie," Terry said. "We were looking for books."

A princess snorted, "Pfft, looking for books?"

"Well, it is the library," Maude mocked, but there was an obvious quiver in her voice.

Terry took a quick look around. Everyone was watching, but no one seemed ready to intervene. In fact, more kids were moving in on either end, blocking Terry and Maude's escape. And where the hell was Zach? He'd told her he wanted to help.

Allison's smile grew. "He's not here," she said, as if she could read Terry's thoughts. "He doesn't care about *you*." She reached up and fingered her gold necklace with manicured nails.

Terry realized the weight of the situation. If Allison was confronting her in a hallway full of witnesses, she must be ready to explode. Terry tried to wet her lips, but her mouth was chalk dry.

Allison took a step closer. Terry could see tiny rainbows reflected off her diamond pendant.

"You think you walk funny now, wait until we—" one of the princesses halted mid-sentence. She looked over Terry's shoulder, her eyes taking on a trance expression. "Who..." she started dreamily, "...who is *that*?"

Standing in the middle of the hallway in designer jeans, a tight black T-shirt and black Dr. Martens was Prince Kamal. His ebony hair fell in layered waves to his shoulders. When he found Terry in the crowd, he smiled, making his cheekbones even more sculpted.

"Someone's been holding out on us," Maude said out of the corner of her mouth. "Who knew all that hotness was under the robe?"

A murmur of approval escaped Allison's half-opened mouth.

"Oh my god," the other princess breathed.

Prince Kamal only had to walk a few steps before the crowd that had gathered to watch a catfight parted for him. Some guys had swag; he had regal confidence.

"Miss Hughes." He practically bowed before Terry. "I hope you don't mind my unexpected presence, but I was worried when you didn't reply to my text."

"Is it my dad?" Terry panicked.

"No. I'm sorry to mislead you. Your father's condition is unchanged. He's still stable. I can take you there at once if you wish." He motioned to the end of the hallway. One of the bodyguards stood rigidly, scrutinizing each student that walked by. "We could talk on the way."

The crowd of passersby was growing as people slowed down to check out the new guy. Terry could feel everyone's stare.

"That is, unless you have other plans with your friends." He cocked his head to the side, noticing Allison and her princesses. "I don't want to take you away from anything."

Maude blurted out, "Take us away ... please!"

Prince Kamal chuckled, showing off one perfect dimple. "You're included as well, Miss Sanchez." He offered her his arm. All the girls were transfixed by his bicep.

"Awesome!" Maude answered, tucking into his side.

Terry started with them toward the main entrance, leaving a stunned trio of beauty pageant wannabes behind. She played with the zipper on her hoodie, hesitant to take his arm. It felt too make-believe — too silly for her to do. Prince Kamal sensed her reluctance and let his other hand hang loosely at his side.

"My car is just outside," he told them when they neared the bodyguard. A second one, also in suit and sunglasses, waited just outside.

"Only a car?" Maude joked. "I was expecting a white horse."

Chapter Twenty-Two

The ICU nurse spoke with Terry as she stood by her father's bedside. The middle-aged woman with the neatly trimmed bob told her the same things Prince Kamal had described in the limo ride to the hospital.

"He's stable," she said. "The blood tests are still carefully analyzed." Terry wiped away a tear. Her father looked so pale. She squeezed his hand, but his fingers were flaccid in her grip. "Diagnosis is a process of elimination," the nurse continued. "The doctors start with a long list of every possibility, then they begin to cross them off one by one."

She smiled thoughtfully at Terry. "Once it's narrowed down, a clear care plan can be drawn up. We're doing our best to get him out of this, don't worry."

A get well card decorated with flowers was standing on the hospital bedside table. "That's from one of his co-workers," the nurse explained to Terry. "She was here all morning. She left her number in case there was any change."

"Long hair and high heels?" Terry asked. She picked up the card and read the sentimental verse. It was signed, *All My Love, Sarah*, in exaggerated loopy swirls. A small ball of heat began at the base of Terry's spine. Sarah was here holding her dad's hand all day while she was forced to go to school.

Gunther Hughes' chest rose and fell. It was the only part of him that was moving. Even his eyelids didn't flutter. Terry thought she'd feel better after seeing him, but it only confirmed her dad was totally helpless.

Dr. Mullaca's words about the missing asp rested heavily on her conscience. She'd hardly done any research, too busy sneaking around the library with Zach and trying to avoid potential paralysis from the wrath of Allison and her consorts.

Terry gave the nurse her cell phone number to add to his file. "I'm his only family," she stressed. She left her father's bedside and found Maude and Prince Kamal on a bench by the elevator leaning over a pile of papers. They both looked up when she approached.

"How is he?" Maude asked brightly. Her smile faded when she read Terry's expression.

"The nurses are turning him every two hours so he doesn't get bedsores," Terry answered somberly.

"He's getting excellent attention while they wait for all the test results," Prince Kamal said.

"But they still have no answers!" Terry stabbed the elevator button. "I feel so useless just standing by his bed, holding his hand. I have to do something."

Maude gathered up the papers and clutched them to her chest. "I'm sure he knows you were there."

The elevator door slid open. "I have to find that stupid asp," Terry announced. "As much as I hate the idea of agreeing with Dr. Mullaca, it's the only thing I've got to go on." She folded her arms and waited for Prince Kamal to voice his concern. Instead he and Maude exchanged a glance that made Terry suspicious. "What is it?" she asked.

"We've been going over the documents from Fraser," Maude began. The elevator stopped and several staff stepped inside. Maude looked at Prince Kamal.

He gave a slight shake of the head. "We can discuss this further in my car," he said.

The trio remained silent until they slipped into the limo. Maude and Terry sat with each other, while Prince Kamal took the seat across from them. They pulled away from the front entrance of the hospital. Terry's good knee started to shake. It was disconcerting for Maude to be so quiet.

Prince Kamal leaned forward in his seat, his elbows rested on the knees of his designer jeans. "The asp was heavily guarded," he started. "It would have been impossible to steal."

"Obviously not," Terry said.

Maude shuffled through the papers and read, "Police are dumbfounded to explain how the Sacred Asp of Cleopatra has vanished into thin air. This comes only two weeks after a night security guard, Gus Tanner, was found unconscious not far from the display. Sources speculate this earlier crime was a staged version primarily as a practice run for the real burglary."

Maude pushed a pink strand of hair behind her ear. "In a bizarre twist, local high school student June Macallum disappeared on a class trip the day of the robbery attempt and has not been seen since."

Maude looked up from the paper. Despite the circumstance, there was a lightness in her voice. "Maybe she took the asp, sold it on eBay and is living in the tropics right now."

Prince Kamal cleared his throat. "The asp has not surfaced in fifty years. If it was bought, my government would know about it. Trust me." His tone left no room for doubt.

Terry studied the black and white school picture of the missing girl. She had simple, straight bangs with a ponytail and wore a plain blouse. Her lips were a thin line, the edges slightly drawn down. Terry recognized the hopeless expression.

"She looks like she could have used the cash," Maude said, still pushing her theory of theft for money.

Terry turned to the tinted window of the car, trying to clear her head. "Forget about the girl," she said. "We're looking for the asp."

Maude took the hint. She folded the papers and shoved them in Terry's backpack. "Okay," she said with a fresh determination. "I'm the cryptoquote champ, after all, so let's tackle this puzzle." She began to count on her fingers. "Because of the first botched burglary, the museum beefed up security. There were guards stationed in front of the exhibit twenty-four hours a day. But none of the police saw anything."

"What do you mean?" Terry asked. Nothing made sense anymore.

"One second the asp was in its locked glass case," Maude said, "and the next it wasn't."

"It really did vanish into thin air?"

Maude motioned with her hands. "Poof!"

Terry frowned. "That's impossible. The guards must be lying."

Prince Kamal nodded to the paper in Maude's hands. "How could all of them be involved? Someone would have talked by now."

Maude pursed her lips. "What is the logical answer in all this mess? It's never resurfaced, but now, fifty years later, we're looking for it again. Why?"

Terry pictured her dad lying in his hospital bed while the doctors and nurses depended on science in their futile search for a cure.

Prince Kamal dropped his chin as if defeated. The simple gesture reminded Terry he was only a few years older than she and Maude. *How will the three of us figure this out?*

"Most burglars brag about a big heist." Maude's eyebrows bunched together. "So maybe whoever wanted the asp wasn't interested in selling it."

The car swerved sharply. Terry instinctively grabbed her right knee. Her life would be so different today if her mother had never discovered that fourth chamber. She would have two good legs, two healthy parents, and instead of a confusing jock with a psycho girlfriend, she would be sneaking off to meet Awad under the

Egyptian stars for midnight kisses.

"Maybe they were going to sell it," Terry said with a tinge of hopeless surrender, "but they fell prey to its curse."

"Do you really think that?" Prince Kamal lifted his gaze, worry furrowing his brow.

Maude glanced back and forth between. "Um ... okay," she said. "I guess we can all agree that the missing asp is one tricky mystery."

The three of them swayed to the side as the car pulled over to the curb. Terry saw the Maudern Style sign glowing against the late February night. Spring seemed years away.

Maude gathered her things, and then gave Terry a quick hug. "Call me later," she whispered.

"Good night, Miss Sanchez," Prince Kamal said.

She slipped out of the back of the limo and jogged to the front of the store. As the car pulled away, Terry wished she was going up to the warm apartment that smelled like apple pie and pot roast.

When she righted herself in the seat again, Prince Kamal smiled back at her. "I'm sorry," he said.

"For what?"

He waved a hand through the air dismissively. "For a lot of things, but right now, I'm sorry for not being a better host."

"You've been very generous." She glanced out the window again, then frowned. "Hold on," she said. "This isn't the way to the Plaza."

Prince Kamal gave her one of his sad smiles again. "I'm sorry, Nefertari," he repeated. "Didn't I tell you? We've got other plans."

Chapter Twenty-Three

Prince Kamal offered no further explanation. The outside blurred as the car sped up. A trickle of panic began to grow inside Terry. She groped her backpack for her phone, desperate to find Maude's name. But the screen was blank — her battery was dead. Prince Kamal's face crinkled in concentration while he texted on his own phone.

The car took a sharp corner, making them both clutch the plush seats. Prince Kamal cursed under his breath. He gave Terry an embarrassed smile.

My kidnapper is blushing. She mentally berated herself for acting so stupidly. She should have listened to Dr. Mullaca. She should have gotten out of the car with Maude when she had the chance. Terry eyed the handle and mentally calculated the physical damage if she jumped out of the racing limo.

"We have an urgent matter to discuss," he said. "I had to wait until Miss Sanchez was gone, obviously."

"Obviously." Terry bit the inside of her cheek. It would have been harder to hide two bodies than one.

The car slowed and came to a stop. Prince Kamal stepped out and offered his hand to Terry.

She stared at his outreached palm. She couldn't stay in the car, but walking along with her would-be killer was the least logical thing to do. Her backpack was only filled with photocopies. She needed something heavy to hit him with.

"Terry?" he prompted, this time using the name she preferred. "Are you all right? You're an interesting shade of green."

Terry tried to keep it together, but her lips began to quiver. "Why?" was all she could say.

"Because the food at the Plaza was getting tiresome." He waved a hand at the restaurant sign behind him.

The Marrakesh Palace.

"Besides," he offered, "I thought you might appreciate this little oasis." He patiently waited for her brain to catch up.

"Dinner," she said, dumbfounded that she had completely forgotten about his earlier text. Every muscle in Terry's body relaxed. She silently berated Dr. Mullaca for making her paranoid.

"Come." He helped her out of the limo. "They're usually closed on Mondays, but the owner is a friend of my family's."

Inside the opulent Middle Eastern restaurant, dark wooden walls were accented with golden drapes and sculpted archways. Blood red tapestries hung from ornamented rods. Delicious aromas from the kitchen triggered her memory. Terry's heart filled up — it even smelled like home. One table in the middle of the sumptuous dining area was already set for two.

The waiter made an incredible fuss over them, pulling out their chairs and placing the napkins on their laps. Prince Kamal replied in Arabic. Terry caught a few phrases, his dialect crisp and perfect, much more understandable than Dr. Mullaca's. Soon they were sitting across from each other with candles lit and a carafe of white wine sangria between them.

"I didn't think Muslims drank alcohol," Terry said. She was comfortable in the familiar surroundings and asked out of sincere curiosity.

He blushed as he filled his glass. "I guess you could say I'm a man who bends the rules sometimes."

Terry almost snorted when he said *man*. The moment felt like dress-up, but she didn't mind; a little escape was exactly what she needed at the end of such a hostile day.

A tapas-style platter of baba ghanoush, hummus and tabbouleh was served first. "I hope you don't mind that I ordered for us," Prince Kamal said. "I texted ahead and told the chef to prepare several courses." A look of concern brushed over his chiseled features. "You don't have any allergies, do you?"

Terry shook her head, not wanting to waste any time on conversation. Using a wedge of pita bread, she dipped into the first dish. The hummus hit her tongue, and her taste buds exploded. She closed her eyes and moaned. It was a long, satisfying chew. When she opened her eyes, Prince Kamal was chuckling.

"Sorry." She dabbed the corner of her mouth with her napkin. "It's been a long time since I've enjoyed something this much."

He raised the wine to his lips then said, "I'm pleased you're enjoying the food."

Terry concentrated on getting the next scoop of hummus.

"You said there was something to discuss," she reminded him.

"I heard some very distressing news today," he dipped a chunk of bread into the bowl of baba ghanoush. "Mayor Harris is pushing for the unveiling of the coffin." His nimble fingers rolled up the morsel, and he took a bite. Terry was impressed with his elegant manners.

"Our history class is getting an advance viewing," Terry told him.

He chewed and his eyes grew wide. "That's … unexpected."

The waiter appeared with more platters, temporarily distracting Terry. She reached across and started on the dolmas. The tender grape leaves filled with rice and fresh herbs were always her favorite. She was on her second helping when she spoke again. "I was going to ask Dr. Mullaca about it … or even Sarah," she said through a mouthful. An uncomfortable image of Sarah weeping over her dad's hospital bed flashed in Terry's mind.

She hastily wiped her hands. "I have no idea what's going on.

129

Are they going to try to open the mummy's case without the asp?
I can't imagine Dr. Mullaca doing anything so reckless," she reasoned. "And why does the mayor have that much say over what
happens?"

Prince Kamal took a long drink of sangria, then put down his
glass. "Dr. Mullaca doesn't confide much in me," he confessed. He
glanced up at Terry. "And that's why I need your help. You seem
to have her ear. I'm here as a delegate, but my heart is invested
in this matter as well. Imagine if it really is the remains of Cleopatra, Egypt's last pharaoh? I can't let anything or anyone endan-
ger what might be inside."

His expression hardened. "Have you seen the news lately? My
country is ripping itself apart. No one trusts the government. The
police are feared..." He dropped his chin. "My people need hope.
We need to remember where we came from. Our souls need to
unite."

Terry had heard her father talking about the state of unrest
in Egypt; the military-backed government violently clashing with
protestors, wrongly jailed journalists, the epidemic of violence toward women. It seemed so opposite to the proud standing monu-
ments in the Valley of the Kings.

Prince Kamal cleared his throat, quickly regaining his regal
composure.

Terry needed to fill the silence. She picked up a kalamata olive and rolled it in her fingers. "It doesn't make sense that Dr.
Mullaca would be going along with the mayor."

"Dr. Mullaca is a herpetologist first and an Egyptologist second."

"Dad mentioned she was into reptiles," Terry said offhanded-
ly. "No wonder she's so obsessed with the asp."

"Her interpretation of the hieroglyphs are more like a Holly-
wood movie. I'm sure your father would be looking for a more rea-
sonable option." He nodded to her empty plate and offered a slice
of roasted eggplant.

Terry tried to imagine what her father would be doing to solve the riddle on the ancient case. "In the last text he sent me," she said, concentrating on the memory, "he mentioned having a hunch about the key."

"And?" Prince Kamal's fingers hesitated over a platter of falafel, waiting for Terry to explain.

"And that was it."

"When did he send it?"

"In the afternoon, I think," Terry pushed her plate away. "I'll check my phone when it's charged again."

Prince Kamal studied her. "I'm sorry," he said. "I've spoiled your appetite. This dinner was supposed to be a chance to talk without Dr. Mullaca pointing her wrinkled old nose at us."

Terry was quiet for a moment, then she asked, "Do you think she's lying about the asp being the trigger?"

Prince Kamal let out a long sigh, then gave her a thoughtful look. "I don't know. I think her need for personal gain is greater than her professional obligation." His voice became serious. "I can't forget the way she looked at you during the examination in the basement that night. She was studying you with such an expression of malice."

Terry kept her reservations about Dr. Mullaca to herself. Still, she couldn't deny the relief at having her suspicions validated.

Prince Kamal leaned back and ran a hand through his dark waves. "Perhaps I'm too superstitious," he said. "I don't have much experience with insane women. You probably don't either."

"You'd be surprised," Terry replied. "High school is full of them."

His features slackened and his mouth dropped open. Terry laughed at his shocked expression. The unexpected moment broke the ominous spell that had settled over their little table. They ate with gusto for the rest of the meal.

The waiter continued to replace their empty platters with lamb kebab, basmati rice, beef shawarma and more delicacies. Terry was stuffed by the time the baklava was served for dessert. Still, she managed to eat every last bite of the honey-soaked phyllo pastry.

Prince Kamal smoothed a hand down his black T-shirt, patting his flat stomach. "Sometimes wearing loose clothing has its advantages. You can eat as much as you want and never worry about looking fat when you get up from the table."

Terry thought of the pictures Maude had found of him on the Internet, overweight and hiding behind sunglasses and long robes. "I bet you're really pleased with how you look now," she said.

His expression faltered. "Pleased? Well, yes, I suppose so."

Terry worried she'd said the wrong thing. Maybe he was sensitive about his overweight teenage years. And how would she explain that she and Maude had looked him up on the Internet? She cringed inside, wishing she had one small bit of social grace. They stood and made their way to the door.

His forehead crinkled with worry. "I hope you don't consider my casual style a reflection on the importance of your company."

The prince's thoughtful articulation left Terry feeling stumped for an appropriately fancy response.

He offered his arm, which she took without hesitating. "Actually," she started, "why did you dress in jeans today? I was under the impression you had to keep it regal."

He gave her a half grin as the maître d held open the front door for them. The bodyguard was waiting by the limo, now bathed in the orange glow of the street light.

"I couldn't very well enter your high school in my royal robes. My father would disapprove. I have to keep a low profile," he told her. "And the best way to stay hidden is to not stand out. If I look like I belong, no one notices."

Terry silently mulled this over. She used her code to stay hidden by being invisible. It was comforting to find they had something in common. "Yeah," she said. "That makes sense."

When they reached the top floor of the Plaza, he escorted Terry to her suite. He leaned against the door frame like it was the most natural pose for him. She'd never seen him so casual and relaxed. *This must be the real Prince Kamal, not the formal delegate I first met in the basement of the museum.*

"Thank you for joining me tonight, Nefertari." His accent made her name sound exotic, much nicer than when Ms. Bernard did attendance. He made no motion to leave. "I hope your knee isn't too sore?" he asked. "I couldn't help but notice your limp was more pronounced this evening."

Terry shoved her hands in her hoodie's pockets. "It's worse when I'm tired," she said. Then because she sensed a connection with him, she confided, "I hate how everyone can see my weakness."

Prince Kamal pushed himself off the wall and gave Terry a serious look. "It is the weight of her burden that makes a woman truly strong." Then he stepped back and slightly bowed.

Terry stayed quiet and watched him make his way down the hallway where a security guard stood by his door. "Thank you," she whispered.

Chapter Twenty-Four

Terry gingerly stepped out of the bubble bath, supporting herself by holding onto the counter, making sure to keep her back to the mirror. The water always made the scars on her leg purple and bulging, like long worms just under the skin. She caught a glimpse of the small bruise on her right upper arm from Dr. Mullaca's fierce grip.

She fastened her brace, then wrapped herself in the hotel's plush bathrobe. Through the doorway Terry glanced at the massive bed, now covered in Fraser's photocopies.

The sketch she'd found in her locker was unfolded and leaning against the lamp on the bedside table. She had stared at it so many times, wishing it really was her mom that her eyes had memorized with every stroke of the pen. It was comforting to look at before she went to sleep — a small part of Terry liked to think her mom was watching over her.

Terry approached the bed carefully, trying to trick her subconscious. Once, during an impromptu archaeology lesson, Her dad had told her, "Even though you're not working on a problem, parts of your brain are still putting the pieces together without you being aware. That's why a solution that's evaded you for a long time will become clear as if out of the blue."

Terry scanned the articles, laid out in order on the bed, hoping the solution would pop out at her unexpectedly. She lifted one and read it through, but only the same things stood out: missing asp, missing girl, no clues. She squinted at the neat columns, making the letters blur — there must be a clue in all those sentences. Maybe she needed to think the way Dr. Mullaca or her dad would interpret hieroglyphics.

"Oh, crap!" Terry had completely forgotten about her cell phone. She grabbed it out of her backpack and plugged it into the charger, waiting until it blinked back to life. There were several messages from Maude, asking where she was. The last one had enough exclamation marks to fill two lines.

Terry texted back.

Battery was dead. All okay. PK took me to dinner. I ordered a Big Mac with large fries.

While she waited for Maude to reply, Terry scrolled through her screen and found the last text her dad had sent.

Enjoy the bball game with yer bestie. Hunch about the key ;) Wish me luck!!

Since when did her dad use slang?

Something was off, but she couldn't narrow her suspicion to anything tangible. The message had been sent just before she and Maude went to the basketball game. Maybe he was so preoccupied with finding the asp he didn't have time to text the whole word like he usually did, she reasoned. It had been several hours after that when Sarah had come to the gym with the police.

Terry rested on the corner of the bed, the photocopies crinkling under her weight. She pictured him bent over the coffin with a magnifying glass. But if her dad had discovered something important, why was he found in the Egypt room? Why wasn't he down in the basement in the examining area? Terry closed her eyes and pinched the bridge of her nose.

Her phone buzzed. There was a new text from Maude.

Big mac? Where RU now, his suite?

Terry replied.

No.

Then she smiled and typed another quick message.

He told me I was a strong woman & then left.

Terry's phone rang five seconds later. Maude was in mid-sentence by the time Terry answered. "— kiss you? Terry, holy shit! He called you a strong woman! Does this mean you get to live in a palace? I knew it! I could tell by how he was looking at you in the limo!"

Maude's voice punctuated the air. Terry could actually see the exclamation points when she spoke. She let Maude continue until she was breathless.

"Um … sorry to burst your *Pretty Woman* bubble," Terry said when there was a break, "but Prince Kamal is too sophisticated for me. And I'm definitely not interested in him *that* way." She pictured Zach's tall frame, his finger lightly touching his eyebrow. She shook her head, trying to focus. "It wasn't romantic, we mostly talked about the asp, but I did get to learn a little about him. At least I trust him more than Dr. Mullaca."

Maude considered this, then said, "Too bad. I was hoping he'd show up at school again in his limo. Then you guys could have a makeout session in front of Allison and her bitch squad."

Terry snorted at the image. "Why not you?" she asked. "A blonde with a pink stripe would be a hot ticket in Egypt."

"Oh please," she said. "I'm so pathetic I can't even cheat on a guy who doesn't know I exist." Maude's tone was light, but Terry could hear the heartbreak behind it.

"Maybe Fraser needs to feel jealous? Then he'll realize what a catch you are."

"You know nothing about guys. They don't get jealous, they move on to the next girl."

"Time for a new guy then," Terry encouraged.

"Sure." Maude's tone was defensive. "Because every guy in school is dying to go out with white trash."

"You're not trash!" Terry's eyes fell on the closest newspaper article. The black and white picture of the missing girl stared back up at her. Plain shirt, sad face, no hope. It was a stark contrast to her friend. "You're the only thing you can be," Terry told her. "You're a Maudern girl."

It was quiet, then Maude chuckled at the other end. "That's a lazy answer," she said. "At least be more *original*."

"I'll leave the T-shirt slogans up to you."

"I made a new one for tomorrow," she confessed.

The conversation flowed easily from that point for the next half hour. After they both yawned goodnight and hung up, Terry leaned back in bed, not caring that she was lying on the photocopies. She hoped the power of osmosis would allow the information to sink through while she slept, then she'd wake with the answer to the missing asp. Probably not, though. *Damn.*

She looked at her cell phone again, concerned Dr. Mullaca hadn't bothered to call her today. An angry swell began to grow inside Terry's chest. Dr. Mullaca had scared her with a groundless warning about Prince Kamal and given her an order to find the missing asp. What right did she have to drop all this into her lap?

Terry made a plan to skip school tomorrow and head straight to the museum to confront Dr. Mullaca. She began to mentally prepare all her questions.

1. What exactly did she and her father discover about the coffin the day he collapsed?

2. How much does Mayor Harris know and why?

3. Why does she think the curse is responsible for her father being in the hospital?

Terry limped around the bedroom suite, building up her fury. She considered calling Prince Kamal for support. Her cell phone rang. The caller ID was unknown.

She envisioned the nice nurse at the hospital calling with bad news. "Hello?" Terry's hands shook so badly she almost dropped the phone.

There was only silence, then she heard his voice. "Terry?"

"Zach?"

Chapter Twenty-Five

"Hey," Zach said. "I tried you earlier, but your phone was off."

"I ... uh, thought you were someone else," Terry said shakily.

"Are you okay?" he asked.

'Okay' was the last word Terry would use to describe her current status. She had to switch gears from crazy Egyptologist to hot guy with crazy girlfriend. Terry tried to picture an Egyptian sunset, concentrating on the three colors. That image always calmed her down. "I'm okay," she said, not wanting to complicate things further. She was sick of complications.

"You sounded a little—" He changed his mind mid-sentence. "I mean, is it a good time to talk? I can call later."

The clock radio on the side table read ten thirty. Terry felt like it was past midnight. "No, I can talk." She left the bedroom and walked into the sitting area. The floor-to-ceiling windows boasted a spectacular view of Devonshire's nightscape. Beyond the city's expansive park, the business towers of downtown stretched up to the stars, creating thin columns of light along the horizon. If she weren't alone and afraid, the view would have been inspiring. "What's up?" she asked.

"I just wanted to let you know your idea worked."

"What idea?"

"The eyebrow trick," he said. "I did it in practice this afternoon before every free throw, and I made every one." His tone was even, but there was an underlying excitement.

She imagined him standing at the line with everyone in the crowd watching him. Then smoothly, deliberately, he'd touch the edge of his eyebrow — just like she'd told him. "Of course," she said. "I'm a basketball genius."

He laughed. "It freaked the guys out a bit, but it worked." Then he repeated more softly. "Every time."

Terry smiled against her phone, his words vibrating against her ear, tickling the skin there. "Every *single* time?" she teased.

"Coach made a big deal about it. He even made up a new game plan for me to get fouled as much as possible."

"Is that good?" she worried. "That seems like a lot of pressure to dump on your shoulders. What about the other players?"

There was the dim background noise of a television. "I'm used to pressure," he said. There was a rustle, and the sound grew quiet. "Sorry, I was just watching a movie."

"Oh," Terry imagined Zach watching a sportscast or something. "Is it about basketball?"

"Seriously? Is that all you think I'm interested in? Have you already forgotten about my piano concerto talents?" There was a playful flirt to his voice.

"So the movie is about piano players?" she teased.

"Of course not, it's about football."

Terry limped closer to the window, her knee brace creaking. She'd forgotten to take her anti-inflammatories after dinner. Now it would be another hour before the pain would subside. "Zach," she sighed. "You're such a..." Terry paused, wishing she could tell him what she was feeling, but her head was so messed up tonight.

"I'm such a what?" he prompted, his voice gentle.

A frustrating enigma. Terry stood in front of the window, her reflection staring back at her. She combed her long bangs to the side with her fingers, thinking about what Prince Kamal had said about carrying a burden.

She took a deep breath, then quickly said, "Did you put that sketch in my locker?"

Terry knew she was going out on a limb. She had no proof. He could have been drawing stick figures with boobs on his notepad for all she knew.

His silence on the other end was unnerving. There was a muffled sound, like he was holding the phone to his chest, gathering his thoughts. He let out a heavy sigh. She wished she'd stayed quiet about the art. Maude was right; she was clueless about guys.

"Um, yeah," he finally said.

"Why didn't you say so? You're amazingly talented. Who cares about getting a scholarship for basketball … you should be an art major!" She laughed at the end, realizing she'd been gushing. "I mean you can do both. Get a scholarship for sports and still take art classes."

"It's complicated," Zach mumbled. "Everything is set up for me to play basketball in college — not draw pictures. And my dad doesn't want anything to distract me from that … basketball, I mean."

"You do more than just *draw pictures*." Terry mimicked his phrase. "Art makes people feel things."

"So does making the winning shot in the last three seconds."

Terry pictured the school gym full of screaming fans, but she also remembered how his portrait of her gave her hope. Even with everything that she'd been through this last few days, his picture still evoked a sense that it was all going to be okay. "I'm not saying you should give up basketball," she admitted. "But you can't turn your back on this talent either. I'm sure there's room in your future for both."

There was another long gap of silence on his end. "I think," he started carefully, "that you can only have one title, you know? What if I'm not good enough to do both? Right now I'm the guy who always sinks the last shot. I can't be anything else — it's too risky."

"Because of the scholarship?"

"No," he said. "The kids at school have a short memory. When I first started Roosevelt High, I was the tall geek who couldn't even get a seat with the chess club at lunch. Then one day in gym, someone put a basketball in my hands."

Terry heard him shuffling his feet. She imagined him pacing in his room. "It was so natural for me," he said. "So easy ... unlike other stuff."

She remembered him squinting in the library, taking time to read Maude's candy hearts. She suspected what he meant by 'other stuff.' There was a simple reason Zach never had a book and always doodled on his notepad. He wasn't lazy or content to let other, smarter kids do the class projects — he couldn't read.

"Other stuff," she repeated. They were venturing into unknown territory now. Having Zach confess he was a kickass artist was one thing, but telling her his greatest secret was another. Terry couldn't ignore the fact he'd switched their conversation to ultra-deep mode. It was as if he wanted her to figure it out so he wouldn't have to say it out loud.

"You can't risk being anything other than the school hero," Terry said tentatively. She leaned against the glass window, the coolness good on her forehead.

"The court is the only place I feel like I'm somebody. Everywhere else, I feel like a loser in a thin disguise. I'm convinced someone will stand up and say, 'Hey that's the nerd from last year.'" He tried to laugh at the end, but the weariness in his voice was unmistakable.

"Would that be so terrible?" she asked point blank.

They shared a few breaths over the phone.

"No," he said. "It was easy flying under the radar. Less expectations meant less pressure. But now..."

Terry wasn't sure what to say next. The evening had a weird vibe that wouldn't go away, but she didn't want to end the conversation either. She racked her brain to come up with something halfway intelligent, something supportive. She wished Maude was here. She'd know exactly what to say; she was a natural cheerleader.

An image of Allison with her friends and their pom-poms sent a shiver down her back. While Zach was perfecting his free throw, his girlfriend was cornering Maude and Terry in the hallway. Why wasn't he on the phone with her? Terry wanted to ask. Why wasn't he quizzing *her* about his 'other stuff.'

Finally Zach said, "I believe this is the part of the conversation where I say something witty that makes you laugh and forget all the complaining I just did. Terry?"

Terry turned away from her reflection and eased into one of the plush chairs. "Sorry, just tired," she said. "My head's all over the place tonight."

"Oh man." He groaned. "I'm such an idiot. Is your dad all right?"

"He's the same, but at least he's stable."

"Can I do anything to help?"

"I doubt it," she said. If he couldn't stop his girlfriend from threatening Terry, he certainly couldn't help her find the missing asp.

There was a pause. "What else is wrong?" he asked.

She put a hand over her forehead and closed her eyes. The pressure was immense, and tears filled her lower lids. "Nothing. Everything. I'm trying to solve a fifty-year-old case, get in touch with a crazy archaeologist, break a curse to keep my dad alive, and keep your girlfriend from…" Terry stopped to take a breath. She didn't know how to finish the sentence. Allison hadn't laid a finger on her. It would sound stupid to say, *your mean girlfriend got her friend to spill milk on me.* "Sorry," she sniffed, "but my life truly sucks right now." She used the tie from her bathrobe to blot her eyes.

"Ex-girlfriend," he replied. "I broke up with Allison."

"Oh." Terry was completely flummoxed. She waited to see if he'd elaborate.

142

There was more silence, then, "You're working on a fifty-year-old case?" he asked. "Does this have anything to do with Fraser's newspaper articles?"

"Um, yeah," Terry answered. Her mind was still reeling from his bombshell about Allison.

"I could come over and help you."

"But it's dark out." Terry's pulse picked up. "And there's a bodyguard outside my door ... and you're a boy." Her gaze flicked to the door, half expecting it to open.

"I'll disguise myself in a rolled-up carpet." Terry could hear the smile in his voice.

"I don't think so."

"Room service?"

"No." She fought to keep her voice steady. She couldn't believe they were actually discussing him coming over. She was in her bathrobe, for crying out loud. How far away was he anyway? Ten, fifteen, twenty minutes? Zach could potentially be standing in her hotel suite. All she had to do was say yes. Damn. Hot damn.

"Candygram?"

"Zach!"

"Yes?"

"Goodnight." She smiled into the phone.

"Goodnight."

She waited. "Zach, hang up."

"You hang up first."

"Why me?"

"Because."

"Oh my god." She tried to sound frustrated. "This is ridiculous. On the count of three we'll hang up together. One, two—"

"That never works," he said. "One person will always fake the other one out. Someone has to hang up first. Or ... we could go with my original candygram idea."

"Goodnight, Zach."

"Good—"

Terry hung up, cutting him off. She pressed the phone to her chest and smiled. Ten seconds later it buzzed with a text from Zach.

Nite. Don't u dare tmb!! Im vbzy wtching mve bout peano plying fb plyers.

Terry smiled in her darkened hotel suite. At least he could text … sort of. It was kind of charming that she could decipher what he meant.

She pushed herself off the chair and went back into the bedroom. Her knee was throbbing, but Zach swooped in and out of her imagination, providing a pleasant distraction.

She gathered the papers off the cushy duvet. *He's just like me. He knows how it feels to be the outsider.* "But now that he's in," she said out loud, "I think he wishes he was invisible again."

Terry froze, and the pure logic of it stunned her for a moment. It was just like her dad said; sometimes the answer came from out of the blue. Everything came together and it all pointed to one answer. The asp wasn't stolen, it was hidden in the museum— right under everyone's noses. Or rather, just above their heads.

She riffled through the papers again, double-checking her theory.

"Holy crap!" she said to the empty room. She dropped the phone, but the second time she managed to complete the call.

Maude's sleepy voice answered after three rings. "Terry?"

"I know where it is! I know where the asp is hidden!"

Chapter Twenty-Six

"I feel like everyone knows." Maude clutched the binder to her chest. Her backpack bulged with supplies for the afternoon. "They're staring more than usual."

"It's your tight T-shirt," Terry teased. "Didn't you notice the big smile the limo driver gave you this morning?"

Maude gripped her binder tighter. "I forgot to try it on before I ironed on the letters. Besides," she huffed, "I didn't have time to put anything else on this morning. I was hauling my butt out of bed when Grandma told me you were waiting in the limo out front."

"Sorry." Terry yawned. "It's my fault. I kept you on the phone until two this morning."

"And," Maude added, dropping her voice, "I had to pack provisions for our you-know-what." A package of red Twizzlers stuck out of the top of her backpack.

Terry glanced at the kids milling in the hallway. Whenever she caught an eye, the person quickly looked away. Maybe Maude was right, maybe their secret plan was written all over their faces. She quickened her shuffle, wanting to escape the weight of their stares.

An uneasy tingle traveled down her spine. A cheerleader and her boyfriend dropped their heads and began to whisper. Terry thought she heard Zach's name.

"I think I'm going to pee my pants. Why do we have to wait until after school?" Maude asked for the tenth time in less than an hour. "Can't we skip class and go straight to the museum?"

Terry didn't answer, distracted by the basketball banner being strung up across the hallway. A lump sifted down her throat, resting in the bottom of her gut. There had been no sign of Zach this morning.

She and Maude continued to drift in a semi-paranoid state down the rest of the hallway and finally into history class. Ms. Bernard's usual blanched complexion was rosy. Terry glanced toward the back. Zach's teammates were roughhousing. One looked up at Terry, and the smile dropped from his face.

"A quick reminder," Ms. Bernard started, while students were still coming in, "that we're going to the museum tomorrow. You'll all need your permission slips brought in or you'll be spending the afternoon in study hall." She motioned to Terry. "Don't worry about the parental consent form, dear," she said. "I was at the museum yesterday finalizing the trip, and Ms. Mathers signed on your behalf." Her eyes squinted behind her glasses. "Sarah is certainly a devoted godmother."

Maude flinched when Ms. Bernard mentioned the museum. Terry immediately felt guilty. She should be doing this on her own. She leaned over and nudged her friend. "Hey," Terry whispered, "let's forget about this afternoon."

Ms. Bernard looked down her pointy nose at the back row. "I must emphasize that this particular field trip is a special honor, and I expect you to behave accordingly. No hijinks will be tolerated."

Allison came into class with a large manila envelope tucked under her arm. She sniffed and handed Ms. Bernard the package. There were a few whispers between them, then Allison took her seat. Terry had barely enough time to register Allison's red-rimmed eyes before Zach came in.

He glided past Terry and Maude and plunked down in a seat

in the back with the other jocks. His snub felt like a slap. Terry replayed their phone conversation. He'd flirted with her, said he'd broken up with his girlfriend, but he hadn't actually said he liked her. An embarrassed blush crept up her neck. She wished she hadn't pinned her hair back today. All she wanted to do was hide.

Ms. Bernard gasped. "Now this," she said, holding out the contents of Allison's envelope, "is what I call an A-plus."

Terry's mouth dropped open.

"The bar has been raised, class," Ms. Bernard stated, holding a colorful pamphlet aloft. "Cleopatra's life and accomplishments as a beauty and fashion entrepreneur." She practically beamed at Allison. "Such originality!"

Terry and Maude exchanged shocked looks. They looked at the back row of jocks. Zach's pale face and expression said it all.

After class, Terry bolted for the door with Maude in tow.

"I can't believe he blabbed our idea to that bitch!" Maude was almost in tears. She rooted through her backpack and withdrew a plastic-covered folder. "Look! I already spent the money on the glossy paper."

Terry's heart broke a little. Maude's beauty magazine article was really slick. "We can still pass it in?" she said.

"We'll get a failing grade from copying Ms. Perfect!" She huffed and shoved the folder under her arm.

Zach caught up to them. "I had no idea—"

"No idea that your ex-girlfriend was going to take away our A-plus?" Maude interrupted. "Do you have any clue how much time I put into this thing?" She pushed the fake magazine at his face. "Now it's worthless. But I guess a superstar jock doesn't care about grades." Maude stormed down the hall, taking her anger to calculus class.

"She doesn't know about the scholarship," Terry murmured.

Zach brushed against Terry's arm. "I might have mentioned something offhand," he started. "You know how important that history mark is to me. I have to make it to the State Championships. I would never do anything to mess that up."

"I know." Terry wished her voice didn't sound so far away, so weak. "But why didn't you sit with us in class?"

"Allison was really upset. I thought I was doing you a favor by staying away." He squeezed her shoulder. She looked up and met his gaze. A million bubbles burst inside her chest.

His voice became soft. "Can we meet after lunch?" he asked. "I have to practice in the gym, but I want to see you after. Um, the library maybe?"

The library. Where people made out in between classes.

"Okay," Terry said. He gave her a smile and squeezed her shoulder again. She limped to English class, not even feeling the floor beneath her feet.

By the time she met up with Maude for lunch, she'd come up with a plan to save their project and make sure Zach got to the State Championships.

"Are you crazy?" Maude screeched. Her outburst earned them a few curious glances in the lunch line. They inched forward.

Terry explained. "The coffin angle is too good not to use. As far as Ms. Bernard is concerned, it's all speculation on my part." She waited for Maude to come around. Terry had the last hour in English to rationalize breaking her promise to her dad about Cleopatra's remains. "Come on, won't it be great to upstage Allison with the scoop of the year?"

"That sounds newsworthy." Fraser's appeared behind Maude. He grinned behind his tortoiseshell glasses. Terry saw he was going for the sloppy chic look today. His blue T-shirt peeked from behind a plaid shirt, which was covered with a tweed vest.

"Go away," Maude ordered. "We're talking about my unicorn article." She was taking on every boy in the world today.

"No, you were talking about the coffin," he playfully insisted. "As in the mysterious one in the museum."

"Hardly." Maude rolled her eyes. "It would be unscrupulous to put top secret international government information in a class project." She gave Terry a pointed stare. "Wouldn't it?"

"Neffie!" he teased. "You broke our deal. I gave you information with the promise you'd do the same for me. I'm brokenhearted, but since I'm an understanding soul, I'll give you and Unicorn Girl a second chance."

"How noble of you," Maude scoffed.

"My pleasure," he said. "'Top secret government information' is my favourite phrase."

They walked a few more steps together, pushing trays along. Terry filled up a large cup with a frothy milkshake. Maude put her attention back on Terry. "It's cheating," she said.

"So?" Terry reasoned. "Allison stole your awesome idea. Same thing."

Fraser made a quick noise at the back of his throat.

"Excuse me?" Allison's voice sliced through the air. She appeared in front of Terry, eyes full of fury. "If anyone is stealing anything it's you, slut."

Every head turned toward Terry. "I don't know what you're talking about," she said.

"I guess that makes you a liar *and* a slut." Allison reached forward and calmly took Terry's milkshake. The whole cafeteria was silent. Terry knew what was coming next. She stood there and watched as Allison poured the thick, freezing milkshake over her head. Even when it was dripping down the back of her neck, Terry stood there, unable to move.

Allison started to cry. The princesses quickly whisked her away before a teacher took notice. The lunch ladies froze in their hair nets, unsure what they'd just witnessed. Only when Maude's voice broke through did Terry come alive again. She reached up and dabbed her eyes. Everything was blurry.

Maude guided her out of the lunch line and away from the snickering students. One of the lunch monitors looked up from his phone and frowned at Terry's sodden appearance. "Get me out of here," she mumbled to Maude. "Please."

A few giggles permeated the tension, triggering the conversations to pick up again. The noise level returned as kids went back to their own lives. A fresh glob of milkshake rolled down Terry's back.

"Did I miss something?" Fraser asked, sounding confused.

"Yeah, chivalry lessons," Maude replied. "Here." She threw her backpack at him. "Make yourself useful." She took Terry by the arm and led her to the closest washroom while Fraser followed behind.

Maude placed her in front of one of the mirrors and turned on the water. Terry kept her gaze down, staring at the sink as it filled.

"Wow," Fraser said, crinkling his nose at the pile of paper towels bursting from the garbage can. "I assumed the girls' washroom would be cleaner, but you're pigs."

Maude snorted. "That's because guys never wash their hands so they never have to dry them."

"As a matter of fact, I always wash my hands. Ask Terry." Then his eyes trailed down and read Maude's tight T-shirt. "Priceless Com*maude*ity? It's punchy," he said. "I like it."

"Shut up," Maude replied. "And stop looking at my chest."

"How am I supposed to read your T-shirt, then?" he asked, completely serious.

Terry hadn't said a word since the milkshake shower. She pulled her soaked sweatshirt over her head, smearing her face with cool goo. "I'm sick of this." Her hair was plastered down on one side, still dripping. She didn't even care that she was only in her bra.

Maude and Fraser grew quiet.

"I'm sick of being weak," Terry confessed to the mirror. "I let her pour it over me, like it was okay for her to do that to me … like I deserved it."

"You're not weak," Maude said. "You're smart." She stood behind Terry's shoulder. Their eyes met in the mirror. "If you had stood up to her, you'd be dead."

"Dead might be an overstatement," Fraser said. He put down Maude's backpack, then began to open her package of Twizzlers.

"Don't be fooled by Allison's tears," Maude told him. "That's a human emotion. I'm pretty sure the devil can't cry." Then she grabbed the licorice out of his hand. "And that's not for you."

Terry rinsed out her hair under the tap while Maude began to work on her sweatshirt. Fraser slipped off his vest and unbuttoned his shirt.

"Good thing I dress in layers," he said, handing Terry his shirt. She put it on, rolling up the sleeves to her elbows. Her long hair hung in wet strands around her shoulders. Maude rummaged through her bag and pulled out some bobby pins and a hair elastic. She held them out, but Terry only blankly stared at them.

Wordlessly, Maude worked on Terry's hair, pulling the longer pieces into a braid, securing the shorter strands with the bobby pins. When she was finished Terry looked in the mirror and lightly patted the pretty hairdo. "Thanks," she whispered.

"Don't be silly. You were in no shape to do your own hair."

Terry cleared her throat. "At least I look better for our trip to the museum this afternoon."

Fraser leaned against a stall. "The class trip is tomorrow," he said. "Unless you two ladies have a private tour planned. Does the principal know about this?"

"Oh god," Maude moaned. "Can you just leave?"

He looked pleadingly at Terry. "I gave you the shirt off my back," he started. "Can't you tell me about the mysterious coffin? Does it have anything to do with the articles I gave you?"

Someone began to push the door open. Fraser moved in a flash, blocking the entrance. "Sorry, toilet overflowed," he said. "Come back later." Then he shut the door and turned the lock. He looked at Terry and Maude and held his hands out by his sides. "I don't know what's going on, but you guys need me."

Maude snorted.

"Or at least my connection to the newspaper. I'm a wealth of information. If you tell me what's going on, I can probably help."

Terry let out a tired breath.

"Neffie," he pleaded. "You still owe me that scoop, remember?"

She shared a look with Maude, who gave her an affirming nod.

"What I'm about to tell you has to stay a secret between us," Terry said. "You can't share this with anyone."

"Even your brother who works at the paper," Maude added.

"Especially him," Terry said.

"Absolutely," Fraser said, placing a hand over his heart. "On my honor as a reporter."

Then Terry and Maude took turns letting him know everything they'd discovered, including where the asp was hidden.

Fraser listened without asking questions until they reached the end. He leaned against the wall and rubbed his bottom lip with his thumb.

"And you think it's still in the museum?"

"It's in the Egypt room," Terry said. "I'm sure of it. When Maude was reading the articles about the robbery, she said there must be a logical explanation. Something can't be stolen if it's impossible to steal. I figured it wasn't taken, just hidden."

"For fifty years?" The skepticism in his voice was obvious.

"I haven't figured that part out yet," Terry said.

"Who cares?" Maude interjected. She wrung out the wet sweatshirt and flicked it a few times. "The important thing is that Terry figured out where the asp is hidden."

"At least where I think it is." She turned to Fraser. "When I was having dinner with Prince Kamal—"

Fraser's jaw dropped. "Dinner with an Egyptian Prince? You had all this stuff happening and you never said anything to me?"

"They're only friends," Maude said importantly. "Nothing romantic happened ... I already asked." Then waved for Terry to continue.

"That evening, Prince Kamal told me the best way to stay hidden is to blend in." Terry began to pace the floor. "Then I thought about my dad and how he had a hunch about the key. They found him collapsed in the Egypt room. The first time my dad took me through that part of the museum, I was freaked out by the old Cleopatra mannequin. And then I remembered the asp on her arm. It was gaudy and painted with thick gold paint. I never would have mistaken it for an actual artifact."

"Perfectly disguised in plain sight," Fraser said, his tone fascinated. He ran a hand through his hair. "Okay, so what's the plan? Obviously we need to go the museum."

"Whoa." Maude held up her hands. "That plan has already been arranged. It's just me and Terry."

Fraser walked up to her. "Scooby-Doo and the gang wouldn't have solved all those mysteries if it were only Velma and Daphne, right?"

"We've already solved it," Maude told him, crossing her arms in front of her T-shirt.

He leaned closer. "I really liked your unicorn article."

"Of course. Anyone would."

"Having an extra guy as a backup while you lovely ladies snoop around the museum would be an asset." He put a hand to his vest and pledged to Maude. "Think of me as your Fred. Plus I have a car. We could leave right now."

Maude glanced at Terry questioningly. Terry pictured Allison pouring the milkshake over her head. The burn of humiliation blazed across her face. She was most embarrassed about believing Zach could keep Allison from bothering her. She couldn't depend on him; she needed to save herself. She needed to save her dad, and she needed to get the hell out of this school.

What would Cleopatra do? She squared her shoulders in the mirror. "I'm ready," she said. "Let's go."

Chapter Twenty-Seven

Riding in the back seat of Fraser's dented hatchback was like sitting inside a mailbox. Piles of papers were stacked like archaeological layers of homework, the earliest at the bottom with the most recent on top. Terry checked out his profile from the back seat, and wondered how someone so disorganized could run a newspaper.

He caught her eye in the rearview mirror. "Let's review the plan," he said, an energy to his tone. He changed lanes quickly and a car blared its horn behind them.

"Can we get there in one piece?" Maude asked, tightening her grip on the door handle. Her voice quivered. "The plan won't matter if we're dead." She was up front with Fraser, something Terry knew terrified and thrilled her at the same time.

He frowned at Maude. "I find your lack of faith in my driving skills troubling."

She pointed to the windshield and said, "Stop looking at me and watch where we're going."

Fraser faced forward, but the frown remained. "I happen to have an IQ of one twenty-nine, you know."

"Is that good?" Terry asked from the backseat.

"Only borderline genius," he said. "I excel at reading, mostly." He snuck a peek at Maude.

She muttered something about priceless commodities and tightened her coat across her chest.

"The plan," Terry started, trying to change the focus, "is that we go to the Egypt room and take the asp off the mannequin."

Fraser snorted from the front seat. "No snags there."

"It doesn't have to be complicated," Terry said. "We'll walk in like we're supposed to be there, and no one will notice us." She leaned forward, putting her head between their front seats. "If we look like we belong, we'll stay hidden."

"I think we should have a code word," Maude suggested. She released her grip on the door handle and began to unwrap a Tootsie Pop. "You know, like if something goes wrong and we all need to run like crazy."

"How about, ABORT!" Fraser joked.

Maude ignored his comment. "Let's go with Twizzlers. No one is suspicious of Twizzlers." She nodded, satisfied with her idea. "All the good burglars have code words."

"We're not burglars." Terry sighed. "I'm not stealing the asp. All I have to do is take it to the basement where the sarcophagus is kept."

Fraser gripped the wheel. "This is epic. Can I be there when it's opened?"

"Easy, your glasses are fogging up," Maude taunted.

"It's the anticipation," he explained.

Maude turned around back to face Terry. "Can't we ask Dr. Mullaca to help?" The nervousness in her question came through clearly.

"As soon as we get the asp, I'm handing it over to her," Terry said. "I don't trust myself to unlock the coffin without her. I could mess it up — I'll only have one chance. It's weird, though, if she was so anxious about me finding the asp, why hasn't she called me again?"

Fraser hit the brakes, and Maude's sucker went flying out of her hand. The seatbelt tightened against Terry's chest as Fraser handled the gearshift quickly, putting it in reverse.

"Watch this," he said. With one arm over Maude's headrest, he twisted his body toward the back. After a few maneuvers he stopped the car. "Fred from *Scooby-Doo* delivered, girls," he boasted.

"Congratulations," Maude said. "You parallel parked. Your medal is in the mail."

"You fail to see the genius of my ways. It's also a prime spot in front of the museum." Fraser unbuckled his belt, looking proud. "In case we need a quick getaway." Then he added, "You're welcome."

Terry entered the museum with Fraser and Maude following close behind. Despite her insistence that nothing would go wrong, her heart was racing. She approached one of the familiar staff at the ticket booth. Luckily it was one of the museum workers who recognized Terry as well.

She smiled back at her automatically, then her expression changed to concern. "Terry," she said, cautiously, "how's your dad? Everybody here is praying for his quick recovery."

"Thanks," Terry said. "He's the same." Then she added, "But the doctors are really nice, and he looks well cared for."

The clerk nodded thoughtfully. Her gaze slipped past Terry, taking in Fraser and Maude.

Terry's palms began to sweat. "These are my friends from school. I just have to get something from my dad's office. Can they come up with me?"

The clerk played with the brass-colored button on her vest, unsure.

"I don't want to go up alone." Terry lowered her voice and explained, "I need a family keepsake. The doctor mentioned that surrounding my dad's hospital bed with familiar things might help him." She stayed quiet. She thought she heard Maude whisper, "Twizzlers."

But the alarm was unnecessary; the girl waved them through. "Sure, go ahead. If anyone asks, tell them I let you in."

Terry thanked her in a way she hoped wasn't too exuberant, then took Fraser and Maude to the elevator.

"Terry?" Maude said hesitantly. "*Do* you want to go to your dad's office? It might make you feel better. Fraser and I can wait outside for you."

Terry stared at the elevator, watching the numbers light up. It would be a relief to sit in her dad's chair and pretend she was waiting for him to walk through the door, but she didn't have time to indulge in such self-pity. The best thing she could do for her dad was to get the asp.

"No," she finally replied. "I want my real dad back, not memories."

With that resolute declaration, all three stood a bit straighter. They marched out of the elevator and down the hallway that edged the open expanse. Terry peeked over the railing. The rotunda was a dizzying five floors down.

When they turned the corner, Maude groaned. The door to the Egypt room was completely blocked off. A huge tarp covered whatever the new archway would be. The glass doors had been blackened out as well.

"What if I give you a boost over?" Fraser suggested to Terry. Then he frowned and said, "You might hit the glass, though."

Maude looked pained. "We'll have to wait until the exhibit opens."

Terry wanted to scream with frustration. "My dad might not have that long!"

A museum staff person came around the corner, making the trio freeze.

"I told you this wasn't the paleontology section," Fraser said to the girls. All three gave embarrassed shrugs to the staff person, then walked as slow as they dared to the elevator.

Terry stepped in and smashed the button.

"Easy, Neffie," Fraser said. "I think you're forgetting a vital piece of information. We're coming back here tomorrow for a field trip, remember?"

Maude started chewing a piece of gum she'd found in her coat pocket. "Are you serious? Steal the asp while Ms. Bernard is in the same room?"

"What else should we do?" he asked matter-of-factly. "Stand there and stare at the asp the whole time? This is our chance. I say we take it."

Maude frowned at him. "But you're not in our history class."

"I can tell them I'm covering the field trip for the school newspaper."

"Why not Tanya?" Maude was suspicious.

"Wow," Fraser mocked, "you've got a question for everything I say. That's so fascinating."

"Why would I care about what fascinates you?"

"There you go again," he pointed out.

"Shut up, you two." Terry leaned against the wall and closed her eyes. Her knee felt like it was ready to burst. Her phone buzzed with a text from Zach.

Wating 4U in liebary. Smthin big 2 shw u.

Terry ignored the text. He'd have to wait for her in the makeout aisle the whole afternoon. Terry was finished being Allison's victim, but she wasn't keen on poking the hornet's nest. Staying away from Zach was probably the best thing for both of them. She looked at the text again. Something tweaked her memory. Her dad's last text had been uncharacteristically full of slang. It wasn't logical. If he was in such a hurry, why take the time to text her at all?

Terry hit the number two button.

"What are you doing?" Fraser asked.

The elevator stopped on the second floor. Terry stepped out and called over her shoulder, "I have to go to my dad's office to check something," she said. "I'll meet you guys in the lobby in a few minutes."

Maude became somber. "Oh, okay. Are you sure?"

"Do I need to have the getaway car ready?" Fraser called out.

Maude huffed and pulled him back as the elevator doors closed.

Terry limped by the mastodon display and made her way down the narrow hallway. The door to his office was closed. Terry tried the doorknob, but it wouldn't budge; his office was locked. Terry considered going down and asking the clerk if she had a key. Then she paused — Sarah's upset voice echoed down the hall. Terry made her way along the wall to the next open door. She spied through the crack, taking care to stay in the shadows.

"I didn't anticipate this much trouble." Sarah's voice shook. She rested an elbow on the desk, the phone tucked close to her ear. "Yes, I understand. Don't worry, he won't be a problem much longer."

Terry's chest grew tight.

Sarah rubbed the back of her neck. "No!" The word pierced the air. "I can't talk reason with him, Kamal." She grew quiet, then traced her finger down a framed picture on her desk.

Sarah pressed her lips together as her face turned red. A sob escaped. "I know." She cried. "But I can't … yes." There was another gap of silence as Sarah dried her tears, slowly nodding her head. "I understand," she finally said. "Yes, I'll wait for your call."

The conversation ended. Sarah closed her eyes and rested her face in her hands.

A surge of adrenaline pounded inside Terry's chest. Before she lost the nerve, she came around the door and walked right into Sarah's office.

"Terry!" Sarah's face drained of all its color. "What … what are you doing here?"

"I wanted to get into my dad's office, but it's locked."

Sarah's gaze narrowed. "Why do you want to get into his office?"

"I need to check his cell phone." Terry glanced around the room. Unlike her cluttered apartment, Sarah's office was painstakingly orderly and clean. Even the books on the shelves were organized by height.

"It's at the hospital," Sarah said, color slowly returning to her cheeks. "The emergency staff found it when the ambulance brought him in. The battery is dead, and I keep forgetting to pick it up."

"I heard you on the phone with Prince Kamal," Terry said.

Sarah opened and closed her mouth a few times. Her fingers flitted over the desk, then to the top button on her blouse.

Terry stayed quiet, knowing Sarah would have to fill in the silence.

There was a groan, then Sarah's posture deflated. "I suppose I have to tell you the truth. Prince Kamal and I were discussing Mayor Harris. He's been increasingly irritating about the sarcophagus." She clasped her hands and rested them on her lap. "My paramount concern is your father, of course, but the mayor has other priorities. Kamal and I were simply agreeing to go ahead with the party, let the mayor cut a ribbon and get his photo op, so we can concentrate on getting your dad better."

"Oh," Terry said quietly. It made sense, but there was something still bothering her about the whole scene. The palpable awkwardness in the room had dissipated, but not completely. She noticed how Sarah's hair was falling out of its bun. Her blouse looked wrinkled, too, and there were dark circles under her eyes. The very opposite of the polished women she met last week.

Sarah pushed herself out of the chair and made her way to Terry. "I wish I could make everything better for you," she said. "I meant to call, but I've been putting in extra hours here and then visiting the hospital."

"Um ... thanks for that." Terry could smell tuna sandwich on Sarah's breath. There was a small stain on the collar of her blouse.

She gently nudged Terry with her elbow. "You've got school to concentrate on. It's important for you to keep a normal schedule. Ms. Bernard told me you're one of the most attentive students in her class."

"That's nice," Terry said hollowly. A rock had lodged itself in her gut. For some reason, standing here exchanging pleasantries with Sarah felt foolish.

"It must be interesting having Ms. Bernard as a history teacher," Sarah probed. "She's one of the museum's most devoted volunteers. It's rumored she believes in reincarnation." Sarah snickered into the back her hand. The silliness of the gesture struck Terry as odd. "I think she wanders around here dreaming she's a famous historical figure." Sarah ended the insult with an eye roll.

Terry snuck a glance at the framed picture, an exact copy of the one her dad had on his desk — the image of Terry with her parents in Giza. She inched away from Sarah. "Huh, well I've got to go. My friends are waiting for me in the lobby."

"I'd love to meet your besties." Sarah beamed. "But I'm a complete mess. I'll be more put together tomorrow. I don't want to embarrass you." She gripped Terry's upper arms and leaned in close, her face somber. "Your mom and I were besties." Her voice dropped to a soft whisper. "You look so much like her."

"Thanks," Terry said. Sarah's fingers were poking the bruise on her upper right arm. The soreness reminded Terry of Dr. Mullaca. "Do you think I might be able to see the sarcophagus in the basement? I had a question for Dr. Mullaca."

Sarah let Terry go. A veiled smile replaced her sad expression. "You're out of luck; she's at the hospital visiting your dad. But I'm sure she'll be happy to see you tomorrow."

Happy was the last word Terry would use to describe Dr. Mullaca. Terry hobbled out of her dad's office, glad to be out of Sarah's embrace.

She found Maude and Fraser waiting by the Velociraptor skeletons in the main lobby.

Terry motioned for them to leave quickly. Once outside, she told them her about her conversation with Sarah.

"It sounds like she's a bit delusional," Fraser said. "Do you think she has thing for your dad?"

"Gross." Terry stumbled into the back seat of Fraser's car and slouched in the back seat. "I think she misses my mom, or at least their old friendship. It's like she talks to me as if we were the ones in school together."

"Interesting," Fraser said, starting the engine. "What did you want to check in your dad's office, anyway?"

Terry traced the seam on the upholstery. "I was hoping to find his cell phone. The last texts he sent were kind of weird, totally out of character. I wondered if someone else had his phone ... or something. I don't know." She hated sounding so hopeless. "I just thought it was worth checking out."

"Maybe it is," Fraser said. "Why don't we go back in and try and get into his office?"

"Apparently his cellphone is at the hospital," Terry explained. "He had it on him when he collapsed, so there goes my mystery text theory."

"Do you want to go to the hospital?" Maude asked her carefully. "Maybe you can catch Dr. Mullaca and see your dad at the same time?"

Terry absentmindedly reached up to tuck a strand of hair behind her ear. It was still stiff with dried milkshake. "No," she said. "I'll see her tomorrow." She knew her knee had pretty much had enough activity for the day. Her mind was shutting down too.

"You haven't eaten, either," Maude addressed. "Maybe you should come back to my house. Grandma keeps asking about you."

"Thanks, but I'm not good company right now."

"We could order at a drive-through," Fraser suggested. "I know a burger place that has really good milkshakes."

Maude glared at him then passed a handful of red Twizzlers to the backseat. Terry's phone rang. Zach had given up on texting and was calling this time. Terry ignored it, content to chew on the end of her licorice, trying to keep her head from exploding.

Fraser worked his car through the heavy traffic in silence. Half an hour later, they pulled up to the Plaza. Terry silently climbed out of the car.

Maude rolled down her window. "Are you sure you're okay to go up on your own?"

Fraser leaned across Maude, both their faces etched with concern as they stared at Terry, waiting for an answer. There was a stab of guilt. These people she barely knew were worried about her. Terry mustered up her best smile, then gave a quick wave and disappeared into the hotel before she started to cry.

Prince Kamal met her as soon as she stepped off the elevator. The brown crew neck sweater looked like cashmere. A gold chain was just visible above the collar. He took a step back. "Are you all right? You look like you've been crying."

Terry waved him off. "No." She quickly wiped away the last tear.

The private floor was buzzing with activity. "Nefertari," he said, all the usual polite formality replaced with anxiety. "My guards caught someone trying to break into your suite."

"What?" Terry had half a string of licorice dangling from her hand.

"I'm sorry to have to put you through this." He put a protective hand on her back and led her to one of the rooms. Various bodyguards and the hotel manager stood around the culprit, questioning him. "He insisted that you knew each other. Don't worry, the police are on their way."

Prince Kamal motioned to one of the bodyguards. They stepped aside, creating an opening.

Terry's backpack slid out of her grasp and hit the floor. "Zach?"

Chapter Twenty-Eight

Zach moved toward her, but the guards put a hand on his chest, warning him.

"You know this boy?" Prince Kamal asked her.

"Of course," she said. "He's in my class."

It took Terry several attempts to convince the hotel manager and Prince Kamal that Zach wasn't a threat. She led Zach to her suite, the questions piling up inside her head.

Prince Kamal pulled her aside. "I'm just down the hall," he told her, "and I'll have a guard outside your door."

His overprotective, brotherly concern made her smile. "I'm perfectly safe," she told him. Prince Kamal did his usual elegant head nod as a way of closing the conversation. Terry stepped back inside her room and quietly closed the door. Zach's expression flickered between discomfort and relief.

She leaned against the wall, using it to prop up her tired body. "Why did those guards think you were trying to break in?"

Zach put up his hands in a defensive gesture. "I wasn't trying to break in," he insisted. "I had to see you."

A warmth started to creep up her neck. Terry limped toward the living area. "Why didn't you just text me?"

"I did." He followed her a few steps then stopped. "And I called you too. But when you didn't reply, I got worried so I came over and waited outside your door." He stopped to gauge Terry's reaction.

"Seems kind of over the top," she said, trying to keep her voice firm, but her half grin betrayed her.

"Then the dudes in suits swarmed me," he said. "They made a big deal of how I'm not on a special list or something."

Terry dropped her backpack and eased herself onto the couch. "Prince Kamal runs a tight ship."

"Prince Kamal can kiss my—"

"Asp?" Terry gave a tired laugh at her own joke. "Oh god, I'm pathetic," she said. The momentum of the day was starting to catch up. Terry took a deep breath. "Listen, Zach, if you're so concerned for my safety, maybe you should talk to your ex-girlfriend." She didn't want him to see her as victim, but everything was wearing her down, and all she wanted was a hot pizza and a hot bath. "Sorry. Today has been … brutal. Thanks for checking on me, but the bodyguards are all the protection I need. You should probably go."

Zach's jaw tightened, but he stayed quiet. He turned toward the door, then stopped and faced her again. "Since I came all this way, I might as well give you these." He held out a small plastic shopping bag.

Terry looked inside. There were several packages of different types of pens; glitter pens, the kind that click, felt-tipped pens and even ones with erasable ink. "You're giving me pens?" she asked.

He gave her a shy shrug. "You never have a real one," he explained. "I borrowed yours the first day. I was going to replace it anyway, but I saw it was from a hotel." Zach cleared his throat, and his tone became softer. "I noticed the next one you used was from another hotel. So I thought … I guess I thought you might need some new ones."

Terry stared at the pile of pens. It seemed too intimate all of a sudden. He'd taken her pen that very first day. He'd noticed how lost she seemed.

He took a few steps closer, then hesitated. "When you didn't show up at the library," he said, "I asked around, and someone told me what happened in the cafeteria. I'm sorry. I knew Allison was upset, but I didn't think she was stupid enough to go after you like that."

"It's not your fault," she said.

The cushion tilted when he sat beside her. "Yeah, it is. Allison's jealous."

"No," Terry said, trying to slow down the automatic rush of her pulse.

He cocked his head to one side, trying to catch her eye. His expression was so intense, a warm pool inside her chest spread down to her toes. "I don't..." she stammered. "I don't understand." Terry hated how pathetic she sounded, but nothing was making sense to her these days. Why would the most popular jock in school find her, an outcast cripple, attractive? What if this was a brilliant ruse put up by Allison?

"You stand out," he said. "You watch the room, keeping track of everyone, but at the same time you want to be invisible." He gave her a half smile. "But I see you. When you talked about Cleopatra that first day, you really came alive, like you could take on anything, and nobody would stand in your way. You were strong and powerful." Then he said, "You were Cleopatra."

Terry shook her head. "You're delusional."

"I'm fooling everyone at school," he said, "but you saw through that. I don't have to be the super jock for you. I can just be me. I like being with you."

"I'll take that as a compliment," she said.

"It is."

Zach stayed quiet, and Terry welcomed the silence. She didn't need her life getting more complicated. Having Zach as a friend was all that she could handle.

She relaxed into the cushions. A blanket of calm covered her. Somehow, everything was going to be okay. "I'm ordering pizza from room service," she told him. "Want to stay?"

It took three slices to fill Terry, and by that time she was convinced that whatever tomorrow brought, it would be manageable. After they got the asp from the Egypt room, she'd deliver it to Dr. Mullaca in the basement. Terry was euphoric that she might have her dad back by this time tomorrow.

She pictured the coffin, still waiting in the cold, stark room. She glanced at Zach in his T-shirt, reaching for his bottle of water. "I think I know how to get an A-plus for our project, but more importantly get you to the State Championships."

He took the last bite of his pizza. "No need. I'm working on it."

"What?"

He laughed at her expression, then reached for his backpack. "I'm serious." He smiled, pulling out a folder. "This is what I wanted to show you in library today."

"Oh," Terry said, now embarrassed by her assumption he'd wanted to kiss her. "Yeah, of course."

He scooted closer and opened the folder. A portfolio of drawings filled Terry's lap. Zach pointed to the first image of Cleopatra dressed for battle. "This is when she decided to fight her brother and reclaim the throne." The artwork showed a familiar scene to Terry. "And this is her being unrolled from the carpet." He spoke in quick intervals as he explained the panels of his comic book.

Terry drank up the images.

"The white blocks are for the text," he told her. "And I left some bubbles for speech." There was a pause. "I thought Maude should be the one to fill in the text, since she has the neatest printing."

Terry stayed quiet, unable to tear her eyes away from his drawings.

His tone was calmer now. "I still have to color in some parts, but that's kind of the idea." He flipped through a few more sheets, then showed Terry the final page — Cleopatra's death scene with the asp.

"Zach," she gasped. "It's brilliant! I've studied this stuff all my life, but I love seeing it in this format. Do you know how many kids would eat this up?" Terry ran her fingertips over Cleopatra's face. "I love her eyes."

"I used you," he admitted. "I drew her so she would have your eyes."

Terry was still looking at the image in her lap, but all of her focus was on Zach, sitting beside her. She became all too aware that their hips were touching. If she turned her head toward him, even the slightest, she wondered if he would kiss her. She could feel his breath on her neck. Terry was falling into that warm pool he'd created inside her. She closed her eyes. Everything was melting.

He leaned in closer and reached up to brush the hair from her shoulder. "You smell sweet."

Terry's eyes flew open, picturing clumps of dried vanilla milkshake in her hair. "Um." She inched away from him. "Maude has all that candy. She gives off waves of sugary odor. It's like cigarette smoke, but different, and more healthy ... I guess."

Zach was momentarily dazed.

Terry peeled herself off the couch, self-consciously smoothing down the side of her hair. The awkwardness was palpable.

"I meant it's nice," Zach stammered. "You're nice to sit next to ... yeah."

"Thank you." Her hands were doing that stupid thing when they hung by her side, useless. Why did conversations with Zach require such complicated choreography? Terry didn't remember ever having this much trouble with Maude or Fraser.

The sudden warmth dissipated, leaving Terry more tired than before. She reasoned it was always going to be like this between them; hot and bothered one moment, followed by jumpy and clumsy.

Zach glanced at his watch, then picked up the portfolio. "Do you think Maude will want to put this on glossy paper before we hand it in?" His tone was cautious.

"I'm pretty sure." She couldn't hide the weary disappointment in her voice. Hadn't they teased each other about him sneaking in rolled up in a carpet? Maybe their chemistry was consistent but short-lived.

Zach pulled on his varsity jacket and shouldered his backpack. "I'll have it ready tomorrow," he promised, heading toward the door. "Then you and Maude can decide on the printing." He reached out and grabbed the doorknob. "You can't expect me to carry you two slackers through this project."

Terry gave him a careful smile, then said, "About the printing." She took in a deep breath. "You deserve help."

"What do you mean?" Zach forced a confused expression, but she heard the slip in his tone.

She took a step closer. "There are tutors trained specially for people who have trouble."

They looked at each other for a long time without speaking. He sniffed and tapped the doorknob. "Is it that obvious?"

"No, you're very good at hiding it. And the fact you've made it this far in school shows how smart you are."

"I can read," he said. "It just takes really long." After a few beats of silence he added, "It makes me feel stupid. I hate it."

Terry tucked her hands behind her back and leaned against the wall. "I'd never be able to function, let alone get through homework," she encouraged. "It's pretty extraordinary you get by like you do."

His expression remained stoic, unmoved by her compliment. "Some teachers give me enough marks to pass so I won't miss basketball — they wouldn't do that if I was going for an art scholarship. I'm only taking the bare minimum to graduate. At first I thought it was perfect." The corner of his mouth curled up, but the smile died on his lips like he'd forgotten the punch line to a boring joke. "It was an easy out. But now, I feel like they're all laughing at me in the staff room."

"It just means you haven't met the right teacher yet."

"Like Ms. Bernard?"

"God, no."

He chuckled. Terry was encouraged by the fact he hadn't left yet. She gave it one more shot. "Ask the guidance counsellor. At least think about a summer program. Maybe something independent from school?"

"Maybe," he whispered. They both stared at the doorknob in his grasp, not sure how to end a conversation with so much weight.

Zach made the first move. He opened the door and walked into the hallway. The bodyguard by the elevator straightened up and pushed the button. Terry leaned against the frame, watching him. "How are you getting home? It's already dark outside."

Zach said. "The bus stop is only a two-minute walk from here."

Terry crinkled her forehead. "Are you sure it's safe?"

His face broke out into a huge grin. It was a true smile. "Why would anyone want to hurt the school's basketball hero?" he joked.

The bodyguard cleared his throat and pointed to the open elevator. "Oh hey, bro," Zach said. "I didn't see you there."

Terry waited until he was gone. She shut her door, then leaned against the wall and closed her eyes. *Everyone has their own limp, but some are more obvious than others.*

She'd been tempted to tell him about her plan for tomorrow, but the less people involved the better. Zach had a full plate, and adding a mysterious curse and a stolen artifact to his list of things to be worried about would be cruel. She let out a breath, trying to adjust to the empty room. A deep ache settled in her chest.

A hurried knock startled Terry. She opened the door, then stood back and let him in.

Zach was red-faced and breathing hard, as if he'd ran up a set of stairs. He dropped his backpack on the floor. "I forgot something," he said. He took Terry's face in his hands and kissed her. She should have been too shocked to kiss him back or at least too unprepared to follow through, but his soft lips felt like the most natural thing in the world. Terry closed her eyes and pressed against him, letting the moment linger. A warm tingle spiraled from her chest, then downwards. She finally took a breath when Zach pressed his forehead to hers. "It's up to you," he murmured. "That can be our first kiss, or our last."

Terry knew she should say no, that everything was too complicated. Maybe even too complicated to be friends. But as the seconds ticked by, she stayed silent, slowly melting into his arms. His words, his kiss, even the sound of his hurried breathing as he waited for her answer, triggered something deep inside.

She was tired of being lonely. She deserved to be kissed. She deserved to be happy. *What would Cleopatra do?*

Instead of stepping out of his embrace Terry reached up and linked her fingers across the back of his neck, pulling him closer.

When they kissed a second time, she was ready. Terry parted her lips, breathing him in. He was a perfect combination of spicy body spray and musky aftershave. His hand slid down her lower back and wrapped around her waist, pulling her closer. Her tongue found his, creating a deliciously dizzy sensation.

How could something that made her feel so strong be bad? She and Zach were alike. They were both outsiders and now they could belong to each other. He held her tightly and leaned back, lifting her feet off the ground, extra careful of her bad knee. All the while his mouth moved softly with hers, savoring the moment. There was a delicate strength to his movements that made her warm all over. After many more kisses, she felt her feet gently return to the floor. His mouth left hers, traveling along her neck. "You're so beautiful," he whispered.

Terry had never felt so precious.

The moment slowed down naturally. He cradled her cheek in his hand. "Is that a yes?" he asked.

Terry laughed against his chest. "Yes, let's just be friends."

With one last kiss to her forehead, and a promise to call her later, Zach left a second time, the smile much grander than his first departure.

Terry floated around her suite, putting the leftover pizza in the fridge, and then finally starting her hot bath. She leaned toward the huge bathroom mirror and pushed her bangs to the side, studying her eyes, trying to find the strength Zach saw in her.

Her phone rang from the bedroom. Terry smiled, picturing Zach calling her from the bus. Maybe they would talk the whole way until he got home. She wondered again, how far away he lived. Terry frowned at the call display.

"Hey, Maude," she said, trying to hide her disappointment.

"Have you heard about Dr. Mullaca?"

"No." The blood started to pound in Terry's ears. She sat on the edge of the bed, her legs suddenly weak. "What happened?"

"Fraser wanted to go back to the museum to see if he could find out anything more about the big lump in front of the exhibit." She paused and Terry could hear a candy wrapper in the background. "He's dead serious on some kind of elaborate plan. Anyway, the first clerk was on break and some other worker wouldn't let us pass, but then Fraser told them we had an appointment with Dr. Mullaca this evening."

"What she say? Why hasn't she called me back? Did you tell her about the asp?" Terry clutched the bed covers.

"No." Maude's voice raised an octave. "She never returned from the hospital. A student nurse found her unconscious in an elevator this afternoon. She's now in the ICU with your dad."

Chapter Twenty-Nine

"Nefertari, you have to eat." Prince Kamal motioned to her breakfast plate. "You need your strength."

They were eating in the hotel's terrarium restaurant on the ground floor. The greenery of the restaurant was a stark contrast with the frozen, barren landscape outside. Late February in Devonshire was like one long, cloudy day interspersed with wind and rain.

Terry speared a sausage with her fork. Her waffle and fresh fruit remained untouched. "I can't," she said, dropping the fork and pushing the food away. She hadn't shared her theory about the asp being in the Egypt room. He'd just say that her father's condition was of a medical nature and therefore best dealt with the hospital staff — not an ancient artifact. Plus, she was a bit hesitant since Kamal and Sarah were closer than she realized. She wondered if this was his overprotective nature manifesting itself; he always seemed to be rescuing her. "I'm scared for my dad," she admitted. "And for Dr. Mullaca. What does this all mean?"

Prince Kamal dabbed the corner of his mouth with his napkin. "I completely understand, but I want you to concentrate on being hopeful. They're getting the same excellent care. And your father won't want to recover and find out you're malnourished, will he?"

Despite being surrounded by large potted ferns and fragrant blooms, Terry felt a chill. She let out a shaking breath. "But my dad isn't getting any better."

He gave her an encouraging smile. "I spoke with the hospital this morning. Dr. Mullaca is still unconscious, but they are optimistic they'll make a breakthrough soon. Please don't worry. Everything will fall into place in the end, I promise."

He said this with such conviction that it gave Terry a little boost. She made herself take a bite of waffle, knowing she needed every bit of strength for today.

Prince Kamal took a sip of orange juice, watching her over the top of his glass. "I was speaking with Mayor Harris."

"Is he reconsidering postponing the party?" Terry asked. She wondered if Sarah had told him about Terry's eavesdropping. Either way, Mayor Harris was hardly her top priority.

"No." His word cut through the air. Clearly Prince Kamal and the mayor were not friends. "He insisted the unveiling will be the museum's biggest fundraiser of the year. It's imperative for the museum to stay operating." Then Prince Kamal grumbled, "It's also imperative it happen before the election."

Terry remembered the sectioned-off areas that weren't on display the first time she toured the building with her dad. Rescuing the museum from bankruptcy would certainly be favorable in the minds of Devonshire's voters.

"The coffin will be on display," he continued, his voice becoming uncharacteristically despondent. "Opened or closed, it makes no difference to him."

Terry visualized taking the asp and fitting it into the grooves of the case. *It will all be fixed today.* She sat a little straighter and gave him a smile. "Don't worry," she told the prince, stealing his line, "everything will fall into place in the end."

Terry spent the rest of the meal concentrating on the image of getting the asp and opening the case. She also embellished her appearance. In her mind, her eyes were lined in kohl and her frumpy hoodie and cargo pants had been traded for skinny jeans and high boots. She would be strong. She would be beautiful. She would have her dad back … and she'd have Zach.

Right after breakfast she called Zach, suggesting they keep their relationship quiet for now. There was no need to mention the obvious fact that his ex-girlfriend and her bloodthirsty princesses would make her existence at school hellish.

"What if I want to hold your hand?" he'd teased.

"If you pretend to trip, I'll reach for you."

"You have a hero complex."

"No. I'm just complex."

Zach's low voice chuckled in her ear. She imagined his breath coming through the phone, breezing against her neck. The thought had sent tingles across her skin. When the call finally ended, Terry was glowing inside. The effect Zach had on her was irrefutably, deliriously wonderful.

The limo ride to school helped Terry keep her focus. Maude skipped out of Maudern Touch wearing a purple knit poncho and a lavender beret. Her pink streak of hair curled tightly, bobbing up and down. The sunlight glinted off the vintage brooch on the front of her beret. Like they planned the night before, she and Maude kept quiet about the museum trip. Once they reached school, they split for the morning and didn't see each other until after lunch.

That afternoon, they made their way to the bus where half their history class was already stomping their feet in the cold afternoon. Terry scanned the crowd; Allison's princesses were by themselves.

Maude seemed to read her mind. "She's not in school today." They climbed on the bus, making their way to the back. Zach was sitting with one of his teammates. He reached up and touched the edge of his eyebrow. She looked away, embarrassed and thrilled at the same time. *We have a secret sign.*

Fraser slipped into the seat behind them, his brown leather jacket crinkling as he leaned forward. "You're certainly dressed for the part, Daphne." Then he turned to Terry. "All systems go, Velma?"

Maude responded with a shush loud enough to make a few

heads peek over in their direction. She hit Fraser with a hard stare. "I knew we shouldn't have told you," she whispered. "You'll ruin everything with your big mouth."

Terry noticed the only ones close by were Tanya and her boyfriend, two seats back and already making out.

He leaned close to Maude's ear. "But I'm your Fred," he reasoned. Roses bloomed in Maude's cheeks. "Plus I'm also the strongest," he continued, "and if anyone asks I can use the press card. Reporters get away with all kinds of stuff in the name of journalism."

Maude rolled her eyes at this one. Fraser leaned back and closed his eyes, content to relax all the way to the museum, full of effortless confidence.

Maude twirled her pink streak tightly around her finger, then released it over and over until the bus pulled up to the museum. The class made their way up the stairs to the fifth floor. Terry had permission to use the elevator, but she didn't want to attract any individual attention. Her knee was threatening to lock by the time they reached the top.

Maude stayed by her side while Fraser lagged close behind. When they turned the corner they saw what had been under the bulky tarp and exchanged uneasy looks.

"Is that what I think it is?" Maude's voice quivered.

Fraser whispered. "What are the odds a metal detector just happened to be set up outside the Egypt room on the very day we—?"

"Shh!" Maude warned. She readjusted her beret, which had drooped somewhat on the trek up the stairs.

"Someone knows," Terry breathed. Her eyes darted around at the faces of her classmates, paranoid one of them could read her guilty expression.

The line inched forward. Two security guards were on either side of the metal detector. Zach walked through the tall panels without incident, but his teammate was stopped. One guard used an electric wand to scan his jacket. He pulled out a pocketknife key chain, which after a quick ruling between the guards he was allowed to keep. Terry noticed they made a note on a clipboard.

"If it picks up a simple pocketknife," Fraser whispered, "there's no way we're leaving the Egypt room with the asp without that thing going off."

"Twizzlers," Maude said, almost weeping.

Tanya and her boyfriend were holding hands up ahead, stealing kisses.

"Maybe we can come back and get that pretty clerk to let us in after hours?" Fraser suggested. "I bet she'd do it if I asked her."

Maude huffed. "Go ahead, ask her out. I bet she'll be impressed with the size of your IQ."

"You're a terrible listener," he said. "I gave no indication I was attracted to her. I don't want to ask her out, I want her to help us out."

"You said she was pretty."

"Yes, it's a subjective observation. I happen to think the Velociraptor exhibit is beautiful too."

"So now she's beautiful?"

"You guys!" Terry whispered harshly.

Fraser leaned closer to Maude. "Excuse me, but I thought we were on the same team?"

"I'm only on one team," Maude said, poking him in the chest. "Team Unicorn." She folded her arms over her chest. Fraser grumbled something incoherent.

"Next!" the guard's voice made Terry jump, and she winced as her knee protested. "Just walk through normally," he instructed.

Terry didn't have time to appreciate the irony of his statement. She limped through as usual. A loud siren began, and a light flashed on both panels. The guards shared a surprised look.

"She has metal in her knee brace!" Maude said, practically jubilant. Terry turned and could almost see the light bulb go over Fraser's head. He'd be the one to steal it, but she'd have to smuggle it out. She'd never been so grateful for that hateful brace. The guard made a tick beside Terry's name on the clipboard and nodded her inside.

"Please take in as much as you can," Ms. Bernard instructed. "The curator graciously allowed us a sneak peek, but we only have one hour before the bus leaves."

There were no plastic coverings, and every display was shined to perfection and well-lit. The walls were painted to look like hieroglyphics, making the visitor feel like they'd just walked into a centuries old tomb.

There were two empty areas that caught Terry's attention. The first was a backlit display showcasing an empty velvet-lined panel. But the labels for Cleopatra's coins were in place. Terry had forgotten how significant that discovery had been, so overshadowed by the events of the last week.

A pull tugged on her soul. She'd never laid eyes on the mysterious coins. Secretly, she blamed their discovery on her mother's death. Their placement in the tomb had encouraged the team to explore deeper into the cave.

Terry moved away from the empty display and pushed down her grief. She needed to concentrate on the one parent she had left.

The center of the Egypt room had a raised area surrounded by glass — but the spot for the museum's secret acquisition was empty. Terry pictured the coffin, waiting for her in the basement.

The Cleopatra mannequin was free of the plastic coverings and on her usual platform surrounded by the red velvet ropes. Ms. Bernard called for everyone's attention as one of the museum staff began to explain the updated exhibit.

Terry and Maude wandered to the farthest corner of the room and stood by a long glass counter, pretending to contemplate the miniature model of the Valley of the Kings. The class shuffled around, roaming from one prominent display to the next. Allison's princesses were actually texting, already bored. Terry had the urge to knock their heads together. They had no idea how much people like her mother sacrificed to unearth history.

Ms. Bernard circled the room, pausing by the students, adding her little tidbits of information. An expression of awe and wonderment lit her features. Terry warmed toward her history teacher, but with her constant attention on the whole class, the opportunity for the perfect moment was quickly dwindling. Fraser had to make his move soon.

Maude poked her in the side, then motioned toward Fraser. He slipped away from the pack and started backing up closer to Cleopatra. Then he locked eyes with Maude, and gave her a quick nod.

Terry's heart was in her throat. There was no turning back.

Maude let out a blood-curdling scream and pointed to the back of the room. "A huge rat just ran by!" She even produced tears and managed to fall to her knees in an attempt to feign weakness.

The class's reaction was immediate: most of the girls ran for the exit, but the guys swarmed the area where the fictitious rat had gone. Ms. Bernard and the museum staff were preoccupied with Maude's fainting. Even Terry temporarily forgot about Fraser until he appeared by her side.

"I'm so sorry," Maude said, getting to her feet and smoothing out her knit dress. "But I really thought I saw a mouse-rat thingy." Ms. Bernard made a low sound in the back of her throat, then stomped into the hallway to retrieve half the class.

Fraser's glasses were smudged. "I couldn't get it," he confessed. He licked his lips and glanced over at the mannequin. "It was stuck on fast. It must be nailed on or something. It wouldn't budge. Maybe it isn't the real asp. Maybe it's only part of the mannequin."

A wave of desperation hit Terry and she gulped down her disappointment.

Fraser and Maude stayed quiet.

"Hey." Zach appeared before them, smiling carefully. He addressed the trio, but his gaze was zoned in on Terry. She stayed silent, too numb to even smile at him. He put his attention on Maude. "Did you have a chance to check out the drawings?" he asked her, his expression hopeful.

Maude lit up. "You're a flippin' genius!" She continued to praise his idea of doing a comic book. Her comments helped soothe the charged air.

When the rest of the class filtered back into the Egypt room, the museum staff finished the lecture. Terry felt the last chance at saving her dad slip away. She stopped in front of Cleopatra. Those kohl-lined eyes gave away no secrets. The glittery asp mocked Terry. Across the room, Tanya and her boyfriend were making out by the empty, fake mummy case with the hollowed-out eyes.

Jealously roared inside Terry. She should be sneaking off with Zach somewhere, not trying to solve a fifty-year-old mystery.

Ms. Bernard announced the trip was cut short and everyone had to make their way to the bus. Maude and Fraser walked out together. Zach gave up trying to catch her eye and left with a few of his teammates.

Terry faced off with Cleopatra again. Her fingers itched to reach up and grab the asp. *It's right here in front of me.* Terry ducked under the red velvet ropes and stepped up onto the platform. The second her fingers touched the asp, it slid off the mannequin's arm.

She stumbled back, staring at the asp in her palm. It felt warm. She glanced around quickly, but no one was watching her. No one saw a thing. Terry slipped the asp up her arm, then pulled down her sleeve.

With the asp snug around her bicep, Terry purposefully walked toward the metal detector. Tanya's boyfriend was behind her, arguing with Ms. Bernard. "She was right beside me," he said, "I swear."

Terry started to whistle. When the detector went off again, she merely pointed to her leg and said, "Knee brace." She didn't even wait for them to question her. Terry waltzed by Maude and Fraser and gave them a big smile. "I'm taking the elevator down." She winked. *Straight down to the basement where the real Cleopatra is waiting.*

A hand grabbed her elbow. "I don't think so, Ms. Hughes." Ms.

Bernard's face was stern. "One student has already gone off by herself. We can't have you go missing too."

"But I need to — I mean my knee is too sore. I have to take the elevator."

"None of the students are permitted to go off by themselves." Ms. Bernard shepherded Terry toward the stairs where the rest of the class had started descending. "Everyone must go to the bus immediately for a head count."

Terry caught up with Maude and Fraser. "Hurry," she instructed. She zigzagged through the crowd of students taking the stairs by twos. Maude breathed heavily behind her, trying to keep up.

They strode across the rotunda. Terry picked up her pace, worried someone would notice the missing asp any second. If she couldn't get to the basement right away, she'd keep it until the time was right.

"Come on, faster," she ordered, grabbing Maude's hand and dragging her to their bus seat.

"What the hell?" Maude said. Her beret was crumpled in her other hand, a light layer of sweat beading her forehead. She gave Terry the strangest look.

Fraser came gasping up the aisle, his wild hair hanging in front of his glasses. "What," he said between breaths, "happened to trying to blend in? Is there some reason you ran like there was a fire?"

Terry pulled up her sleeve.

"Holy shit," he whispered. "How..."

Maude's face grew pale. "You ran," she said to Terry.

"Uh-huh," Terry said distractedly. The first few students had finally caught up to them and were getting on the bus. She pulled her sleeve back down, careful to conceal the asp.

"I mean you *ran*," Maude repeated. "Without limping."

Chapter Thirty

"Forty-two seconds," Maude said, staring at her watch. "I don't believe it." Her voice echoed in the concrete stairwell.

Terry leaned over with her hands on her knees, taking in a few deep breaths. "Best score yet," she said. "It's like I'm getting faster each time. I don't even feel tired!" She lifted up her pant leg and frowned at her brace. "This thing looks so battered," she said. "I'll have to take it off before my super powers break the joint in half."

Maude shouldered her backpack. "It's freaking me out. You ran up all twenty-five floors of the Plaza." She reached for the door handle and gave it a firm tug. "Ten trips is enough. I'm not timing you anymore. We've been doing this for a half hour. Fraser will think we've gone missing too."

"I can't help it." Terry followed her into the plush surroundings of Prince Kamal's private floor. "You have no idea how amazing it is for me to actually run." She pushed a strand of hair off her sweaty forehead. She loved the feeling of moving fast, almost like she could fly. "It would take me at least twice that long to normally walk up only one flight of stairs! If I wasn't wearing the brace I bet I'd go even faster."

"Exactly," Maude said, stopping outside Terry's suite. She glanced at the men in suits guarding the elevator, then leaned in, dropping her voice. "What you can do isn't normal."

Terry ignored Maude's ominous tone and walked into the room. Fraser was sitting in the middle of the plush couch. The old newspaper articles were strewn around him like a fan. A can of Coke sat on the table in front of him.

"Can you fly yet?" he asked, not even looking up from his reading.

"All I'm saying is that I don't trust that thing." Maude pointed toward Terry's arm.

Terry pushed up her sleeve. The asp was smooth against her skin. She smiled as her fingers trailed over its golden surface. A few flecks of paint came off. She was in awe of it being hidden under cheap paint for all these years. She was the one who figured it out. She was the one who found it. Fraser couldn't even make it budge — she was the one who claimed it.

Maude sat beside Fraser and picked up one of the articles he'd covered with underlines and circles. "Hmm," she said, studying his notes. "Interesting pattern."

Terry unscrewed the cap off a bottle of water and leaned against the wall. "Maude's the cryptoquote champ," she teased. "She's got a big trophy and everything."

A corner of Fraser's mouth curled up. He nudged Maude with his knee. "Letters are my thing too."

Terry waved her bottle at the old clippings. "I have a priceless artifact on my arm, plus superpowers. So maybe we could put away yesterday's news and make a plan for how I'm supposed to get to the sarcophagus."

"I never took you for the insensitive kind." Fraser gave her a chastising look. "We did lose a classmate today, remember?" He picked up the remote and turned on the flat-screen TV. A female reporter in a bright red scarf and double-breasted wool coat stood outside the museum with a microphone in her hand. The sound came on, catching her in mid-sentence, "—unavailable for comment. However, sources say police haven't ruled out foul play."

In the top corner of the screen, Tanya Godfrey's school picture appeared with the words 'Local Missing Girl' printed neatly underneath. Her black lipstick and piercings were hard to miss. Terry's heart tightened for Tanya's family.

The reporter continued. "A few students I interviewed indicated skipping out on field trips is not unusual behavior. Authorities are encouraging anyone with information to call the Devonshire police department immediately."

Maude paused the TV with a huff of disgust. "Skipping out? Who would tell a reporter such a stupid thing?"

Tanya's picture stayed on the screen. "It's so weird," Terry murmured. "She was with her boyfriend practically the whole time. I saw them making out right before I took the asp."

Fraser took a sip of his drink. "Weird doesn't begin to describe today."

"You don't sound worried," Terry noticed. "Everyone thinks she ditched out early. You know Tanya from the newspaper office. Do you think she just took off for fun?"

Fraser put down his Coke. "I don't know, but we're going to do for Tanya what no one did for June fifty years ago."

Terry looked at the old articles, fanned out. "How is June connected to what happened today?"

Maude ran a finger over the black and white photo of the plain girl. She glanced up at the TV. Tanya's goth image stared back. "They didn't exactly have a lot in common," she said. "What made you think of June?"

"While you were flexing your muscles, I figured out a few things; both girls went missing in the same building the same time the asp was stolen," Fraser declared.

"But the asp was hidden, not stolen," Terry said. "And this time I did the stealing. I certainly didn't have anything to do with Tanya disappearing."

Fraser underlined a name in the article. "I'm going to talk to Gus Tanner."

"Who's he?" Maude asked.

"The security guard who was working the day June went missing." Fraser made a note, then tucked the piece of paper into his jacket pocket.

Terry let out an exasperated sigh. "Seriously? You think this is useful? How are you ever going to find him? That was fifty years ago."

Fraser slipped his satchel over his shoulder, then adjusted his glasses. "He's in the phone book. I got him on the first try while you were playing Supergirl in the stairwell." He made his way to the door. Maude gave him a smile of approval and followed.

Terry watched them walk towards the door. "How does this help me?"

"He was the last person to see June alive, apparently," Fraser answered.

Maude shivered. "This is getting creepy. What if her bones are in his backyard or something?"

Terry stepped in front of them, blocking their path. "How does looking for a geriatric runaway help me get into the museum?"

"That's cold," Maude lectured, zipping up her pink backpack. "What about Tanya?"

"Look, I hope she's okay, but opening up that coffin should be our priority." She put a hand on Maude's arm. "Please," she begged. "Like the reporter said, Tanya probably just skipped out. My dad and Dr. Mullaca need our help more."

Maude's eyes got bigger. She turned to Fraser. "Terry's right."

Fraser studied Terry. "Have you taken that off yet?" he asked, pointing to the asp.

Terry put a protective hand over the gold piece. "No. This seems like the safest place." She frowned back at him. "Why?"

"I was wondering what kind of enhancements it would give Maude." His tone was challenging

Maude threw him a disgusted look. "I hate boob jokes."

"I wasn't talking about your precious *commaudities*," he said, looking slightly insulted. "More like you sprouting wings and turning into a unicorn or something."

"They're *priceless*, not precious," she said, rolling her eyes. "I thought you excelled at reading."

"Books, not boobs."

"Can you two just shut up?" Terry urged.

"And just because I have an IQ of one twenty-nine, it doesn't mean I'm not a regular guy."

Maude threw down her backpack and tugged off her coat. "I have no idea what that means, but it sounded pathetic." She rolled up her sleeve and held out her arm to Terry. "Let's have it, then," she said. "I hope I do have super strength so I can knock that smirk off his face."

Terry hesitated, then straightened her arm until her fingers touched Maude's, creating an uninterrupted connection. She slipped the asp down her arm, pausing at her wrist. Her instinct was willing her to stop. Fraser nodded for her to continue. In one quick motion she slid the asp off her hand and up Maude's arm.

Terry crumpled to the floor, clutching her knee. Her bones felt like they were flying apart. She rolled onto her back, her mouth contorted in a silent scream as if being tortured.

Maude panicked. "Oh, god! Terry!"

Fraser grunted as he wrenched Terry's hand away from her knee. He shoved the cool, hard spiral of the asp over her knuckles, scraping the skin. Terry went limp, taking in mouthfuls of air. Maude put an arm around her shoulders and helped her sit up.

"I guess running isn't such a good idea," Terry admitted. She sniffed as two fat tears rolled down her cheeks. They splattered on the expensive Persian rug. She hit Fraser with a stare. "Did you know that would happen?"

"No," he said quietly. He sat with his back against the wall. "I was worried you wouldn't be able to take it off."

"She can't!" Maude said, now starting her own set of tears.

"It'll kill her."

Terry wiped a hand down her face, and composed herself. "I'll be okay," she said. "Once I rest my knee and take my medicine. I just won't be able to run again."

The trio stayed on the floor, each one quiet with their own thoughts.

Fraser spoke first. "Terry," he began, "I think what happened fifty years ago is important to helping your dad and Dr. Mullaca. You're a part of this somehow."

"So what do we do now?" she asked.

"We have to find out what happened the first time," he said. "We have to find out what really happened to June."

Chapter Thirty-One

Terry accepted the mug of tea and wrapped her fingers around its warmth. Gus Tanner's kitchen was homey and quaint. Maude cooed when she saw the cherry wallpaper and Kit-Cat Clock, with its rolling eyes and pendulum tail.

"Thanks again for agreeing to see us, Mr. Tanner," Fraser said. His leather jacket was draped over the chrome kitchen chair. He pushed up his glasses and gave his best 'trust me, I'm harmless' smile.

"I'm not sure if I can help you kids," Gus replied. His white hair was cut short, and even though it was late afternoon there were still crisp pleats in his slacks. He leaned against the spotless counter with his own mug of tea steaming in his hand. "You said over the phone it was urgent."

Terry and Maude hit Fraser with a worried stare. He didn't even flinch. "Like I said in our earlier conversation, our friend is missing," he began smoothly. "And we know this isn't the first time something odd happened in that museum."

Gus placed a plate of cookies on the table. Terry noticed the tiny roses painted around the plate's edges. "Go ahead." He motioned to sweets. "My daughter makes them for me."

"Thank you." Terry took a bite, then stopped mid-chew. She looked at Fraser, who had taken one as well. She guessed she was wearing the same hesitant expression.

Gus chuckled at their reaction. "Gluten-free," he explained. "My daughter thinks it will help my arthritis."

Fraser swallowed. "And raisins too," he said.

Maude leaned back, distancing herself from the healthy snack. She counted out and added five sugar cubes to her tea, clinking her spoon against the cup's edge as she stirred.

Terry squirmed in her chair. "We're here because of June Macallum," she said.

"I thought as much." Gus put down his mug and looked out the window over the sink. A collection of salt and pepper shakers lined the sill. "June loved the museum and spent every weekend there. She knew more about the exhibits than most of the staff." His voice took on a nostalgic quality. Terry thought she could see the young man he used to be under the wrinkles. "I teased her and said she should work at the museum. But she told me she wanted to get far away from Devonshire. That she needed to be free."

Terry gripped the edge of her chair.

"So you think she ran away?" Maude sounded hopeful.

He dropped his head. "I can't imagine a young girl being able to disappear that easily. If she did run away," he paused and all the lines came back to his face, "I think someone or something got to her soon after."

"Maybe the same thing that knocked you out?" Fraser asked.

"I don't know," Gus said hollowly. "I heard noises in the Egypt room, but I didn't see anyone. The asp was perfectly safe under its glass case. Then everything went black. I woke up with the fire department standing over me and one hell of a bump on the back of my head." He shrugged. "Glass shards covered the entire floor, but the asp was still in place. Two weeks later, it went missing for good."

"And they never found any fingerprints or any other clues?" Maude asked.

Gus shook his head. "The police scoured the area, but all they found was a pink sweater crumpled up in the girls' bathroom, one of the sleeves ripped and missing a few buttons." His voice sound heavy, like he'd told this story too many times. "It was June's."

The bitter wind howled outside. The Kit-Cat Clock ticking away the seconds was the only sound inside the little kitchen. Gus straightened up and put his hands in his pockets. "You say your friend is missing now?" he asked.

Fraser nodded.

"Wait here." Gus left the kitchen and walked down the short hallway. After a few minutes he returned with a worn shoebox. "It's too late for June, but maybe this can help your friend."

Fraser took off the lid and gingerly lifted out a yellowed article from the top of the clippings. "I don't remember seeing these before." Terry caught the excitement in his voice.

"I saved all the articles in the crime section after June disappeared. Everything from purse snatches to armed robberies. There's up to a year's worth in there."

"I only checked headlines pertaining to the museum and June," Fraser said, his tone uncharacteristically solemn. He shot the girls an apologetic glance, then turned to Gus. "Thank you, sir. I'll make sure these return to you." He stood, and the group followed him out of the kitchen.

"No need," Gus said, seeing them to the door. "I don't want them anymore. It's a reminder of a dark time in my life."

"Being a suspect must have been horrible," Maude said.

Gus's mouth turned down at the edges. "The police questioned me a few times, but I was never arrested. But that night..." His voice dropped. "I saw something ... something unnatural."

It seemed like all of the air in the room had been sucked out. "I never told the police," he confessed. "I thought they'd lock me up in an asylum for good, or maybe they'd think I was trying to cover up my supposed guilt." He raised his white eyebrows and let out a sigh. "But that was a long time ago, and I think it's worth sharing with you now. The truth is, I think it was June."

"You think *what* was her?" Maude asked.

"An angel or something," he said. "She was beautiful, but she looked dangerous too. There was a snake tattoo on her arm that glowed — she even kissed me." A gnarled finger grazed his cheek.

Fraser looked at the two girls for direction, but no one made a move. The asp pulsed warmly against Terry's skin, but Gus's description sent a shiver straight through to her bones.

Gus blinked a few times, coming back to the present. He ran a hand over his short hair. "I only thought of her as a smart high school girl before, but after that kiss, I was completely in love with her. I spent the following few years wondering about her constantly," he said, more composed. "I was obsessed. I drifted away from my family and friends. I couldn't even hold down a job."

He gave them a sheepish grin. "One day, I almost walked out in front of a cab. It would've killed me for sure. That's the day I realized my life had to continue. It pained me, but I put away all the newspaper articles and stopped dreaming about June. After a few more years I met a nice girl and got married."

Maude looked around the modest apartment, everything neatly in place, right down to the crocheted doilies on the flowered armchair. "I really love your wife's taste," she praised. "It's very cozy chic."

"Oh," Gus said softly, his cheeks growing pink. "Thank you. She passed away last year."

"So did my mom," Terry said. She stepped forward and gave him a hug. He smelled like Ivory soap.

Gus tapped the shoebox in Fraser's hand. "I hope you find your friend."

"Thank you, sir." Fraser nodded.

Terry pulled her hoodie tightly against the high winds as they made their way to Fraser's car. They got into their usual spots and slammed the doors. Maude rubbed her hands together.

Fraser handed Maude the shoebox and started the ignition. "Anyone else thinking what I'm thinking?" he asked, pulling away.

"That if you'd checked the crime sections we might have solved this thing on the first day?" Terry replied.

"No, but thank you for showcasing my oversight. I'm thinking about—"

"Hot chocolate?" Maude guessed hopefully.

He nodded. "Well, I'm thinking of that now, but I mean about Gus and his glowing angel."

Terry hugged her arms, and the asp's heat penetrated the fabric. Gus's story had left her chilled. "What if June was wearing the asp the night of the burglary, but Gus thought it was a tattoo? It would explain how the robbers were easily defeated."

Maude made a face. "That doesn't make any sense. The asp didn't go missing until two weeks later. If she wore the asp for the burglary, why put it back in its case?"

Terry stayed quiet. The snake tattoo sounded familiar, but she couldn't remember why. The elusiveness made her uneasy.

Maude took the lid off the shoebox and started rummaging through yellowed newspaper clippings. "Maybe there's something—"

"Hey!" Fraser made a grab for the cover. "Wait until we can spread everything out and categorize."

Maude moved it out of his reach. "Will you just drive!"

"Those are fragile. You're going to mess them up," he insisted. He made another grab, and she swatted his hand away. The wipers started to swish across the windshield. A horn blared at them from behind.

"God, Fraser! You're going to kill us before we can find out the truth!" Maude slammed the lid on the box and handed it back to Terry.

"It's impossible to drive with you freaking out." He thrust the gear into the next shift. "Calm down and pull out some of your candy to suck on."

"Shut up," Maude said, "or I'll give *you* something to suck on."

The car came to a red light. There was total silence. Fraser turned to Maude, a careful grin tugging at the corner of his mouth. "And what exactly am I supposed to suck on?" His eyebrows went up. "Hmm?"

Maude held up a hand toward his face. "Oh, god," she muttered. "Just drive."

"Why are you mad?" he teased. "You offered."

Maude raised her voice. "I'm not mad!"

"Clearly, you are," he said. "You're yelling at me, and your cheeks are flushed. That's hardly an indication—"

"Just drive!"

"—of calm serenity."

When the light turned green, Fraser moved with the rest of the traffic. Maude put her Hello Kitty backpack on her lap and kept her gaze out the window. Terry drooped in the backseat. Her phone buzzed in her front hoodie pocket. There was a quick text from Zach. The asp pulsed a little quicker.

RU OK?

She wasn't sure how to answer that one.

Call u soon

She stared at the screen waiting for his reply. Waves of warmth spread from the asp, pulsating through her. Terry remembered how his kiss had lifted her off her feet. Her phone buzzed again with his reply.

XOXO

"Price Kamal?" Maude playfully asked, now turned in her seat, staring at Terry in the back. She still hadn't given up on teasing Terry about a royal fairy tale wedding.

"Uh … no," she said, pocketing the phone. "Spam."

"Sure," Maude said. "Spam makes me blush all the time too. Is the spam asking you out on another dinner date?"

"Date?" Fraser caught Terry's eye in the rearview mirror. His shocked expression felt like an insult.

"Is it so unbelievable that I would have a date?" she asked.

"You two love twisting my words." He let out the exhausted sigh of a beaten soldier. "No, I don't find it unbelievable that you'd have a date. I wonder if you've forgotten Gus's story about how the last girl to wear the asp merely kissed him on the cheek and he was obsessed with her for years. It almost ruined his life."

"So?" Maude said.

Fraser came to another red light. "It should be obvious," he said. He turned around from the front seat and stared at Terry. "Be careful who you make out with while wearing that thing."

Chapter Thirty-Two

Terry stopped at the doorway to the ICU. The whispers of the nurses were interrupted by the soft beeps from the monitors.

"Nefertari." Prince Kamal came up behind her. His leather jacket was unzipped, showing off his tight T-shirt underneath. A warm smile spread across his face. "You're limping less today."

"Oh," she stammered, silently reprimanding herself for forgetting to limp. "I've … uh, cut out gluten."

"I'm glad," he said. "Seeing you struggle is not something I enjoy. I sincerely hope it continues working for you."

Prince Kamal's grand politeness was comforting. They made their way to Gunther Hughes' bedside. Terry stared. "He looks like he's sleeping," she said.

Prince Kamal lifted the vital chart from the slot at the foot of the bed. There was a graph with a line that spiked at regular intervals. "See this point?" He indicated a sharp increase in her father's pulse. "It happens roughly once a day."

Terry studied the graph. "Why?" she asked.

"The nurses said it probably means that whatever toxin is in his system is growing weaker."

Terry took her dad's hand and squeezed, but there was no reaction. "So he's waking up?" She squeezed his hand harder, staring at her his eyes, willing them to open.

"Perhaps," he said.

"But they don't know for sure, do they?" Terry was tired of waiting for science to help her dad.

Prince Kamal dropped his gaze then backed away, giving her privacy.

Terry bent over here dad's bed. "I've got the asp," she whispered. There was no movement from his fingers. "I'm going to make everything better, then you can get out of here and we'll be a family again."

Terry waited for a response, hoping that maybe the sound of her voice could reach deep down to where her dad's consciousness was. But he remained still. She pressed her forehead against his hand. He seemed so weak, so vulnerable...

The idea came to Terry so quickly, her head snapped up, making a cracking sound. After a glance around the room to make sure no one was watching, Terry shifted all of her weight to her good leg then slowly, carefully slipped the asp off her arm.

Instantly, her right knee began to throb. She held her breath against the pain then moved the gold piece over her dad's hand, pushing it up as far up as it would fit his arm, just below the elbow.

Terry let out a slow breath through pursed lips. She squeezed his hand again and waited.

Ten seconds.

One minute.

Nothing.

Terry pulled off the asp and slipped it back on her own arm again. The instant relief of pain from her knee did nothing to ease her desperation.

Prince Kamal's deep voice came from the opposite side of the room. He was speaking with a nurse at another bed. A heavy weight settled across Terry's shoulders. Dr. Mullaca looked so feeble and tiny in the bed, surrounded by all the monitors, her gray hair fanned out on the pillow like a ghostly flower. The frail woman seemed much less threatening than the tyrant in the wheelchair.

Terry had to fix all this. She needed to get to that sarcophagus in the locked room. She needed the code for the number pad.

She gingerly made her way to the bedside, stepping around the little wheelchair. A small, black zip-up bag hung off the back. She rested her hand over Dr. Mullaca's bony one — it was warmer than her dad's. Prince Kamal and the nurse had moved around the curtain out of view.

Terry leaned down and whispered, "Can you hear me?" There was no response. "Dr. Mullaca." A little louder this time. "It's Terry, I've got the asp." A bony finger curled around Terry's hand.

The monitors began dinging at a high pitch. A rush of white uniforms and lab coats spilled into the small area. Terry stepped back, watching them assess Dr. Mullaca. She stumbled and tripped over the wheelchair. A clear vial and several syringes fell out of the black bag. A strong hand cupped her elbow and helped her stand. "Are you all right?" Prince Kamal's eyes were wide with concern. "We should leave."

Terry nodded. "Yes, just help me with this." They righted the wheelchair and slipped the supplies back in the pouch.

They waited in the visitors' lounge area until a nurse let them know that Dr. Mullaca was stable, but there were no further signs of consciousness. Prince Kamal thanked the staff and led Terry to the elevator.

They were quiet the whole ride back in the limo. He only spoke when they were outside her suite. "That's unfortunate," Prince Kamal said.

"I know." Terry sighed, leaning against the door frame. She was exhausted. "I was so close to speaking with her." She stopped herself from saying, "*and getting the code and opening up the sarcophagus.*"

Prince Kamal's eyebrows came together. "I mean about the vials and syringes. I assume she's diabetic. I have an uncle who has to inject insulin three times a day or he will die. It will complicate her condition, I'm afraid."

Terry pictured the tiny vials. "Right," she said. "Of course." She used her card key and opened the suite. The light in the hallway was on. She appreciated not coming back to a dark room.

Prince Kamal stayed in the hallway. "I don't want you to lose hope."

His unfailing optimism was a comforting contrast to the unsettling meeting with Gus Tanner. Terry appreciated having Prince Kamal on her side. She gave him a smile, grateful for his words. "Thanks, I won't."

"Sleep well, Nefertari." Then he made his way back to his suite.

Terry locked the door and grabbed her phone, punching in Zach's number. It went straight to voicemail. After leaving a message for him to call her later she made her way to the bathroom, removed her brace and slowly lowered herself into the tub. She gritted her teeth and then slipped off the asp, hoping a long hot soak would ease the ache in her knee, but it still throbbed by the time she toweled off.

Terry wrapped herself up in the plush bathrobe and checked her phone. There was still no reply from Zach. She frowned at the blank screen, absentmindedly rubbing her sore knee. Her fingers traced the deepest scar.

She folded back the robe and looked down at her legs, one strong and straight, the other lumpy and disfigured from the thigh down. Grotesque. Terry leaned back on the pillow and covered her face with her arm. Who was she kidding? Zach might want to kiss her, but he'd never want to see this part of her — ever. No one would. Only in her dreams.

Her bottle of anti-inflammatories was on the bedside table beside the asp. The ache in her knee kept traveling up and down her whole leg. If she didn't take something soon, her entire side would be knotted up all night. Instead, Terry reached for the asp and slipped it on her arm. Waves of relief washed over her. She sighed as every muscle relaxed. She kept it on all night and lay under the fluffy duvet dreaming of Egyptian sunsets.

Chapter Thirty-Three

Terry found Maude waiting by her locker. "Where were you this morning that you didn't need a drive to school in the limo?" Terry asked. "The text you sent me was purposely ambiguous."

"Fraser picked me up."

"Oh, really?"

Maude ignored her innuendo. She pulled out a glossy booklet. "This is why I wasn't home this morning. I had to pick it up from the printers. Look!"

"Wow." Terry took the comic book from Maude. "It's amazing!" The cover was almost identical to the drawing Zach had given Terry, except smaller parts of the story were represented in the four corners around Cleopatra's portrait; a bloodied sword for gathering an army to defeat her brother, an adorned barge for her first meeting with Mark Antony, a golden headdress for her reign as a sovereign monarch, and the asp — representing her death.

"It's like an *Indiana Jones* movie poster," Terry gushed. "But so much better."

"I know," Maude giggled. "Zach is a genius."

Terry's fingers lightly traced Cleopatra's image.

"We'll totally get a better mark than stupid Allison and her stupid pamphlet."

"Yeah," Terry said in a fog. She couldn't wait to show Zach.

She hoped he would be proud and recognize how smart he was. He still hadn't called her back, and a sliver of doubt had been pestering her all morning.

Maude dropped her voice and leaned in close. "You've got to skip school this afternoon." Her voice was mysterious.

"Are you kidding? We've got to show this to Zach." Terry unloaded her books into the locker, and then carefully placed the comic book inside her empty backpack.

"No, I'm serious, Fraser's waiting for us in the library." Maude gripped her arm. When she felt the asp through Terry's shirt, her hand flew away. "Why are you still wearing that thing?"

"I kind of forgot I was wearing it," Terry said truthfully. "Besides, it's good for my body to take a break from all those anti-inflammatories. Think of how happy my liver is right now."

"I don't like it, you're becoming dependent."

Terry shut her locker loudly. "Once you've been in chronic pain for a year we'll have this discussion, but until then stop talking to me like I'm some kind of drug addict."

Maude clutched the books to her chest. "Okay," she said. "Message received."

"Good," Terry said, a little less forcefully.

Maude put all of her attention on picking at a unicorn sticker on her folder. "It's just that I'm worried about you."

Terry's heart warmed. She'd never had a close friend before. It was weird to have someone her own age say something parental. Maude was the only person close enough to be like family.

"I'm sorry," Terry said. "Once we find June everything will make sense, and then I can get rid of this thing." She motioned to her arm.

Maude smiled and offered her a piece of gum. "You're not going to believe what Fraser and I found out last night."

"That you're actually compatible?"

Maude tugged on her arm and led her down the hall to the library. "Hardly," she said. "You of all people should realize why I can never date Fraser."

Terry had no idea what she was talking about, and waited for
her to elaborate.

Instead, she wordlessly led Terry to one of the private study
rooms. The table was covered with Gus's yellowed articles. Fraser
had his back to them, sitting at a computer. "We're here," Maude
announced unnecessarily.

Fraser slowly turned in his chair to face them, as if he was the
villain in a James Bond movie. "Good, close the door," he ordered.

"Yes, Dr. Evil," Terry said. She plopped her backpack on the
nearest chair. The window at the top of the door gave Terry an
unobstructed view of the entrance to the library. "If you wanted
things to be so secret, why aren't we in the newspaper office?"

Fraser stood and put all his attention was on the table. He
was wearing a fitted Oxford shirt and a plaid bowtie. The tail of
his shirt hung over his skinny black jeans.

He said, "The police took Tanya's computer, and I had to get
an old yearbook from the student archives." He nodded to the articles. "We organized by date."

Terry noticed there was a labeled folder for each pile. "I
thought you had every article about the asp?" She was careful not
to put anything out of order.

"Gus kept anything in the news that was unexplained or in
the crime column." He pushed up his glasses. "Like robberies and
such." There was a long row of clippings. "Right after June disappeared there was a sharp increase in assaults."

Maude pointed to one particular article. "But some people
were calling it vigilantism. A few shop owners reported instances
where the robbers left the store with a bundle of cash or packs of
cigarettes, only to get beaten up in the parking lot. Muggers
would be found with stolen wallets, unconscious in the park." She
shrugged. "Stuff like that."

"When did you guys do all this?" Terry asked, feeling a little
left out.

"Last night at Maude's house," Fraser answered matter-of-factly. "I stayed for supper." He looked at Terry and smiled for the first time. "Have you eaten there? Her grandma can't feed you enough."

Terry grinned back. "I know!"

"I was deliciously stuffed with gluten."

"Anyway," Maude prompted. "Show her what else we found."

"Right." Fraser handed Terry a slip of newspaper. He pointed to a name halfway down the page. "Read that quote," he said.

Amy Sue Veinot, a classmate of June's, stated, "She was always by herself, never talked to anyone. The last time I saw her was in the bathroom."

Terry glanced up. "So?"

"It reminded me what some of our less than tactless students told the reporter about Tanya usually ditching school." She nodded to the black and white school picture of June. "What kind of student does an interview after a classmate goes missing? Especially a classmate that didn't have any friends."

"Someone who likes the spotlight," Terry said.

Maude pointed at her. "Exactly!"

Fraser held up an old yearbook. "I didn't put much thought into Maude's instinct until we looked up Amy Sue."

Terry caught sight of the library door opening. Zach walked in and looked around. He saw her through the glass window, his smile unmistakably genuine. She grabbed their history project and raced out. "I'll be right back" she called over her shoulder.

"What the f—"

The door shut behind Terry, cutting off Fraser in mid-swear.

Chapter Thirty-Four

Terry forced herself not to run to him. He was wearing his light blue Henley shirt again, the first few buttons undone. He motioned for her to follow him down the farthest aisle.

One of Allison's princesses looked up from her study pod. Terry brushed her bangs in front of her eyes. She took the long way around, turning corners and pausing every few aisles, pretending to look for a title. Hands smoothed around her waist. Zach hugged her from behind. His chin rested on the top of her head. The comic book dropped to the floor. He carefully stepped around Terry, keeping her in the embrace. He smiled down at her, then swept her long bangs off to the side. "I missed you," he whispered.

At his touch the asp sent tingles down Terry's arm. "I called you last night," she said.

"Sorry." He shuffled his feet, sneaking even closer. "My dad had me practicing until late. When I called you back you'd already turned your phone off." He touched her chin, tilting up her face. "You have early sleeping habits. I'm going to have to change my schedule accordingly."

Terry's hands smoothed over his Henley shirt, resting on his chest. The fabric *was* soft. The asp began to pulse a tempo through Terry's veins.

Zach frowned down at her. "Are you okay?" he asked. "It must be hard with your dad in the hospital," he said. "I'm sorry I wasn't there for you last night. I hate the thought of you being alone."

His voice triggered that part of her that ached to be a normal girl who just wanted to be liked by a cute boy. He made her feel like it was okay to forget about curses and missing girls and mean-spirited bullies. His hands moved to the waist of her cargo paints. Terry snuggled into his arms, laying her cheek against his chest. She closed her eyes and breathed in. "You smell nice," she said.

He chuckled and tightened his grip around her waist. They stayed in the embrace. Terry became aware of every bit of their bodies that were touching. The asp throbbed faster, creating an adrenaline rush. Waves of heat rolled over her skin.

Her hands slid around and started moving over his back. Zach murmured into her hair. He cupped the back of her head. The asp sent ripples of electricity through the length of her body.

Zach leaned back, putting an inch of space between them. He stared at Terry, then traced her lower lip with his thumb. She rose up on her tiptoes, meeting him halfway. All she wanted was one kiss. One kiss and he'd be hers forever.

Forever.

A tiny moan escaped Zach's lips.

"Oh god!" Terry pushed hard on his chest, sending him crashing into the opposite bookcase.

He righted himself and touched the back of his head. "What?" he asked, a little stunned.

"I thought I saw someone." She fumbled with the lie and pointed down the empty aisle. "We have to be more careful, right? No PDAs." He did a double take of both ends of the empty aisle. Terry wrung her hands, too embarrassed to look him in the eye. The bright glossy comic book lay on the floor. She smiled nervously then bent down and picked it up. "I also wanted you to see this."

Zach's expression of confused hurt dissolved into shock. He

stared at the front cover. A crooked grin spread across his features. He turned the page and his eyes lit up. "This is good," he said.

"Good?" Terry tucked into his side. "It's amazing!" She watched his face, and a new kind of hurried pulse ran through her: one that had nothing to do with how good he smelled or how amazing his kisses felt. "Maude said you're a genius."

Zach glanced at her with a sarcastic look. "No one's ever said that."

"Shut up." She punched his arm. "Our history project is totally boss ... and so are you."

"Boss?" He laughed. He flipped through it again, drinking up every detail. "The glossy pages make it look real." He sighed and handed it back to her. "It's a good thing I'm doing all that practicing, since this project guarantees I'm going to the State Championships. There's no way Ms. Bernard will give us anything less than a B."

Terry pushed it back to him. "You can hand it in," she told him. "It was your idea, and you did like ninety per cent of the work."

"Ninety-eight." He took her hand. "Thanks, Terry. I never would have come up with this if it wasn't for you."

They had another staring contest. The kind that sent tingles all the way to her toes. And even though Terry knew she should look away, she couldn't.

He squeezed her hand. "I really want to kiss you," he said.

She swallowed, trying to ignore the asp waking back up. "Not here."

"When?" He sounded desperate. "Can you come to practice this afternoon? Please?"

"I can't."

"Tonight?"

Terry handed him her phone. "Give me your address," she said. "I'll visit you this time."

"I'll make sure your name is on the safe list for the body-guards in the lobby so you don't get arrested," he grinned. Then Zach handed back her phone and slipped his arms around her for a quick hug. It was impossible for Terry to ignore her heightened awareness of him — the pressure of his fingers, the smell of his shampoo, the vibration of his voice against her ear as he whispered, "You drive me crazy."

Terry squeezed her arms around him. All she could think of was one word — *closer*.

A strangled cry erupted from Zach. He held his side and gave her a quizzical look. "Easy, girl." He winced. "I think you almost cracked a rib. Man, you're stronger than you look."

Terry's hands flew up to her mouth. "Oh my god. I'm sorry."

He rubbed his side and did a quick stretch. "You can't injure me before the big game," he teased. "Maybe I should avoid you until after the State Championships. I can't play in a full body cast." He studied Terry's dismayed expression, then his smile fell. "I'm only kidding. I really want to see you tonight."

A freshman turned the corner and came into the aisle, a large encyclopedia-sized book under her arm.

"Um ... so don't forget to pass that in, okay?" Terry used an unusually loud voice.

Zach held up the comic book and gave her wink. She watched him walk by the freshman who, was so concerned with balancing a second volume, she and Zach could have been making out and the girl wouldn't have noticed.

Terry dragged herself back to the study room, missing the electricity Zach charged up in her.

Fraser looked up from the table. "How's the school's golden boy these days?"

"We're working on the same project for history," Terry said. She looked at Maude, hoping for backup.

"Anyway," Fraser said, "before you ran out with your pants on fire for your homework buddy, I was about to show you this."

Fraser held up an old yearbook from Roosevelt High. "Guess who was the homecoming queen fifty years ago?"

"I have no clue," Terry said, reaching for the yearbook.

Fraser pulled it out of her reach. "Amy Sue Veinot."

"The girl from the interview," Maude reminded her. She was also dating the star quarterback — he was voted king."

Terry shrugged. "So?"

Fraser pointed to another article in the crime section. "Two weeks after June disappeared, Amy Sue was attacked. The blunt trauma to her head was so severe, she sustained permanent brain damage."

Terry's stomach threatened to push up its contents. She wasn't expecting *that* twist. "Who would do that to her?"

Fraser's tone softened. "Remember the rash of vigilantism? The police thought it was random violence and chalked it up to that. She had no enemies and was never able to identify her attacker."

The room cooled. Terry asked, "Do you think who ever attacked Amy Sue is also responsible for June's disappearance?"

Fraser and Maude shared a look. "We're not sure," he said, "but we're going to see her today."

He opened the yearbook and slid it across the table. A black and white photo of a young girl took up nearly a whole page. Her blonde hair was in an elegant twist and topped with a tiara. She wore pearl earrings and a perfect smile. Under the picture was written "Amy Sue Veinot, Homecoming Queen 1963."

Fraser asked. "Does she look like any other debutant you might know?"

"Oh my god," Terry breathed. "She looks exactly like Allison."

Chapter Thirty-Five

"What do you think, Daphne?" Fraser turned off the ignition and wiggled his eyebrows at Maude.

The three friends stared out the windshield at the Victorian mansion. Ivy dusted with snow crawled up the sides, softening the corners. From the street it looked like an estate, but up close the fire escapes and wheelchair ramps were more obvious.

"It certainly looks like a place a former homecoming queen would live out her old age," Maude said.

"Except she's not that old," Terry said. "She's only in her late sixties."

"Same as my grandma," Maude said quietly.

They furtively made their way up the impressive stairs, careful to avoid the icy patches. A brown paper bag was tucked under Fraser's arm. He held open the massive oak door for the girls. "Okay, let me do all the talking," he told them.

"Sure thing, Fred." Maude rolled her eyes.

The foyer was grandly decorated with tall ferns and expensive rugs, but the smell of disinfectant and medicine lingered — as beautiful as this building was, it was still a hospital. A woman with a smart-looking bun and glasses looked up as they approached the nurses' station. Fraser put on his best smile. There was a rustle of paper as he pulled out a box of chocolates. From the impressed expression on Maude's face Terry guessed they were high quality.

"I hope you can help me," he began, his voice full of innocence. "I'm visiting the city, and my aunt wanted me to make sure I saw an old school friend of hers. I'm sure she won't know who I am, but I do have a little something for her." He gave a pained smile and held up the expensive chocolates.

The nurse tilted her head. "That's so thoughtful. What's the name of your aunt's friend?"

Fraser checked his pocket and pulled out a crumpled note. "Hold on, I've got it written down." He pretended to read the blank piece of paper. "Amy Sue Veinot."

The nurse's smile fell. "Are you sure?"

"Maybe I mispronounced the last name?" He laughed.

Maude and Terry shared a glance. The nurse craned her neck around Fraser, studying them.

"My friends and I drove all night," he explained. "We're in Devonshire for college interviews." Maude and Terry smiled widely and nodded. Fraser angled closer to the nurse. "I'm pre-med, and she's kinesiology, but my other friend," he waved a hand at Maude, "she's going for plumber's apprentice."

Maude shrank under the nurse's gaze. "I'm super handy," she added quickly. The nurse narrowed her eyes. "I'll see that Ms. Veinot gets the chocolates. What's the name of your aunt, again?"

"Trina Baker," he answered. "Well, Baker is her married name, I guess you should tell Miss Veinot the chocolates are from her good friend, Trina Colby."

The nurse made a note and took the box from Fraser.

He backed away, then stopped. "Oh geez, I almost forgot. Here," he said, pulling out a larger box of chocolates from the paper bag. "My aunt is a retired nurse, and she made sure that I bring something for the staff as well."

"Oh my goodness." The nurse stood up and took the sweets. She gave Fraser a second scan.

He nodded shyly. "Please make sure to tell her that my aunt

still laughs about the time they let the frogs escape from bio lab. She also wanted me to pass along that Bud Wilson turned out to be gay after all."

Fraser paused, then patted his pockets. He pulled out another sheet of paper and began to read. "And tell her that Shirley Buchannon married a plastic surgeon and finally got her nose fixed, and Craig Jackson confessed to putting the dog—"

"I have an idea," the nurse interrupted. She smoothed a hand over her already perfectly tight bun. She returned the smaller box of chocolates to Fraser. "Go ahead and tell her yourself. Only five minutes," she warned. "Ms. Veinot gets agitated easily."

"Thank you," Fraser said. "I promise, just a quick hello."

After getting the room number from the nurse, they took the grand wooden staircase up to the first floor. Terry fought the urge to run up the steps. Once they turned the corner and entered a quiet area, Maude hauled off and punched Fraser.

He rubbed his shoulder, looking shocked. "That's a weird way to say thank you."

"A plumber's apprentice?" she hissed. "Why can't I go to college? Is that because you think I'm not smart enough?"

Fraser stopped so quickly, Terry almost ran into the back of him. Maude placed her hands on her hips, ready for a showdown. "That just popped in my head," he said. "Your grandma pulled out her toolbox the other night, I guess that image stuck in my brain. And in case you didn't notice it, I was busy tap-dancing naked in front of that nurse to get us up here."

"You said you'd do all the talking," Maude reminded him. "I assumed you had a plan, instead of randomly pulling stupid crap out of your butt."

"It's always about the butt with you plumbers, isn't it?"

Maude snatched the box of chocolates out of his hands. "You're not worthy to carry these."

Terry tried to hush them.

The trio walked to the end of the hallway, then turned the final corner. "Seriously, though," Fraser whispered to Maude, "do you have any idea how much plumbers make an hour? Especially on a holiday?"

"I wish you'd be quiet," Maude answered.

"Is this the part where you threaten to give me something to suck on to keep me quiet?" Fraser was straight-faced, but the smallest hint of tease curled his words at the end into a smile.

"Stop," Terry whispered harshly. She pointed to a nameplate across the way. A plaque with Amy Sue's full name in fancy cursive confirmed they found the right room. All the built-up tension between Maude and Fraser dissipated, a new sense of foreboding taking its place.

"What's the plan now?" Terry asked. It had been all too easy to say they'd question Amy Sue when they were sitting in the little room in the library, but now they were about to meet her face-to-face. Questioning her about a fifty-year-old case now seemed ridiculous.

"I'm going to ask her about June," Fraser said. He removed his glasses and cleaned them off on his shirttail. He lightly knocked on the door, and they all walked inside.

It was like stepping into a teenage girl's room. Everything was pink and sparkly. There was more makeup than on Maude's vanity. The bed was lined with stuffed teddy bears, and there was a black and white poster of some heartthrob in a suit and tie singing into a microphone. Terry squinted at the poster and saw the name Paul Anka along the bottom.

Fraser cleared his throat "Miss Veinot?"

A delicate-looking woman with a blonde updo sat in a recliner pointed toward the large-screen TV on the wall. A soap opera was taking her full attention. Terry could see, even now, the striking resemblance of her upturned nose and fine profile to Allison.

Fraser tried again. "We're from Roosevelt High and I wonder if we could ask you some questions?" He took a step closer and offered her the chocolates. She finally turned toward him. Terry sucked in her breath, unprepared for what she saw.

Chapter Thirty-Six

Amy Sue's hair was smooth and shiny, and her makeup was impeccable — on the right side of her face. Her left eye was missing, a caved-in crater of flesh covering what should have been a matching baby blue. She started to mumble, but her sounds were garbled. Her hands fidgeted under her pink shawl, and a remote control emerged. She pressed a button, turning down the volume. She turned to Fraser again and mumbled a second time, her voice rising.

Terry swallowed hard. She poked Fraser in the back. "Let's go," she whispered.

"Um … Roosevelt High," he repeated. He tried to hand her the chocolates again, but she only stared back at him with one eye. Her thick, mascara-laden lashes blinked slowly.

Maude stepped forward and took the package. She unwrapped the plastic and crouched beside the recliner. She opened up the box and pointed to one of the largest chocolates, decorated with swirls. "This one is a praline," she said. "And this one with the white stripes is a caramel."

Amy Sue picked the praline chocolate and ate it daintily. Her baby blue eye winked at Maude then she pushed away the shawl, revealing a plastic board covered in the alphabet. A pink fingernail tapped out a word a letter at a time.

T-H-A-N-K-Y-O-U

Maude smiled widely. "You're welcome." She turned and gave Fraser an encouraging nod.

"Like I said," he began, "we're from Roosevelt High and we know you were friends with—"

"New visitors?" An older nurse in a white cardigan walked into the room. "I understand you're relatives of a former school chum of our Ms. Veinot." She was smiling, but Terry could hear the authority in her tone.

Fraser put his hands in his pockets and rocked back on his heels. "Yup," he said.

The nurse stood there waiting for more of an explanation. Fraser decided to stay quiet. Terry thought this was wise since he might blurt out Maude's plumbing ambitions again.

The nurse moved beside Amy Sue. She noticed the open box of chocolates in Maude's hands. "And you brought a treat as well."

Maude gently placed the box on the corner of the bed and slunk back with Terry. "Twizzlers," she whispered.

The nurse's attention was soon taken by the soap opera on the television. "I bet Nicholas will find out Brooke is lying about her pregnancy," she said. "And then he'll blackmail her into marrying his brother." Amy Sue tapped on her board again.

S-L-U-T

"Mm-hmm," the nurse replied.

Maude touched Fraser's elbow, but he shook her off, reluctant to go. Terry glanced around the pink room. On the wall were a few framed photographs. The largest was of Prince William and Kate's famous wedding kiss from the balcony of Buckingham Palace. The second largest, though, was a newspaper clipping of a handsome man in a suit accepting some kind of award.

She recognized the mayor. A heat burned inside Terry. Maybe if the mayor hadn't been pushing to ensure everything was in order for the unveiling, her father wouldn't be in the hospital.

The ending theme of the soap opera filled the room. The nurse made a frustrated noise. "Why do they always leave us hanging?" she asked. Amy Sue helped herself to another chocolate.

The music switched over to the local news channel. Tanya's photo appeared in the corner of the screen while a well-coiffed reporter recapped details of her disappearance.

Amy Sue stopped chewing. The front of the museum filled the television. She let out a garbled scream and started jabbing the plastic board.

"It's all right," the nurse tried to soothe. Amy Sue continued to scream. The nurse pressed a button on the wall. Terry and Maude backed out of the room. Another nurse arrived. Over Fraser's shoulder Terry could see Amy Sue's face frozen in fear. One of the nurses produced a needle.

Fraser turned and grabbed them both by the hands, leading them down the hallway and down the stairs. The frigid winter air hit them as they rushed to his car, sweat freezing on their goose bumps.

He peeled out of the parking lot, white as a ghost.

"God, that was horrible." Maude leaned over, hugging her stomach. "Let's promise to never, ever, do that again."

"That was weird," Terry said, trying to catch her breath in the backseat. "And I've seen some pretty weird stuff on digs with my parents."

Fraser rolled down his window and wiped an arm across his forehead. He steered the car down a quiet street.

Maude leaned back. "That poor woman," she said. "I mean, that could be my grandma."

"You're grandma's awesome," Fraser said.

"And even how the room was decorated," Terry continued, still in a daze. "Did you see the picture on the wall?"

"I guess she likes royalty," Maude said. "Maybe Prince Kamal could pay her a visit." She turned to Fraser, but he had no reaction to her attempt at humor.

Terry scooted forward. "No, I mean the one of the mayor. It

looked like a newspaper clipping."

Maude crinkled her nose. "Mayor Harris?"

"Yeah, but it was framed like a real picture. Isn't that weird?"

"Why is he on Amy Sue's wall?" Maude asked.

"And why does Allison look so much like her?" Terry replied.

Fraser finally spoke, his tone detached. "Two years ago my older brother had to do an interview for the newspaper. If he did a good job, he'd get hired permanently. The mayor was running for election, so my brother's room was covered with sticky notes full of facts."

His voice softened. "For fun I memorized all the notes and then hid them. I was hoping my brother would let me tag along if I convinced him I knew all the facts."

"Nerd alert," Maude murmured.

"It worked," he continued. "He had to take me. I even got to ask a few questions." Fraser signaled and turned right. He slowed down and pulled into the parking lot of a convenience store.

"So?" Maude prompted.

"It may interest you to know that the mayor will be forty-nine in three months," he said. "And that he was adopted." Fraser backed into a space, and turned off the engine. The only sound was the ticking of the car cooling down.

Maude broke the silence. "Are you saying Mayor Harris is Amy Sue's illegitimate son?"

He rested a wrist on the steering wheel, staring through the windshield. "Is it so impossible to imagine that the homecoming queen got knocked up by her quarterback boyfriend? I mean, people did have sex in high school back then, probably just as much as today."

Maude's ears turned bright red. "Still." She cleared her throat. "It doesn't explain why she'd give him up. I mean, there are a lot of girls who kept their babies, even though they didn't get married."

Fraser tapped the wheel. "If you look at the timeline, Amy Sue was already pregnant when she was attacked." There was a long pause. "Half of her face was smashed in and she became totally dependent. Do you think anyone would want to marry her after that? They'd spend their whole life watching her pound out words on her board."

Terry's head weighed a thousand tons. "It seems the more we uncover, the less I understand. How can this help my dad? How does this even relate to the museum?"

Fraser started a list on his fingers. "Allison got the class into the museum for a preview. During that trip Tanya went missing. Mayor Harris is pushing for an early unveiling for the fundraiser that will apparently save the museum."

"Is he looking to be the hero by ensuring the museum stays open?" Maude suggested. "Is this just about getting more votes and getting reelected next year?"

"I don't think it's that simple," he said.

A chill rippled through Terry. Instinctively she wrapped her fingers over the asp.

Fraser stared through the windshield again. "When the news came on," he said, "Amy Sue wasn't bothered by Tanya's picture. She became upset when they showed the museum."

"Upset?" Maude said. "She beat up her little alphabet board." Her voice lowered. "And ruined some perfectly good chocolates, I might add."

"She wasn't beating it up," Fraser replied. He frowned as if watching the whole scenario again. "You couldn't see because you were behind me, but she was spelling the same name over and over again."

The hairs raised on the back of Terry's neck.

"Whose name?" Maude asked apprehensively.

He turned to her and said, "June."

Chapter Thirty-Seven

Terry rested her head on a pink pillow and stared at Maude's bedroom ceiling. Glow-in-the-dark stars were randomly placed in the space above the bed. Terry could barely make out their shapes. Even though it was early evening, the lamp made the room too bright to see them properly.

"I was going to do an actual constellation," Maude explained, "but my neck got sore." She sat at her desk doodling on a piece of paper. June and Amy Sue's names had been written out several times. Maude was convinced she was missing something, that a clue was staring her in the face.

"What do you think you're going to find?" Terry asked dozily. The sausage lasagna and sweet potato casserole Maude's grandma made for supper had a soporific effect.

"There must be a connection," Maude insisted. She chewed the end of her pencil. "I mean, why would a picture of the museum freak out Amy Sue?"

Terry closed her eyes. "I don't know," she mumbled. "Because there's lots of dead stuff?"

Maude pursed her lips together. "Remember that quote in the paper by Amy Sue about how the last time she saw June was in the bathroom?" She waited a few beats, then continued. "Do you think Amy Sue was the type of girl to notice a loner like June …

in the bathroom?"

Maude's tone caught Terry's attention. She raised herself up on her elbows, sensing Maude had a theory. "Spill it," she said.

Maude made little circles on the paper with her pen. "I kind of get her, you know?" she started. "June, I mean. A loner made fun of at school, someone who doesn't exactly fit in. I've met Allison many times in the bathroom, and she's never once complimented me on anything. She's only humiliated me."

Terry sat up and swung her legs over the bed. She didn't care about Amy Sue or June anymore. This time was all about Maude. "Why does Allison hate you so much?" Terry asked.

Maude let out a long sigh. "Because of a stupid bake table in grade eight."

"Sounds scandalous."

"She made a big deal about these chocolate cupcakes that she was bringing, convinced everyone that she would sell the most and fund the school trip for the whole class." Maude shrugged. "I brought in Grandma's vanilla cupcakes with her special rainbow swirled icing."

"And everyone wanted those," Terry guessed.

"Plus, I'd sold them in Mom's shop and around the neighborhood. I ended up making way more money so I used the extra for the local food bank. The teacher awarded me that week's 'Exemplary Samaritan Award.' I even got my picture in the paper. Allison was so mad."

"Uh-oh."

Maude nodded. "Allison came to school the next day and told everyone that my grandma was never married, and never went to college. Then she said the same about Mom. I didn't care about that, but then she called me a slut and said I'd get pregnant and drop out of high school too. I came home crying because none of the other kids would talk to me. When Mom asked what was wrong, I told her I was ashamed of my family."

Terry kept quiet.

Maude's shoulders curled inward. She let out a long sigh, like she was slowly deflating. "Once I saw the look on my mom's face, I regretted ever opening my mouth. It wasn't my lack of a father that made me ashamed, it was how Allison convinced me that I should be. Allison started calling me white trash, and it stuck." Maude dropped her pencil. "I guess the fact her biggest crush asked me out probably didn't help much."

"At least you got some revenge," Terry suggested carefully.

"I was too young to date," Maude explained. "I was only thirteen. That was three years ago — plenty of time for rumors to circulate," she said. "I've never had a decent guy ask me out since."

"I hate mean girls," Terry said. Out of habit, she placed a hand on her knee and started rubbing. "At least there's one good thing about all this weird stuff with June and Amy Sue — you and Fraser seem to be spending a lot of time together."

Maude made a pathetic sound. "Please, he's never going to ask me out. And if he did, I'd turn him down."

"Are you kidding? I thought you liked him."

She pushed away the notepad full of squiggles. "I gave him too much of an awesome personality before we met," she said. "My fantasy Fraser can't compete with the real, unromantic, stuck-up genius who thinks a dinosaur exhibit is more beautiful than me.."

"Fantasy Fraser?" Terry teased. "What's he like?"

A smirk spread across Maude's face. "He's awesome; he compliments me, holds open doors, takes my hand in the hallway, carries my books for me…"

"Oh, him!" Terry said. "Amy Sue has his poster on her wall, his name is Paul Anka."

Maude picked up a pillow from the floor and tossed it at her face. "I know my worth." She laughed. "There's nothing wrong with having high standards. Every girl deserves to be kissed by a boy she loves. The kind of kiss that lifts you off your feet, you know?"

"Yeah," Terry sighed. Her stomach swooped as she thought

about Zach.

There was a glint in Maude's eye. She studied Terry for a moment. "You mean, 'yeah I wish,' or 'yeah I know'?"

"More like 'I wish I knew,'" Terry said, rolling her eyes. Maude didn't press the issue, and the room became quiet. Secretly, she hoped Maude would soon make a move on Fraser. Terry felt she couldn't be completely happy about her relationship with Zach until Maude was happy as well. If she shared about her kiss about Zach it would feel like bragging.

Terry glanced at Maude's M&Ms alarm clock. "Um ... I have to get back to the Plaza." With a package of cookies from Maude's grandma, she called a cab and gave the driver directions to Zach's home instead.

The drive to Zach's took less than five minutes. Terry had no idea he lived so close to Maude.

The brick apartment building was on the opposite side of town from where the Plaza and the upscale homes of Devonshire were. It was completely dark now. Terry squinted through the window for details of the neighborhood. Modest homes with well-kept lawns blurred past, then there was a section of brick apartment buildings. She appreciated how long a bus ride he had taken after he saw her that night at the Plaza.

Terry paid the driver, then made her way into the clean foyer. The rusticated masonry and arched doorway were elegant yet understated. Past the glass doors she could see the elevator, flanked by two large potted ferns. She studied the panel of names and easily found the Bretons — they were on the fifth floor. Terry pressed the buzzer and waited to be let up.

After several more attempts there was still no answer. She drummed her fingers on the panel, trying to decide what to do next. Leaving wasn't an option. She'd been waiting since this morning to see him. Terry flexed her bicep. The fifth floor wouldn't be too high to climb, she thought with a grin. And secretly, she'd been aching to test her new strength again. She'd just have to be careful not to break her brace.

Around the back of the building a basketball court was scraped clear of ice and snow. Several raised garden beds were covered with burlap. An iron fire escape snaked up the height of the complex. She counted up five floors. One window, two over from the right, flickered with the blue glow of a television. The window was barely cracked open, but the sounds of shooting echoed down to her.

If Zach was in his bedroom watching a movie, he wouldn't have heard the buzzer, she reasoned. Terry tucked the cookies into her front pocket and jumped for the rung of the first iron ladder. She wasn't surprised the climbing came effortlessly. Her body hummed with the electrical current of the asp.

Keeping her back to the wall, she inched her way along the fire escape's ledge and peeked in the corner of the window. Her pulse, already racing with the exercise, picked up even more when she saw Zach sitting on his bed in front of an Xbox 360. He was playing some kind of dystopian warfare zombie game. Terry grinned, enjoying how he pulled different faces while he played.

She pulled out the bag of cookies and munched a few, contemplating climbing through the window. He'd be shocked, of course, but before he could ask her how she managed to climb up the building, she'd wrap her hands around his neck and kiss him. The warmth from the asp grew in her chest with the thought of making out with Zach.

Terry would have to take the asp off. She had no idea if Fraser's theory about its love addiction properties were true, but she wasn't willing to mess with Zach's mental state.

It began to drizzle freezing rain. His phone lay on the bed beside him. She rolled her eyes to the sky. She was so stupid. Why hadn't she just called him from downstairs?

She started to dial, but he was already picking up his phone. He paused his game and looked at the screen. The expression on his face was hard to read. Terry canceled her call and watched.

She could barely hear his voice. "Hi," he answered. "Um …
no." He closed his eyes and pinched the bridge of his nose with his
thumb and finger. Terry strained to hear bits of the conversation.
"… you have to see me in person?"

Terry's insides began to squirm. The bag of cookies dropped
from her hand.

There was an excruciating long pause, then he said, "Okay.
Five minutes." He ended the call and sat on the bed, motionless.

Chapter Thirty-Eight

Terry took a few steps back and punched in his number. She watched him as he considered her caller ID. Finally, on the fourth ring, he answered. "Hey," he said brightly. It scared her how upbeat he sounded. "Where were you this afternoon? Ms. Bernard wondered why you and Maude weren't in class."

Terry was caught off guard by his question. She wasn't expecting to be the one on the hot seat. "Maude threw up at lunch and had to go home."

"Gross. Nothing worse than being sick at school." He made a face. "So where were you?"

Terry huffed from the far corner of the cold fire escape. "She threw up on me. I had to go with her to change."

"Oh."

He checked his watch, then grabbed his varsity jacket from the end of the bed. "I have to go out and throw a few hoops."

Terry looked down at the abandoned basketball court five floors below. "Isn't it too cold?" she asked.

"Every bit of practice I can get helps."

"Awesome," she said. "Do you still want me to come over?" A jealous curiosity began to take root. If he was going to lie to her, she wanted to catch him in the act with whoever he was going to meet.

He checked his watch and turned off the Xbox. "I was expecting you'd call earlier," he said, completely sidestepping her question.

"I was with Maude."

"Right. Still, it's kind of late for you to be out alone. Why don't you come over after school tomorrow instead?" As Zach left his room, she could hear his footsteps quicken. "Listen, I have to go, but I'll call you when I'm done, okay? Make sure you leave your phone on this time," he said. Then Zach ended the call.

With blood roaring through her ears, Terry scaled down the side of the building, not even bothered by how slick the icy rain made the railings. She crept around the corner of the building and waited in the shadows. Zach came out and stood under the street-lamp, his varsity jacket buttoned up against the weather. He shuffled his feet nervously on the sidewalk.

A red car sped into view and pulled over. Terry read the license plate: 2GOOD4U. Allison stepped out from the driver's side, the streetlight illuminating her blonde hair. She tightened her red coat against the rain. She and Zach nodded to each other, then started to walk up the sidewalk. The bare branches of the trees on either side of the street drooped under the weight of the freezing rain.

Terry followed the pair, careful to stay hidden. Zach's hands were deep in his jacket pockets while Allison's moved in the air as she talked. Terry pulled back her hood, straining to hear her exact words, but they were swallowed by the wind.

They paused by a deserted ball field. Icicles dripped from the dugout roofs.

Terry watched from the shadows, wishing she had super hearing as well. Frozen pellets stung her checks.

A black SUV with tinted windows roared by, making Terry shrink back farther from the street. When it drove out of sight, she moved closer to the curb, trying to get a better view.

" ... crazy," Zach said, stepping away from Allison. His loud voice echoed through the quiet night. Allison reached for him, but he took another step backward. "No. I don't care," he said. "Go home." He pointed in the direction of her car. Then Zach turned on his heel and started up the street in the opposite direction, leaving Allison crying on the sidewalk. He passed under a street-light with his head bowed into the wind, then he was swallowed up by the darkness.

Terry guessed that after a huge fight, you don't want to walk your ex-girlfriend back to her car. She watched Allison head back down the street, her boots taking short, quick steps. When she made it back to her car, she took out her cell phone. Terry was close enough to hear her. "Now," was all she said before she hung up.

Tires squealed on the slippery surface before getting a grip. Allison's car fishtailed slightly, then straightened and slowly disappeared down the street. Terry stayed hidden until the red sports car turned the corner and finally disappeared.

She looked up the street, waiting for Zach to backtrack and appear under the next streetlamp. She'd come up with an excuse to explain her sudden appearance — she just needed to see him. But after waiting for two minutes Terry decided to go after him. Her sneakers made crunching noises over the icy sidewalk, and she squinted at the ground, following the trail of Zach's footsteps. The wind whistled through her hoodie and around her neck. She paused. Tires squealed again. Car doors slammed. The asp began to pulse more quickly.

Someone screamed up ahead. Terry froze. She raised her face, taking the full assault of the freezing rain. The cozy houses on the other side of the street were a blurry mix of lighted windows. She squinted into the distance, willing him to reappear. She remembered how he looked standing outside her suite with his tousled light brown hair and boyish grin, after he'd shown her his drawings — and right before he had returned to kiss her. He'd joked that it was perfectly safe to walk home after dark.

Why would anyone want to hurt the school basketball hero?

Terry sprinted into the wind. Zach's lone pair of footprints turned sharply around a corner. She followed the trail and soon a mash of many footprints appeared. She felt the thick crack of her brace snapping in two; only the Velcro kept it from sliding off her leg. The scream came again, and this time it was much closer. Terry followed the scuffle and found Zach up against the side of the black SUV. One guy was punching him while another stood by with a tire iron at his side.

Terry went for the first guy, pulling him off Zach and tossing him to the ground. The man let out a garbled swear as his face collided with the ground. His partner ran forward, swinging the tire iron over his head. She grabbed it from him and flung it into the darkness. His fist came from the right, but her reflexes were faster. She dodged the hit, making him stagger off balance. Terry kneed him in the stomach, then kicked him to the sidewalk, where he stayed motionless.

Zach pushed himself up against the car. She put a hand around his waist, helping him stand. "Terry?" He winced.

"It's going to be okay," she babbled, her tears mixing with the freezing rain. The asp pulsated frantically, adrenaline surging through her muscles.

He stared back, confused, then his eyes shifted behind her. "Run!" he screamed, pushing her away. The first thug with the scraped-up face rushed toward Zach and mashed his cheek into concrete wall.

Zach cried out. "Run, Terry!"

In one quick motion Zach's arm was twisted upward behind his back. There was a sickening crunch as he screamed and dropped to his knees.

Terry clawed her fingers into the thug's hair and pulled back. He flew past her like a rag doll and landed on top of the hood of the SUV. She knelt beside Zach, resting his head in her lap. His arm lay at an awkward angle by his side. He mouthed something, then his eyes flickered and closed.

Chapter Thirty-Nine

"Why was the legend of Osiris and Isis so important to Cleopatra?" Ms. Bernard's voice was enthusiastic. Her eyes scanned the classroom. Terry sunk lower in her chair, staring at her desk, wishing to be invisible. It felt like the first day all over again.

1. Don't attract attention.
2. Don't get involved.
3. Don't make trouble.

But of course, everything was different now.

Ms. Bernard cleared her throat. "The legend tells us Osiris was murdered by his brother Seth, and his body was chopped into pieces and scattered all over Egypt."

Allison sniffed from behind Terry.

"But Isis, wife and sister of Osiris, tricked the sun god Re and was able to resurrect him," Ms. Bernard continued. "They became lovers again for his short second life on Earth. But it was long enough for her to bear him a son. Horus eventually avenged his father's death by slaughtering his Uncle Seth."

There was a murmur from the back of the class. Terry pictured Zach's teammates huddled together, leaning over their desks, red-faced and ready for revenge.

Ms. Bernard pressed her mouth into a hard line. "Before Cleopatra died, she negotiated with Octavian to allow her to bury Mark

Antony in Egypt, so that her corpse could be buried with his, allow-ing them to reenact the legend of Isis and Osiris."

She waited for a reaction, but it was clear no one cared about Cleopatra this morning. She let her shoulders fall, clearly defeat-ed. "All right," she said, "I understand most if you are upset about the news of your classmate. And since there seems to be several conversations going on already, the best thing would be for all of us to share our thoughts."

At the invitation to speak up, everyone grew quiet. Ms. Ber-nard motioned to the back of the class where the jocks sat. They squirmed in their chairs, busy studying the floor.

Tanya's boyfriend spoke. The dark circles under his eyes made him look older. "It's just weird, isn't it?" he said. He licked his lips and frowned at the front of the room, but his eyes weren't fo-cused. "First Tanya disappears, and now Zach gets the crap beat-en out of him? Why is this happening?"

"Dude, use your head," one of the other jocks said. "It's not a coincidence that our captain got his arm broken a few weeks be-fore the State Championships." He tilted his chin up and scanned the classroom. "Those pricks from West Mount Academy did this. They're our biggest competition."

Ms. Bernard put her hands up again. "I will not condone that language in my classroom."

"It's true, though," another voice added. "I heard they were bragging about it on Facebook. Something like, without Zach that trophy is theirs for the taking."

Terry's fingernails dug into her palms as she tightened her fists under the desk. Those two thugs weren't from some rival school. She knew who was responsible for Zach's broken arm.

"It's so sad," one of the princesses said. There was a bundle of markers in her hands and a large pair of scissors. "The cheerlead-ers are too devastated to even make posters for the game. No one will want to go see us lose to West Mount."

A disgruntled ripple of morbid agreement moved through the

class. Terry could sense Maude watching her out of the corner of her eye. Earlier, in the limo ride to school, Terry had divulged everything to Maude about the night before. "They broke his arm on purpose," Terry had said. "Allison is behind it."

"You beat off Zach's attackers, then carried him unconscious to the hospital?" Maude had replied, her eyes filling up. "You could have been killed by those guys."

Terry had stayed quiet, trying hard to stop the sound of Zach's bone breaking from replaying in her mind. Maude didn't ask any more questions but stayed by Terry's side, giving her concerned looks. Now, in history class, with everyone talking about Zach, Terry's heart was squeezed so tight, it hurt to breathe.

A dainty cough a few desks back made everyone quiet. "This school will come together and be strong," Allison said. "Zach would never want to see that trophy go to West Mount. We can win." She mustered up a sweet smile. "And we *will* win."

"Allison," Ms. Bernard beamed, "you're an example for us all."

Terry closed her eyes and gritted her teeth.

"Thank you." Allison sniffed. "I spoke with his parents this morning. He's home now, and he doesn't remember anything. My father promises to improve funding for more policing, and he vows to make sure this never happens again."

"I'd never go walking alone at night," one of the princesses added.

"Me neither," Allison sighed in agreement. "But Zach always felt untouchable."

Terry turned in her seat. Allison stared back at her. "I guess he was wrong."

After class, Terry went straight to her locker, not even bothering to pretend to limp. Her face was hot from holding in her urge to scream at the top of her lungs. She opened the locker and leaned in, taking long slow breaths. The asp throbbed against her skin, the episode from last night playing over and over in her mind.

Maude put a hand on her back. "Please, you've got to be careful," she warned. "Bad things are happening. That asp should be back in the museum, not on your arm making you into some kind of—"

"Some kind of what?" Terry snapped.

"I don't know…" Maude's ears turned bright crimson, almost matching her wavy pink streak. "I'm just so scared. It's like the asp makes you think you're strong enough to fight everyone."

"I *am* strong enough." She put an arm on Maude's shoulder. "Look, I can handle this. As long as I'm wearing the asp, no one can hurt me. Besides, I broke my brace last night, if I didn't have the asp I wouldn't be walking." Maude opened her mouth to object, but Terry continued. "You don't understand, and that's why it scares you. But I'm not scared, and that's all that matters."

Terry turned away. She needed to be alone. She marched at a quickened pace. It felt good to move this fluidly without her brace.

Ms. Bernard turned the corner, her nose in a book. "Oh!" she said, running into Terry. The book dropped from her hands. Her surprised expression melted into sympathy. "I've been meaning to ask, how's your father?"

The anger that had fueled Terry's energy quickly ebbed, leaving her weak. "He's stable," she said. "But there's no real change. I mean, he's not awake yet." She pictured his vital graph, with occasional spikes in his pulse.

"I'm glad to hear that." The teacher smiled.

Terry bent down and picked up the book. She recognized Osiris's image on the cover. The title flashed at her before Ms. Bernard tucked it under her arm.

The Osiris Cult of Resurrection

"Be strong," Ms. Bernard said. She patted Terry's arm, pausing to let her fingers curl around the asp hidden under her sleeve. The touch only lasted a few seconds, but the expression of wanting on Ms. Bernard's face lingered.

Terry moved backward. "I don't want to be late," she stammered. Without waiting for a reply, she spun on her heel. The asp vibrated weirdly. Terry needed to splash some water on her face. She pushed through the washroom, heat rising from the asp.

Allison glared at one of her princesses. "You said you locked the door."

Maude was on her knees being held by one of the princesses. Blonde curls littered the tiled floor. A section of her hair was short and bristly on one side of her head. Allison had a fist of Maude's hair in one hand and a long pair of scissors in the other. She gave Terry a murderous stare. "Do you know what the first rule of power is, Nefertari?" Allison sneered. She licked her lips. "It's fear! This little bitch thinks it's funny to accuse innocent people of committing a crime. She needs to be taught a lesson."

"You won't get away with this or hurting Zach," Maude said defiantly.

There was a crunching snip and Maude's perfectly wavy, beautiful pink streak fell to the floor beside the accumulating pile of hair, leaving another chunk of her head sheared.

"There," Allison laughed, "a proper mullet to go with your white trash image."

Terry launched at Allison, grabbing her by the throat. The scissors dropped to the floor. Allison's eyes grew wide. Terry squeezed tighter, lifting her off the floor. "I know what you did," Terry said, her voice like gravel. "I'm sick of you hurting the people I care about."

Allison's feet kicked pathetically in the air.

"Is this what you meant?" Terry smiled grimly. "Are you afraid, Allison? Because I'm feeling pretty powerful right now."

A hand reached around Terry, fingers clawing at her to let go. Terry elbowed the person away hard. A body careened across the bathroom floor.

In the mirror, Terry saw one of Allison's princess standing stunned. Maude was crumpled on the floor, holding the back of her head. She pulled her hand away and saw blood. "Terry?" she said weakly.

Terry let go of Allison, who collapsed to the floor, struggling for breath.

"What's wrong with you?" Maude cried. She cowered away from Terry. Allison's princess started to back up, her eyes darting between Terry and the door.

A raspy sound came from across the room. Allison had pushed herself up, sitting against the wall. The evil smile slipped into place. "You don't scare me, freak," she whispered. "You're so dead."

Chapter Forty

Terry stood in the basketball court behind Zach's apartment building, ignoring the cold wind. Earlier she had rung the buzzer, but chickened out when Zach's dad answered the intercom.

What would she say?

"Hi, Mr. Breton. You don't know me, but I'm the one who carried your son to the hospital last night and then left before the nurses could question me. Don't worry, I have the ability to crush bones, but I'm perfectly safe to be around Zach."

Or am I?

Maude's terrified expression was burned into her memory. In a daze, Terry had left school and run as fast as she could. She ended up at Zach's. All she needed was to see that he was going to be okay and that the asp was capable of helping her do good things. It couldn't only be about fighting, she hoped. There must be something to the power she felt — there must be a deeper meaning.

Terry pushed aside her fear and peered up through the rain at Zach's window. *Just one look*, she promised herself. She easily scaled the fire escape, making sure to move fast enough to avoid detection. She paused outside Zach's window. The bag of cookies from Maude's grandmother lay in a crumpled, frozen mess, mostly picked over by crows.

A stone dropped in Terry's stomach, reminding her how Maude had tried to warn her about the asp. And then, more painful, was the image of Maude clutching her bleeding head, looking at Terry like she was a monster.

Terry moved in front of the window as much as she dared. The bedroom door was closed. Zach was lying in bed asleep with the covers up to his waist. His left arm was in a cast and propped up on a pillow. Terry counted the slow rising and falling of his bare chest. The asp began to throb. *Just one touch.*

Terry pushed up the window enough to slip her good leg through first. The toe of her sneaker touched the hardwood floor, and the rest of her followed soundlessly. His room was bigger than she expected. The high, vaulted ceilings and corniced edges gave it a regal feel, but the modern decorating was all Zach. A stray sport sock was bunched up in the corner by the door. His gaming system was a tangle of cords, shoved between the television and a pile of comic books. She stood at the foot of his bed.

Now that it was daylight, more details emerged. His bottom lip was cut and his right eye was purple and swollen. Tears welled up in Terry's eyes. Her anger for Allison began to growl again, tearing through the guilt about Maude.

His breathing kept the same steady rhythm. Her eyes traveled down the length of his long legs, outlined under the blankets. At least those seemed free of injury. She reached out and smoothed a wrinkle from the blanket.

"See anything interesting?" Zach had his good eye open. "I thought I was dreaming when you first slipped in through the window," he said. A grin pulled up the corner of his mouth. "But since you're still dressed, I guess this is real."

That half smile made all of Terry's anxiety disappear. He was okay, and he was happy to see her. Nothing else mattered at that moment. She wanted to slip into his arms, close her eyes and let the rest of the world take care of itself.

His hand opened, palm facing upward, motioning for her.

"Hey," she said, trying to blink away her tears. She linked her fingers through his and gingerly perched on the side of his bed.

Terry's attention wandered around his room. One wall was covered with *Sports Illustrated* posters of basketball stars. Zach stayed quiet.

A small pile of meticulously folded laundry covered an oak study desk along the wall. A corkboard on the wall had numerous layers of sketches on regular lined looseleaf, tacked in place. Mostly were action shots, fight scenes between overly muscular characters. A glass was filled with pens and pencils. *There should be an easel here,* Terry thought.

She realized he was watching her. "How do you feel?" she asked.

"Like I've been beaten up."

Amy Sue's face came to her mind. "I've seen worse," she told him. Now that she knew he was all right, she should leave before things got more complicated.

Her other hand lightly touched his cast. "I'm sorry." The words seemed too small for what she was feeling.

"You're not the one who broke my arm."

There was a palpable shift in the atmosphere. Terry knew she had to tread carefully. "How much do you remember?" she asked.

"I told the police I went for a walk to clear my head because I was anxious about the State Championships coming up. The gang must have hit me from behind." His voice was almost robotic. "The next thing I remember is waking up in the hospital with my mom leaning over me crying."

Terry wasn't sure to be relieved or upset that he'd forgotten about her so easily. And why was he lying about Allison? "There's a rumor at school that some kids from West Mount did this to you," she said.

He leaned back into his pillow and stared at the ceiling with his good eye.

Terry squeezed his hand. "I'm sorry," she repeated.

"You're not the one who ruined my chance at a scholarship …

a chance at a worthwhile future."

She inched closer to him. "Don't say that. Your arm will heal, you'll play basketball again."

"I missed my chance," he said. His voice was starting to crack. "Without that ticket to a good school, I'm nothing."

"You're so much more than a basketball player. I wish you could see that."

He let go of her hand. It lay there useless on the blanket. "I wish I hadn't gone with with Allison last night." He fixed her with a challenging stare. "She said she had information that could help your dad. She insisted I see her in person."

"My dad?" Terry hadn't been expecting that answer. "What did she say?"

He dropped his eyes. "She was lying. It was only to get me to that ball field. She knew I'd get mad and leave her. I was so stupid. I literally walked into her trap."

"But you told the police—"

"Exactly what they needed to hear. Her dad's the mayor. She's untouchable."

"Why are you protecting her?"

"I'm keeping her out of it," he snapped, "because that's what she wants. Life is much easier when she gets her way."

Terry felt complicated layers of relief and guilt; Zach had only met Allison to get information to help her dad. He waited for her response, softly curling his fingers around her hand.

The familiar warmth pulsed from Terry's heart. She was afraid the next thing out of her mouth would be a confession of how she'd saved him. She reminded herself Zach should never know about the asp — too many people she cared about were getting hurt.

"It doesn't matter anyway," he said. "Without that scholarship I'll be stuck living with my parents, playing video games by day and doing some lousy back shift work at a factory where reading isn't required."

"Do you truly believe that?" Terry asked. She couldn't imagine Zach being so lifeless and dull. Everything about him was electric.

He winced and cradled his cast. "At least that's what my dad thinks. I heard him say those exact words to my mom in the hospital."

Terry was aghast. Her parents had always been enthusiastic about every tiny thing she did. How could Zach's dad have so little faith? "Maybe he was in shock?" she suggested.

"Look around this place. There's no way we'd be able to live here if Dad wasn't the superintendent. He's not going to waste thousands of dollars to send a kid to college who can barely make it through high school."

His bedroom door began to open. Terry slipped into his closet lightning fast. She watched through the slats in the door. Zach's mom came in with a small glass of water. She had a flowered apron tied around her waist. In her other hand was a pill bottle. "Are you hungry? Can I make you something? Maybe a grilled cheese?"

He shook his head and reached for the water.

She fussed with his pillow, then said, "I thought I heard voices. Were you on the phone?"

He looked at his phone sitting on the bedside table, its blank screen staring back at him. "Maybe I was talking in my sleep."

She frowned and looked at the pill bottle. "I wonder if these are too strong for you. The doctor said to take them only as needed."

"I need them." He held out his hand.

She gave him two pills and stayed while he swallowed them. She shivered and crossed the floor. "It's freezing in here," she said, closing the window. Her eyes wandered to the basketball posters, then flitted away nervously. "Oh," she said with nervous enthusiasm, "I forgot to tell you, Allison called again."

"We broke up," he replied.

"I know, honey." She bent down and picked up the bunched

sport sock from the corner. "But she's such a thoughtful girl and always dresses so prettily. It's obvious she's still in love with you." She straightened a pile of papers and used the edge of her apron to dust the edge of a picture frame. From where Terry stood, she guessed it was a team photo. Zach's mom gave him a weak smile. "I heard the team is going to dedicate the final game to you."

Zach squirmed in his bed, his gaze flicking toward the closet. "Actually, Mom, I think I'll have that grilled cheese."

Relief took over her face. "With a side of pickles and chocolate milk?" He nodded. She tucked the sock into her apron pocket and whisked out of the room.

Terry waited until she heard the soft click of the door closing. When she came out, Zach was staring at her. "I feel like I'm dreaming and that none of this is true." His body shuddered as he tried to swallow a quiet sob.

She was by his side in an instant. Her finger traced the edge of his eyebrow. He gently pressed his cheek into her touch, then reached up and covered her hand with his, keeping it there. Terry leaned forward, their foreheads touching. Being this close to him was intoxicating.

"Please," he begged. "Tell me the truth. Why were you there last night? I know what I saw."

Terry's heart was being ripped in two. Allison was too dangerous to ignore. For all the special powers the asp gave her, she was nobody's hero. She couldn't even keep the people she cared about safe. All of this was an illusion. She didn't belong on the arm of the school hero, or deserve to have a best friend. Asp or no asp, Terry was destined to watch life from the sidelines, slunk down in her chair, hiding under her hoodie.

"I'm not the person you think I am," Terry said, swallowing her tears. She imagined his expression if he ever saw her leg. "And I'll never be the person you want me to be."

A low moan came from Zach. He nudged her, moving his

mouth closer to hers. The asp began to throb again. "Please. I shared things with you that I've never told anyone. You know about my reading problems and I showed you my drawings." His breath feathered her lips. "You can trust me. Tell me how you beat up those guys last night."

"I can't." Terry dropped her head and moved back. "I'm sorry."

His hand fell to his side as if wounded. "Yeah," he said. "The whole world is sorry." He turned his head toward the wall, silently dismissing her.

Terry disappeared out the window, making sure to close it this time.

She arrived at the hospital completely frozen through. Her sneakers made sucking noises as she made her way down the corridor to the ICU. There was only one way to fix this horrible mess, and that was to open the coffin. But to do that she needed the code — and only one person knew it.

A scream echoed up ahead as a stretcher was wheeled down the corridor. Several medical staff ran alongside. A woman's shrieks filled the hallway.

"It's all right, May," one of the nurses said. "I'm giving you something for the pain." The nurse used a syringe to inject drugs into the intravenous.

Terry pressed herself along the wall as the stretcher wheeled past. Her eyes grew wide. "Dr. Mullaca?" she said. "What happened?"

The patient looked back at Terry with a blank expression. The staff continued toward the elevator. The nurse who injected the medicine recognized Terry. "She can't answer you," she said.

"She's awake!" Terry couldn't hide her enthusiasm.

The nurse nodded. "She woke up a few hours ago."

Terry tried to make sense of the nurse's crestfallen tone. "That's good, right?" she asked.

"She fell and possibly broke her hip, she's going for an X-ray."

Terry's forehead bunched up. "I don't understand," she began.

"How could she walk? She has a wheelchair."

"She has amnesia. She tried to get out of bed and fell to the floor. She simply forgot she was paralyzed. She can't even remember her name." The nurse continued to talk, but the dull roar inside Terry's head blanked her words out.

Terry dragged herself to her dad's bedside, feeling like she had no one else to turn to for comfort. He'd been lying in this bed for almost a week. How much damage had been done to his body? To his brain?

She stared at his serene expression and felt a sudden stab of jealousy. She hadn't slept the night before, and this evening was shaping up to be the same. All Terry wanted at that moment was to close her eyes and fall asleep too — maybe even never wake up.

"Nefertari." There was a gentle tap on her shoulder. Prince Kamal stood behind her. "I need to speak with you, please." He wore a wool blazer with a long striped scarf looped loosely around his neck. He ran a hand over the stubble across his chin.

Terry had only ever seen him clean-shaven. This tired, worried version of the prince made her anxious. She didn't think she could take any more bad news. He led her out into the hallway, away from the nurses' ever watchful eyes.

His voice lowered. "I haven't been able to reach you on your phone. I had no idea where you were. And then last night, you didn't answer your door..." He paused and waited for her to respond.

Terry felt like she was slipping into her own coma. She leaned against the wall for support and the tears started to fall.

Prince Kamal wrapped an arm around her shoulders, then jumped back. "You're absolutely freezing!" Terry mumbled something about the weather. He removed his jacket and laid it over her shoulders. "When was the last time you ate? Please, let's go back to the Plaza for a hot meal and change of clothes."

Terry pulled away. "I can't leave without seeing Dr. Mullaca," she insisted. "I need the code for the room in the basement of the museum."

"Whatever for?" He looked perplexed.

"I need to see the coffin," she said. "Please." She sniffed. "It was my mother's legacy, and it makes me feel like she's with me." Terry crossed her fingers behind her back, hoping he would believe her lie.

He narrowed his eyes. "And if I help you with this, do you promise to eat something and get a proper rest tonight?" he asked.

"I promise," Terry replied.

"Good," he answered. Then he made his way down the hall. "Do you want to change before or after I take you to the museum?"

Terry looked back at the ICU. "But we need to talk with Dr. Mullaca when she gets back from X-ray."

"No need," he answered. "I have the code as well."

Chapter Forty-One

Terry stood behind Prince Kamal. There were a few beeps followed by a clunk as the door unlocked. She wasn't sure what the plan was at this point. Her main objective since this whole mess began was to fit the asp into the special grooves of the coffin. With Prince Kamal by her side, whatever came next, he would be a part of the consequences.

Terry had to tell him the truth. "Remember how Dr. Mullaca said the missing asp was the only thing that could open the case?" she began tentatively.

"Yes, of course," he said, frowning in the dimness. His hand smoothed along the wall, looking for the light switch.

"I have a confession." Terry's hands were clasped in front of her as if in a desperate prayer.

With a click the room was suddenly a blinding white. Terry squinted as her eyes adjusted. One look at the empty room made her want to collapse into a crying heap. "Where is it?" She panicked.

"I don't understand," Prince Kamal said. He glanced around, as if a huge, elaborate coffin could be hiding in the corner or misplaced behind a shelf of cleaning utensils.

Hurried footsteps echoed down the hallway. Sarah appeared in the doorway, out of breath. Instead of her usual fitted outfits, she wore jeans and a sweatshirt. "I was told you came down. I'm assuming you're looking for the mummy case?"

Both Terry and Prince Kamal nodded eagerly. Sarah smiled tiredly and patted back a strand of hair that had come out of its ponytail. A smudge of mascara was under her right eye. "It's already on display in the Egypt room."

Terry's jaw dropped open. She felt numb all over. "It's been opened?"

"No, of course not." Sarah's patronizing tone pierced the air. "But the exhibit is still quite impressive." She held up a ring of keys and gave Prince Kamal a nod. "It's closed until tomorrow night, but I can let you in."

"Ms. Hughes and I would be forever in your debt," he said.

Terry's gazed flitted back and forth between them. The formal politeness didn't make sense; both of them had been arguing about Mayor Harris only a few days ago.

They took the elevator to the fifth floor and made their way to the rom. "The unveiling will be a special dress-up party," Sarah said, her gaze falling on Terry. "You know, like a costume ball."

Prince Kamal gave Terry a half grin. "And what disguise will you be wearing?"

"I'm invited?" A party was the last thing on Terry's schedule.

Sarah made an attempt to smooth out her sweatshirt. "How about an Egyptian serving girl?" she suggested to Terry. "I need more volunteers to help with the cocktail reception."

"Have you asked Ms. Bernard yet?" Terry couldn't keep the edge from her voice. Like Zach, she'd begun to believe everyone was lying to her.

The trio came to the Egypt room. Sarah went through first and began turning on the display lights.

The creepy mummy case with the hollowed-out eyes seemed to be staring across the room at the Cleopatra mannequin. Terry felt for the asp, the hard coils under her shirt comforting.

Sarah flicked on a few more switches, spotlighting the new

exhibits. On the raised platform in the middle of the room, the coffin was encased in a long glass box. Terry walked up to the red velvet rope that encircled it, the urge to get closer overwhelming.

"Isn't it beautiful?" Sarah stated. "Mayor Harris will be hosting the party tomorrow night. For all the anxiety he's created, it was completely worth it."

Terry questioned Sarah's lack of tact.

"It's so wonderful the museum has this piece." Her voice became dreamy, almost trancelike. It was a sharp contrast to Terry's building anxiety. "With the dignitaries and socialites coming, the fundraiser will make the world of difference for us. It will be everything I've hoped for — everything I deserve."

"Why the glass case?" Terry interrupted.

Sarah's smile melted. "It's to protect the coffin."

Terry slipped under the red ropes, ignoring Sarah's gasp. "Is it breakable?" she asked, resting her fingertips on the top.

"I believe it's very strong." Sarah looked up at Prince Kamal. "Maybe even bulletproof."

"Then there's nothing to be worried about," he smiled. "I'm quite sure Ms. Hughes does not own a gun." He waited two seconds then laughed. A smile slowly crept across Sarah's lips. He stepped away and took Sarah by the elbow. Their hushed voices continued along the wall, pausing at a different exhibit.

Terry splayed her hands over the top of the glass, directly over the three grooves, identical to the ones now spiraling her upper arm. She curled her fingers into fists. She felt certain that she could break through the thick case. Her eyes flitted over to Sarah, now leaning on one hip, gazing up at Prince Kamal, hanging on his every word.

Terry put her attention back to the case, letting out a regretful sigh. *Not now. Not with Sarah in the room.* Her mother gave her life for the discovery of this sarcophagus. If she was about to open the case that might hold the remains of Egypt's last pharaoh, she wasn't going to do it in front of crazy Sarah.

Her mother had put her faith in science, not curses. She'd never condone Terry doing something like this on her own.

What if nothing happens? What if everything happens?

Terry stepped back. Smashing the glass and jamming the asp into the case at this moment didn't seem right.

She walked around the case and saw the other display that had been updated since the class trip. The simple flat panel was backlit from behind, illuminating text … and a photograph of Terry's mother. It must have been scanned from the picture on her dad's desk and then enlarged. Her dark eyes were crinkled at the edges in a smile. A few curls had come loose from her hair tie, framing her high cheekbones. A heavy ache spread through Terry's bones — she missed her mother so much, it physically hurt. There was nothing the asp could do to fill that gap.

Below the photograph was a detailed description of how the sarcophagus had been located, complete with a map and several quotes from her mother, and finally the artifacts Terry had thought brought them to Devonshire — the coins her mother had discovered with Cleopatra's profile. The most shocking part was the image of the famed queen with a large hooked nose. It was a far cry from the legendary goddess history had crowned as a seductive opportunist.

Even though Terry knew all the facts by heart reading them so unexpectedly and finding them in such a public place, opened the wound fresh. It was like hearing about her mother's death for the first time; she remembered lying in the hospital, her leg a throbbing mess. When her dad's face had come into focus by her bedside, his eyes were red and teary.

Terry blinked hard. Her fingers traced her mother's image on the display. A quote underneath read:

"We've been looking for the real Cleopatra since the last century, spurred on by the legend of her beauty and fortune, but for all the proof archaeologists have uncovered, there is nothing that shows her as a truly aesthetically pleasing woman.

Every chronicle details how her warfare strategy, her health and fashion influences, and of course her love for her country fortified her as an icon.

She simply wasn't that beautiful, but instead emitted a strength that others found empowering and inspiring. I hope that's a message about humanity people take from this discovery."

A handkerchief appeared in front of Terry. She hadn't realized she was crying. "Your mother was very wise," Prince Kamal said softly.

"Thank you." Terry sniffed, taking it from him. Sarah stood outside the room in the hallway.

"You have her eyes," he said. Terry blew her nose in protest. Sarah's presence left her in a bad mood. "Now that you've seen the coffin," he began, "will you finally come back to the Plaza and get out of those clothes before you catch pneumonia?"

Terry nodded tiredly. There was nothing else to do. She was at another dead end.

Sarah walked them to the main doors. The museum had already closed for the night. "And what will you be dressed as for the party tomorrow night?" she asked Prince Kamal.

"I thought I'd come as an Egyptian Prince," he answered.

Terry smiled behind the handkerchief, appreciating his stab at humor. When they settled into the backseat of the limo, her stomach growled. Prince Kamal pulled out his phone and started texting.

"Ordering your costume for tomorrow night?" she asked. "I thought you had a full closet of royal robes to wear."

He laughed. "Maybe I'm ordering your servant's costume."

Terry couldn't care less about dressing up. "Parties aren't my thing," she said. "Although, I wonder if I can get in for another tour before the benefit starts?" Prince Kamal didn't respond, too intent on texting.

When Terry checked her own phone, she saw there were no messages or calls. It was a terribly hollow feeling. She had to acknowledge that Maude and Zach were probably finished with her. She turned off her phone and tucked it deep into her pocket.

Once they reached the private floor, Prince Kamal put a hand on her elbow before she entered her suite. "I have food coming to my room," he told her. "Please join me after you've had a chance to change."

Terry wavered, the key card halfway into its slot.

He noticed her hesitation. "It's from The Marrakesh Palace." Terry's mouth started to water. She agreed then quickly disappeared into her room.

Chapter Forty-Two

After a hot shower, she slipped on a cozy pair of sweatpants and the long-sleeved fleece top she'd gotten with her dad at Old Navy. She didn't once think of her knee. Wearing the asp all the time made everyday activities effortless.

Terry wasn't a fashion expert, not by a long shot, but sometimes she wanted to be the girl who showed up in the beautiful dress that everybody noticed. Her stomach growled again. Instead of drying her hair, she pulled it into a ponytail and secured the stray bits with clips.

Down the hall, she made her way to the door with two bodyguards stationed out front. They simply nodded and let her into Prince Kamal's suite.

Terry took in the sumptuous surroundings; his suite seemed to encapsulate the entire corner of the Plaza. "Hello?" she called out. A waft of delicious, spicy food led her to the dining area. A table covered in white linen had been set for two. Covered platters were arranged on a cart to the side. The pile of dolmas was too tempting. She took one of the stuffed grape leaves and popped it in her mouth.

Through a pair of French doors she saw Prince Kamal watching the big-screen television. The sound was off, but the video of protestors being pushed back by police in riot gear was powerful enough. Cairo had made headline news again. A scene of an emergency center being overwhelmed with victims was the last thing Terry saw before the television was turned off.

She quickly backed up, pretending not to see. She returned her attention to the platters of food.

"It's good to see you finally eating," Prince Kamal said, his eyes were red rimmed.

He took the covers off the platters, revealing all of Terry's favourites from the restaurant, plus a few new entrées. "I hope you can help me put a serious dent in all this food," he said, handing her a plate. "Baba ghanoush?" he asked. Terry nodded, the news footage still fresh in her mind.

Prince Kamal methodically served Terry and himself until both their plates were piled high. He gathered their silverware and motioned to the room beyond the French doors. "The table is too formal for tonight," he said.

Terry followed him into a sitting room with a huge squashy sectional. They sat with the plates balanced on their knees. She noticed Prince Kamal still managed to be meticulous, while she was constantly wiping up drips of olive oil from her fingers. She was grateful the television stayed off.

He leaned back, careful to keep his tone even. "Are you going to tell me where you were last night?"

The image of Zach falling unconscious in her arms and the horrible gut-wrenching feeling that he'd die before she could reach the hospital washed over her. A cool sweat peppered her skin.

Terry pushed her plate away. "I was helping a friend," she said truthfully.

"A friend from school?" he asked, his tone softer this time. She nodded, unsure which category Zach fit into. Friend? Boyfriend? Ex-friend? The image of Maude's scared face surfaced. Terry rubbed her temples. Her mind wouldn't stop replaying the horrible memories of the last few days.

"I understand." Prince Kamal ran a hand through his dark

waves. "I'd do anything for my friends back home." He smiled. "In fact I'd do anything for my home. I love my country. I miss so much about it when I travel." He let out a relaxed laugh. "You have no idea how many tourists come to Cairo, shocked that we are a modern city. They think it's all about Indiana Jones and lost treasure."

Terry leaned back and tucked her bad leg underneath her. "I miss the marketplace," she told him. "I miss shopping there with my mom. I miss..." she bit her lip. 'Home' was the word that came to mind.

"Egypt is close to my heart, but it has its troubles too." Prince Kamal sounded uncharacteristically hopeless. "There's so much political unrest these days. The people need a common goal. Something to believe in ... something to unite them."

Terry pictured him standing on a balcony addressing a crowd, inspiring a new generation. "Maybe you're Egypt's next pharaoh," she said, half teasing.

He smiled, then crossed his hands behind his head and stretched out his legs. "That's why this discovery of your mother's is so important. It's a reminder of how great and strong my country used to be. Maybe that's what the people need," he said. "A modern-day Cleopatra."

"What do you mean?"

If he was surprised by her question, his expression didn't give him away. "Some people believe the last pharaoh of Egypt will reign again through resurrection," he said, matter-of-factly.

Terry couldn't gauge if he was bored by the subject or thought it was bogus. She pictured Ms. Bernard's book. "Do you know anything about the cult of Osiris?" she asked.

Prince Kamal tilted his head. "You're familiar with the legend, I assume," he said. "The cult practices the belief that after their deaths, the gods allowed Cleopatra to live with Mark Antony in another form of existence so they would have eternal life together."

"So they believe their queen is still alive?"

He lifted a shoulder. "In a way, I suppose."

The asp began to pulse around Terry's arm. "Does the cult still exist?"

"I don't believe in such things," he said. "There are all kinds of theories about the afterlife, but I'm more concerned with everyday miracles."

She smiled back at him, relieved to abandon the subject of death and resurrection. Prince Kamal had a way of taking a morbid subject and turning it into something of beauty. "Like what?" she prompted.

He seemed pleased with her question. "Simple things, really," he began. "A spider having the ability to make a web purely on instinct, how a mother knows her baby's own cry, and of course the colors of the sunset." He looked across the room, staring into nothing. "And when two strangers smile and fall in love."

Zach's pained expression haunted her memory. It was unbearable that he thought she'd given up on him. "You make it sound like falling in love is easy," she said dully.

"You're cynical for one so young. Men crossing the desert for the smile of a loved one is the stuff of legends."

Terry snorted. "Oh really? Have you ever crossed the desert for someone?"

"Once," he laughed. "She's one of the things I miss most about home."

Terry smiled. "That's so sweet. Maybe next time you visit, you can bring her too."

"I'm not sure Devonshire is big enough, she prefers New York."

"Who wouldn't," Terry joked easily. He made her feel secure. Through every crisis, Prince Kamal had been there to pick her up and give her what she needed. He reminded her of all the things she loved and missed about Egypt. When she was with him it felt like she was home. And she supposed that was why he was the only one she could trust right now. "I need to see the sarcophagus before the unveiling. Can you help me?"

"Of course. I'll be busy most of tomorrow, but I promise to escort you to the museum. I hope you seriously consider staying for the party. We'll be honoring your mother's work. You should be there to represent your family."

Terry had no idea what chain reaction would be caused by her putting the asp into the grooves of the mummy case, but she didn't plan on hanging around to watch the mayhem. "Um ... I'll think about it."

Prince Kamal nodded. He walked her back to her room. When she opened the door to her suite, he placed a protective hand on her shoulder. "Don't worry," he soothed, "when the time comes, you'll know what to do. And then everything will fall into place." Then he gave her his regal goodnight smile and bowed slightly.

Terry got herself to bed. The last thing she looked at was the Zach's portrait of herself as Cleopatra. She closed her eyes and fell asleep, dreaming of home.

Chapter Forty-Three

Terry woke the next day from a vague dream. She and Prince Kamal had been standing on a balcony high above a mass of people. His expression had been solemn, but she'd spoken to the crowd, not him. The image lingered in her memory, leaving her slightly anxious.

The magnitude of what she was planning suddenly hit her. She was going to open a sarcophagus that might hold the most famous and tragic monarch of all time. What if nothing happened when she put the asp in the case? What if everything happened? Terry might have superpowers, but she was clueless … and quite frankly terrified.

It was Saturday, and she had slept in just past noon. She slipped into the fluffy bathrobe and ordered a small lunch tray from room service. She was halfway through her orange juice when there was a knock at the door.

Two of Prince Kamal's bodyguards stood at attention with a garment bag and several large boxes. "For the benefit tonight, Ms. Hughes," the taller one said. "The prince had them delivered specially." Then he handed her an elegant, slim envelope edged in gold.

Terry took the packages to the bedroom. The fancy envelope contained a card with her name on it and the official insignia of the museum — apparently tonight's event was by invitation only. Inside the first box was a pair of gold sandals. In the next was a diadem decorated with an asp. With shaking fingers Terry unzipped the garment bag. The dress was something out of a fashion magazine. From the halter-top neckline, white fabric cascaded to the floor. Everyone would be able to see the asp on her arm, but it would look part of the costume.

Terry held the dress up. There was a long slit up the side, but it was on her left side; her right leg, with all its bumps and scars, would be hidden. It was obvious who Prince Kamal wanted her to be tonight. She leaned in close to the mirror, studying her eyes. She tried to remember Zach's soft voice when he told her she inspired him.

"When you talked about Cleopatra that first day you really came alive, like you could take on anything and nobody would stand in your way. You were strong ... you were Cleopatra."

Terry had to build up her courage — her dad was depending on her. She looked at the drawing on the bedside table, then back at the mirror. It would take some work, but she'd be able to pull it off. Tonight, she would be Cleopatra.

Terry put the drawing down beside her phone. She turned it on and quickly dialed Maude's number before she lost the nerve. Even if Maude never wanted to speak with her again, Terry had to apologize before she went to the museum — everything could change after tonight..

It rang three times, then finally Maude answered.

"Thank god!" Maude's voice was full of relief. "We thought you were dead!"

"I'm sorry." There was a long pause. "How's your head?" Terry asked carefully. "I mean, is it sore?"

Maude snorted. "I look so bad, it's painful."

"Yeah, but..." Terry wasn't sure how to proceed so she just came out and said it. "I pushed you back, you hit your head ... there was blood."

There was a long sigh at the end. "I'm fine. Well, I am now. I was a bit freaked out by your Hulk impersonation. Fraser and I have been trying your phone all night. I even called Prince Kamal, but he wasn't answering either."

"I turned it off. We were at the hospital," Terry said. Maude stayed quiet as she mulled over this bit of information. "I'm sorry you and Fraser were worried about me, but I'm okay." Then she added, "By the end of tonight, everything will fall into place." She liked using Prince Kamal's words.

Maude squealed. "Yes! We're back on track. Fraser was trying to come up with a plan for tonight, but it involved a pulley system and some kind of fireworks distraction. For a guy who's smart he can be so lame."

"Tell Fraser there's no need."

"No kidding." Maude laughed. "He makes everything so complicated. I'm like, 'Genius, how can you smuggle fireworks into the benefit?'"

Terry interrupted her. "I mean, there's no need because I'm doing this without you."

"Whoa, what?"

"This is about the asp, not June — and certainly not Amy Sue." Terry turned and looked at herself in the mirror. "I can't risk anyone else getting hurt for something that I can do on my own."

"On your own? Are you crazy?" Maude began to panic. "We're in this together. Remember?"

Terry closed her eyes. The image of Maude holding her bleeding head resurfaced from Terry's memory like a nightmare stuck on replay. "It doesn't matter. You guys can't get in anyway," she reasoned. "It's by invitation only."

Maude didn't miss a beat. "Fraser will get us in."

Terry took in a deep breath and held it. She had a speech prepared to explain why she couldn't accept Maude's help anymore, but it was too hard once she heard her friend's voice. All Terry could get out was one word. "No."

Maude pleaded. "Please, you can't do—"

Terry turned off her phone. Roosevelt High and Maude weren't really part of her life; her true home was back in Egypt. Tears came, and Terry let them fall until she was numb with exhaustion. After a while she looked at her puffy face in the mirror and called the concierge for a late afternoon appointment at the hotel spa and beauty center. If she was going to pretend to be a queen, she had to look the part.

It was darkening by the time Terry entered her suite again. She purposely stayed away from the mirror while the spa staff did her hair and makeup. Careful not to smudge her face, Terry slipped the white dress over her head. The fabric was like a waterfall over her skin. The cut of the dress was such that the right side had gathered pleats running down the length, while the other side showed off her good leg almost to the hip. With both arms bare, the asp was in full view. Terry was grateful for the chips of glitter paint stuck fast; it still looked fake. The sandals fit perfectly, and she marveled at how Prince Kamal knew her exact size. She saved the plastic diadem for last and crowned herself Queen of Egypt in the middle of an empty hotel room.

Terry made her way over to the mirror. "Wow," she whispered. The esthetician had done her eyes Egyptian-style, with the dark kohl extending outward. Her hair was cut straight across the back, and the stylist had used a flatiron to make it shiny. She had shorter bangs now — she was unable to hide from the world anymore.

A shaking breath came out as she took in her whole image. For the first time since the accident, Terry felt beautiful.

When Prince Kamal knocked on the door five minutes later, he took in Terry's complete transformation with admiration. His eyes lingered on the asp.

"It was in the box with the crown," Terry said. "I thought it was tacky, but Cleopatra knew more about fashion than me."

"I agree," he said. "Besides, we make a perfect match." He'd dressed as Mark Antony, complete with brass breastplate over a red tunic, and leather apron with heavily studded lappets. The hilt of a dagger peeked out from a strap around his calf. She stayed silent in the limo drive to the benefit, fighting off the chill from her earlier dream.

They entered the museum flanked by his usual bodyguards. The rotunda was filled with guests already drinking and eating finger foods. Terry hadn't bothered to check the time, but by the count of heads swiveling in their direction, she guessed they were fashionably late. The men were in tuxedos or fine suits, but almost all of the woman had fashioned their attire to reflect the ancient Egyptian style. Several asps decorated arms.

Prince Kamal leaned close to her ear. "I have to mingle here first, but I'll get you into the Egypt room shortly," he told her. "Are you all right on your own for a moment?"

"Yes." She had to concentrate to keep her voice steady. An unsettling suspense made her squirm inside.

He leaned closer and whispered, "Don't worry, everything will fall into place." His fingers were inches from her hand, but he didn't touch her. Terry instinctively stepped to the side, letting him pass.

She watched him walk through the partygoers with his usual royal confidence, parting the crowd automatically.

"Samosa?" A server in roman style sandals was wearing a golden King Tut mask and robe. She held out a tray of triangular pastries.

Terry's stomach was full of knots. Food was the last thing she needed right now. "No, thank you."

"Terry?" King Tut tilted his head, then pulled up the mask slightly. "I didn't recognize you at first."

"Ms. Bernard?" Terry was taken aback to see her history teacher dressed so dramatically. She was used to seeing her in tweed skirts and sweater sets.

"I'm head of the volunteer committee," she said. Her voice was shrill and excited. "I wouldn't miss this unveiling for the world!" Her eyes grazed the length of Terry's dress. "You look like a queen."

"Thank you." Terry stepped back. Ms. Bernard smiled and slipped the mask back in place. She left Terry and spun around the floor, offering rich socialites Middle Eastern appetizers.

Terry looked up through the open rotunda to the rooftop skylight. Her gaze focused on the fifth floor. She didn't want to wait for Prince Kamal any longer. She'd do this without his help.

Terry picked her way through the crowd. She stumbled over someone's foot. Another King Tut server growled under their breath. Terry saw this particular server was in bare feet. "Oh, sorry," Terry said. A hard stare through the mask was the only reply from the server.

No more delays. Terry kept her eyes trained on the elevator and prayed the metal detector wouldn't be loud enough for the guests in the rotunda to hear. A hand circled her arm, just below the asp. She spun around, expecting Prince Kamal. Instead a blonde roman dancing girl greeted her.

"Hey, stranger," Maude said. "Remember me?" She was wearing a toga-style dress with a large brooch at the shoulder. Her hair had been meticulously curled into spirals and put into an updo. The headband was decorated with gold glitter. Terry reasoned Maud's mother had worked in extensions, or maybe the whole thing was a wig. It broke her spirit seeing her friend without her pink streak.

"I told you I'd do this on my own," Terry said harshly, hoping to scare her off with fake anger.

"I love your makeup," Maude said, leaning in closer, completely ignoring Terry's warning.

Fraser came up behind Maude. "Neffie," he said, "you look like you stepped out of a Turner classic movie." Everything except his head was wrapped in several layers of gauze bandages. He was holding a large glass jar filled with what looked like cauliflower and red Kool-Aid.

"It's my brain," he told her. "I'm a mummy ... get it?" He reached over and took a falafel off a tray. Another masked King Tut bowed and handed him a serviette as well. Fraser declined and wiped his fingers on the gauze instead.

"How did you guys get in?" Terry asked.

Fraser pulled a lanyard out from his bandages, showing off an official *The Daily Devonshire* card with a newspaper's insignia. "I'm with the press," he grinned.

Maude explained. "Fraser's brother got us these. We had to promise to keep a low profile." She shrugged. "And you know, actually write an article or something."

"You two? A low profile?" Terry said, unconvinced.

"I can be totally professional," Maude rebuffed. "I promised Fraser's brother a top ten list on the best things about a museum benefit. You know, like Buzzfeed."

"Buzzfeed?" Fraser looked insulted. "I'm not interested in appealing to the lowest common denominator."

"You're such a snob," Maude huffed.

"Please," Terry begged her friends. "Leave now before anything bad happens. Look what happened to Zach."

"That was his crazy psycho ex-girlfriend," Fraser said. "Not you."

Maude pulled Terry to the side, away from the crowd. "You don't have to do this all by yourself."

"Yes," she insisted. "I do. Have you forgotten what I did to you in the bathroom? No one is safe around me."

"You saved me from a scissor-wielding monster." Maude took her by the shoulders. "We started this together, and we'll end it together. You're the closest friend I've had in high school. There's no way I'm letting you do this freaky thing without me."

Fraser gave Terry an obvious look. "I'm with Daphne on this one. We make too good a team to split up before our first case is solved."

With her two friends declaring solidarity, Terry drew strength from their confidence. She glanced up to the fifth floor. It would all be over soon anyway. All she needed was to get into the Egypt room. "All right," Terry decided. "You can stick around, but please stay in the rotunda."

Fraser laughed. "You're cute when you pretend to be in charge. I think that crown has gone to your head."

"Why did I bring you?" Maude said.

"Because I was your ticket in here, plus I drive the getaway car." He smiled. "And let's not forget about my incredible charm and snobbishness."

Terry saw Prince Kamal was talking with Sarah. She was in a tight-fitting black dress that reached the floor. She turned and focused on Terry. There was a glint in Sarah's eye that suggested she was enjoying a private joke. Terry looked away quickly and ushered her friends toward the elevator.

"We have to move now," she told Maude and Fraser.

"Awesome," Fraser said. The Kool-Aid brains jiggled as he switched the jar to his other arm.

Maude followed behind, her hand self-consciously touching her wig. "By the way," she asked Terry, "what's your plan for *after* the asp is in place and the coffin opens?"

Terry hit the button for the fifth floor. Her jaw tightened. "Run like hell."

Fraser grinned. "Classic Scooby-Doo."

Chapter Forty-Four

Terry rubbed her bare arms. The asp didn't feel warm enough to fight the sudden chill.

Fraser tucked the jar under his arm. "All right, Neffie," he said. "Maude and I will help you construct some kind of trap."

"Enough with the Scooby-Doo," Maude moaned. "Besides, Fred's plans never work."

"Yeah, but they always catch the thief," he insisted.

"Except in this case *we're* the thieves," Maude said. "Well, sort of." She pulled out a Tootsie Pop from her clutch and began to unwrap it methodically.

If Maude and Fraser were set on following her, it would be safer for them to at least know what she was about to do. She gave them the details of her simple plan. "I have to break through the bulletproof case first—"

"You're going to smash it with your Hulk fists?" There was admiration in Fraser's voice.

"Yes," she said. "Then I'll fit the asp into the grooves and leave everything else up to two-and-a-half-thousand-year-old engineering."

"Flawless," he said. "But who gets to unmask the thief?"

Maude groaned. "Why are you still talking?"

"You want me to shut up?" he asked her. "I'm wondering if

your original offer still stands."

Maude wrinkled her brow. Terry sensed things were about to get crazy between her two friends. The elevator seemed stuck between the first and second floors.

"You told me that if I didn't stop talking you'd give me something..." He paused and pretended to look confused. "What was your exact wording? Something to suck on?" He waved a hand toward her outfit. "Once you put something like that out there — ugh!"

Maude had thrust the Tootsie Pop into his mouth. Fraser winced and swore around the sucker. Maude's look of satisfaction slowly disappeared, morphing into an expression of shock.

"I'm sorry," Maude muttered as she pressed the two button on the elevator panel. "I just..."

The elevator door opened. Maude pushed by him, running down the hallway.

Fraser looked stunned. "Where are you going?" he called out.

Terry followed Maude's flowing dress around the corner. She hesitated at the entrance to the dinosaur and fossils gallery. Maude was standing by a model of a triceratops with her hands covering her face. Terry could tell by the movement of her shoulders she was crying.

Fraser came up behind Terry, out of breath and still holding his glass jar. "It's not every day you see a Roman dancing girl leaning against something from the Jurassic Period," he said. "When time machines go awry."

Terry remained stone-faced.

"Why does she hate me?" he asked, his voice sounded small in the large room. "What's her problem?"

"She doesn't hate you," Terry sighed. "She likes you ... really likes you. That's the problem."

"Hold my brains," he said, passing over the jar.

Terry hugged the jar to her chest and stayed by the doorway.

Fraser walked up to Maude, still holding the sucker. She kept her back to him. He lightly touched her bare shoulder. "Excuse me, there's no crying in the paleontology department."

Maude wiped under her eyes. "Go away."

He let out a ragged sigh. "I'm sorry."

"What are you sorry for?"

"That's the standard response for the boy to say when the girl is crying."

"I'm the one who shoved a sucker in your mouth." Maude sniffed. "I'm so desperate to get any kind of reaction from you, I'll settle for fighting just so you'll talk to me."

Fraser tried to turn her around to face him, but Maude was stubborn. "Well, to be honest," he said, "I always thought it was playful banter. You know, almost like hate flirting ... or something."

Maude slowly turned and peeked over her shoulder at him.

Fraser tried again. "You insult me all the time and end every sentence with a huff — but I'm still hanging around."

Maude took in a deep breath and stood taller. "For your information, when I was nice and sweet, and generally being my usual self, you totally ignored me. You only started paying attention when I showed no interest. If you like the," she paused and scrunched up her nose, "hate flirting thing, then you'll be disappointed because that's not what I want."

Fraser stared back at Maude. "Once," he told her, "I spent a whole afternoon trying to decide if I should use a semicolon or not. After the article was published in the school paper, I saw a simple spelling mistake."

Maude didn't respond. He tried again. "What I'm saying is that I don't notice everything around me. It's not that I've never liked you before, I was just too busy looking at semicolons. But now," he gave her a crooked smile, "I'd like nothing better than to spend an afternoon contemplating you."

Terry looked back and forth between Maude and Fraser. She had the feeling they didn't even remember she was still in the room.

Maude lifted an eyebrow. "An afternoon listening to you critique my vocabulary while bragging about your IQ?" she said flatly. "No thanks."

Fraser ran a hand through his hair, clearly frustrated. "What do I have to say to convince you that I think you're special?"

"It's not rocket science," Maude said. "If you think I'm special, then treat me that way. Tell me I'm pretty, offer to carry my books for me, hold my hand in the hallway, just generally be a nice human being."

Terry silently cheered her on. Maude was channeling her own Cleopatra.

"I see you," Fraser said. His tone had lost its usual superiority. "And you know what? You're absolutely perfect. You're absolutely … maudevelous."

Maude dropped her chin and smiled at her sandals. "That's so corny," she said. Fraser stepped closer, filling in the space between them.

Terry put down the jar and ducked out of the room, sensing the need to give her friends privacy — and to ditch them and get to the Egypt room. She wandered over to the railing and looked down onto the rotunda below. The reception was still in full swing.

Prince Kamal was talking off to the side with the mayor. Terry instinctively leaned back. The mayor, dressed in a sharp tuxedo, was flanked by two stylish blonde women. Terry assumed the older one with the pinched expression was his wife. A splinter of fear wedged itself under Terry's skin. Allison's impossibly long hair cascaded down the back of her strapless dress. But instead of her usual air of superiority, Allison kept her eyes on the floor, ignoring any of the conversation. One of the museum officials whispered in Prince Kamal's ear. He nodded, and with the mayor by his side, made his way to the elevator.

Allison pulled on her father's arm, making him turn around.

He leered down at her, his face rigid. They were speaking at the same time. Allison shook her head quickly, making her golden tresses sway. Mayor Harris grabbed her elbow then marched through the crowd, away from Prince Kamal, leaving Mrs. Harris standing alone, smiling apologetically to her hands.

Terry's pulse began to race. She didn't have time to worry about Allison and her father. If she didn't go now, the Egypt room would be crawling with partygoers. Knowing the elevator would be full, she opted for the stairs, having full confidence that her speed would get her to the Egypt room in time.

She slipped into the stairwell. Terry began to run up the stairs, then she stopped. Sobbing echoed from the ground floor. "…supposed to be here! My boyfriend just broke up with me! How am I supposed to act, Daddy?"

Terry peeked over the railing. Allison had her back against the concrete wall, and her mascara was smudged under her eyes. Mayor Harris pointed a finger at her face. "I don't care," he growled. "We're the first family of this city. A lot of important people are here tonight — influential people."

"I don't care about being the best anymore!" she shouted. "I'm sick of being on display for your stupid voters. I just want to go home." Allison covered her face with her hands and continued to cry.

His hands clenched into fists by his sides. He took a deep breath, his nostrils flaring. Terry fought the urge to jump over the railing and get between Allison and her dad.

"Go then," Mayor Harris finally said. He ran a hand over his head, smoothing down his already perfect hair. "Go home and cry like a baby. Go wash your face too. You look like a whore in all that makeup. Now get out of my sight."

Allison shook in the corner. "What about Mom?"

"She's waiting for me by the elevator." He turned and pushed open the door that led to the rotunda on the ground floor.

"But…" Allison sputtered. "I need money for a cab." Her voice went high on the end like a question.

"That's your problem," he said. "Take the bus for all I care." The door closed behind him.

Terry remained still. Allison's sobs soon quieted. There was the beeping of a cell phone, then Allison's voice. "Hi, Rosetta. I'm coming home early from the museum. Daddy wanted to make sure I call you before I leave, I know you like to turn in early after you finish the ironing. Can you call me a cab and wait up until I get home?" There was a pause, and then, "Oh, thank you. I'll pay you back. Daddy only brought his credit card tonight."

The call ended. Then Allison wiped under her eyes and slipped back out to the empty rotunda.

A knot tightened inside Terry. She tasted blood and realized she'd been biting her cheek. "Focus," she whispered. She had to push aside what she'd just witnessed and get to the Egypt room. She started to race up the stairs. She had enough time — as long as there weren't any more distractions.

She easily reached the fifth floor. Terry pulled the heavy door open and smacked straight into Zach.

Chapter Forty-Five

Zach winced, then readjusted the sling across his chest. He wore a light green Hollister T-shirt and jeans.

He stared at Terry. "Wow," he said.

Her hand flitted over the white fabric of her costume. She was embarrassed and thrilled that her appearance had elicited that kind of reaction from him.

His bad eye was less swollen but still purple and sore looking. "Can you see all right?" she asked. It seemed like the safest thing to ask.

"Perfectly." Zach's stare trailed down the length of her dress. "My drawings could never do you justice."

The asp began to beat a tempo against Terry's skin. She saw a lanyard around his neck, the end tucked in behind his sling. "What are you doing here?"

"Fraser left me a press pass at the front desk. He said something about needing a Shaggy for the group."

"For someone who's borderline genius, he really is dumb." Terry looked around wildly. Voices came down the hall from the elevator.

"I called Maude when I couldn't get you on the phone last night. She told me this was the best place to find you." He reached for her waist, his face growing serious. "We need to talk."

Terry closed her eyes, trying to ignore the tingles going all the way to her toes.

His voice was soft. "I know you were there that night. Maude told me you were the one who brought me to the hospital," he said. "She couldn't explain everything, but she told me I definitely wasn't seeing things."

Terry hung her head and studied her gold sandals. The sound of partygoers grew louder. Zach pulled her closer. "I know you're the reason I'm not in a coma. Please, tell me what's going on."

"No." She put her hand on his chest, just above the sling. "You can't be here."

Terry's splayed fingertips could feel Zach's heartbeat under his T-shirt. The asp adjusted its rhythm to match. He reached up with his good hand, covering hers, keeping it in place. Terry stared at their laced fingers.

Using the asp to summon all of her strength, she lightly pressed on his chest, pushing him away.

"This isn't right," he pleaded. "Please, you have to let me help you. I don't want to lose you." He searched her face for some kind of hint, but Terry remained placid, her mask of stone barely intact. "What do you want?"

"I want you to leave," she said.

There was an expression of resistance, then a reserved kind of surrender settled on his face. Zach took a step backward.

"Nefertari?" Prince Kamal came up from behind and stood beside her. "Have you been waiting outside the Egypt room for me all this time? I'm sorry." His curious gaze then focused on Zach. "You're the one my bodyguards caught, correct?"

Zach nodded. "No worries. I won't be dropping by anymore."

Prince Kamal looked back at Terry. She tried to smile. "Shall we go in together?" he softly asked. "Everyone is waiting."

Without a backward glance, Terry continued with Prince Kamal to the Egypt room. There was a sharp pain in her chest, like an elastic band between her and Zach was being pulled to the breaking point. Each step felt like she was walking in liquid concrete. *Run back to Zach*, all her cells screamed at once.

"I know you wanted to see the room privately before this," Prince Kamal said. "But it was impossible with all the security checks. You'll have your opportunity afterward, though." He searched her face. "I hope that's satisfactory."

Terry kept her head down, biting her lower lip to keep it from trembling. They walked through the metal detector together. When the alarm went off, both guards instinctively looked at Terry. There was no reason to frisk the royalty. Prince Kamal waved them off. "She has a knee brace." Terry felt a jolt of panic. She wasn't wearing the brace. It was broken. If they asked to see it, she'd be stuck trying to explain why her 'fake' jewelry had set off the alarm. The asp warmed her skin. Prince Kamal put a protective hand on her back and led her through. Then he leaned down and joked, "You're not carrying a gun tonight, are you, Nefertari?"

The Egypt room was packed. The mayor waited by the glass case. He smiled at Prince Kamal, then his eyes slid to Terry. She trembled in her dress, remembering his vile words to his own daughter. And had Allison told him about the choking incident in the bathroom?

He smiled, then reached out and shook her hand, red-faced and smelling of brandy. It was obvious that he didn't remember meeting her in her dad's office. Terry's skin recoiled at his touch. Amy Sue's face flashed in her memory.

Prince Kamal extended his arms to the crowd. On cue, one of the museum officials welcomed all the guests and began a speech about funding and how generous support from benefactors had helped the museum to stay open.

Terry glanced around the room and found Fraser and Maude huddled in a small space against the wall on the opposite side of the Egypt room. Some of Fraser's bandages had come loose, and Maude's cheeks were flushed as red as her favorite Tootsie Pop.

"I'm so pleased to see all of you here," Prince Kamal began.

"But there are several important people who are not able to join us for this special event. The first is a world-renowned herpetologist and Egyptologist, Dr. May Mullaca. Her commitment to help interpret the hieroglyphics brought her all the way from her home in Egypt. And we hope to have her continuing her work as soon as she is able."

From across the room Terry noticed Maude's face fall. She grabbed Fraser's arm and pulled him closer, talking quickly. One of the more elegantly dressed women in the crowd gave them a sneer and pressed a finger to her lips for them to be quiet.

A smattering of applause politely acknowledged the woman that Terry had feared from the very beginning. She focused on the coffin and the three grooves. The asp was warming her whole body, pulsating waves of energy.

Movement across the room caught Terry's attention. Maude was waving something — a long red Twizzler.

"Naomi Hughes," Prince Kamal said. His arms were spread wide taking in the whole room. He had everyone's attention. "She sacrificed her life to uncover one of Egypt's most legendary leaders." Terry felt the eyes of the room slowly settle on her. She wanted to look proud, but she felt *foolish* standing behind the prince, dressed like it was Halloween. He continued to speak of his government's commitment to share the priceless artifact with the world. His words became muffled as Terry's memory of that day in the cave replayed.

"This is it." Her mother's voice was high, quivering with excitement. Her breaths came in short gasps. "The fourth chamber—"

Terry wished she could step into history and pull her mother backward and out of the cave instead of urging her to move forward.

Without warning, a roar boomed across Terry's face. Her leg burst open. There was a blinding flash of white light.

She hated the memory of the white flash most of all. It marked the definitive moment of her life; before the accident and after the accident

"—last pharaoh." Prince Kamal's words poked through Terry's haze, bringing her back to the present.

The asp began to pulsate faster. Terry stared at the coffin under the glass. Her fists were clenched behind her back. Prince Kamal finished his speech and motioned for Mayor Harris to say a few words. Terry made her way through the dresses and suits across the room.

Fraser took her hand and pulled her closer. "Where's Maude?" he asked, the panic in his voice unfamiliar. "She was on her way to talk to you."

"Is this about the Twizzler?" she whispered back.

Fraser showed her his gauze-covered arm. "When Maude heard Dr. Mullaca's first name was May, she grabbed her eyeliner pencil and started drawing all over me."

"What are you talking about?" Terry titled her head, trying to read the letters Maude had scratched over his arm.

"May is the month before June." He pointed to the letters. "See? Mullaca spelled backwards is acallum, now add her first initial and it spells, Macallum."

"Oh my god," Terry said.

"Dr. Mullaca is June Macallum!" Fraser hissed under his breath.

Terry's mind reeled. "But if she is June Macallum, why did she disappear fifty years ago, and what's her connection to the asp?"

The color drained from Fraser's face. "I think maybe Amy Sue knows," he said. "Maude thought we should call the hospital."

"But Dr. Mullaca isn't dangerous," Terry said. "She's in the hospital with a broken hip. Plus she has no memory." She moved through the room, looking around the crowd for a glimpse of Maude's wig or flowing costume. "Maybe Maude left to call the ICU," she guessed.

"And tell them what?" Fraser said, following behind. "That the paralyzed Egyptologist might be a missing girl from fifty years ago because their names are similar?"

Terry's eyes darted around the room. "She couldn't have disappeared into thin air."

He ran a hand over his face. "I'm so stupid. I should have gone with her."

Terry had known something horrible like this would happen. She fought the panic and took a deep breath. She couldn't freak out. Too much depended on her tonight.

She scanned the room, and her eyes focused on the upright mummy case with the hollowed-out eyes.

A scene flickered from Terry's memory — Tanya and her boyfriend had been in the same area right before she went missing. "Fraser, look!" On the floor at the foot of the case was Maude's cell phone. Terry picked it up. A couple standing close by whispered for them to be quiet. The wife's lips were drawn tight.

Terry ran her fingers along the edge of the mummy case, looking for a gap to pry her fingers into, but there nothing to grasp.

Fraser peeked through the eye sockets. "I can't see anything. Can you use your bionic woman thing?" he asked. The woman with the lemon face actually made a 'tsk' noise this time.

"This is useless," Terry whispered. "We have to start searching." She and Fraser headed for the exit. Prince Kamal's eyes followed them, but he stayed beside the mayor.

The rotunda far below was empty except for a few staff cleaning up smudged wine glasses and crumpled napkins. "We have to split up," Terry said. "You take this floor, and I'll start on the fourth."

Fraser nodded vigorously, then raced down the hallway to search the other exhibits. Terry ran to the elevator, slipped inside and hit the button for the fourth floor.

She swallowed the sob that had been threatening to erupt. *Keep it together. You need to concentrate on Maude.* Terry made an effort to calm her breathing. The doors slid open. She made her way along the corridor, blinking away the rush of tears. She knocked into someone and stumbled backward. A strong, thin hand grabbed her forearm to steady her. It was one of the King Tut servers, the one with the bare feet she'd bumped earlier.

"Uh ... sorry," Terry stammered, almost dropping Maude's cell phone.

The server tightened their grip. "Well done, Nefertari," the raspy voice said, pulling off the mask.

"Dr. Mullaca?"

Chapter Forty-Six

Terry stared back at Dr. Mullaca dressed in the server's costume. "How are you standing?" she asked. "And why aren't you in the hospital?"

"I warned you about Prince Kamal," she said. "You have no idea how close you came to disaster tonight." She paused, letting the sting of her words linger. "However, now that I'm here, you can give the asp to me and run away freely."

"To you?" Terry took a step back, but Dr. Mullaca kept a firm grip. The blue hospital gown peeked from the bottom of the server's robe.

Dr. Mullaca sneered at the King Tut mask and tossed it over the railing. There was a spectacular crunching sound as it hit the marble tiles four floors below. "I suspect the staff at the hospital are dumbfounded by my sudden disappearance from the X-ray department." A hint of pride to her voice that gave Terry goose bumps. "The ICU is crawling with staff. It's nearly impossible to leave without being detected, but radiology is more lax, especially if they think you can't walk."

Terry's head was swirling. "Why did you fake being paralyzed?"

"No one ever suspects the cripple, do they, Nefertari?" Her eyes were afire. "I heard the nurses talking about the handsome basketball star who was mugged and mysteriously delivered to the emergency room." Her voice was tinged with suspicious antici-pation. "That same night another rumor filtered up through the staff that a pair of local hooligans also arrived unconscious and beaten up ... and that's when I knew for certain."

Terry was surprised at the old woman's strong grip on her arm. "One scream from me and security will be down here," Terry threatened, "including Prince Kamal."

"We both know you could toss me over the railing if you want-ed," Dr. Mullaca said. "But I'm not the one you need to fight, Nef-ertari. As soon as Prince Kamal knows you have the asp, you're as good as dead."

"You're crazy." Terry ripped out of her grip. "Why should I lis-ten to you?"

"Because I'm the only one who can tell you the truth." Dr. Mullaca rolled up her sleeve, showing a faded asp tattoo. "I know exactly what's going on. Because the same thing happened to me fifty years ago."

The asp tattoo. Terry suddenly remembered Sarah had men-tioned she'd seen it on Dr. Mullaca's arm when she was slipping on her lab coat. The same tattoo Gus Tanner had seen glowing.

Terry took in a slow breath, letting her confidence recharge. "You'll have to do better than that, Dr. Mullaca." She paused, rel-ishing the feeling of gaining an upper hand. "Or should I say, June Macallum."

The veil of fearlessness fell. Dr. Mullaca's lips quivered. "That girl hasn't existed for a very long time."

Terry pushed. "What happened the day you disappeared?"

Dr. Mullaca's eyes became cloudy. She stared over Terry's shoulder as if watching a movie of her past. "It was a class trip, but I thought I could hide from them. I loved this museum and knew every corner of it, but she still found me."

"Who?"

"Amy Sue Veinot," Dr. Mullaca looked like she'd swallowed

poison. "I was poor and unloved, and that was enough reason for Amy Sue and her friends to tease me and laugh behind my back. It made her feel important, I think. I never stood up for myself ... no one did."

Terry stayed quiet.

"I spent study breaks by myself in an empty classroom or a reading nook in the library. I was invisible to everyone. One of those times, I overheard Amy Sue crying to her friend that she was pregnant. They thought they were alone."

Her voice grew cold. "When they discovered me, I promised to keep her secret, but I could see it would do no good. Amy Sue would use fear to assure I stayed quiet."

"By the time the class trip to the museum happened, the teasing had escalated to daily bullying. After the particularly cruel session at the hands of Amy Sue and her friends, I stayed in the museum's bathroom, wishing I could disappear."

"Your ripped sweater," Terry whispered.

"The only nice thing I owned." She took in a long breath through her nose. "I ended up falling asleep on the cold tiles. When I woke up, it was after hours, and the museum had closed — no one had looked for me, no one missed me. I panicked, knowing my foster mother wouldn't be pleased if I called her for help." Her voice had a bitter edge. "But I was about to discover my destiny."

"Destiny?" Pins and needles shot down Terry's spine.

Dr. Mullaca's mouth twisted into a grin. "I wandered around the exhibits, then a loud noise came for the Egypt room. I found the security guard slumped against the wall, unconscious. Three men in black surrounded the smashed case, holding the asp. I was frozen to the spot, terrified they would see me. But when they started to discuss selling the irreplaceable piece, an anger I'd never felt before pushed me forward."

A light laugh escaped her. "The expression on the robbers' faces when I ran toward them, screaming like a warrior! I grabbed the asp from their hands and ran as fast as I could. Its golden coils were warm when I slipped it on."

Terry cupped the asp on her arm protectively.

Dr. Mullaca looked up to the fifth floor. "The men caught me and we struggled. I fell over the railing."

Terry's eyes grew wide. "But...?"

"The fall should have killed me, but the impact didn't happen. Instead, there was a flash of white light. I was no longer in the rotunda, but in front of an exotic woman dressed in white robes. She told me she was the asp's priestess and that it had chosen me to be its next protector."

A flash of white light. A dull roar began inside Terry's head.

"The asp chooses a protector. It has for thousands of years." Dr. Mullaca's fingers grazed her faded asp tattoo, her voice becoming eerily calm. "It bestowed its mark upon me. It came with an ancient power that few throughout history have been able to possess. I was chosen to protect Cleopatra's most valuable piece and prevent it from falling into the hands of those who would abuse its power for profit or gain."

She smiled at Terry, her chin tilted up. "Those robbers ran screaming from the museum when I turned up in the Egypt room very much alive and ready for revenge. I slipped the asp off my arm and placed it back inside the broken case. Then I pulled the fire alarm." She lifted a shoulder as if bored with this part of the story. "I stayed by the security guard until I heard the sirens grow close."

"But why did you disappear?" Terry asked. She pictured Gus Tanner as a young man, obsessed for years.

"Because for the first time in my whole miserable life, I saw a future I only thought possible in my dreams. Me, June Macallum, whom nobody ever bothered with except to tease or torment. And even though I wasn't in possession of the asp, it had marked me. The tattoo gave me the same physical strength."

Dr. Mullaca's face morphed into a helpless expression.

"Besides, no one missed me," she said hollowly. "All I needed for a disguise was a simple wig and some new clothes. I had to steal everything, but I was so fast no one saw me." A ghost of a smile touched her lips. "I think the hangers must have still been swinging by the time I was out of the department store with a bundle of skirts and blouses under my arms. I could have anything I ever wanted, clothes, jewelry, money..."

There was an eruption of laughter from the fifth floor, but Terry ignored it, concentrating on Dr. Mullaca's story. Maude was somehow thrown into this mess, and Terry was certain Dr. Mullaca had information that would save her.

Chapter Forty-Seven

"No one would suspect the young woman at the boarding house with expensive clothes and shoes was the dowdy missing girl." Dr. Mullaca's voice took on a boastful quality. "But I was meant for a purpose. I spent my nights fighting back for all those too weak to save themselves. It was exhilarating at first, leaving robbers for the police to find. The power was intoxicating." Her features darkened. "It was like a comic book. I was invincible ... or so I thought."

Terry hugged her elbows. Dr. Mullaca's story was uncomfortably familiar.

"Then, two weeks after I first tried on the asp, while doing my usual night patrol, I saw Amy Sue and her friends smoking and sharing beers in the park with their boyfriends. One of the football players had a theory I'd gone crazy and was hiding in the basement of the school, living on rats."

She merely rolled her eyes. "Soon their talk turned morbid. Someone said I must have been murdered by the security guard, and one day they'd find my dismembered skeleton in his backyard. Amy Sue said they were all wrong. She told them I'd killed myself after I found out I was pregnant."

Dr. Mullaca's breaths came faster. "She said I didn't know who the father was because I'd given myself to every boy in school. One of the football players bragged that his older brother

279

had been at a party were I was passed around."

Terry swallowed hard, remembering Maude's own experience with vicious rumors.

Dr. Mullaca's voice was thick. "I'd never even been kissed, but everyone believed what she said about me." She blinked and two tears rolled down her cheeks. "They didn't even care that I might be dead."

She unclenched her fists and hastily wiped her face. "I followed her home that night, and waited until she was alone." The lines tightened around Dr. Mullaca's mouth. "She laughed and said that no matter how pretty my clothes were, I was still an ugly whore that no one would ever love."

She stopped and looked at Terry. "It was only one punch," she confessed, "but it was filled with all the hate and fear I'd kept inside from all the bullying."

Terry remembered Amy Sue's face. She brought a hand to her mouth.

"She lay on her driveway, twitching," Dr. Mullaca continued, more composed. "I ran to a pay phone and called in an anonymous tip. The police were there within a minute. I was terrified that I'd killed her or hurt her unborn baby. I was afraid of my powers. I didn't want to have anything to do with the asp; I was convinced it was cursed. But I was still its protector, so I hid it in the in the safest spot I could think of. No one would ever notice a fake asp had been replaced by the real thing."

"The Cleopatra mannequin," Terry said unexpectedly. She was so engrossed in the story she forgot why she was wearing the asp.

Dr. Mullaca nodded. "I left the city and found someone who could give me fake identification for the right price. Then I boarded a plane for Egypt, the only place that had any future for me."

Terry tried to take a deep breath, but the air felt heavy. She was still no closer to finding Maude. "But why come back now?" she asked.

"Because after decades of feeling nothing, last year I woke up with my heart racing and this pulsating." Dr. Mullaca touched her asp tattoo. "Some of the strength I once had returned as well. I went into work and my colleagues told me an American archaeologist and her husband had unearthed what might be Cleopatra's final resting place."

Blood flooded Terry's chest. She wasn't expecting this inclusion of her parents.

"Your mother's discovery changed everything. You see, the asp is not only a conduit for power, but it's also an alarm. The closer she got to the coffin, the stronger my tattoo pulsated. When I learned of her death, I kept a close eye on you and your father, assuming he would continue to pursue her work.

"I put my name forward and made sure I was the expert chosen to study the hieroglyphics. And when I discovered the truth about the asp being the key to opening it, I made arrangements with the government for it to be brought here." She stopped and tilted her head, now recovered from her confession. "Do you understand now, Nefertari?"

"No." Terry's voice sounded wounded. "If you're the one who hid the asp, why did you ask me to find it? Why did you pretend you didn't know where it was?"

A look of embarrassment flashed across Dr. Mullaca's usual stone expression. "It wouldn't respond to my touch anymore. I couldn't pull it off the mannequin. I suspected that you were the new protector. I needed you to get it for me."

"That's impossible."

"No more impossible than surviving a cave-in that should have crushed you in half. There's no other explanation for you to still be alive, Nefertari. I knew you were destined to get the asp. When you seemed reluctant, I had to make you desperate enough to not only find it, but steal it as well. I had to take away something you loved."

Terry stared back unbelievingly at the old woman. "My dad?"

"I know all about snake venom; how much will induce a coma,

how much will kill a grown man. It would show up on the blood tests, but I planned to have your father recover after a few days."

Her boastful tone sent chills across Terry skin. "You poisoned my dad!"

"And myself!" she rebutted. "I had to keep administering the venom; he was starting to wake up. His pulse rates were being questioned by the staff. I had to be closer to him to keep him in his unconscious state."

"The vials," Terry murmured, her brain aching with all the revelations. "Prince Kamal assumed you were diabetic."

"He'd make a terrible physician," she huffed. "When you told me you'd found the asp, I had to act quickly, but I knew I couldn't show up at the Plaza — not with Kamal's bodyguards. I had to wait until the benefit party. Then yesterday, I pretended I'd fallen. I made a great fuss about a painful hip. While I was waiting for an X-ray, lying on a stretcher with no one watching me, I knew I'd found my perfect escape. This morning I gave your father his last dose and had another fake fall." Dr. Mullaca held her hands out to her side. "And you know the rest."

"Last dose!" Terry's voice rose. "You killed my dad?"

"Of course not." She reached for Terry's hands. "By tomorrow morning he'll have woken up completely, and by that time the asp and I will have disappeared." She smiled. "Again."

Terry stared at their clasped hands. "None of this makes any sense. You don't even care about the coffin. All you want is the power of the asp."

Dr. Mullaca threw her head back and laughed. "Spoken like a true protector," she praised. "But you're too young. You'll make the same mistakes I did. I have to take it back to Egypt, give it a proper burial — something I should have done fifty years ago. If I don't, another tragedy will happen. I'm only doing this to protect you."

"No. I'm not the next protector." She tried to step back, but Dr. Mullaca's wouldn't loosen her grip.

"It fell into your hands easily, yes?"

Terry nodded.

"You felt a surge of energy and power like never before. And the priestess in white robes appeared in a bright light, yes?"

"No," Terry said. She looked up to the fifth floor.

Dr. Mullaca tightened her grip. "Are you sure? There's always a priestess."

"Help!" Terry screamed, willing Prince Kamal's face to appear over the railing above them.

"Quiet! We don't have much time." Dr. Mullaca's eyes looked hungrily at Terry's arm. "Of course," she said. "The transfer of power isn't complete. That's why you're not marked with a tattoo. Your life must be in danger. That's how the asp knows you're willing to die for it."

"What are you talking about?"

"I've learned a lot in the last fifty years, Nefertari. I don't want you to make the same mistakes. You must give it back to me. I'm the only one you can trust." Dr. Mullaca's fingers clawed at her arm, trying to pry to asp off.

"You're crazy!" Terry pulled away, but Dr. Mullaca's strength was more than Terry was prepared for. She felt the railing press against her back. The King Tut mask was smashed to bits on the rotunda below.

Dr. Mullaca's face contorted with adrenaline. The sleeve of her hospital gown had bunched up, and her asp tattoo was pulsating. She lunged at Terry, pushing her back into the railing, forcing her feet off the ground. "You have to be willing to die for it!" Dr. Mullaca screamed. "It's the only way to save us both!" Dr. Mullaca's face froze, then her mouth made a silent scream in the shape of an 'O.' She crumpled to the floor. A red blossom spread across her gown. A jeweled hilt stuck out the side of her neck at an awkward angle.

Prince Kamal pulled out the dagger and tucked it back into his leg strap. He reached for Terry. "Are you all right?"

Terry's whole body started to shake. "You … you killed her."

"*She* was trying to kill *you*!" He glanced up to the fifth floor.

"Come," he said, leading her into the elevator. "We don't have much time."

"We have to call an ambulance," Terry sputtered.

He wrapped a protective arm around her as the elevator descended.

Terry's body wouldn't stop shaking. She grabbed Prince Kamal's breast plate. "We have to call the ICU." She felt like she was screaming. "She's been poisoning my dad!"

"You never have to worry about her again."

"And Maude! We need to find Maude!" Her pitch was frantic.

"Of course." The elevator doors opened. Terry buried her face in his shoulder, letting the tears fall. She continued to lean into him, letting him blindly lead her along. "Shh, it's all right," he soothed, patting the back of her head.

Soon Terry felt the air grow colder. She pulled her face away and wiped her tears, blinking against the starkness of the white examining room.

"Why are we in the basement?" she asked.

"Don't worry. Soon everything will fall into place." Prince Kamal pulled her across to another door which he unlocked with an ancient looking key. "This is where the asp belongs."

Still in shock from Dr. Mullaca's death, Terry stumbled behind Prince Kamal. The floor seemed to be tipping at dangerous angles. He led her down another corridor, much darker and smelling of damp earth. "Wait ... how did you know I had the asp?"

"See for yourself." He waved a hand at the final corner.

They walked into the chamber together. Torches along the walls of the circular room cast gruesome shadows on the faces of the hooded figures, whose mouths moved in unison as they began to chant.

Prince Kamal pulled Terry close. The back of his fingers lightly stroked her cheek. "It's time for the resurrection, my queen."

Chapter Forty-Eight

The air was smoky with incense. A stone table was positioned in the middle of the blackened floor. Hooded figures lined the perimeter, chanting.

"What is this?" Terry whispered. She was still in Prince Kamal's embrace, but all the feeling had left her body. She was like a puppet in his hands.

"Your destiny." There was a hunger to his voice.

"Please stop. This is a sick joke, Prince Kamal." Terry regained her footing and stepped back. "I don't want anyone else to get hurt. You have no idea the powers I possess."

"Oh, really?" Sarah stepped out from the shadows, pointing a gun at Terry. Her red lips pulled back from her teeth in a malicious smile. The sequins on her long black gown sparkled in the torch light. "I'm quite certain the asp doesn't make you bulletproof," she said.

Terry's head swiveled between Sarah and Prince Kamal. "I don't understand. What's going on?"

"I'm only righting what should have happened twenty years ago," Sarah said. Her pose was a glaring opposite to the hooded chanters.

"Twenty?" Terry said. "But the asp was stolen fifty years ago."

Sarah threw her head back and laughed. "I'm talking about

your parents ... or rather, the man who was supposed to be my husband. Your mother stole him from me, so now I'm taking back what's rightfully mine."

"What?" She looked at Prince Kamal. "You killed Dr. Mullaca because of Sarah and my dad?"

"Sarah has her own agenda." The prince's elegant features were still there, but a darker, more primal quality had taken over his voice. "However, in order for both of us to get what we want, the unpleasant business of murder had to occur. Dr. Mullaca was under the impression we'd let her have the asp if she opened the coffin for us."

"Excuse me," Sarah said, "but that snake freak messed up the first day. Gunther passed out immediately instead of after they'd gone to the fifth floor. I'm the one who suggested we sneak him up the passageway to the Egypt room. And I'm the one who faked a text from Gunther about the key."

"My dad was already poisoned when that text was sent?" Terry moaned. She imagined him lying on the floor of the Egypt room while Sarah sent that ridiculous text full of exclamation marks. Terry ground her teeth — she should have been more suspicious.

"Admit it," Sarah said. "You never would have figured out where the asp was if you didn't have that little clue."

Terry blinked, stunned. Prince Kamal stepped closer. He continued to watch her reaction with a perverse curiosity. "You asked me last night if I'd ever crossed a desert for love. I didn't lie." His finger traced the asp. "But I crossed an ocean for this — and for you."

The chanting stopped, and the room became deathly quiet. One by one each of the hooded figures revealed themselves. Terry wasn't surprised to see most of Prince Kamal's bodyguards among them, but the last figure jolted her. "Ms. Bernard?"

She bowed to Terry, "It is an honor to be with you tonight."

The elegant address hinted at a craziness that Terry suspected would be the death of her. "Me?" she asked.

"Of course," Ms. Bernard said, her matter-of-fact demeanor more chilling than Prince Kamal's stare. "You're the chosen one. The new Cleopatra."

Prince Kamal motioned to his bodyguards. "My staff will assure their military confidants of our lineage, and a new king will be crowned." His eyes grew larger. "And you will be right by my side."

Terry felt the room swirl. "But I don't love you," she said numbly. "And you already have a girlfriend back home!"

"That's inconsequential, Nefertari," he said. "This is about me getting the throne, not your heart."

"And I'll be there to nurse your dad back to health." Sarah smiled. "Don't worry, honey. He'll be fully recovered by the time you two tie the knot. We wouldn't dare miss your royal wedding, especially if I'm to be mother of the bride!"

"You'll never be my mother."

"No, but I am opportunistic," Sarah smiled. "And with your dad working by my side, the museum will become one of the most popular in the country. You can make damn sure we'll be the new power couple of Devonshire."

Ms. Bernard clutched a worn book, the thick pages made of papyrus. "Life repaid, life relived, life resurrected," she said devotedly.

A commotion made every head turn. Terry squinted through the haze of incense. From the far end of the room, another mummy case with hollowed-out eyes stood up against the wall. The lid flung open. Mayor Harris came through, disheveled and sucking air. He brushed off his tuxedo, then looked around. When he saw Terry and Prince Kamal, his mouth dropped open.

For a moment Terry thought he was going to save her, but then he said, "You haven't even started yet? They just found the old lady. The police will be here any minute."

"We're in a secure area." Prince Kamal narrowed his eyes. "We only have one chance to perform the ritual. There's no need to be careless and rush the process. You can wait to the side."

"You don't give me orders," Mayor Harris snapped. "If it weren't for my support, the closest you'd get to the throne is to clean it."

Prince Kamal turned an alarming shade of purple. "You ignorant buffoon! Let me remind you, I hold the most important piece to your future victory."

"Boys!" Sarah said. "Stop with the spitting contest and get busy. We can't be missing for too long." She stepped closer to Terry, keeping her at point blank range.

Mayor Harris wet his lips. He pointed a finger at Terry's arm. "Can you confirm it will still have power after the resurrection spell is completed?"

"Bit late to be asking, Mayor Harris." Prince Kamal's face turned darker. "Your intentions are less than honorable. Don't pretend to be more than you are."

"I'll be more of a king than you'll ever be. That thing will give me power over the city, its businesses, the voters, and more importantly ... the banks." Mayor Harris gave the room a self-satisfied grin at the end.

"Banks?" Terry's head was in a fog from all the incense. She had to concentrate on keeping sharp. She noticed the rest of the figures in the room had glazed eyes.

Prince Kamal chuckled. "The mayor is having cash flow problems."

Terry glared at Mayor Harris. Her inhibitions were slowly crumbling. "It must be expensive to keep Amy Sue in that hospital," she said.

Mayor Harris stared hatefully at the asp. "That thing stole the life I was supposed to have," he said, his voice full of loathing. "I could have grown up the son of a professional football player and the local beauty queen. Instead I was raised on a pig farm, working in slop every morning, surrounded by simple people." His face contorted between self-pity and uncontrolled rage.

"But you're the mayor of Devonshire," Terry said.

"I could have been president of the country!" he spat out. His right eye twitched.

Terry took in the handsome man, seeing only the selfish shell of a human being. "You did all this for revenge?" she asked.

"And greed," Prince Kamal said. "When I discovered the government was shipping the coffin to Devonshire, I did a little investigating, knowing that I'd need a few inside associates to help me find my newly reincarnated wife." He grinned openly, gesturing to Sarah and Mayor Harris. "Not only did I find a corrupt politician, but a jilted curator with an unfathomable lust for an old flame."

Terry pleaded with Sarah. "But my dad would have fallen in love with you anyway. I mean, you're such a great cook." Terry knew her only chance of escape was to distract Sarah long enough to grab the gun without getting shot. Her reflexes were fast enough to beat up a couple of thugs, but she wasn't willing to test them with a gun pointed at her head.

"Nice try." Sarah pressed the barrel of the gun harder into Terry's temple. "I know you hate my guts. No worries, the feeling is mutual. That's why it's important you board a plane with your fiancé tonight. Gunther can't very well forget about 'perfect and brilliant Naomi' if her lookalike daughter is moping around him all the time. Once you're out of sight, your dad and I will be the perfect team. We might even open that art gallery he once promised me."

"You're nuts," Terry said. "You're all nuts!"

Mayor Harris glowered at Terry. "I'm only getting what is rightfully mine. And you'll get to live in a palace, so shut up and let's get this started."

Prince Kamal's mouth was a hard line. "You're blinded by your American ignorance. You'll never understand the importance of what's about to happen."

Terry's eyes flicked back and forth between her arguing cap-

tors. She focused her gaze on the upright mummy with the hollowed-out eyes — just like the one in the Egypt room. She had a
suspicion where it led.

The mayor smoothed out his tuxedo. "Where are the other girls?"

A grunt came from the darkened corner of the room. Out of
the shadows one of the hooded figures came forward. An unconscious girl wearing ripped jeans and a black jacket was draped
over his arms.

Terry gasped as Tanya was placed on the stone tablet. She
was pale and had smudges of dirt all over her face and clothes,
but she was still breathing. Prince Kamal whispered to Terry,
"Please see that this is our destiny."

She protectively put a hand over the asp. "You're delusional!"

His biting tone was a sudden contrast. "You cannot stop what
is about to happen. Make no mistake, Nefertari, you will be my
wife."

Terry's stomach twisted. She took in shallow breaths. The
cloaked figures put their hoods back up and began chanting
again. Ms. Bernard stood apart from the others, watching over
the ceremony. Her unmistakable pointed nose and sharp features
stood out. "What were you promised?" Terry asked.

Her stoic expression flashed with excitement. "To see history
come to life," she said. "I've waited a very long time for this moment."

"What do you think is going to happen?" Terry was dumb-
struck at the insane logic. They actual thought she was going to
have Cleopatra's soul.

"The same thing that happened fifty years ago," she answered. Terry remembered the shadow that had crossed Ms. Bernard's face that very first day in class when she mentioned the
museum. Terry had mistaken her expression for fear; however, in
the flicker of the torches, she now recognized what must have
been painful anticipation.

"I'll be stepping back in time to ancient Egypt," Ms. Bernard added breathlessly, "just like that girl, June." Her eyes were misty. Prince Kamal gave her a reassuring nod.

The image of Dr. Mullaca lying in a pool of blood filled Terry's head with a thousand screams. She swallowed down the wave of nausea.

Prince Kamal's fingers tried to coax her grip from the asp. "This is not the treasure, my queen. You are," he said. "Everyone in this room has worked to make sure this moment happens. You need to show us who you really are."

Terry tilted up her chin. "You can't get the asp unless I give it to you," she said. "Even Dr. Mullaca couldn't pry it off my arm."

He motioned to Ms. Bernard. She came forward, a nervous smile strained across her lined face. The papyrus-bound book shook in her hands. She read, "As Cleopatra spilled her blood with the fangs of the asp, so shall the next pharaoh. Only she who is the daughter of Isis shall be the chosen one. Three of pure blood must cleanse the asp to complete the circle."

She gazed adoringly at Terry. "Life repaid, live relived, life resurrected." Ms. Bernard was joined by the rest of the hooded figures as they continued the chant.

"Life repaid, live relived, life resurrected." Their deep, monotone voices signaled the end for Terry. She felt woozy again, the room a jumble of disjointed images.

Prince Kamal squeezed her hand. "Don't be afraid," he tried to soothe. "This is your destiny, just as your mother intended."

"What?" Terry snapped alert.

"Dr. Mullaca had a theory about you being the new protector, but that's not true." He paused, enjoying her full attention. "In fact, it's quite the opposite."

Terry searched his face. "What is the truth?" she asked. "Please."

Prince Kamal stroked the asp with his thumb. "I want to share everything with you," he said. "But none of this can move forward if you resist giving me what I need."

He nodded toward Tanya. "If you give me the asp now, she'll be in a hospital in less than an hour. And we'll be on my private jet, where I'll tell you everything you want to know."

"Including how my mother is involved?"

"Of course."

Terry knew her father would be all right by tomorrow morning; his life didn't depend on the asp anymore. Tanya lay unconscious on the stone pillar.

Terry hesitated.

"Enough sweet talk." Sarah pointed the gun at Tanya. "We're losing valuable time. Hand Kamal the asp or Tanya joins Dr. Mullaca in the morgue."

Terry swallowed hard and slid the asp off her arm.

Chapter Forty-Nine

The second the asp left her skin, Terry's knee roared in pain. She bit the inside of her cheek and tasted blood. Her knee, weakened from all the running and without the support of the brace, buckled under her weight. She instinctively reached out, grabbing Prince Kamal's arm. He smiled back at her.

"Now you shall see the first secret," he said. With the asp in his hands, he pulled off the snake head, revealing two golden fangs, each one an inch long.

"Life repaid, life relived, life resurrected," the hooded figures continued to chant.

Mayor Harris' eyes darted around the room. He checked his watch and licked his lips again.

Prince Kamal loomed over Tanya. He pushed her leather jacket and shirt to the side. Her soft white skin was practically luminescent in the darkened room. She slept on, oblivious. There was a twitch on the corner of Prince Kamal's lips. He positioned the fangs above her heart, and then with one quick thrust, he pushed it into her flesh.

The chant continued, the voices became stronger. Tanya's eyes stayed closed, but her back arched off the stone table. Terry watched helplessly.

Prince Kamal withdrew the asp, now coated with Tanya's

blood. Two small trickles ran down her chest, disappearing under her jacket. A hooded bodyguard lifted Tanya and disappeared with her through the corridor that led to the white examining room.

"Good work," Prince Kamal praised Terry. "The ambulance will find her soon."

Terry stayed quiet about the ambulance he was supposed to call for Dr. Mullaca. What if he was lying about Tanya now too? Her insides knotted up. Sarah turned the gun back on Terry again.

"Next," Prince Kamal ordered. A second bodyguard carried over another unconscious victim and placed her on the stone table.

Terry bit back a scream. Her best friend was still in her toga, but the wig was gone. The roughly cropped sections of scalp were now exposed, ugly and harsh. Maude's eyelids flickered.

Prince Kamal pulled aside the toga and placed the asp's fangs on Maude's bare skin.

"No!" Terry lunged for his arm. She clenched her teeth as her knee crunched painfully. "Let me take her place," she begged.

"Not to worry, my queen," he smiled. "You're the third pure blood. She won't remember a thing. In fact you'll only be a distant memory for her. You're not a silly schoolgirl, Nefertari — you never were. Egypt is your past and your future. It is your home, and we will build up a nation together."

Mayor Harris's forehead was slick with sweat. "Can we hurry this up?"

Prince Kamal impaled Maude's chest with the golden fangs. Her eyes flung wide open. A garbled scream came from the back of her throat while one of her hands flapped uselessly at her side.

"Life repaid, life relived, life resurrected," the chant continued.

Terry put her hands to her ears, wishing she could block them out. She was helpless without the asp.

"Nefertari must get on the table," Ms. Bernard said, her voice regaining some of its usual authority. The book was now steady in her hands.

"No," Prince Kamal snapped. "I'll hold her in my arms." Terry was helpless. All of her weight was on her good leg. Prince Kamal pulled her close. He hooked a finger in the white fabric of her dress and dragged down the neck line. His pupils dilated, reminding Terry of bottomless black wells. The razor-sharp tips of the golden fangs pressed against her flesh.

"Your heart is racing as fast as mine," he said, his breath ragged. He didn't take his eyes off Terry when the prongs of the fangs pierced her. She hardly flinched; the pain in her knee was overwhelmingly worse.

Prince Kamal couldn't hide his wicked grin. "That's my queen," he praised. Terry fought the urge to throw up. He recapped the ancient snake head back in place, locking Terry's blood inside its secret compartment forever.

"Hand it over." Mayor Harris held out his palm. "Now," he ordered.

"Not so fast." Sarah pointed the gun toward Mayor Harris's shocked face. "I didn't plan this for six months only to have to most valuable possession in my museum go to a gambling addict. Prince Kamal promised the asp to me."

"What?" The mayor was frozen under the gun's aim.

Prince Kamal ignored them and turned to Terry. He took the asp and slipped it back on her arm. The relief was instant. Prince Kamal declared, "There is one last step before I can crown my queen." His hand slipped behind Terry's neck. He moved in and closed his mouth over hers. Terry purposely went slack in his arms. "My queen," he murmured against her lips as he kissed her. When he pulled away, his eyes were wild.

Terry's body was on fire. The room was silent as if the very walls were holding their breath. His fingertips trailed down her throat. "Say something, my queen."

"Twizzlers," she whispered.

The prince didn't see the first punch. Terry's fist connected with his confused expression, sending him sprawling into Sarah. They slid across the floor, his body pinning Sarah's as they smashed into the wall. Terry's arms swung like a windmill in a hurricane, landing on anything that approached. Hooded figures flew back in blurs. Ms. Bernard screamed in the background.

Terry grabbed Maude off the table and swung her over her shoulder, fireman style. She blazed toward the open mummy case, cutting a path through the hooded figures, sending them to the floor with her fists. Mayor Harris lunged out of the way.

Terry sprinted through the mummy case and ran up a darkened stairway. She stumbled when Maude's feet hit a wall. Frantically, Terry felt around and realized this was only the turn in the stairs. She continued her ascent up the second flight. "Hold on, Maude," she grunted, hefting her best friend's drooping body higher up on her shoulder.

Angry voices echoed after her. Terry blindly clambered up the stairs. She was running so fast now that her feet were only hitting the occasional step. Terry squinted into the darkness. Two tiny pricks of light beckoned her. She clenched her teeth and put her head down, racing upward.

She and Maude smashed through the mummy lid and into the middle of the Egypt room. There were screams as delegates and socialites scattered.

"Terry?" Zach whirled around, standing still as the crowd panicked in a rush to get out.

Fraser pushed by Zach, and ran toward her. "Oh my god! What happened to Maude?"

"Take her ... get out now!"

Fraser cradled Maude in his arms. "Wait ... what?" A gunshot zinged through the air, hitting the ceiling and sending a shower of plaster on top of Fraser's head. "Oh shit!"

"Just do it!" Terry screamed. She scrambled over to the coffin. She held her fists above the glass case, then brought them down with all her strength. Shattered bits blew out in all directions. Another gunshot cracked through the air. Terry's bad leg felt like it was ripped in two. At her feet, a trail of blood began to trek across the floor.

"Nefertari!" Prince Kamal stood at the opening of the passageway. He aimed the gun directly at her head. "Give me the asp or everything we've created tonight will be lost."

"My mother didn't die so you could force me to be your queen!"

"You're mine now," Prince Kamal said through clenched teeth. "And soon all of Egypt will be ours."

"Egypt belongs to no one. And neither do I." Terry pulled off the asp. The pain from her knee was white hot. She gritted her teeth and gripped the edge of the case, the broken glass piercing her palms.

"No!" The gun shook in Prince Kamal's hands. He hesitated, his eyes pleading with Terry. Then, like a plume of smoke, his compassion disappeared.

Terry focused through her tears, the asp shaking in her grip, hovering above the three grooves.

Prince Kamal cried out as Zach's voice suddenly grunted and cursed with his. Another gunshot fired off. Terry slammed the asp into place. There was a clicking sound. She crumpled to the floor. The bottom half of her dress was soaked in blood. The pool steadily spread. Across from her, Zach and Prince Kamal lay in an unmoving pile on the floor. The room began to fade into blackness. Terry let out one last breath.

There was a flash of light, then a voice said, "The asp has chosen."

Chapter Fifty

When Terry opened her eyes, she was no longer in the Egypt room, lying in a pool of her own blood. She stared down at her legs, but there was only swirling mist, as if she was floating. There was no pain and everything was quiet. She squinted against the whiteness.

"The asp has chosen," the voice said again. A nervous tremble trickled down Terry's spine. She recognized that voice.

The clouds parted to reveal a woman dressed in white robes. Naomi Hughes gave Terry a knowing look.

"Mom?" Terry tentatively reached out, the ends of her fingers shaking. "Are ... are you a ghost?"

"In a way." She tilted her head, studying Terry. "Each time a protector is chosen, a small part of their spirit is absorbed by the original priestess, thereby making the asp more powerful. It is my image and my memories that are being used to communicate with you."

"So you're not really my mom," Terry said heavily.

Her mother reached for her hand and pulled her close. The sleeve of Naomi's white robe flowed. "I'm real enough," she replied, squeezing Terry in a hug.

Terry collapsed into the familiar embrace and let out a long string of sobs.

"There, there." Her mother patted her back.

When Terry finished, she stepped back and stared at her mother's face. She forgot how beautiful she was. "Does this mean I'm dead too?" Terry asked.

"No. You've been chosen as the next protector."

"Protector?"

Naomi smiled wisely and bowed. "The asp chooses the protector. It always has, for thousands of years, as proclaimed by Cleopatra with her last dying breath."

The asp.

A collage of images sped through Terry's mind; her father's hospital bed, Dr. Mullaca bleeding, Maude's garbled scream, Zach lying unmoving … and the coffin.

She reached up and felt her forearm, but the asp wasn't there. "I don't have it anymore," Terry said. Was she supposed to keep it? Had she made the wrong decision? Was everyone she loved hurt because of her mistake?

Naomi's luminescent form smiled at Terry. "You do not have to be in possession of the asp in order to be its protector. But I must warn you, it comes with an ancient power that few can comprehend and control."

"But I wasn't protecting the asp," Terry said. "I was using it to open the coffin."

Naomi's ivory-smooth features crinkled into a look of amusement. "Your actions must have been noble, or you wouldn't be standing in front of me."

Terry stammered. "I'm confused. If I've only just been chosen as the protector, how come the asp responded to my touch the day I stole it from the museum?"

"Because I relinquished my right and passed the honor to be the next protector onto you." She clasped her hands in front of her. "But you had to prove yourself before the asp would mark you for life."

"You? I thought Dr. Mullaca was the last one to wear the asp."

A somber expression clouded Naomi's features. "June proved less than noble with her violent temper. It cost her the power of the asp."

"But she was strong enough to fight me," Terry said, desperate to fit all the puzzle pieces together.

"She wasn't always vengeful. The original priestess allowed her to keep some of the power, stored in the mark of the asp on her arm ... for one last battle."

"I should have given it to her," Terry said, deadpan. "She'd still be alive."

Naomi stayed quiet.

Terry mulled over what her mother was telling her. She frowned. "If the asp was always in the museum, how could the priestess offer you to be its next protector? Dr. Mullaca said your life had to be in danger."

The dark curls of Naomi's hair swirled in the mist. "The asp, the coffin and Cleopatra are connected. Protecting one means protecting the other. My decision was magnanimous, but it came at a risk — it always does. That's how the asp knows."

A wave rippled through Terry. "The cave-in..." she whispered.

Naomi nodded. "When the original priestess appeared, telling me I'd been chosen as the next protector, you and I were dying under the rubble of the cave-in. Only one of us could survive. I asked for your life to be spared if I passed the power of the asp on to you."

"No." Terry shook her head, disbelieving. Her memory of the accident came into focus. The collapse had been followed by a bright light — the priestess. Until now, she always assumed the flash of light had been part of the collapse.

"The priestess granted my request but still absorbed a small part of my spirit, knowing that you'd be connected to the asp until the day you proved yourself worthy."

Terry was drowning in guilt. If she hadn't insisted on going up front that day, her mother would have the power of the asp and still be alive. *How different life would be.*

Her mother's voice became solemn. "And now you have been chosen to protect Cleopatra's most valuable piece and prevent it from falling into the hands of those who would abuse its power for profit or gain. This is your destiny. Do you accept?"

Terry wanted to scream until she had no breath left. Her insistence to be on the dig that day with her mother had ruined so many futures. Everything was her fault: her dad's poisoning, Zach's broken arm and loss of a scholarship, Maude's assault, and Dr. Mullaca's murder.

"Do you accept?" Naomi prompted.

"I'm not worthy." There was a heavy lump in Terry's stomach. "I wish I'd died in that cave too."

"Nefertari Hughes!" She gave Terry a stern look. "I'm shocked you'd be so selfish."

"Everyone in my life is hurt because of me."

"Everyone is in your life because they love you." Her features softened. "The people who surround you are not there by accident, sweetheart." She touched Terry's cheek. "I died peacefully knowing you and your dad still had each other."

Terry wanted to bury her face in her mother's robes and cry until she fell asleep. "I just … I just miss you so much. And I miss how everything used to be." Terry's spirit lifted, considering a new possibility. "If I choose to be a protector, will I be able to talk with you like we used to … like in real life?" she asked hopefully.

"No," Naomi answered softly. "What you see now is a memory of who I was before I died. Life is dynamic. Things have to change to evolve." She paused and put a finger under Terry's chin. "The asp has chosen. Do you accept?"

Terry pictured her father, recovering from Dr. Mullaca's snake venom poisoning. Would he wake up in the morning only to learn his daughter had bled to death on the museum floor? "What happens if I say no?" she asked.

"Then you return to your body, and the asp waits until another protector can prove herself."

"Are you happy?" Terry swallowed. "Or do you regret your decision?"

"I died saving you. I can't think of a more noble cause." Her mother took in breath and stood taller. "Cleopatra absorbed life and emitted energy. Her greatest talent was not holding onto power but how she made everyone around her feel powerful. She inspired the world."

"Still does," Terry added.

"No matter what you decide, it will always be a part of you," she said. She took hold of Terry's hands. "Keep your head up, Nefertari. Empower those around you, and you'll find your own destiny." Then she added, "Protector or not."

Terry stepped in for one last hug. The protector even smelled like her mother. "I wish it really was you," she said.

"My real spirit is always with you," she said. "Now close your eyes and let your heart decide."

Terry let herself sink into her mother's arms. She silently made a promise, then the darkness came.

Chapter Fifty-One

Someone squeezed her hand. "I think she's waking up!"

The mental fog began to ebb. She tried to sit up, but waves of pain pushed her back down. "It's okay, Terry." Her dad's face came into focus. He was unshaven, with red, puffy eyes.

Terry's mind flashed back to the cave accident. She had had a dream about her mother, but she couldn't quite remember everything. "I saw Mom," she whispered.

There was a strangled kind of gasp from her dad. "It's all right," he said. "You're in the hospital." Mr. Hughes carefully leaned in from a wheelchair beside her hospital bed. "The doctors told me I have to build up my strength from lying in bed so long."

"How long…" Terry began, uncertain. She tried to push herself up again, but she had no strength.

"Easy now." A nurse fluffed Terry's pillow. "Just relax."

Mr. Hughes said, "I woke up yesterday." His expression was pained.

"He's been by your bedside since then." The nurse smiled. "Against doctor's orders," she teasingly added.

There was something forced about her manner that made Terry suspicious. She studied the woman in the white uniform, but there was nothing ominous about her. A shudder ran through Terry. She wondered if she'd be paranoid about everyone from now on.

"Honey," Mr. Hughes started, "there was a lot of blood loss." He reached out and held her hand. "Your leg was so badly damaged, we almost lost you..."

Terry squirmed a bit on the bed. "My knee hurts."

Her dad shared an uncomfortable look with the nurse. "I'll call the surgeon," she said above Terry in a whisper. Then the nurse produced a syringe. "I can give you pain medication through your IV," she offered.

"Surgeon?" Terry asked.

The lines on her dad's forehead deepened. "The doctor did everything she could, but the first accident left your knee compromised. I'm so sorry, Terry. There was no way you would walk again if she didn't amputate."

Terry moved, but only her good knee came up — the sheets were flat on the right side. "Dad?" she said, her voice quivering.

The nurse pressed the call bell. Terry whipped back the sheet. Her thigh was heavily bandaged, but from there down was nothing.

"Dad!" Terry stared in horror at the stump that used to be her leg.

"I'm here," he said, his expression caving. She reached for him, clawing at his arms as he struggled to comfort her. A nurse appeared in the doorway. He exchanged a glance with the other nurse by Terry's beside. A small dose from the syringe went into Terry's IV.

The new nurse placed a cool cloth on Terry's forehead. "It's a shock," he began, "and I know you can't imagine anything worse, but you would have died. The damage from the bullets was too extensive."

Terry's dad had been wearing the same desperate face when she woke up from the cave in that killed her mother. Her mother, forever one with the spirit of the priestess. Terry took in a deep breath.

" —you're still alive," her dad was saying, his voice was shaky.

"I don't know what I'd do if I lost you too."

Empower those around you and you will find your own destiny.

The nurse with the syringe put a hand on Terry's shoulder. "It'll be tough, but you're young and strong." She waited to gauge Terry's response, then she added with an unnecessary gusto, "The staff at the rehabilitation center will have you running again in no time. I bet they'll even have one of those handsome Paralympic sprinters to pay you a visit!"

The medication started to peel off the top layers of fearfulness. Terry's breathing slowed as she relaxed her grip on her father's hand. "I feel so weak."

"You lost a lot of blood," the second nurse told her, "but you'll bounce back." Terry liked his matter-of-fact tone. "It's rare for someone to be this alert so soon after your type of surgery." He looked at Terry's dad. "You've got a fast healer in this one."

"Thank god," he said.

"How's the pain now?" the first nurse asked.

"Another half dose," the male nurse instructed. "She should be sleeping."

"Excuse me." A tired-looking man in a wrinkled suit and a younger version with more stylish clothes stood in the doorway. They held up police badges. "Could we could hold off the medication for a moment?" the older one asked.

Mr. Hughes sat up straighter. "She just woke up," he said, the hard edge to his voice unmistakably protective.

The second nurse assessed the shrinking space in the room and made his way to the door. "Ring the bell again if you need me," he said to both Terry and the other nurse.

The older man with the police badge said, "I'm sorry, but she's our key eyewitness." He positioned himself at the foot of Terry's bedside. "I'm Detective Hogan. My partner and I need to ask you a few questions." The younger detective with blond stubble across his chin pulled out a notepad. They both looked like they had slept in their clothes.

Mr. Hughes let out an angry sigh.

"It's okay," Terry said. She reached up and felt a tube under her nose.

"That's oxygen," the first nurse whispered. "It will help with the healing." She gave Terry another one of her overly excited smiles. Terry wondered if she was picturing herself starring in a crime show.

Detective Hogan cleared his throat. "How did you end up in the museum basement?"

Terry took a deep breath, the oxygen helping her focus. "Prince Kamal took me there."

"For what purpose?" he prompted.

"I'm not sure. He wasn't making much sense." She paused. "How are Tanya and Maude? He kidnapped them too."

The younger detective looked up from his notepad. "They're fine," he said. "And they're back home. We have everyone's statements, but we require your side in case any further charges need to be laid."

"Prince Kamal is in prison," Detective Hogan explained.

"With a broken jaw," the second one added. "Don't worry. He won't be able to hurt you."

Detective Hogan gave his younger partner a sharp look, then he smoothed out his tie and put his attention back on Terry. "Whatever you can tell us would be appreciated."

"He stabbed Dr. Mullaca," she said. A huge lump swelled in her throat. She imagined a younger June, cowering in the bathroom from the bullies gripping her pink sweater. The second detective scribbled madly.

"He said it was in defense," Detective Hogan said. "That she was going to push you over the railing."

"No," Terry lied. "She was trying to warn me about Prince Kamal. In case you haven't noticed, he's crazy."

"Was there anyone else in the basement you recognized?" Detective Hogan asked. There was a hopeful lilt to his question.

"Prince Kamal's bodyguards, Ms. Bernard from school, and the museum curator, Sarah..."

"Sarah Mathers," Mr. Hughes finished, his voice hard. His features grew dark and he squeezed Terry's hand tightly.

Terry waited as the second detective continued to write. Neither officer looked surprised. "And Mayor Harris."

Both men stayed stone-faced, but the curt glance between the two of them didn't go unnoticed. Taking her time, Terry explained the ritual as simply as possible, careful not to over explain.

"So Prince Kamal was the only one who used the asp to wound you and the other two girls?" Detective Hogan probed.

Terry cringed. "Yes."

The younger detective stopped writing. "And where did the asp come from?"

"I assume the museum." Terry shrugged. She squirmed again and winced. The nurse held up the syringe and gave the detectives a huff.

The younger one tucked away his notepad. "Thank you, Miss Hughes," he said. "That should be enough for today." They nodded to Terry's dad, then left the room.

"This will make you a bit sleepy," the nurse said, pushing the medicine into Terry's IV.

"Don't worry," Mr. Hughes said. "I'm not leaving your side."

Terry's eyelids grew heavy. A calming pulse from her arm lulled her back to sleep as the darkness surrounded her.

When Terry opened her eyes again, the room was empty, but on the bedside table was a bouquet of roses. The tiny oxygen tube under her nose was gone, but her IV was still in. Terry had no idea what day it was.

She tentatively pulled back the sheets, steeling herself. The stump was still there. Her left leg looked awkward on the bed, perfectly free of scars and lumps — except that it was alone now.

"Hey, sleepyhead." Mr. Hughes appeared in the doorway holding a white box. He was in a baggy sweater and jeans. He was clean shaven and color lightened his cheeks.

"You're walking." She smiled.

"Like a snail." He gingerly sat in the chair by her bed. "How are you feeling?"

She covered up her stump again and shrugged. Laughter came from the hallway. She thought she could smell toast. Her stomach grumbled. "I'm hungry," she said.

"That's good," he said. He opened the white box and revealed delicious-looking cupcakes. "Your friend Maude has been dropping off treats for the nurses. I think she's hoping to be allowed to sneak in."

A mix of anxiety and love filled Terry. "How is she?"

"A little hyper, but I think she's a nice girl."

"No, I mean..." Terry wasn't sure how to express what she was feeling. Did Maude still want to be friends after everything that had happened to her? She never would have ended up in that basement if it weren't for getting mixed up with Terry.

"She's worried about you," he said. Terry let herself smile. It felt like a lifetime since that had happened. "And she's waiting outside."

Terry panicked. "No." She shook her head. "Not like this, Dad. Please."

Mr. Hughes held up his hands in surrender. "I won't force you. Besides, now that you're feeling better we can catch up." His tone alerted Terry. She waited anxiously as he deliberately took his time picking out a cupcake. "For instance," he motioned to the roses, "who's Zach?"

Terry's face grew hot. "Just a friend," she replied. She was certain there would never be a future with him now. She plucked the tiny white envelope from the stems and read the card.

ICU

"Uh-huh," her dad replied, unconvinced. "According to the police, he probably saved your life when he fought Prince Kamal for the gun." He took a bite of cupcake and chewed languidly. Terry stayed quiet, determined to win this battle of patience. She had no idea how much the police had figured out.

She hoped to change the subject. "Has Detective Hogan been back?"

He swallowed the last bite and wiped the crumbs from his hands. "They found it very interesting that you and Dr. Mullaca have the exact same tattoo on your arms."

Terry raised the sleeve of her hospital gown. There, faintly outlined in gold, was an image of the asp. She pressed her lips together, fighting the smile. She remembered falling into her mother's arms, then closing her eyes and making the promise.

She met her father's gaze. "What did you tell them?"

"I told them that you got it when we were still in Cairo." He gave her hand a squeeze. "You'll tell me the whole story one day, right?"

Terry was hesitant. She wanted to keep her mother's image a secret just a little longer. "One day soon, Dad. I promise."

He studied her for a moment, then gave her one slow nod.

Terry glanced at her tattoo again. "Where's the asp?"

"Someplace safe," he simply said. Then he stayed quiet, as if challenging her.

Terry mimicked his slow nod in return, realizing they both had secrets ... for now.

"Okay," he said, clapping his hands loudly, signaling a new topic. "I'm officially discharged tomorrow, and you're going to start physio next week, so I need to start looking for a new job."

"The museum fired you?"

"No," he said. "Now that Sarah is in jail, they want me to be the curator. They've offered a raise and substantial bonus. I think they're hoping we won't sue." He dropped his voice. "But I can't imagine you wanting to stay here, not after everything that's happened."

"Sarah was crazy, Dad," Terry said. "She always hated Mom and wanted to marry you."

He shuddered. "Even if I hadn't met your mom, I wouldn't have dated Sarah."

"Nice instincts. Think of the crazy kids you would have produced with her." She smiled weakly. The wind picked up outside.

Mr. Hughes chuckled. "Although making her your godmother out of guilt probably wasn't the best choice."

"Maybe you should give up guilt," Terry said. Then she added. "But not gluten."

They laughed lightly, then the gap of silence grew and filled up the small hospital room. Mr. Hughes blinked, and his eyes became misty. "Oh Terry, I'm so sorry you had to go through everything alone."

Terry looked at the roses and the box of cupcakes. Her fingertips edged the tattoo. "I wasn't alone," she said. "And I think you should at least consider what the museum is offering." The snow became heavier, swirling and whipping around in sheets. "I mean, how can you turn your back on tropical weather like this?"

He motioned his head toward the hallway. "Maude's been waiting all day," he said. "She knows about your leg. She just wants to make sure you're all right."

Terry said, "Me too."

"Good." He eased himself out of the chair and shuffled out of the room.

"Dad, wait! What was inside the coffin?"

He paused and put on hand on the door frame. "I'll let Maude tell you."

Chapter Fifty-Two

Terry perched on her bed. The mid-morning sunlight filled the room. The rehab center where she'd spent the last three weeks learning to walk again was much cozier than the hospital. It was almost April, and the trees outside her window had begun to form buds. A small duffel bag was zipped up and waiting by the door.

She looked at the clock. It was two minutes past the time she'd last checked. She crossed her good leg over her stump. *Yeah, that will fool him.* Terry rubbed her forehead, already regretting this meeting. But she knew she had to see him eventually. She owed him that at least, considering he'd risked his life for her.

Waiting for him was making her crazy. She pulled over the tote bag full of newspaper clippings and spread them out on the bed, feeling a little like Gus Tanner.

"Hey, Peggy!" Fraser strode into her room. His tweed blazer was paired with ripped jeans and black loafers. You would assume he was an aloof assistant to some English professor. There was a folded up newspaper tucked under his arm. He pulled out a Tootsie Pop from his pocket, totally ruining the image. Maude, who had followed in behind, had transformed him into a sugar junkie.

Her new hairstyle took some getting used to at first, but now Terry thought the closely cropped pixie with the long fringe of pink bangs suited her best friend perfectly. At Maude's insistence, her mom called the punk-inspired haircut the 'Cleo.'

Maude snapped her pink bubble gum. Her gaze fell on Terry's pinned-up sweatpants leg. "Hey," she asked, "where's your new leg?"

Fraser said, "It doesn't make sense if I call you Peggy and you don't even have a peg leg."

"That was last year's model," Terry sassed. "I'm getting the one that fires lasers." She turned to Maude. "It still needs one more adjustment. They promised it would be ready by next week."

"Poo." She wrinkled her nose. "I wanted to take you shopping to celebrate. Forever 21 is having a sale." Maude was determined to give Terry a makeover for her triumphant return to Roosevelt High. She was certain the slim-legged prosthesis would be easy to slip a pair of skinny jeans over compared to the old bulky knee brace.

"Needing an adjustment, huh?" Fraser added suspiciously. "More like a good cleaning. According my brother, there are rumors at *The Devonshire Daily* about suspicious markings around a bound and gagged mugger a few nights ago."

Terry gave him an innocent shrug. "And?"

"At least try and stay out of the mud. It narrows the suspects down considerably when the police are looking for someone with a carbon-fiber running blade for a right foot."

Maude's mouth dropped open. "You said you weren't going out again until you were discharged!" she chastised. "How would you explain sneaking back in to the rehab staff?"

"That's why I make sure I'm not caught. I couldn't sleep, so I went for a run," Terry defended. "What was I supposed to do, let that creep attack the gas station attendant?" Her friends stayed tight-lipped. They knew it was useless to argue with her. "Besides, nobody ever suspects the cripple."

Fraser's eyes lit up. He totally loved having an inside scoop for a friend. He craned his neck around Maude and motioned to the clippings. "Reliving fun times?"

Terry read the headline she held in her hands: *Disgraced mayor admits to gambling addiction and stealing city funds, forced to step down.*

Fraser had found out from his newspaper connections that the mayor had made a deal with the district attorney to keep his involvement in the museum debacle quiet if he pled guilty to charges with less evidence. He'd be serving jail time, at least.

They also discovered that all of Amy Sue's expenses had been paid by Dr. Mullaca, anonymously, from the very beginning. Staff at the posh hospital told Maude and Fraser that Mayor Harris had only visited a few times.

"I can't imagine my grandma in a home with no one to visit her," Maude said, reaching for another article.

Fraser crunched down on his sucker. "Although the last time we spoke with the nurses, they told us Allison drops in regularly now."

"I can't believe Mayor Harris kept his birth mother a secret all those years," Maude said.

"Not everyone is as awesome as your family," Terry replied. Her eyes fell on Dr. Mullaca's obituary. A hollow feeling carved into her heart at the smallness of it. Terry's dad had written the piece. There was no mention of June Macallum.

When Terry had finally told her dad everything, it felt like it took a hundred years until he spoke. He only wiped his eyes, then hugged her. Then he had threatened softly that questions were coming — once he digested everything.

"I called Gus," Maude said.

Terry's mouth gaped open. "What did you say?"

Tears welled in Maude's bottom lids. "I told him that we discovered June had in fact run away that night, but went on to live her dream … he seemed happy about that."

Fraser picked up the headline that had crushed Terry the most. *Wild chase through museum reveals empty coffin.*

Maude studied her friend. "Are you okay?" she asked.

Terry said, "My mom would have been disappointed that Cleopatra's remains are still undiscovered. But Dad said the hieroglyphs inside the case will be studied for years. It proves her servants were loyal enough to keep her final resting place a secret. They must have risked so much to go behind Octavian's back."

"And your dad is certain it really is her coffin?" Fraser asked, suppressing a thrill in his voice that Terry recognized from the very first time they met.

"You're still looking for that famous headline, aren't you?"

He flashed his boyish grin. "I already got my next scoop: top ten reasons unicorns are better than zombies."

Maude rolled her eyes, but Terry could tell she was fighting a proud grin. "I expect an autographed copy," Terry said.

There was a natural gap in the conversation as the three friends looked through the articles again. "Still," Maude said. "It would have been cool to find at least something inside. You know, like a golden crown or a pair of earrings."

Terry put a hand on one of her crutches. "Cleopatra didn't spend her time trying to dig up someone's treasure; she was too busy making an empire. Maybe I need to be more like that — instead of hunting for the past, I'm going to start living in the present."

"Cliché," Fraser coughed.

"Don't listen to him," Maude soothed. "I think it's a spectacular mantra. Grandma will love it." She winked at Terry. "She told me the best revenge is not having any revenge at all and that nothing bad ever happens when you put kindness out into the world."

"Your grandma is the best," Fraser said.

"Yeah," Maude agreed. "Although I don't think I'll be sharing cupcakes with Allison anytime soon."

"By the way," Fraser said, handing her the folded up paper from under his arm, "your boyfriend made the news again."

Terry ignored his jab and read the latest about the Prince Kamal. "He's not really a prince?" she said.

Maude played with her pink infinity scarf. "Remember when we looked him up on the Internet and we saw the fat guy with the sunglasses? Well, that was the real Prince Kamal."

"But he had all those bodyguards," Terry said. "And he seemed so regal." She looked out the window, the late March sky gray. She thought she saw a few snow flurries.

"He had me fooled too," Maude sympathized. "He's actually a second cousin of the real prince and like twentieth in line for the throne or something."

"The royals have enough cash to spread around." Fraser twisted the wrapper of the Tootsie Pop. "Apparently he was trying to start a familial coup. From what I've heard, he has a reputation for elaborate schemes. Whether he truly believed in the whole reincarnation idea or not, he was convinced it would ensure him a fast track to the throne. But all that's waiting for him in Egypt is a trip to jail."

Terry rubbed her tattoo. "He was so intense." She grimaced at the memory of their kiss. "Dad said he's demanding the prison guards allow him a phone call with me. He gives them letters, too, but those go straight to his lawyer."

"Hmm," Maude said, an eyebrow arched. "Was it the asp or your kissing expertise?"

"I can't believe you chose him over Zach," Fraser teased.

Maude swatted him. "Terry was kidnapped!."

"Zach's a stubborn fellow, thank God." Fraser pointed his sucker at her. "You're lucky I found him brokenhearted on the fifth floor. I convinced him we should go back to the Egypt room and force open the mummy case."

"And you're lucky I rammed it open with my head to save your girlfriend," Terry rebutted. She busied herself gathering all the news clippings, hoping they couldn't see her blush.

"Is that how it's going to be, Peggy? You're all tough and super strong now, so I have to agree with everything you say?"

"Pretty much."

"Fascinating." He took a loud bite from the sucker.

Terry glanced at the clock again. "Uh … my dad should be here soon. I'll call you guys later, okay?"

Maude didn't move. "Where's your new apartment?"

Terry drummed her fingers on her thigh. "Not sure. He's going to surprise me."

A nurse popped her head in the doorway of Terry's room. "How's my favourite patient?" she asked brightly. The fact that Terry was an impossibly fast healer whose muscles seemed to crave the tedious exercises had made her popular with the staff at the rehab center. Plus, Maude kept bringing in her grandmother's sweets to share. The nurse motioned to the duffel bag. "Almost ready to go home?"

Home.

That word used to hollow out a hole so deep in her soul, Terry had thought it would never be filled. She had convinced her dad to take the job at the museum. It was easy once he met Maude and saw how close they were.

"Uh, yeah." Terry started to gather up the clippings. She was planning on putting them with Gus's old ones in the shoebox. She wasn't sure why, but it felt right to keep them all together.

"Good," the nurse beamed. "But do you have time for another visitor?"

Terry's mouth went dry. She ran her fingers through her hair a few times, then licked her lips and prayed for a cool demeanor.

Zach's head almost reached the top of the door frame.

"Greetings, Shaggy," Fraser said. "How's the new cast?" He pointed to Zach's arm.

"White and hard," Zach said.

Terry grabbed the tote bag of news clippings and put it on her lap, fighting the urge to roll up in the bed sheets with only her head peeking out.

Maude gave Zach a quick hug. "Did you get my message?" Terry knew Maude and Fraser had been hanging out with him these last few weeks. Almost dying together created unlikely bonds, apparently. "How long before this one comes off?" Maude nodded to his arm.

"Another two weeks." He sounded tired. Terry noticed he was wearing a thick cable-knit sweater under a jean jacket instead of his usual varsity attire. Was he giving up basketball entirely? Had the break permanently damaged his chance to play again?

Terry steeled herself for his gaze. "Why did you need another cast?" she asked.

Zach seemed to be focused on the space right above her head. "They had to make sure I didn't do any more damage after I fought with Prince Kamal."

"Oh," Terry said.

"Plus there was blood all over it," Fraser added. He turned to Zach. "It's just Kamal, actually, but that hardly matters to us now."

Zach's forehead scrunched up even more. Maude rocked back on the heels of her flowered Dr. Martens. "Fraser and I promised Grandma a drive to the park — the crocuses are finally out — so we better get going." She pulled on his elbow.

"I thought your grandma was teaching Zumba all morning at the gym."

Maude made a funny noise and motioned to the door.

"Oh, right!" Fraser said. He patted Zach on the shoulder. "We have to leave you guys alone now."

Maude grumbled under her breath as she dragged him out of the room. "This is the start of something big, Peggy!" Fraser called out from the hallway. "I can feel it."

"That's what he said the first time we met," she mumbled to the floor. The room was quiet after that — too quiet.

Terry considered standing so Zach wouldn't have to look down on her, but then he'd see the pinned up sweatpants, and it would freak him out. She was frozen on the edge of the bed, unable to look him in the eye. "Thanks for coming," she said.

"Thanks for finally letting me." His sneakers closed the space between them. He perched carefully on the corner of the mattress. "I've got something to show you," he said. Zach slipped off his backpack and pulled out their history project.

Terry opened the front and a tiny laugh escaped. "An A-plus," she said. "Although I think Ms. Bernard might have been a bit biased."

"Another teacher did the grading," he said. "Ms. Bernard is in the hospital."

Terry's stomach dropped. Ms. Bernard's hope to time travel now seemed so sad and pathetic. *How miserable she must be to realize her lifelong dream will never happen*, she thought silently.

"I've never gotten anything higher than a B," he told her. "And that was in gym."

She handed him back the folder. "Well done."

It was almost unbearable having him see her like this. The asp tattoo grew warm. Terry steadied herself for the speech she'd been practicing all morning. "I know you're responsible for saving my life, and I wanted to thank you."

"I think you're confusing me with the surgeon. Besides, anyone would have slammed into Prince Kamal. Sorry, just Kamal."

She'd known it would be like this; him acting polite, gently letting her know they'd just be friends. It was exactly what she wanted. It would make things much simpler. The roses were sent a lifetime ago. He'd sent them so soon after the museum party, he had probably still been picturing her in the Cleopatra dress. She started to drum her fingers on her thigh again. "Um ... how's school?"

Zach put the history project on the bedside table. "There was some crazy gossip, but mostly people are over it."

She nodded. Her head felt stupid bobbing up and down. All the words she wanted to say broke apart, refusing to come together. Terry didn't have a coherent thought in her brain. He didn't seem to have anything else to say either. The reality of it hurt more than she'd expected, but it was what she needed to carry this through. She couldn't force him to love her.

"So … I guess everyone at school knows I lost my leg." She swallowed the threat of tears, letting anger step into its place. "I bet Allison's loving that news."

Zach stiffened beside her. "Considering her dad's in jail and the family is totally broke, I think there's more on her mind these days."

Terry wished she hadn't put the conversation in this direction, but his last sentence made her see red. "Maude told me you're not going to press charges against her."

"I can't prove anything. She's out of my life now, and that's how I want to keep it. If she posed a threat to you, of course I'd follow up with the police." He tilted his head. "But from what Maude tells me, you're more than capable of taking care of yourself."

"How much did Maude tell you?"

"Well, everything." He looked pointedly at her right arm where the tattoo warmed gently under her long sleeves. "Explains how you fought those goons who broke my arm."

Terry squirmed on the bed, unable to keep eye contact. "Look." She sighed. "School is going to be a freak show when I go back, and I totally understand if you want to watch from the sidelines. I mean, you've done more than anyone could have ever asked. You don't owe me anything."

His expression clouded over. "I hate to bust your ego, but you're old news. The game against West Mount took everyone's attention. They ended up beating us and took us out of the State Championships."

Terry was hit with a wave of selfishness. Zach had had all his hopes on getting to the finals. She had listened to the play-by-play on the radio beside her bed, practically crying the whole time. Roosevelt High lost, but it was Zach's game to lose and he had to watch from the bench.

"I'm sorry," she whispered.

"You have to stop apologizing for that," he said. "It's not your fault." He reached out and put his hand over hers. His thumb brushed over her knuckles. "None of this is your fault."

She closed her eyes. "Zach," she started, "you're making this so hard."

He squeezed her hand. "Look at me, Terry."

"I only want you to be happy," she said.

"What makes you think I won't be happy with you?" His stare wandered over her thighs. His silence was unnerving. She was tempted to tell him to get it over with and just leave.

"I only have one leg!"

He seemed to hold his breath. "The sexy one or the limpy one?" he asked, completely straight-faced.

"The sexy one."

"Good," he said. "That was my favorite of the two. I'm also particularly fond of the rest of you, especially your eyes." He tucked a stray hair behind Terry's ear. "So, if you're in a knife fight and one of your eyes gets poked out, I'm telling you right now, we'll be through."

Terry's resolve began to melt. "You're a … a very frustrating enigma," she said, unable to hide her smile. "And a bit insane."

"That's because I haven't kissed you in over four weeks." He gently lifted her chin. "You don't want to be responsible for sending me to the psych ward with Ms. Bernard, do you?"

"No." Terry shook her head as he leaned in closer. A warm pool inside her heart flooded over, sending a blush to her skin. "Wait," she said, putting her hand against his chest. "There's a slight chance you might become obsessed with me if we kiss."

"Excuse me?"

"Well, it's just a theory of Fraser's, and it's only if I was actually wearing the asp, but the tattoo is responding to you and …

uh, well … I thought I should warn you."

"Hmm," he frowned. "Let me see it. I want to see your tattoo."

Terry pushed her sleeve all the way up to her shoulder. Zach's finger traced the asp on her skin. Terry's toes on her left foot curled as electricity buzzed through her. She stared at his mouth, wishing she could kiss him. His body spray had a different scent than his usual spicy brand. This one was more like the forest after it rained.

"I hope you don't take offense," he said, pulling down her sleeve. "But I didn't feel anything. Was it supposed to shock me or something?"

"No. It likes you."

He chuckled at this. "So you think if we kiss, the tattoo might have the same effect as the real asp?"

"Maybe," she whispered.

"Then we only have two choices, Terry: kiss and risk having me obsessed with you or not kiss and never know." He leaned closer. "I've become a bit of a thrill seeker since I started hanging out with you, did you know that? I say let's go for it."

Zach kissed her long and soft. A thrill ran up and down Terry. She combed her fingers through his hair, deepening the kiss. When they parted, dizzy and out of breath, Terry raised her eyebrows at him. "Feel any different?" she asked.

"Hard to tell. I was crazy about you already," he said. "But for the sake of our experiment, I'd say it's a failure. I'm not obsessed with you … well, at least not yet."

Terry flashed him a grin. "Maybe we should double check, just to make sure." Zach's smile barely brushed against hers when Terry's dad walked in.

Zach stood up so quickly, he practically tripped over his backpack. "Hi, Mr. Hughes," he stammered. "Um … is everything all set?"

Terry's dad looked like he just stepped in fake dog poop — slightly amused, but not exactly happy. "Yes, everything is ready." He read Terry's confused expression. "Zach was able to find us a great apartment," he told her. "It's in a nice neighborhood, and not too far from Maude."

"Well, my parents helped too," Zach added. "They know the landlord, so you guys were able to skip the waiting list." He shouldered his backpack, then reached down for Terry's duffel bag.

Terry gripped her crutches. "What's it like?" she asked.

"Old-fashioned," Terry's dad began. "Cast-iron radiators, high ceilings, wood floors throughout…"

"And there's a basketball court in the back," Zach interjected, now taking the tote bag full of newspapers. "Plus there's a built-on fire escape, so it's really safe." He winked at Terry.

"Are you sure you can't carry anything else?" Terry's dad asked him. She could tell he was joking, but his expression made Zach stammer again a few times.

Terry stood and tucked the crutches under her arms. She remembered a time when that simple task would have sent jolts of pain through her bad knee. But now she stood solidly, with her head up — just like her mother encouraged. Terry appreciated the irony of losing a leg to stand straighter.

She let Zach take in her whole image. "Are you sure?" she asked him. It was a coded message, but he knew exactly what she was saying.

Sure about us? Sure about dating a girl with one leg? Sure about dating a girl who has superpowers?

He held up his cast. "When this comes off I'll need you to help me get back into practice … neighbor." Then he reached up and lightly touched the edge of his eyebrow. Terry didn't even care that her dad could probably see her ears redden.

His questioning gaze slide back and forth between Terry and Zach, but he stayed quiet. Then he gave Terry a careful smile. "So," he said. "Are you ready to check out your new home?"

Home.

For the first time in a long time, Terry didn't think of Egyptian sunsets. Instead, an image of Maude's pink hair, Fraser's dented-up car, and then finally Zach's drawings swirled together, creating an overwhelming tug at her heart, anchoring her spirit. Terry realized home wasn't an address or a place to search for on a map — it was being surrounded by the things that made her happiest.

"Home?" Terry repeated back to her dad. "Yeah," she said. "I like the sound of that."

Acknowledgements

Asp of Ascension would not exist without the encouragement of numerous valiant readers. Thank you to Arianna Sanchez for hosting the short story contest that gave this story its first breath. And thank you to my three amigos armed with lattes and red pens: Barbara MacDougall, Tricia Dauphinee Bishop and Shannon Macgillivray.

I am indebted to fellow writers, Jen Swann Downey and Ann Marie Walker, for their early advice and direction.

The biggest nod of gratitude goes to Fierce Ink for pulling this novel out of the slush pile and helping coax the best parts of the story to the surface.

To Penelope Jackson, rock star editor and all around genius, I humbly pledge my eternal devotion to your extraordinary guidance.

Thank you as well to Sarah Sawler, marketing executive and tireless cheerleader. I also applaud designer, Emma Dolan for creating a spectacular cover.

I'm grateful to my siblings, Brad Bishop and Cynthia Flack, for their endless encouragement. And thank you again and again to my parents, Eric and Ethel Bishop, for their unwavering praise and near-embarrassing endorsements.

And most of all to my family — Ken, Ruth and Adam — my most patient and understanding supporters, thank you.

BR Myers is a young adult author who appreciates a design in her cappuccino, loves shopping for vintage jewelry and dreams in color. Always in the mood for a good scare, she spent most of her teen years behind the covers of Lois Duncan, Ray Bradbury and Stephen King. When she's not putting her characters in compromising situations, she works as a registered nurse in Halifax, Nova Scotia, where she lives with her husband and two children.

(Photo credit: Tanya Reynolds Photography)

Untitled

June pressed her palms against the washroom stall, staring down at her scuffed penny loafers perched on the toilet seat.

"We know you're in here, skank." Amy Sue's unmistakable snarl reverberated off the walls.

June held her breath.

"That pimply security guard wants your phone number," Amy Sue teased. "The one you were swooning over by the mummies and junk."

June stayed quiet. She'd been nervous when the guard approached her — he'd noticed her particular interest in the Sacred Asp. But as they talked about the main exhibit, it was obvious she knew more about Egyptology than him.

Now, stuck in the bathroom stall, June wished she'd stayed home.

"Let's go," one of the Amy Sue's minions sighed. "Mrs. Obeck will flip her wig if we're gone for too long."

June's hand slipped. She caught herself, but it was too late. A simple lock didn't keep them out. June closed her eyes, hoping it would be quick this time. Someone pulled her roughly, dragging her across the tiles. There was a distinctive rip when her sweater sleeve let go. June closed her eyes tighter.

"Stand up, skank!" Amy Sue ordered. Her voice was laced

with a breathy excitability. "We're going to fix you up for your date."

Two sets of arms held June prisoner as something cold was smeared across her lips. Fingers roughly rubbed her eyelids and mauled her face. They ordered her to open her eyes.

June blinked at the clown in the mirror. Thick make-up covered her face in swirls of color.

A teacher's voice bellowed from the hallway, gathering the students for departure. The girls, over-heated and a bit disheveled, touched up their perfect faces before rejoining the class.

June was frozen to the spot, staring at her reflection. Her pants were too short and her t-shirt was a hand-me down from her foster brother. The pink sweater, now ripped at the shoulder and missing two buttons, was the only pretty thing she owned.

A second announcement to return to the school bus snapped June to attention. She frantically pumped the dispenser, but the small drop of soap only made the greasy make-up smear. She scoured her face with rough paper towels, but it was useless.

Hideous. Hopeless. Unloved.

June curled into a ball in the far corner. She buried her face in the crook of her arm and cried herself to sleep. The image of the Sacred Asp glowed behind her swollen eyelids.

June jerked awake. Her neck was stiff. She carefully stood up, wondering how long she'd been asleep. The hallway outside the washroom was dark and silent. She leaned over the railing and looked four floors down into the rotunda. The museum was empty — it was after hours.

She was in big trouble. A knot tightened inside her chest. She imaged the hard line of Miss Edna's mouth. Her foster mother said all the right things in front of the other tenants, but when the apartment door closed the shouting began.

A sudden noise from above made June jump — something was happening in the Egypt room. Panic at being stuck inside the museum overnight was replaced with another kind of urgency.

June raced up the stairs to the fifth floor landing. She gasped. The young security guard she'd spoken with earlier was slumped against the wall, unconscious.

Further into the Egyptian exhibit, three men in black masks hovered over a display case, carefully cutting a hole in the glass. The Sacred Asp, believed to have been worn by Cleopatra the night she first seduced Mark Antony, shined brightly.

The men discussed selling the irreplaceable piece. June took in angry breaths as heat rose through her skin. She peeled off her ripped sweater and ran toward the men.

The robbers were dumbfounded by the surprise attack. June raced by and snatched the piece from their grasp. The Asp throbbed in her hand, urging her faster. She slipped the golden coil up her arm as she sprinted back toward the landing.

Angry voices shouted after her, bearing down on her like a locomotive. June was forced against the railing. The marble tiles of the rotunda stared up at her — four floors below. Red welts lined her arm as the men wildly grabbed for the Asp.

"No!" She twisted out of their grip. The motion propelled her backward. The burglars' eyes grew wide as June teetered over the railing and fell into nothing but air.

The floor came quickly.

June blinked against a bright light. No longer in the rotunda, she now stood in a swirling mist. An exotic woman in white robes gave her a critical look.

"The Asp has chosen," the woman said.

"Am I dead?" June asked. The fall should have killed her, but she stood in her second hand t-shirt looking and feeling very much alive.

"No." Her voice was smooth. "You have been deemed worthy to be the new Protector of the Asp."

"Me?" June pinched her arm, certain she was still asleep in the bathroom.

"The Asp chooses its Protector, it always has ... for thousands of years. It will bestow its mark upon you, giving you a power few can comprehend; a power to protect what others would destroy for profit or gain. This is your destiny. Do you accept?"

June thought of her ripped sweater. Protector? Powerful? For the first time in her whole miserable life, she saw a future she'd only thought possible in her dreams.

The woman prompted again. "Do you accept?"

"Yes."

Later, the police questioned the revived security guard, but he was unable to explain how three men were tied up and trapped in the lion diorama on the second floor. The Sacred Asp was safely in its place, although the glass appeared to be compromised.

June smiled at the night sky from the rooftop of the museum, a golden tattoo of an asp now encircled her upper arm. "The power to protect," she whispered. "My destiny."

CPSIA information can be obtained at www.ICGtesting.com
Printed in the USA
LVOW06s0145031015

456755LV00004B/93/P